SCO #1

D0596038

4/2012

Bantam Books by David Brin

STARTIDE RISING
SUNDIVER

SUNDIVER

DAVID BRIN

BANTAM BOOKS
TORONTO · NEW YORK · LONDON · SYDNEY

SUNDIVER
A Bantam Book / February 1980
2nd printing .... April 1980
3rd printing ... November 1981

Illustrations by David S. Perry

ISBN 0-553-20760-1

Published simultaneously in the United States and Canada

Bantam Books are published by Bantam Books, Inc. Its trademark, consisting of the words "Bantam Books" and the por-
trayal of a rooster, is Registered in U.S. Patent and Trademark
Office and in other countries. Marca Registrada. Bantam
Books, Inc., 666 Fifth Avenue, New York, New York 10103.

PRINTED IN THE UNITED STATES OF AMERICA

12 11 10 9 8 7 6 5 4

To my brothers Dan and Stan,
to Arglebargle the IVth . . .
and to somebody else.

CONTENTS

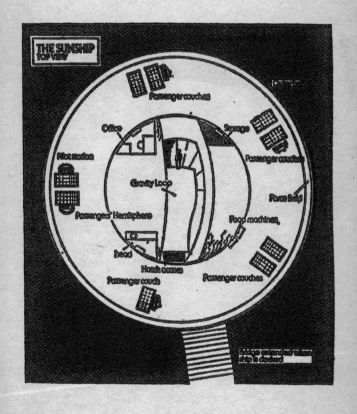

PART I

... it is reasonable to hope
that in the not too distant future
we shall be competent to understand
so simple a thing as a star.

A. S. Eddington, 1926

1.

OUT OF THE WHALE-DREAM

"Makakai, are you ready?"

Jacob ignored the tiny whirrings of motors and valves in his metal cocoon. He lay still. The water lapped gently against the bulbous nose of his mechanical whale, as he waited for an answer.

One more time he checked the tiny indicators on his helmet display. Yes, the radio was working. The occupant of the other waldo whale, lying half submerged a few meters away, had heard every word.

The water was exceptionally clear today. Facing downward, he could see a small leopard shark swim lazily past, a bit out of place here in the deeper water offshore.

"Makakai . . . are you ready?"

He tried not to sound impatient, or betray the tension he felt building in the back of his neck as he waited. He closed his eyes and made the delinquent muscles relax, one by one. Still, he waited for his pupil to speak.

"Yesss . . . let'sss do it!" came the warbling,

squeaky voice, at last. The words sounded breathless, as if spoken grudgingly, in lieu of inhalation.

A nice long speech for Makakai. He could see the young dolphin's training machine next to his, its image reflected in the mirrors that rimmed his faceplate. Its gray metal flukes lifted and fell slightly with the swell. Feebly, without their power, her artificial fins moved, sluggishly under the transient, serrated surface of the water.

She's as ready as she'll ever be, he thought. If technology can wean a dolphin of the Whale-Dream, now's the time we'll find out.

He chinned the microphone switch again. "All right, Makakai. You know how the waldo works. It will amplify any action you make, but if you want the rockets to cut in, you'll have to give the command in English. Just to be fair, I have to whistle in trinary to make mine work."

"Yesss!" she hissed. Her waldo's gray flukes thrashed up once and down with a boom and a spray of saltwater.

With a half muttered prayer to the Dreamer, he touched a switch releasing the amplifiers on both Makakai's waldo and his own, then cautiously turned his arms to set the fins into motion. He flexed his legs, the massive flukes thrust back jerkily in response, and his machine immediately rolled over and sank.

Jacob tried to correct but overcompensated, making the waldo tumble even worse. The beating of his fins momentarily made the area around him a churning mass of bubbles, until patiently, by trial and error, he got himself righted.

He pushed off again, carefully, to get some headway, then arched his back and kicked out. The waldo responded with a great tail-slashing leap into the air.

The dolphin was almost a kilometer off. As he reached the top of his arc, Jacob saw her fall gracefully from a height of ten meters to slice smoothly into the swell below.

He pointed his helmet beak at the water and the sea came at him like a green wall. The impact made his helmet ring as he tore through tendrils of floating

4

kelp, sending a golden Garibaldi darting away in panic as he drove downwards.

He was going in too steep. He swore and kicked twice to straighten out. The machine's massive metal flukes beat at the water to the rhythmic push of his feet, each beat sending a tremor up his spine, pressing him against the suit's heavy padding. When the time was right, he arched and kicked again. The machine ripped out of the water.

Sunlight flashed like a missile in his left window, its glare drowning the dim glow of his tiny instrument panel. The helmet computer chuckled softly as he twisted, beak down, to crash into the bright water once again.

As a school of tiny silver anchovies scattered before him, Jacob hooted out loud with exhilaration.

His hands slipped along the controls to the rocket verniers, and at the top of his next arc he whistled a code in trinary. Motors hummed, as the exoskeleton extended winglets along its sides. Then the boosters cut in with a savage burst, pressing the padded headpiece upward with the sudden acceleration, pinching the back of his skull as the waves swept past, just below his hurtling craft.

He came down near Makakai with a great splash. She whistled a shrill trinary welcome. Jacob let the rockets shut off automatically and resumed the purely mechanical leaping beside her.

For a time they moved in unison. With each leap Makakai grew more daring, performing twists and pirouettes during the long seconds before they struck the water. Once, in midair, she rattled off a dirty limerick in dolphin, a low piece of work, but Jacob hoped they'd recorded it back at the chase boat. He'd missed the punch line at the crashing end of the aerial cycle.

The rest of the training team followed behind them on the hovercraft. During each leap he caught sight of the large vessel, diminished, now, by distance, until his impact cut off everything but the sounds of splitting water, Makakai's sonar squeaking, and the rushing, phosphorescent blue-green past his windows.

Jacob's chronometer indicated that ten minutes had

passed. He wouldn't be able to keep up with Maka-kai for more than a half hour, no matter how much amplification he used. A man's muscles and nervous system weren't designed for this leap-and-crash routine.

"Makakai, it's time to try the rockets. Let me know if you're ready and we'll use them on the following jump."

They both came down into the sea and he worked his flukes in the frothy water to prepare for the next leap. They jumped again.

"Makakai, I'm serious now. Are you ready?"

They sailed high together. He could see her tiny eye behind a plastic window as her waldo-machine twisted before slicing into the water. He followed an instant later.

"Okay, Makakai. If you don't answer me, we'll just have to stop right now."

Blue water swept past, along with a cloud of bub-bles, as he pushed along beside his pupil.

Makakai twisted around and dove down instead of rising for another leap. She chattered something al-most too fast to follow in trinary . . . about how he shouldn't be a spoilsport.

Jacob let his machine rise slowly to the surface. "Come dear, use the King's English. You'll need it if you ever want your children to go into space. And it's *so* expressive! Come on. Tell Jacob what you think of him."

There were a few seconds of silence. Then he saw something move very fast below him. It streaked upward and, just before it hit the surface, he heard Makakai's voice shrilly taunt:

"Ch-chase me, ch-chump! I fly-y-y!"

With the last word, her mechanical flukes snapped back and she leaped out of the water on a column of flame.

Laughing, he dove to give himself headway and then launched into the air after his pupil.

Gloria handed him the strip chart as soon as he finished his second cup of coffee. Jacob tried to make his eyes focus on the squiggly lines, but they swam back and forth like ocean swells. He handed the chart back.

"I'll look at the data later. Can you just give me a summary? And I'll take one of those sandwiches now, too, if you'll let me clean up."

She tossed him a tuna on rye and sat on the countertop, her hands on the edges to compensate for the swaying of the boat. As usual, she was wearing next to nothing. Pretty, well endowed, and with long black hair, the young biologist wore next to nothing very well.

"I think we have the brainwave information we need now, Jacob. I don't know how you did it, but Makakai's attention span in English was at least twice normal. Manfred thinks he's found enough associated synaptic clusters to give him a boost in his next set of experimental mutations. There are a couple of nodes that he wants to expand in the left cerebral lobe of Makakai's offspring.

"My group is happy enough with the present. Makakai's facility with the waldo-whale proves that the current generation can use machines."

Jacob sighed. "If you're hoping these results will persuade the Confederacy to cancel the next generation of mutations, don't count on it. They're running scared. They don't want to have to rely forever on poetry and music to prove that dolphins are intelligent. They want a race of analytical tool users, and giving codewords to activate a rocket waldo just won't qualify. Twenty to one Manfred gets to cut."

Gloria reddened. "Cutting! They're people, a people with a beautiful dream. We'll carve them into engineers and lose a race of poets!"

Jacob put down the crust of his sandwich. He brushed crumbs away from his chest. Already he regretted having said anything.

"I know, I know. I wish things could go a little slower, too. But look at it this way. Maybe the fins'll be able to put the Whale-Dream into words someday. We won't need trinary to discuss the weather, or Aborigine-pidgin to talk philosophy. They'll be able to join the chimps, thumbing their metaphorical noses at the Galactics while we put on an act of being dignified adults."

"But . . ."

Jacob raised his hand to cut her off. "Can we discuss this later? I'd like to stretch out for a little while, and then go down and visit with our girl."

Gloria frowned for a moment, then smiled openly. "I'm sorry, Jacob. You must really be tired. But at least today, finally, everything worked."

Jacob allowed himself to return her grin. On his broad face the toothy smile brought out lines around his mouth and eyes.

"Yes," he said, rising to his feet. "Today everything worked."

"Oh by the way, while you were down, there was a call for you. It was an Eatee! Johnny was so excited about it that he barely remembered to take a message. I think it's around here somewhere."

She pushed aside the lunch dishes and plucked up a slip of paper. She handed it to him.

Jacob's bushy eyebrows knotted together as he looked down at the message. His skin was taut and dark from a mixture of ancestry and exposure to sun and saltwater. The brown eyes tended to narrow to fine slits when he concentrated. He brought a calloused hand to the side of his hooked, amerind nose and struggled with the radio operator's handwriting.

"I guess we all knew that you worked with Eatees," Gloria said. "But I sure didn't expect to get one on the horn out here! Especially one that looks like a giant broccoli sprout and talks like a Minister of Protocol!"

Jacob's head jerked up.

"A Kanten called? Here? Did he leave his name?"

"It should be down there. Is that what it was? A Kanten? I'm afraid I don't know my aliens that well. I'd recognize a Cynthian or a Tymbrimi, but this one was new to me."

"Um . . . I'm going to have to call somebody. I'll clean up the dishes later so don't you touch them! Tell Manfred and Johnny I'll be down in a little while to visit with Makakai. And thanks again." He smiled and touched her shoulder lightly, but as he

8

turned his expression quickly relapsed to one of worried preoccupation.

He passed on through the forward hatch, clutching the message. Gloria looked after him for a moment. She picked up the data charts and wished she knew what it would take to hold the man's interest for more than an hour, or a night.

Jacob's cabin was barely a closet with a narrow fold-down bunk, but it offered enough privacy. He pulled his portable teli out of a cabinet near the door and set it on the bunk.

There was no reason to assume that Fagin had called for any other purpose than to be sociable. He had, after all, a deep interest in the work with dolphins.

There had been a few times, though, when the alien's messages had led to nothing but trouble. Jacob considered not returning the Kanten's call.

After a moment's hesitation, he punched out a code on the face of the teli and settled back to compose himself. When he came right down to it, he couldn't resist an opportunity to talk with an E.T., anywhere, anytime.

A line of binary flashed on the screen, giving the location of the portable unit he was calling. The Baja E.T. Reserve. Makes sense, Jacob thought. That's where the Library is. There was the standard warning against contact with aliens by Probationary Personalities. Jacob looked away with distaste. Bright points of static filled the space above the blankets and in front of the screen, and then Fagin stood, en-replica, a few inches away.

The E.T. *did* look somewhat like a giant sprout of broccoli. Rounded blue and green shoots formed symmetrical, spherical balls of growth around a gnarled, striated trunk. Here and there tiny crystalline flakes tipped a few of the branches, forming a cluster near the top around an invisible blowhole.

The foliage swayed and the crystals near the top tinkled from the passage of air the creature exhaled.

"Hello, Jacob," Fagin's voice came tinnily out of midair. "I greet you with gladness and gratitude and

9

with the austere lack of formality upon which you so frequently and forcefully insist."

Jacob fought back a laugh. Fagin reminded him of an ancient Mandarin, as much for the fluting quality of his accent as for the convoluted protocol he used with even his closest human friends.

"I greet you, Friend-Fagin, and wish you well with all respect. And now that that's over, and before you say even a word, the answer is no."

The crystals tinkled softly. "Jacob! You are so young and yet so perspicacious! I admire your insight and ability to divine my purpose in calling you!"

Jacob shook his head.

"Neither flattery nor thickly veiled sarcasm, Fagin; I insist on speaking colloquial English with you because it's the only way I have a chance of avoiding getting screwed whenever I deal with you. And you know very well what I'm talking about!"

The alien shook, giving a parody of a shrug.

"Ah, Jacob, I must bow to your will and use the highly esteemed honesty of which your species should be so proud. It is true that there is a slight favor for which I had the temerity to ask. But now that you have given me your answer . . . based no doubt on certain past unpleasant occurrences, most of which nevertheless turned out for the best . . . I shall simply drop the subject.

"Would it be possible to inquire how your work with the proud Client species 'porpoise' proceeds?"

"Uh, yes, the work is going very well. We had a breakthrough today."

"That is excellent, I am certain that it could not have happened without your intervention. I heard that your work there was indispensable!"

Jacob shook his head to clear it. Somehow Fagin had taken the initiative again.

"Well, it's true I was able to help out early on with the Water-Sphinx problem, but since then my part hasn't been all that special. Hell, anyone could have done what I've been doing here lately."

"Oh, that is something that I find very hard to believe!"

Jacob frowned. Unfortunately it was true. And

from now on the work here at the Center for Uplift would be even more routine.

A hundred experts, some more qualified in porppsych than he, were waiting to step in. The Center would probably keep him on, partly out of gratitude, but did he really *want* to stay? Much as he loved dolphins and the sea, he'd found himself more and more restless lately.

"Fagin, I'm sorry I was so rude at first. I'd like to hear what you called me about . . . provided you understand that the answer is still probably no."

Fagin's foliage rustled.

"I had the intention of inviting you to a small and amicable meeting with some worthy beings of diverse species, to discuss an important problem of a purely intellectual nature. The meeting will be held this Thursday, at the Visitors Center in Ensenada, at eleven o'clock. You will be committed to nothing if you attend."

Jacob chewed on the idea for a moment.

"E.T.'s, you say? Who are they? What's this meeting about?"

"Alas, Jacob, I am not at liberty to say, at least not by teli. The details will have to wait until you come, if you come, on Thursday."

Jacob immediately became suspicious. "Say, this 'problem' isn't political, is it? You're being awfully close."

The image of the alien was very still. It's verdant mass rippled slowly, as if in contemplation.

"I have never understood, Jacob," the fluting voice finally resumed, "why a man of your background takes so little interest in the interplay of emotions and needs which you call 'politics.' Were the metaphor appropriate, I would say that politics is 'in my blood.' It certainly is in yours."

"You leave my family out of this! I only want to know why it's necessary to wait until Thursday to find out what all of this is about!"

Again, the Kanten hesitated.

"There are . . . aspects of this matter which would best not be spoken over the ether. Several of the more thalamic of the contesting factions in your culture might misuse the knowledge if they . . . overheard. However, let me assure you that your part would be purely technical. It is your knowledge we wish to tap, and the skills you have been using at the Center."

Bull! Jacob thought. You want more than that.

He knew Fagin. If he attended this meeting the Kanten undoubtedly would try to use it as a wedge to get him involved in some ridiculously complicated and dangerous adventure. The alien had already done it to him on three occasions in the past.

The first two times Jacob hadn't minded. But he'd been a different sort of person then, the kind who loved that sort of thing.

Then came the Needle. The trauma in Ecuador had changed his life completely. He had no desire to go through anything like it again.

And yet, Jacob felt a powerful reluctance to disappoint the old Kanten. Fagin had never actually lied to him, and he was the only E.T. he'd met who was unabashedly an admirer of human culture and history. Physically the most alien creature he knew, Fagin was also the one extraterrestrial who tried hardest to understand Earthmen.

I should be safe if I simply tell Fagin the truth, Jacob thought. If he starts applying too much pressure I'll let him know about my mental state—the experiments with self-hypnosis and the weird results I've been getting. He won't push too hard if I appeal to his sense of fair play.

"All right," he sighed. "You win, Fagin. I'll be there. Just don't expect me to be the star of the show."

Fagin's laughter whistled with a flavor of woodwinds. "Do not be concerned about that, Friend-Jacob! In this particular show no one will mistake you for the star!"

The Sun was still above the horizon as he walked along the upper deck toward Makakai's quarters. It loomed, dim and orange among the sparse clouds in the west—a benign, featureless orb. He stopped at the rail for a moment to appreciate the colors of the sunset and the smell of the sea.

12

He closed his eyes and allowed the sunlight to warm his face, the rays penetrating his skin with gentle, browning insistence. Finally, he swung both legs over the rail and dropped to the lower deck. A taut, energized feeling had almost replaced the day's exhaustion. He began to hum a fragment of a tune— out of key, of course.

A tired dolphin drifted to the edge of the pool when he arrived. Makakai greeted him with a trinary poem too quick to catch, but it sounded amiably nasty. Something about his sex life. Dolphins had been telling humans dirty jokes for thousands of years before men finally started breeding them for brains and for speech, and began to understand. Makakai might be a lot smarter than her ancestors, Jacob thought, but her sense of humor was strictly dolphin.

"Well," he said. "Guess who's had a busy day."

She splashed at him, more weakly than usual, and said something that sounded a lot like "Br-r-a-a-a-p you!"

But she moved in closer when he hunkered down to put his hand into the water and say hello.

2.

SHIRTS AND SKINS

The old North American governments had razed the Border Strip years ago, to control movements to and from Mexico. A desert was made where two cities once touched.

Since the Overturn, and the destruction of the oppressive "Bureaucracy" of the old syndical governments, Confederacy authorities had maintained the area as parklands. The border zone between San Diego and Tijuana was now one of the largest forested areas south of Pendleton Park.

But that was changing. As he drove his rented car southward on the elevated highway, Jacob saw signs that the belt was returning to its old purpose. Crews worked on both sides of the road, cutting down trees and erecting slender, candy-striped poles at hundred-yard intervals to the west and east. The poles were shameful. He looked away.

A large green and white sign loomed where the line of poles crossed the highway.

New Boundary: Baja Extraterrestrial Reserve
Tijuana Residents Who Are Non-Citizens
Report to City Hall for Your Generous
Resettlement Bonus!

Jacob shook his head and grunted, "Oderint Dum Metuant." Let them hate, so long as they fear. So what if a person has lived in a town his entire life. If he hasn't got the vote, he's got to move out of the way when progress comes along.

Tijuana, Honolulu, Oslo, and half a dozen other cities were to be included when the E.T. Reserves expanded again. Fifty or sixty thousand Probationers, both permanent and temporary, would have to move to make those cities "safe" for perhaps a thousand aliens. The actual hardship would be small, of course. Most of Earth was still barred to E.T.'s, and non-Citizens still had plenty of room. The government offered large reparations as well.

But once again there were refugees on Earth.

The city suddenly resumed at the southern edge of the Strip. Many of the structures followed a Spanish or Spanish-Revival style, but overall the city showed the architectural experimentation typical of a modern Mexican town. Here the buildings ran in whites and blues. Traffic on both sides of the highway filled the air with a faint electric whine.

All over the town, green and white metallic signs, like the one at the border, heralded the coming change. But one, near the highway, had been defaced with black spray paint. Before it passed out of sight, Jacob caught a glimpse of the raggedly written words "Occupation" and "Invasion."

A Permanent Probationer did that, he thought. A Citizen wasn't likely to do anything so kinky, with hundreds of legal ways to express his opinion. And a Temporary Probie, sentenced to probation for a crime, wouldn't want his sentence lengthened. A Temporary would recognize the certainty of being caught.

No doubt some poor Permanent, facing eviction, had vented his feelings, not caring about the consequences. Jacob sympathized. The P.P. was probably in custody by now.

Although he was not particularly interested in politics, Jacob came from a political family. Two of his grandparents had been heroes in the Overturn, when a small group of technocrats had succeeded in bringing the Bureaucracy tumbling down. The family policy toward the Probation Laws was one of vehement opposition.

Jacob had been of a habit, the last few years, of avoiding memories of the past. Now, though, an image came forcefully to mind.

Summer school in the Alvarez Clan compound in the hills above Caracas . . . in the very house where Joseph Alvarez and his friends had made their plans thirty years before . . . there was Uncle Jeremey lecturing while Jacob's cousins and adopted cousins listened, all respectful expressions on the outside and seething summer boredom within. And Jacob fidgeted in the back corner, wishing he could get back to his room and the "secret equipment" he and his step-sister Alice had put together.

Suave and confident, Jeremey was then still in early middle age, a rising voice in the Confederacy Assembly. Soon he would be leader of the Alvarez clan, edging aside his older brother James.

Uncle Jeremey was telling about how the old Bureaucracy had decreed that everyone alive would be tested for "violent tendencies" and that all who failed would from then on be under constant surveillance—Probation.

Jacob could remember the exact words his uncle had spoken that afternoon, when Alice had come sneaking into the Library, excitement radiating from her twelve-year-old face like something about to go nova.

". . . They went to great efforts to convince the populace," Jeremey said in a low rumbling voice, "that the laws would cut down on crime. And they *did* have that effect. Individuals with radio transmitters in their rumps often think twice about causing trouble to their neighbors.

"Then, as now, the Citizens loved the Probation Laws. They had no trouble forgetting the fact that they cut through every traditional Constitutional guarantee of due process. Most of them lived in countries that had never had such niceties anyway.

"And when a fluke in those laws allowed Joseph Alvarez and his friends to turn the Bureaucrats themselves out on their ears—well, the jubilant Citizens just loved Probation testing even more. It did the leaders of the Overturn no good to push the issue at the time. They were having enough trouble setting up the Confederacy. . . ."

Jacob thought he would scream. Here was old Uncle Jeremey gabbing on and on about all that old nonsense, and Alice—lucky Alice whose turn it was to risk the oldsters' ire and listen in on the tap they'd placed on the house deepspace receiver—what was it she had heard!

It *had* to be a starship! It would be only the third of the great slow vessels ever to come back! That was the only possible explanation for the call up of the Space Reserves or for all the excitement in the east wing, where the adults kept their labs and offices.

Jeremey was still expounding on the public's continuing lack of compassion, but Jacob neither saw nor heard him. He kept his face rigid and still as Alice leaned over to whisper—no, gasp in her excitement—into his ear.

". . . *Aliens,* Jacob! They're bringing extraterrestrials! In their own ships! Oh, Jake, the Vesarius is bringing home Eatees!"

It was the first time Jacob had ever heard that word. He had often wondered if Alice was the one to coin it. At ten years of age, he recalled, he had wondered if "eatee" implied that someone else was to be designated "eaten."

As he drove above the streets of Tijuana, it occurred to him that the question still hadn't been answered.

In several major intersections one corner edifice had been removed and a rainbow-colored "E.T. Comfort Station Kiosk" installed. Jacob saw several of the new low open-decked busses equipped to carry humans and aliens who slithered, or walked three meters tall.

As he passed City Hall, Jacob saw about a dozen "Skins" picketing. At least they looked like Skins: people wearing furs and waving toy plastic spears.

Who else would dress that way in this sort of weather?

He turned up the volume on the car's radio and pressed the voice-select.

"Local news," he said. "Key words: Skins, City Hall, picketing."

After only a moment of delay a mechanical voice spoke from behind the dashboard with the slightly flawed inflection of a computer-generated news report. Jacob wondered if they'd ever get the voice tone right.

"Newsbrief summary." The artificial voice had an Oxford accent. "Precis: today, January 12, 2246, oh-nine forty one, good morning. Thirty seven persons are picketing the Tijuana City Hall in a legal manner. Their registered grievance is, summarized in abstract, the expansion of the Extraterrestrial Reserve. Please interrupt if you wish a fax or verbal presentation of their registered protest manifesto."

The machine paused. Jacob said nothing, already wondering if he wanted to hear the rest of the precis. He was already well acquainted with the Skins' protest against the implication of the Reserves: that some humans, at least, weren't fit to associate with aliens.

"Twenty-six of the thirty-seven members of the protest group carry probation transmitters," the report continued. "The rest are, of course, Citizens. This compares to a ratio of one probationer per hundred and twenty-four Citizens in Tijuana in general. By their demeanor and dress the protestors can be tentatively described as proponents of the so-called Neolithic Ethic, colloquially, 'Skins.' As none of the citizens has invoked privacy privilege, it can be said for certain that thirty of the thirty-seven are residents of Tijuana and the rest are visitors . . ."

Jacob stabbed the cutoff button and the voice died in mid-sentence. The scene at City Hall had long ago passed out of sight and it was an old story anyway.

The controversy over the expansion of the E.T. Reserve reminded him, though, that it had been almost two months since he last visited his Uncle James in Santa Barbara. The old bombast was prob-

18

ably up to his protruding ears, by now, in lawsuits on behalf of half of the probies in Tijuana. Still, he would notice if Jacob left on a long trip without saying good-bye, either to him or to the other uncles, aunts, and cousins of the rambling, rambunctious Alvarez clan.

Long trip? What long trip? Jacob thought suddenly. I'm not going anywhere!

But that corner of his mind he'd set aside for such things had caught scent of something in this meeting Fagin had called. He felt a sense of anticipation, and simultaneously a wish to suppress it. The feelings would have been intriguing, if they weren't already so familiar.

He rode on for a time in silence. Soon the city gave way to open countryside, and traffic reduced to a trickle. For the next twenty kilometers he drove with the sunshine warm on his arm and a pattern of doubts playing tag in his mind.

In spite of the restlessness he had felt recently, he was reluctant to admit that it was time to leave the Center for Uplift. The work with dolphins and chimps was fascinating, and far more equable (after the first tumultuous weeks during the Water-Sphinx affair) than his old profession as a scientific-crime investigator had been. The staff at the Center was dedicated and, unlike so many other scientific enterprises on Earth these days, they had high morale. They were doing work that had tremendous intrinsic value and would not be made instantly obsolete when the Branch Library in La Paz became completely operational.

But most important, he had made friends, and those friends had been supportive during the last year or so as he began the slow process of knitting together the schismed portions of his mind.

Gloria especially. I'm going to have to do something about her if I stay, Jacob thought. And more than the comradely heavy breathing we've done so far. The girl's feelings were becoming obvious.

Before the disaster in Ecuador, the loss that had brought him to the Center in the first place seeking work and peace, he would have known what to do and had the courage to do it. Now his feelings were a morass. He wondered if he would ever again consider more than a casual love relationship.

It had been a long two years since Tania's death. It had been lonely, at times, in spite of his work, his friends, and the ever fascinating games he played with his mind.

The ground became hilly and brown. Watching the cacti go by, Jacob sat back to enjoy the slow rhythm of the ride. Even now, his body swayed slightly with the motion as if he were still at sea.

The ocean glistened blue beyond the hills. The nearer the curving road took him to the meeting place, the more he wished he was aboard a boat out there: watching for the first hunched back and raised fluke of the year's Grey Migration, listening for the whale's Song of the Leader.

He rounded one hill to find the parking strips on both sides of the road lined solid with little electric runabouts like his own. On the crests of the hills up ahead were scores of people.

Jacob pulled his vehicle over into the automatic guideway on the right, where he could cruise slowly and take his eyes off the highway. What was going on here? Two adults and several children unloaded a car by the left side of the road, taking out picnic baskets and binoculars. They were clearly excited. They looked like a typical family on a weekday outing, except that all of them wore bright silver robes and golden amulets. Most of the people on the hill above them were similarly garbed. Many had small telescopes, aimed up the road at something that was obscured from Jacob's view by the hill on the right.

The crowd on that hill wore their caveman gear with panache. These Compleat Cro-Magnons compromised. They had their own telescopes, as well as wristwatches, radios, and megaphones, to back up their flint axes and spears.

It wasn't surprising that the two groups settled on opposite hilltops. The only thing that the Shirts and Skins ever agreed on was their hatred of the Extraterrestrial Quarantine.

A huge sign spanned the highway at the crest between the two hills.

BAJA CALIFORNIA EXTRATERRESTRIAL
RESERVE
Probationaries Not Admitted Without
Authorization
First Time Visitors Please Stop At The
Information Center
No Fetishes Or Neolithic Garments
Please
Check "Skins" in at Information Center.

Jacob smiled. The "papers" had had a field day
with that last command. There were cartoons on
every channel, which depicted visitors to the Reserve being forced to peel off their dermis, while a
pair of snakelike E.T.'s looked on approvingly.

The parked cars jammed together at the top. When
Jacob's car reached that point, the Barrier came into
view.

In a wide swatch of barren ground that stretched
from east to west, another line of barber poles ran,
this one complete. The colors had faded from many
of the smooth posts. Dust coated the round lamps
that capped the tops.

The ubiquitous P-trackers acted here as a visible
sieve, allowing Citizens to pass freely in and out of
the E.T. Reserve but warning probationers to stay
out, and aliens to stay within. It was a crude reminder of a fact that most people carefully ignored:
that a large part of humanity wore imbedded transmitters because the larger part didn't trust them. The
majority didn't want contact between extraterrestrials and those deemed "prone to violence" by a
psychological test.

Apparently, the Barrier did its job well. The crowds
on both sides grew thicker up ahead, and the costumes wilder, but the mob stopped in a clump just
north of the line of P-posts. Some of the Shirts and
Skins were probably Citizens, but they kept on this
side with their friends—out of politeness or perhaps
as a protest.

The crowds were thickest just north of the Barrier. Here the Shirts and Skins shoved signs at
quickly passing motorists.

Jacob kept in the guideway and looked about, shading his eyes from the glare and enjoying the show.

A young man on the left, wrapped in silver sateen from throat to toe, held up a placard that said, "Mankind Was Uplifted Too: Let Our E.T. Cousins Out!"

Just across the roadway from him a woman held a banner tacked to a spearshaft: "We did it Ourselves ... Eatees off Earth!"

There was the controversy in a nutshell. The whole world waited to see if the believers in Darwin, or those who followed Von Daniken, were right. The Skins and Shirts were only the more fanatical fringes of a split that had divided humanity into two philosophical camps. The issue: how did Homo-Sapiens originate as a thinking being?

Or was that *all* the Shirts and Skins represented?

The former group took their love of aliens to almost a pseudo-religious frenzy. Hysterical Xenophilia?

The Neoliths, with their love of caveman garb and ancient lore; were their cries for "independence from E.T. influence" based on something more basic—fear of the unknown, the powerfully alien? Xenophobia?

Of one thing Jacob was sure. The Shirts and Skins shared resentment. Resentment of the Confederacy's cautious compromise policy towards E.T.'s. Resentment of the Probation Laws which kept so many of them in a form of coventry. Resentment of a world in which no man any longer knew his roots for certain.

An old, unshaven man caught Jacob's eye. He squatted by the road, hopped up and down and pointed at the ground between his legs, shouting in the dust kicked up by the crowd. Jacob slowed down as he approached.

The man wore a fur jacket and hand-sewn leather breeches. His shouting and jumping grew more frenzied as Jacob neared.

"Doo-Doo!" He screamed, as if delivering a terrible insult. Froth appeared on his lips and he again pointed to the ground.

"Doo-Doo! Doo-Doo!"

Puzzled, Jacob slowed the car almost to a stop.

Something flew past his face from the left and

cracked against the window on the passenger side. There was a bang on the roof and within seconds a fusillade of small pebbles was striking the car, making a drumming that pounded in his ears.

He ran up the window on his left side, yanked the car out of automatic, and surged ahead. The flimsy metal and plastic of the runabout dimpled every time a missile struck it. Suddenly there were faces leering in Jacob's side windows; young tough faces with drooping moustaches. The youths ran along the side of the car as it sluggishly accelerated, hammering on it with fists and shouting.

With the Barrier only a few meters away, Jacob laughed and decided to find out what they wanted. He eased off a trifle on the accelerator and turned to mouth a question at the man who ran next to him, an adolescent dressed as a twentieth-century science fiction hero. The crowd by the side of the road was a blur of placards and costumes.

Before he could speak the car was shaken by a jolting bang. A hole had appeared in his windshield and a burning smell filled the little cab.

Jacob gunned the car toward the Barrier. The row of barber poles whizzed by and suddenly he was alone. In his rearview mirror he saw his entourage gather together. The youths shouted as he drove off, raising fists from the sleeves of futuristic robes. He grinned and opened the window to wave back.

How am I going to explain this to the rental company? he thought. Shall I say that I was attacked by forces of the Imperial Ming or do you think they'll believe the truth?

There was no question of calling the police. The local constabulary would be unable to make a move without starting with a P-Search. And a few P-Transmitters among so many would be lost for sure. Besides, Fagin had asked him to be discreet in coming to this meeting.

He rolled down the windows to let a breeze carry away the smoke. He poked at the bullet hole in his windshield with the tip of his small finger and smiled bemusedly.

You actually enjoyed that, didn't you? he thought.

It was one thing to let the adrenalin flow, and quite

23

another to *laugh* at danger. His sense of elation during the fracas at the Barrier worried a part of Jacob more than the mysterious violence of the crowd did ... a symptom out of his past.

A minute or two passed, then a tone sounded from the dashboard.

He looked up. A hitchhiker? Out here? Down the road, less than half of a kilometer away, a man by the curb held his watch out into the path of the guidebeam. Two satchels rested on the ground beside him.

Jacob hesitated. But here inside the Reserve only Citizens were allowed. He pulled over to the curb, just a few meters past the man.

There was something familiar about the fellow. He was a florid little man in a dark grey business suit and his paunch jiggled as he heaved two heavy bags to the side of Jacob's car. His face was perspiring as he bent over the door on the passenger's side and peered in.

"Oh boy, what heat!" he moaned. He spoke standard English with a thick accent.

"No wonder no one uses the guideway!" he went on, mopping his brow with a handkerchief. "They drive so fast to catch a little tiny breeze, don't they? But you are familiar, we must have met somewhere before. I am Peter LaRoque . . . or Pierre, if you wish. I am with *Les Mondes*."

Jacob started.

"Oh. Yes, LaRoque. We've met before. I'm Jacob Demwa. Hop in, I'm only going as far as the Information Center, but you can get a bus from there."

He hoped that his face didn't show his feelings. Why hadn't he recognized LaRoque when he was still moving? He might not have stopped.

It wasn't that he had anything in particular against the man . . . other than his incredible ego and his inexhaustible store of opinions, which he would thrust upon anyone at the smallest opportunity. In many ways he was probably a fascinating personality. He certainly had a following in the Danikenite press. Jacob had read a number of LaRoque's articles and enjoyed the style, if not the content.

But LaRoque had been a member of the press corps

24

that had chased him for weeks after he'd solved the Water-Sphinx mystery, and one of the least tactful at that. The final story in *Les Mondes* had been favorable, and beautifully written as well. But it hadn't been worth the trouble.

Jacob was glad that the press hadn't been able to find him after the still earlier Ecuadorian fiasco, that mess at the Vanilla Needle. At that time LaRoque would have been too much to bear.

Right now he was having trouble believing La-Roque's obviously affected "Origin" accent. It was even thicker than the last time they'd met, if possible.

"Demwa, ah, of course!" the man said. He stuffed his bags behind the passenger seat and got in. "The maker and purveyor of aphorisms! The connoisseur of mysteries! You're here maybe to play puzzle games with our noble interplanetary guests? Or perhaps you are going to consult with the Great Library in La Paz?"

Jacob re-entered the guideway, wishing he knew who had started the "National Origins Accent" fad, so he could strangle the man.

"I'm here to do some consultant work and my employers include extraterrestrials, if that's what you mean. But I can't go into details."

"Ah yes, so very secret!" LaRoque wagged a finger playfully. "You should not tease a journalist so! Your business I might make my business! But you, you must surely wonder what brings the ace reporter of *Les Mondes* to this desolate place, no?"

"Actually," Jacob said, "I'm more interested in how you came to be hitchhiking in the *middle* of this desolate place."

LaRoque sighed.

"A desolate place, indeed! How sad it is that the noble aliens who visit us should be stuck here and in other wastelands such as your Alaska!"

"And Hawaii and Caracas and Sri Lanka, the Confederacy Capitols," Jacob said. "But as to how you came to be . . ."

"How I came to be assigned here? Yes, of course, Demwa! But maybe we can amuse ourselves with your renowned deductive talents. You perhaps can guess?"

25

Jacob suppressed a groan. He reached forward to pull the car out of the guideway and put more weight onto the accelerator pedal.

"I've got a better idea, LaRoque. Since you don't want to tell me why you were standing there in the middle of nowhere, perhaps you'd be willing to clear up a little mystery for me."

Jacob described the scene at the Barrier. He left out the violent ending, hoping that LaRoque hadn't noticed the hole in the windshield, but he carefully described the behavior of the squatting man.

"But of course!" LaRoque cried. "You make it easy for me!

"You know the initials of this phrase you used, 'Permanent Probationer,' that horrible classification which denies a man his rights, parenthood, the franchise . . ."

"Look, I agree already! Save the speech." Jacob thought for a moment. What were the initials?

"Oh . . . I think I see."

"Yes, the poor fellow was only striking back! You Citizens, you call him Pee-Pee . . . so is it not simple justice that he accuse you of being Docile and Domesticated? Ergo the doo-doo!"

Jacob laughed, despite himself. The road began to curve.

"I wonder why all those people were gathered at the Barrier? They seemed to be waiting for somebody."

"At the Barrier?" LaRoque said. "Ah yes. I hear that happens every Thursday. Eatees from the Center go up to look at non-Citizens and they in turn come down to look at an Eatee. Droll, no? One doesn't know which side throws the peanuts!"

The road turned around one hill and their destination was in sight.

The Information Center, a few kilometers north of Ensenada, was a sprawling compound of E.T. quarters, public museums and, hidden around back, barracks for the border patrol. In front of a broad parking lot stood the main structure where first-time visitors took lessons in Galactic Protocol.

The station was on a small plateau, between the highway and the ocean, commanding a broad view over both. Jacob parked the car near the main entrance.

LaRoque was chewing, red-faced, on some thought. He looked up suddenly.

"You know I was joking, just then, when I spoke about peanuts. I was only making a joke."

Jacob nodded, wondering what had got into the man. Strange.

3.

GESTALT

Jacob helped LaRoque carry his bags to the bus station, then made his way around the main building to find a place outside to sit. Ten minutes remained before he was due at the meeting.

Where the compound overlooked a small harbor he found a patio with shade trees and picnic tables. He chose one table to sit on and rested his feet on the bench. The touch of the cool ceramic tile and the breeze off the ocean penetrated his clothing and drew away the redness from his skin and the perspiration from his clothes.

For a few minutes he sat quietly, letting the hard muscles of his shoulders and lower back relax one by one, sloughing off the tension of the drive. He focused on a small sailboat, a daycraft with jib and main colored greener than the ocean. Then he let a trance come down over his eyes.

Floating. One at a time he examined the things his senses revealed to him and then he canceled them. He concentrated on his muscles one by one, to cut off sensation and tension. Slowly his limbs grew numb and distant.

An itch in his thigh persisted, but his hands remained in his lap until it left of its own accord. The salt smell of the sea was pleasant but equally distracting. He made it go away. He shut off the sound of his heartbeat by listening to it with undivided attention until it became too familiar to notice.

As he had for two years, Jacob guided the trance through a cathartic phase, in which images came and went startlingly fast in healing pain, as two pieces, split apart, tried again to fuse whole. It was a process that he never enjoyed.

He was alone, almost. All that remained was a background of voices, murmuring subvocal snatches of phrases at the edge of meaning. For a moment he thought he could hear Gloria and Johnny arguing about Makakai, then Makakai herself chattering something irreverent in pidgin-trinary.

He guided each sound away gently, waiting for one that came, as usual, with predictable suddenness: Tania's voice calling something he couldn't quite understand as she fell past him, arms outstretched. He still heard her as she fell the rest of the twenty miles to the ground, becoming a tiny speck and then disappearing . . . still calling.

That little voice too faded, but this time it left him more uneasy than usual.

A violent, exaggerated version of the incident at the Zone Boundary flashed through his mind. Suddenly he was back, this time standing among the Probationers. A bearded man dressed as a Pictish Shaman held out a pair of binoculars and nodded insistently.

Jacob picked them up and looked where the man pointed. Its image warped by heat waves rising from the highway, a bus rolled to a stop just on the other side of a line of candy-striped poles that stretched to each horizon. Each pole seemed to reach all the way up to the sun.

Then the image was gone. With practiced indifference, Jacob let go of the temptation to think about it and allowed his mind to go completely blank.

Silence and Darkness.

He rested in a deep trance, relying on his own internal clock to signal when the time to emerge was near. He moved slowly among patterns that had no

29

symbols and long familiar meanings that eluded description or remembrance, patiently looking for the key he knew was there and that he'd someday find.

Time was now a thing like any other, lost in a deeper passage.

The calm dark was pierced, suddenly, by a sharp pain driving past all of his mind's isolation. It took a moment, an eternity that must have been a hundredth of a second, to localize it. The pain was a bright blue light that seemed to stab at his hypnosis sensitized eyes through closed lids. In another instant, before he could react, it was gone.

Jacob struggled for a moment with his confusion. He tried to concentrate solely on rising to consciousness while a stream of panicky questions popped like flashbulbs in his mind.

What subconscious artifact had that blue light been? A corner of neurosis that defends itself so fiercely has to mean trouble! What hidden fear did I probe?

As he emerged, hearing returned.

There were footsteps ahead. He picked them out from the sounds of the wind and sea, but in his trance they seemed like the soft padding ostrich feet might make if clothed in mocassins.

The deep trance finally broke, several seconds after the subjective burst of light. He opened his eyes. A tall alien stood in front of him, a few meters away. His immediate impression was of tallness, whiteness, and huge red eyes.

For a moment the world seemed to tilt.

Jacob's hands flew to the sides of the table and his head sank as he steadied himself. He closed his eyes.

Some trance! he thought. My head feels as if it's about to crash through the Earth and come out the other side!

He rubbed his eyes with one hand, then carefully looked up once again.

The alien was still there. So it was real. It was humanoid, standing at least two meters tall. Most of its slender body was covered by a long silvery robe. The hands, folded in front in the Attitude of Respectful Waiting, were long, white and glossy.

A very large round head bowed forward on a slender neck. The lidless, red, columnar eyes and the lips of the alien's mouth were huge. They dominated the face, on which a few other small organs served purposes unknown to him. This species was new to Jacob.

The eyes glowed with intelligence.

Jacob cleared his throat. He still had to fight off waves of dizziness.

"Excuse me. . . . Since we haven't been introduced, I . . . don't know how I'm to address you, but I assume you're here to see me?"

The big, white head nodded deeply in assent.

"Are you with the group the Kanten Fagin asked me to meet?"

Again, the alien nodded.

I suppose that means yes, Jacob thought. I wonder if he can speak, what with any imaginable kind of mechanism lurking behind those huge lips.

But why was the creature just standing there? Was there something in its attitude . . . ?

"Am I to assume that, that yours is a client species and you are waiting for permission to speak?"

The "lips" separated slightly and Jacob caught a glimpse of something bright and white. The alien nodded again.

"Well then speak up, please! We humans are notoriously short on protocol. What's your name?"

The voice was surprisingly deep. It hissed out of a barely widened mouth with a pronounced lisp.

"I am Culla, Shir. Thank you. I have been shent to make sure that you were not losht. If you will come with me, the othersh are waiting. Or, if you prefer, you can continue to meditate until the appointed time."

"No, no let's go, by all means." Jacob rose to his feet unsteadily. He closed his eyes for a moment to clear his mind of the last shreds of the trance. Sooner or later he would have to sort out what had happened, while he'd been under, but that would have to wait.

"Lead on."

Culla turned and walked with a slow, fluid gait toward one of the side doorways to the Center.

Culla was apparently a member of a "client" species—one whose period of indenture to its "patron" species was still active. Such a race rated low on the galactic pecking order. Jacob, mystified as he still was by the intricacies of galactic affairs, was glad that a lucky accident had won for humanity a better, if insecure, place on the hierarchy.

Culla led him upstairs to a large oaken door. He opened it without announcement and preceded Jacob into the meeting room.

Jacob saw two human beings and, besides Culla, two aliens: one short and furry, the other smaller still, and lizardlike. They were seated on cushions between some large indoor shrubs and a picture window overlooking the bay.

He tried to sort his impressions of the aliens before they noticed him, but had only a moment before someone spoke his name.

"Jacob, my friend! How kind it is for you to come and share with us your time!" It was Fagin's fluting voice. Jacob looked quickly about the room.

"Fagin, where . . . ?"

"I am here."

He looked back at the group by the window. The humans and the furry E.T. were rising to their feet. The lizard-alien remained on its cushion.

Jacob adjusted his perspective and suddenly one of the "indoor shrubs" was Fagin. The old Kanten's silver tipped foliage tinkled softly as if there were a breeze.

Jacob smiled. Fagin presented a problem whenever they met. With humanoids, one looked for a face, or something that served the same purpose. Usually it took only a little time to find a place in an alien's strange features on which to focus.

There was almost always a part of the anatomy that one learned to address as the seat of another awareness. Among humans and very often among E.T.'s, this focus was in the eyes.

A Kanten has no eyes. Jacob guessed that the bright silver objects that made the sound of tiny sleigh bells were Fagin's light receptors. If so, it still didn't help. One had to look at the whole of Fagin, not at some cusp of the ego. It made Jacob wonder which was the larger improbability: that he liked the alien despite this handicap, or that he still felt uneasy with him despite years of friendship.

Fagin's dark leafy body approached from the window in a series of twists that brought successive root-knots to the fore. Jacob gave him one medium-formal bow and waited.

"Jacob Alvarez Demwa, a-Human, ul-Dolphin-ul-Chimp, we welcome you. It pleases this poor being to sense you today, once again." Fagin spoke clearly, but with an uncontrolled singsong quality which made his accent sound like mixed Swedish and Cantonese. The Kanten did much better speaking dolphin or trinary.

"Fagin, a-Kanten, ab-Linten-ab-Siqul-ul-Nish, Mihorki Keephu. It pleases me to see you once again." Jacob bowed.

"These venerable beings have come to exchange their wisdom with yours, Friend-Jacob," Fagin said. "I hope you are prepared for formal introductions."

Jacob set his mind to concentrate on the convoluted species names of each alien, at least as much as on their appearance. Patronymics and multiple client names would tell a great deal about the status of each. He nodded for Fagin to proceed.

"I will now formally introduce you to Bubbacub, a-Pil, ab-Kisa-ab-Soro-ab-Hul-ab-Puber-ul-Gello-ul-Pring, of the Library Institute."

One of the E.T.'s stepped forward. Jacob's initial gestalt was of a four-foot, gray teddy bear. But a wide snout and fringe of cilia around the eyes belied that impression.

This was Bubbacub, director of the Branch Library! The Branch Library at La Paz consumed almost all of the meager trade balance which Earth had accumulated since contact. Even so, much of the prodigious effort of adapting a tiny "suburban" Branch to human referents was donated by the huge galactic Institute of the Library, as a charity, to help the "backward" human race catch up with the rest of the galaxy. As head of the Branch, Bubbacub was one of the most important aliens on Earth! His species name also implied high status, higher even than Fagin's!

The "ab" something-to-the-fourth meant that Bubbacub's species had been nurtured into sentience by another which had in turn been nurtured by another, and so forth back to the mythical beginning at the time of the Progenitors . . . and that four of these generations of "Parentals" were still alive somewhere in the galaxy. To be derived from such a chain meant status in a diffuse galactic culture whose every spacefaring species (with the possible lone exception of humanity) was brought up out of semi-intelligent savagery by some previous, space-traveling race.

The "ul" something squared said that the Pil race had in turn fostered two new cultures on their own. This too was status.

The one thing that had prevented the complete snubbing of the "orphan" human race by the Galactics was the fortunate fact that man had himself fostered new intelligent races twice before the Vesarius had brought Contact with the E.T. civilization home to Earth.

The alien made a slight bow.

"I am Bubbacub."

The voice sounded artificial. It came from a disc that hung from the Pil's neck.

A Vodor! The Pil race required artificial assistance to speak English, then. From the simplicity of the device, much smaller than those used by alien visitors whose native tongues were twitters and squeaks, Jacob guessed that Bubbacub could actually pronounce human words, but in a frequency range beyond human hearing. He decided to assume that the being could hear him.

"I am Jacob. Welcome to Earth." He nodded.

Bubbacub's mouth snapped open and shut a few times silently.

"Thank you," the Vodor buzzed, in clipped, short words. "I am happy to be here."

"And I to be of service as your host." Jacob bowed ever so slightly deeper than he had seen Bubbacub do when he came forward. The alien seemed to be satisfied and stepped back.

Fagin recommenced his introductions.

"These worthy beings are of your race." A twig and a bunch of petals gestured vaguely in the direction of the two human beings. A gray-haired gentleman, dressed in tweed, stood next to a tall brown woman, in handsome middle age.

"I will now introduce you," Fagin continued, "in the informal manner preferred by humans.

"Jacob Demwa, meet Doctor Dwayne Kepler, of the Sundiver Expedition, and Doctor Mildred Martine, of the Department of Parapsychology at the University of La Paz."

Kepler's face was dominated by a substantial handlebar moustache. He smiled, but Jacob was too amazed to reply to his pleasantries with more than a monosyllable.

The Sundiver Expedition! The research on Mercury and in the solar chromosphere had been a football in the Confederacy Assembly, of late. The "Adapt & Survive" faction said that it made no sense to spend so much for knowledge that could be pulled out of the Library, when the same appropriation could employ several times as many unemployed scientists here on Earth with make-work projects. The "Self-Sufficiency" faction had so far had its way, though, in spite of abuse from the Danikenite press.

But to Jacob it was the *idea* of sending men and ships down into a star that sounded like insanity of the first degree.

"Kant Fagin was enthusiastic in his recommendations," Kepler said. The Sundiver leader smiled, but his eyes were reddened. They bore puffy outlines from some inner worry. He pressed Jacob's hand in both of his own and pumped quickly as he spoke. His voice was deep but it did not hide a quaver.

"We came to Earth only for a little while. It's an answered prayer that Fagin was able to persuade you to meet with us. We really hope you can join us on Mercury and give us the benefit of your experience in interspecies contact."

Jacob started. Oh no, not this time you don't, you leafy monster! He wanted to turn and glare at Fagin but even informal intrahuman propriety required that he face these people and make small talk. Mercury indeed!

Dr. Martine's face fell easily into a pleasant smile

but she looked a little bored as he shook her hand.

Jacob wondered if he could ask what parapsychology had to do with solar physics without sounding as if he were interested, but Fagin beat him to it.

"I intrude, as is generally considered acceptable in informal conversations among human beings when a pause has occurred. There remains one worthy being to introduce."

Oops, thought Jacob, I hope this Eatee's not one of the hypersensitive ones. He turned to where the lizardlike extraterrestrial stood, to his right, next to a multicolored wall mosaic. It had risen from its cushion and now moved on six legs toward them. It was less than a meter in length and about twenty centimeters high. It walked right past him without a glance and proceeded to rub itself against Bubbacub's leg.

"Ahem," Fagin said. "That is a pet. The worthy whom you are about to meet is the estimable client who brought you to this room."

"Oh, I'm sorry." Jacob grinned, then forced a serious expression onto his face.

"Jacob Demwa, a-Human, ul-Dolphin-ul-Chimp, please meet Culla, a-Pring, ab-Pil-ab-Kisa-ab-Soro-ab-Hul-ab-Puber, Assistant to Bubbacub of the Libraries and Representative of the Library with the Sundiver Project."

As Jacob had expected, the name had only patronymics. The Pring had no clients of their own. They were of the Puber/Soro line, though. Someday they would have high status as members of that old and powerful lineage. He had noticed that Bubbacub's species was also out of the Puber/Soro and wished he could recall if the Pila and Pring were Patron and Client.

The alien stepped forward but did not offer to shake hands. His hands were long and tentacular with six fingers each at the ends of long slender arms. They looked fragile. Culla had a faint odor, a bit like the smell of new mown hay, that was not at all unpleasant.

The huge columnar eyes flashed as Culla bowed for the formal introduction. The E.T.'s "lips" curled back to display a pair of white, gleaming, grindermashie things, one on top and one on the bottom. The partially prehensile lips brought the cleavers together with a white porcelain "clack!"

That can't be a friendly gesture where he comes from, Jacob shuddered. The alien probably pulled his huge dentures out to imitate a human smile. The sight was disturbing and at the same time intriguing. Jacob wondered what they were for. He also hoped that Culla would keep his . . . lips curled back in the future.

Nodding slightly he said, "I am Jacob."

"I am Culla, Shir," the alien replied. "Your Earth ish very pleasant." The great red eyes were now dull. Culla backed away.

Bubbacub led them back to the cushions by the window. The little Pil sprawled into a prone position with his quadrilaterally symmetric hands dangling over the sides of the cushion. The "pet" followed and curled up next to him.

Kepler leaned forward and spoke hesitantly.

"I'm sorry we dragged you away from your important work, Mr. Demwa. I know you're already heavily engaged . . . I only hope that we can persuade you that, that our own little . . . problem is worth your time and worthy of your talents." Dr. Kepler's hands were knotted together on his lap.

Dr. Martine looked on Kepler's earnestness with an expression of mildly amused patience. There were nuances here that bothered Jacob.

"Well, Dr. Kepler, Fagin must have told you that since my wife's death, I've retired from the "mystery business," and I am pretty busy right now, probably too much so to get involved in a long journey off planet . . ."

Kepler's face fell. His expression became so bleak so suddenly that Jacob was moved.

". . . However, since Kant Fagin is a perceptive individual, I'll be happy to listen to anyone he refers to me, and decide on the merits of the case."

"Oh, you'll find this case interesting! I've been saying all along that we need fresh insight. And, of course, now that the Trustees have agreed to let us bring in some consultants . . ."

"Now, Dwayne," Dr. Martine said. "You're not being fair. I came in as a consultant six months ago, and Culla brought the services of the Library even earlier. Now Bubbacub has kindly agreed to increase the Library support for the project and come personally with us to Mercury. I think the Trustees are being more than generous."

Jacob sighed.

"I wish someone would explain what this is all about. Like you, Dr. Martine, perhaps you can tell me what your job is . . . on Mercury?" He found it difficult to say the word "Sundiver."

"I am a consultant, Mr. Demwa. I was hired to perform psychological and parapsychological tests on the crew and environment on Mercury."

"I assume they had to do with the problem Dr. Kepler mentioned?"

"Yes. It was thought at first that the phenomena were a hoax or some sort of mass-hallucination. I've eliminated both of those possibilities. It's clear now that they're real and actually take place in the solar chromosphere.

"For the last months I've been designing psi experiments to take down on solar dives. I've also been helping as a therapist for a number of Sundiver staff members; the pressures of conducting this kind of solar research have been telling on many of the men."

Martine sounded competent, but there was something about her attitude that put Jacob off. Flippancy, perhaps. Jacob wondered what else there was to her relationship with Kepler. Was she his personal therapist as well?

For that matter, am I here just to satisfy the whim of a sick, great man who must be kept going? The idea wasn't very attractive. Nor was the prospect of getting involved in politics.

Bubbacub, head of the entire Branch Library on Earth—why is he involved in an obscure Terran project? In some ways, the little Pil was the most important E.T. on the Planet outside of the Tymbrimi Ambassador. His Library Institute, the biggest and most influential of the galactic organizations, made Fagin's Institute of Progress look like a drum and tambourine outfit. Did Martine say he's going to Mercury?

Bubbacub stared at the ceiling, apparently ignoring the conversation. His mouth worked as though singing in some range inaudible to humans.

Culla's bright eyes were on the little Library Chief. Perhaps he could hear the singing, or perhaps he too was bored by the conversation so far.

Kepler, Martine, Bubbacub, Culla . . . I never thought I'd be in a room in which *Fagin* was the least strange!

The Kanten rustled nearby. Fagin was obviously excited. Jacob wondered what could have happened in the Sundiver project to get him so fired up.

"Dr. Kepler, it just might be possible that I could spare the time to help you out . . . maybe." Jacob shrugged. "But first, it would be nice to find out what this is all about!"

Kepler brightened.

"Oh, didn't I ever actually say it? Oh my. I guess I just avoid thinking about it these days . . . just skirt around the subject, so to speak."

He straightened and took a deep breath.

"Mr. Demwa, it appears that the Sun is haunted."

PART II

In prehistoric and early times the
Earth was visited by unknown beings
from the cosmos. These unknown
beings created human intelligence by a
deliberate genetic mutation. The
extraterrestrials ennobled hominids
"in their own image." That is why we
resemble them and not they us.

Erich Von Daniken
Chariots of the Gods

The sublime mental activities, such
as religion, altruism and morality, all
evolved, and have a physical base.

Edward O. Wilson
On Human Nature
Harvard University Press

4.

VIRTUAL IMAGE

The *Bradbury* was a new ship. It used a technology far ahead of its predecessors on the commercial line, taking off from sea level under its own power instead of riding to the station at the top of one of the equatorial "Needles," slung beneath a giant balloon. *Bradbury* was a huge sphere, titanically massive by earlier standards.

This was Jacob's first trip aboard a ship powered by the billion-year-old science of the Galactics. He watched from the first-class lounge as the Earth fell away, and Baja California became first a brown rib, separating two seas, then a mere finger along the coast of Mexico. The view was breathtaking, but a bit disappointing. The roar and acceleration of a jetliner, or the slow majesty of a cruise-zep had more romance. And the few times he had left Earth before, rising and returning by balloon, there has been the other ships to watch, bright and busy as they floated up to Power Station or back down the pressurized interior of one of the Needles.

Neither of the great Needles had ever been boring. The thin ceram walls that held the twenty-mile towers at sea-level pressures had been painted with gigantic murals—huge swooping birds and pseudo science-fiction space battles copied from twenty-century magazines. It had never been claustrophobic.

Still, Jacob was glad to be aboard the *Bradbury*. Someday he might visit the Chocolate Needle, at the summit of Mt. Kenya, for nostalgia's sake. But the other one, the one in Ecuador—Jacob hoped never to see the Vanilla Needle again.

No matter that the great tower was only a stone's throw from Caracas. No matter that he would be given a hero's welcome, if ever he came there, as the man who had saved the one engineering marvel on Earth to impress even the Galactics.

Saving the Needle had cost Jacob Demwa his wife and a large portion of his mind. The price had been too high.

Earth had gained a visible disc when Jacob went off to look for the ship's bar. Suddenly he was in the mood for company. He hadn't felt that way when he came aboard. He'd had a rough time making excuses to Gloria and the others at the Center. Makakai had raised a fit. Also, many of the research materials on Solar Physics he'd ordered had not arrived and would have to be forwarded to Mercury. Finally, he'd let himself get into a stew wondering how he'd been talked into coming along in the first place.

Now he made his way along the main corridor, at the ship's equator, until he found the crowded, dimly lit Saloon. Inside he squeezed past clots of talking, drinking passengers to get to the bar.

About forty persons, many of them contract workers bound for skilled labor on Mercury, crowded into the Saloon. More than a few, having drunk too much, spoke loudly to their neighbors or simply stared. For some, departure from Earth came hard.

A few extraterrestrials rested on cushions in the corner set aside for them. One, a Cynthian with shiny fur and thick sunglasses, sat across from Culla, whose great head nodded silently while he sipped daintily with a straw between his huge lips, from what appeared to be a bottle of vodka.

Several humans stood near the aliens, typical of the Xenophiles who hang on every word of an eavesdropped E.T. conversation and who wait eagerly for chances to ask questions.

Jacob considered edging through the crowd to get to the E.T. corner. The Cynthian might be someone he knew. But there were too many people at that end of the room. He chose instead to get a drink and see if anyone had started storytelling.

Soon he was part of a group listening to a mining engineer tell an enjoyably exaggerated tale of blow-ins and rescues in the deep Hermetian mines. Though he had to strain to hear over the noise, Jacob still felt he could conveniently ignore the headache that was coming on ... at least long enough to listen to the end of the story, when a finger jabbed in his ribs made him jump.

"Demwa! It's you!" Pierre LaRoque cried. "How fortunate! We shall travel together and now I know that there will always be someone with whom I can exchange witticisms!"

LaRoque wore a loose shiny robe. Blue PurSmok drifted into the air from the pipe he puffed with earnest.

Jacob tried to smile but with someone behind him stepping on his heel, it came out more like gritting his teeth.

"Hello, LaRoque. Why are you going to Mercury? Wouldn't your readers be more interested in stories about the Peruvian excavations or ..."

"Or similar dramatic evidence that our primitive ancestors were nurtured by ancient astronauts?" LaRoque interrupted. "Yes, Demwa, such evidence shall soon be so overwhelming that even the Skins and skeptics who sit on the Confederacy Council will see the error of their ways!"

"I see you wear the Shirt yourself." Jacob pointed to LaRoque's silvery tunic.

"I wear the robe of the Daniken Society on my last day on Earth, in honor of the older ones who gave us the power to go into space." LaRoque shifted pipe and drink into one hand and with the other straightened the gold medallion and chain that hung from his neck.

Jacob thought the effect was a bit theatrical for a grown man. The robe and jewelry seemed effeminate,

45

in contrast to the Frenchman's gruff manner. He had to admit, though, that it went well with the outrageous, affected accent.

"Oh come on, LaRoque," Jacob smiled. "Even you have to admit we got into space by ourselves, and *we* discovered the extraterrestrials, not they us."

"I admit nothing!" LaRoque answered hotly. "When we prove ourselves worthy of the Patrons who gave us our intelligence in the dim past, when they acknowledge us, *then* we'll know how much they have covertly helped us all these years!"

Jacob shrugged. There was nothing new in the Skin-Shirt controversy. One side insisted that man should be proud of his unique heritage as a self-evolved race, having won intelligence from Nature herself on the savannah and shoreline of East Africa. The other side held that homo sapiens—just as every other known race of sophonts—was part of a chain of genetic and cultural uplifting that stretched back to the fabled early days of the galaxy, the time of the Progenitors.

Many, like Jacob, were studiously neutral in the conflict of views, but humanity, and humanity's client races, awaited the outcome with interest. Archeology and Paleontology had become the great new hobbies since Contact.

However, LaRoque's arguments were so stale they could be used for croutons. And the headache was getting worse.

"That's very interesting, LaRoque," he said as he began to edge past. "Perhaps we can discuss it some other time . . ." But LaRoque wasn't finished yet.

"Space is filled with Neanderthaler sentiment, you know. The men on our ships would prefer to wear animal skins and grunt like apes! They resent the Older Ones, and they actively snub sensible people who practice humility!"

LaRoque made his point while jabbing in Jacob's direction with the stem of his pipe. Jacob backed away, trying to stay polite but having difficulty.

"Well, now I think that's going a little too far, La-Roque. I mean you're talking about astronauts! Emotional and political stability are prime criteria in their selection . . ."

"Aha! What you do not know about the very things

you just mentioned! You joke, no? I know a thing or two about 'emotional and political stability' of astronauts!

"I'll tell you about it sometime," he continued. "Someday the whole story will come out, about the Confederacy's plan to isolate a large part of humanity away from the elder races, and from their heritage in the stars! All the poor 'unreliables'! But by then it will be too late to seal the leak!"

LaRoque puffed and exhaled a cloud of blue Pur-Smok in Jacob's direction. Jacob felt a wave of dizziness.

"Yeah, LaRoque, whatever you say. You've got to tell me about it some time." He backed away.

LaRoque glowered on for a moment, then grinned and patted Jacob on the back as he edged his way to the door.

"Yes," he said. "I'll tell you all about it. But meanwhile, better you should lie down. You don't look so good at all! Bye bye!" He slapped Jacob's back once more then slipped back into the bar.

Jacob walked to the nearest port and rested his head against the pane. It was cool and it helped to ease the throbbing in his forehead. When he opened his eyes to look out, the Earth was not in sight . . . only a great field of stars, shining unblinking against blackness. The brighter ones were surrounded by diffraction rays, which he could lengthen or shorten by squinting. Except for the brightness, the effect was no different than looking at the stars on a night in the desert. They didn't twinkle, but they were the same stars.

Jacob knew he should feel more. The stars when viewed from space should be more mysterious, more . . . "philosophical." One of the things he could remember best about his adolescence was the asolopsistic roar of starry nights. It was nothing like the oceanic feeling he now got through hypnosis. It had been like half-remembered dreams of another life.

He found Dr. Kepler, Bubbacub, and Fagin in the main lounge. Kepler invited him to join them.

The group settled around a cluster of cushions near the view ports. Bubbacub carried with him a cup of something that looked and, from a chance whiff, smelled noxious. Fagin ambled slowly, twisting on his root-pods, carrying nothing.

The row of ports that ran along the curved periphery of the ship was broken in the lounge by a large circular disc, like a giant round window, that touched floor and ceiling. The flat side protruded into the room about a foot. Whatever lay within was hidden behind a tightly fixed panel.

"We are glad that you made it," Bubbacub barked through his Vodor. He had sprawled on one of the cushions and, after saying this, dipped his snout into the cup he carried and ignored Jacob and the others. Jacob wondered if the Pil was trying to be sociable, or if he came by his charm naturally.

Jacob thought of Bubbacub as "he" because he had no idea at all about Bubbacub's true gender. Though Bubbacub wore no clothes, other than the Vodor and a small pouch, what Jacob could see of the alien's anatomy only confused matters. He had learned, for instance, that the Pila were oviparous and did not suckle their young. But a row of what appeared to be teats lay like shirt buttons from throat to crotch. He couldn't even guess at their purpose. The Datanet did not mention them. Jacob had ordered a more complete summary from the Library.

Fagin and Kepler were talking about the history of Sunships. Fagin's voice was muffled because his upper foliage and blowhole brushed against the soundproofing panels on the ceiling. (Jacob hoped that Kanten were not prone to claustrophobia. But then, what were talking vegetables afraid of anyway? Being nibbled on, he supposed. He wondered about the sexual mores of a race whose lovemaking required the intermediary of a sort of domesticated bumblebee.)

"Then these magnificent improvisations," Fagin said, "without benefit of the slightest help from outside, enabled you to convey packages of instruments into the very Photosphere! This is most impressive and I wonder that, in my years here, I never knew of this adventure of your period before Contact!"

Kepler beamed. "You must understand that the bathysphere project was only . . . the beginning, long before my time. When laser propulsion for pre-Contact interstellar craft was developed, they were able to drop robot ships that could hover and, by the thermodynamics of using a high temperature laser, they could dump excess heat and cool the probe's interior."

"Then you were only a short time away from sending men!"

Kepler smiled ruefully. "Well, perhaps. Plans were made. But sending living beings to the Sun and back involved more than just heat and gravity. The worst obstacle was the turbulence!

"It would have been great to see if we could have solved the problem, though." Kepler's eyes shone for a moment. "There were plans."

"But then the Vesarius found Tymbrimi ships in Cygnus," Jacob said.

"Yes. So we'll never find out. The plans were drawn up when I was just a boy. Now they're hopelessly obsolete. And it's probably just as well. . . . There would have been inescapable losses, even deaths, if we'd done it without stasis. . . . Control of timeflow is the key to Sundiver now, and I certainly wouldn't complain about the results."

The scientist's expression suddenly darkened. "That is, until now."

Kepler fell silent and stared at the carpet. Jacob watched him for a moment, then covered his mouth and coughed.

"While we're on the subject, I've noticed that there isn't any mention of Sun Ghosts on the Datanet, or even in a special request from the Library . . . and I have a 1-AB permit. I was wondering if you could spare some of your reports on the subject, to study during the trip?"

Kepler looked away from Jacob nervously.

"We weren't quite ready to let the data off Mercury yet, Mr. Demwa. There . . . are political considerations to this discovery that, uh, will delay your briefing until we get to the base. I'm sure that all of your questions will be answered there." He looked so genuinely ashamed that Jacob decided to drop the matter for the moment. But this was not a good sign.

"I might take a liberty in adding one piece of information," Fagin said. "There has been another dive since our meeting, Jacob, and on that dive, we are told, only the first and more prosaic species of Solarian was observed. Not the second variety which has caused Dr. Kepler so much concern."

Jacob was still confused by the hurried explanations Kepler had given of the two types of Sun-creatures so far observed.

"Now I take it that type was your herbivore?"

"Not herbivore!" Kepler interjected. "A magnetovore. It feeds on magnetic field energy. That type is actually becoming rather well understood, however . . ."

"I interrupt! In the most unctious wish that I be forgiven for the intrusion, I urge discretion. A stranger approaches." Fagin's upper branches rustled against the ceiling.

Jacob turned to look at the doorway, a bit shocked that *anything* would bring Fagin to interrupt another's sentence. Dismally he realized that this was still another sign that he had stepped into a politically tense situation, and he still knew none of the rules.

I don't hear anything, he thought. Then Pierre LaRoque stood at the door, a drink in his hand and his always florid face further flushed. The man's initial smile broadened when he saw Fagin and Bubbacub. He entered and gave Jacob a jovial slap on the back, insisting that he be introduced right away.

Jacob internalized a shrug.

He performed the introductions slowly. LaRoque was impressed, and he bowed deeply to Bubbacub.

"Ab-Kisa-ab-Soro-ab-Hul-ab-Puber! And two clients, what were they, Demwa? Jello and something? I'm honored to meet a sophont of the Soro line in person! I have studied the language of your ancestrals, whom we may someday show to be ours as well! The Soro tongue is so similar to Proto-Semitic, and Proto-Bantu also!"

Bubbacub's cilia bristled above his eyes. The Pil, through his Vodor, began to make voice with a complicated, alliterative, incomprehensible speech. Then the alien's jaws made short, sharp snaps and a high pitched growling could be heard, half amplified by the Vodor.

From behind Jacob, Fagin answered in a clicking and rumbling tongue. Bubbacub turned to face him, black eyes hot as he answered with a throaty growl, waving a stubby arm in a slash in LaRoque's direc-

50

tion. The Kanten's trilling reply sent a chill down Jacob's back.

Bubbacub swiveled and stamped out of the room without a further word to the humans.

For a dumbfounded instant, LaRoque said nothing. Then, he looked at Jacob plaintively. "What is it I did, please?"

Jacob sighed, "Maybe he doesn't like being called a cousin of yours, LaRoque." He turned to Kepler to change the subject. The scientist was staring at the door through which Bubbacub left.

"Dr. Kepler, if you haven't any specific data on board, perhaps you could lend me some basic solar physics texts and some background histories on Sundiver itself?"

"I'd be delighted to, Mr. Demwa." Kepler nodded. "I'll send them to you by dinner time." His mind appeared to be elsewhere.

"I too!" LaRoque cried. "I am an accredited journalist and I demand the background upon your infamous endeavor, Mr. Director!"

After a moment's startlement, Jacob shrugged. Have to hand it to LaRoque. Chutzhpa can be easily mistaken for resiliency.

Kepler smiled, as if he had not heard. "I beg your pardon?"

"The great conceit! This 'Sundiver Project' of yours, which takes money that could go to the deserts of Earth for reclamation, or to a greater Library for our world!

"The vanity of this project, to study what our betters understood perfectly before we were apes!"

"Now see here, sir. The Confederacy has funded this research . . ." Kepler reddened.

"Research! Ree-search it is. You re-search for that which is already in the Libraries of the Galaxy, and shame us all by making humans out to be fools!"

"LaRoque . . ." Jacob began, but the man wouldn't shut up.

"And what of your Confederacy! They stuff the Elders into reservations, like the old-time Indians of America! They keep access to the Branch Library out of the hands of the people! They allow continuation

51

of this absurdity that all laugh at us for, this claim of spontaneous intelligence!"

Kepler backed away from LaRoque's vehemence. The color drained out of his face and he stammered.

"I ... I don't think ..."

"LaRoque! Come on, cut it out!"

Jacob grabbed his shoulder and pulled him over to whisper urgently in his ear.

"Come on man, you don't want to shame us in front of the venerable Kanten Fagin, do you?"

LaRoque's eyes widened. Over Jacob's shoulder Fagin's upper foliage rustled audibly in agitation. Finally, LaRoque's gaze dropped.

The second embarrassment must have been enough for him. He mumbled an apology to the alien, and with a parting glare at Kepler, took his leave.

"Thanks for the special effects, Fagin," Jacob said after LaRoque was gone.

He was answered by a whistle, short and low.

5.

REFRACTION

At 40 million kilometers, the Sun was a chained hell. It boiled in black space, no longer the brilliant dot that the children of Earth took for granted and easily, unconsciously, avoided with their eyes. Across millions of miles it pulled. Compulsively, one felt a need to look, but the need was dangerous.

From the Bradbury, it had the apparent size of a nickel held a foot away from the eye. The specter was too bright to be endured undiminished. To "catch a glimpse" of this orb, as one sometimes did on Earth, would invite blindness. The Captain ordered the ship's stasis screens polarized and the regular viewing ports sealed.

The Lyot window was unshuttered in the lounge, so that passengers could examine the Lifegiver without injury.

Jacob paused in front of the round window in a late night pilgrimage to the coffee machine, half awake from a fitful sleep in his tiny stateroom. For minutes he stared, blank faced, still only half conscious, until a lisping voice roused him.

"Dish ish the way your shun looksh from the Aphelion of the orbit of Mercury, Jacob."

Culla sat at one of the card tables in the dimly lit lounge. Just behind the alien, above a row of vending machines, a wall clock read "04:30" in glowing numbers.

Jacob's sleepy voice was thick in his throat. "Have . . . um, . . . are we that close already?"

Culla nodded. "Yesh."

The alien's lip grinders were tucked away. His big folded lips pursed and let out a whistle each time he tried to pronounce an English long "s." In the dim light his eyes reflected a red glow from the viewing window.

"We have only two more days until we arrive," the alien said. His arms were crossed on the table in front of him. The loose folds of his silver gown covered half of the surface.

Jacob, swaying slightly, turned to glance back at the port. The solar orb wavered before his eyes.

"Are you all right?" the Pring asked anxiously. He started to rise.

"No. No, please." Jacob held up his hand. "I'm just groggy. Not 'nuff sleep. Need coffee."

He shambled toward the vending machines, but halfway there he stopped, turned, and peered again at the image of the furnace-sun.

"It's red!" he grunted in surprise.

"Shall I tell you why while you get your coffee?" Culla asked.

"Yes. Please." Jacob turned back to the dark row of food and beverage dispensers, looking for a coffee spout.

"The Lyot window only allowsh in light in monochromatic form," Culla said. "It ish made of many round platesh; some polarizersh and some light retardersh. They are rotated with reshpect to one another to finely tune which wavelength ish allowed through.

"Itsh a most delicate and ingenioush device, although quite obsholete by Galactic standarsh . . . like one of the 'Shwiss' watchesh some humansh shtill wear in an age of electronicsh. When your people become adept with the Library such . . . Rube Goldbersh? . . . will be archaic."

Jacob bent forward to peer at the nearest machine.

54

It looked like a coffee machine. There was a transparent panel door, and behind that a little platform with a metal grill drain at the bottom. Now, if he pushed the right button, a disposable cup should drop onto the platform and then, from some mechanical artery would pour a stream of the bitter black beverage he wanted.

As Culla's voice droned on in his ears, Jacob made polite sounds. "Uh, huh . . . yes, I see."

At the far left, one of the buttons was lit with a green light. On impulse, he pressed it.

He watched the machine blearily. Now! That was a buzz and a click! There's the cup! Now . . . what the hell?

A large yellow and green pill fell into the cup.

Jacob lifted the panel and took out the cup. A second later a stream of hot liquid spilled through the empty space where the cup had been, disappearing in the drain below.

Dubiously, he glowered down at the pill. Whatever it was, it wasn't coffee. He rubbed his eyes with his left wrist, one at a time. Then he sent an accusing glance at the button he'd pressed.

That button had a label, he now saw. It read "E.T. Nutrient Synthesis." Below the label a computer card stuck out from a data slot. The words "Pring: Dietary Supplement—Coumarin Protein Complex" were printed along the protruding end.

Jacob looked quickly at Culla. The alien continued his explanation while he faced the Lyot window. Culla waved one arm toward the Sun's Dantean brilliance to emphasize a point.

"Thish ish now the red alpha line of Hydrogen," he said. "A very useful shpectral line. Inshtead of being overwhelmed by huge amountsh of random light from all levelsh of the Shun, we can now look at only those regions where elemental Hydrogen absorbsh or emitsh more than normal . . ."

Culla pointed to the Sun's mottled surface. It was covered with dark reddish speckles and feathery arches.

Jacob had read about them. The feathery arches were "filaments." Viewed against space, at the solar limb, they were the prominences that had been seen since the first time a telescope was used during an eclipse. Culla apparently was explaining the way these objects were viewed head-on.

Jacob considered. Throughout the voyage from Earth, Culla had refrained from eating his meals with the others. All he would do is sip an occasional vodka or beer with a straw. Although he had given no reasons, Jacob could only assume that the being had some cultural inhibition against eating in public.

Come to think of it, he thought, with those mashies for teeth it *could* get a little messy. Apparently I've barged in while he's having breakfast and he's too polite to mention it.

He glanced at the tablet which still lay in the cup in his hand. He dropped the pill into his jacket pocket and crumpled the cup into a nearby trash bin.

Now he could see the button which was labeled "Coffee–Black." He smiled ruefully. Maybe it would be best to skip the coffee and not run the risk of offending Culla. Although the E.T. had made no objections, he *had* kept his back turned while Jacob visited the food and beverage machines.

Culla looked up as Jacob approached. He opened his mouth slightly and for an instant the human caught a glimpse of white porcelain.

"Are you lesh . . . groggy, now?" the alien asked solicitously.

"Yesh, uh yes, thanks . . . thanks also for the explanation. I always thought of the Sun as a pretty smooth place . . . except for Sunspots and prominences. But I guess it's actually pretty complicated."

Culla nodded. "Doctor Kepler ish the expert. You will get a better explanation from him when you go on a dive wid ush."

Jacob smiled politely. How carefully these Galactic Emissaries were trained! When Culla nodded, was the gesture personally meaningful? Or was it something he had been taught to do at certain times and places around humans?

Dive with us!?

He decided not to ask Culla to repeat the remark.

Better not to press my luck, he thought.

He started to yawn. Just in time he remembered to stifle it behind his hand. No telling what a similar gesture would mean on the Pring home planet! "Well, Culla, I think I'm going to go back to my room and try for a little more sleep. Thanks for the talk."

"You are mosht entirely welcome, Jacob. Good night."

He shuffled down the hall and barely made it to bed before he was fast asleep.

6.

RETARDATION AND DIFFRACTION

A soft, pearly light suffused through the ports, illuminating the faces of those who watched Mercury glide beneath the descending ship.

Almost everyone who did not have a duty to perform was in the lounge, held to the row of viewing windows by the planet's terrible beauty. Voices were hushed, and conversations settled into small groups gathered around each port. For the most part the only sound was a faint crackling which Jacob couldn't identify.

The surface of the planet was gouged and scratched with craters and long rills. The shadows cast by the mountains of Mercury were vacuum sharp in their blackness, set against bright silvers and browns. In many ways the place resembled the Earth's moon.

There were differences. In one area a whole piece had been torn off in some ancient cataclysm. The scar made a deep series of grooves on the side that faced the Sun. The terminator ran starkly along the edge of the indention, a sharp borderline of day and night.

58

Down there, in places where shadow did not fall, a rain of seven different types of fire fell. Protons, x-rays spun off from the planet's magnetosphere and the simple blinding sunshine itself mixed with other deadly things to make the surface of Mercury as unlike the moon as anyplace could be.

It seemed like a place where one could find ghosts. A purgatory.

He remembered a line from an ancient pre-Haiku Japanese poem that he had read only a month before:

> More sad thoughts crowd into my mind
> When evening comes; for then,
> Appears your phantom shape—
> Speaking as I have known you speak.

"Did you say something?"

Jacob started from the mild trance and saw Dwayne Kepler standing next to him.

"No, nothing much. Here's your jacket." He handed the folded garment to Kepler, who took it with a grin.

"Sorry, but biology strikes at the most unromantic times. In real life space travelers have to go to the bathroom too. Bubbacub seems to find this velour fabric irresistible. Every time I put my jacket down to do something I come back to find that he's gone to sleep on it. I'm going to have to purchase some for him when we get back to Earth. Now what were we talking about before I left?"

Jacob pointed down at the surface below. "I was just thinking . . . now I understand why astronauts call the moon 'The Playpen.' You certainly have to be more cautious here."

Kepler nodded. "Yes, but it's a whole lot better than working on some stupid 'make-work' project at home!" Kepler paused for a moment, as if he were about to go on to say something scathing. But the passion leaked away before he could continue. He turned to the port and gestured at the view below. "The early observers, Antoniodi and Schiaparelli, called this area Charit Regio. That huge ancient crater over there is Goethe." He pointed to a jumble of darker material in a bright plain. "It's very close to the North Pole, and underneath it is the network of caves that makes Hermes Base possible."

Kepler was the perfect picture, now, of the dignified scholarly gentleman, except for the times when one end or the other of his long sandy-colored moustache was in his mouth. His nervousness appeared to ease as they approached Mercury and the Sundiver Base where he was boss.

But at times during the trip, particularly when a conversation turned to uplift or the Library, Kepler's face took on the expression of a man with a great deal to say and no way to say it. It was a nervous, *embarrassed* look, as if he were afraid of expressing his opinions out of fear of rebuke.

After some pondering, Jacob thought he knew part of the reason. Although the Sundiver chief had said nothing explicit to give himself away, Jacob was convinced that Dwayne Kepler was religious.

In the midst of the Shirt-Skin controversy and Contact with extraterrestrials, organized religion had been torn apart.

The Danikenites proselytized their faith in some great (but not omnipotent) race of beings that had intervened in man's development and might do so again. The followers of the Neolithic Ethic preached the palpable presence of the "spirit of man."

And the mere existence of thousands of space-traveling races, few professing anything similar to the tenets of the old faiths of earth, did grievous harm to concepts of an all-powerful, anthropomorphic God.

Most of the formal creeds had either co-opted one side or another in the Shirt-Skin conflict or devolved into philosophical theism. The armies of the faithful had mostly flocked to other banners, and those who remained were quiet amid all of the uproar.

Jacob had often wondered if they were waiting for a Sign.

If Kepler were a Believer, it would explain some of his caution. There was enough unemployment among scientists these days. Kepler wouldn't want to risk adding his own name to the rolls by getting a reputation as a fanatic.

Jacob thought it a shame that the man felt that way. It would have been interesting to hear his views. But he respected Kepler's obvious wish for privacy in that area.

What attracted Jacob's professional interest was the way in which the isolation might have contributed to Kepler's mental problems. Something more than just a philosophical quandary was at work in the man's mind, something that now and then impaired his effectiveness as a leader and his self-confidence as a scientist.

Martine, the psychologist, was often with Kepler, reminding him regularly to take his medication from the vials of diverse, multicolored pills that he carried in his pockets.

Jacob felt old habits coming back, undulled by recent quiet months at the Center for Uplift. He wanted to know what those pills were, almost as much as he wished to know what Mildred Martine's *real* job was on Sundiver.

Martine was still an enigma to Jacob. In all of their conversations aboard ship he failed to penetrate the woman's damnable friendly detachment. Her amused condescension toward him was just as pronounced as Dr. Kepler's exaggerated confidence in him. The dark woman's thoughts were elsewhere.

Martine and LaRoque hardly glanced out their port. Instead, Martine was talking about her research into the effects of color and glare on psychotic behavior. Jacob had heard about this at the Ensenada meeting. One of the first things Martine had done on joining Sundiver was to have environmental psychogenic effects brought to a minimum, in case the "phenomena" turned out to be a stress-illusion.

Her friendship with LaRoque had grown over the trip out as she listened, rapt, to story after contradicting story about lost civilizations and ancient visitors to Earth. LaRoque responded to the attention by calling up the eloquence for which he was famous. Several times their private conversations in the lounge had gathered crowds. Jacob listened in a couple of times, himself. LaRoque could evoke a great deal of sensitivity when he tried.

Still Jacob felt less comfortable around the man than he did with any of the other passengers. He preferred the company of more straightforward beings, such as Culla. Jacob had come to like the alien. Notwithstanding the huge complex eyes and incredible dental work, the Pring had tastes akin to his on a wide range of subjects.

Culla had been full of ingenuous questions about Earth and humans, most of all regarding the way humans treated their client races. When he learned that Jacob had actually participated in the project to raise chimpanzees, dolphins and, recently, dogs and gorillas, to full sapiency, he began to treat Jacob with even more respect.

Culla never once referred to Earth's technology as archaic or obsolete, although everyone knew that it was unique in the galaxy for its quaintness. No other race in living memory had, after all, had to invent everything itself from ground zero. The Library saw to that. Culla was enthusiastic about the benefits the Library would bring to his human and chimpanzee friends.

Once, the E.T. followed Jacob into the ship's gymnasium and watched, with those huge red disc oculars, as Jacob went into one of his marathon conditioning sessions, one of several during the trip out from Earth. During rests Jacob found that the Pring had already learned the art of telling off-color jokes. The Pring race must have similar sexual mores to those of contemporary humanity, for the punch line ". . . now we're only haggling over the price," seemed to have the same meaning for both.

It was the jokes more than anything else that made Jacob realize how very far away from home the slender Pring diplomat was. He wondered if Culla was as lonely as he would be in that situation.

In their subsequent discussion of whether Tuborg or L-5 was the best brand of beer, Jacob had to struggle to remember that this was an alien, not a lisping, overly polite human being. But the lesson had been brought home when, in the course of a conversation, they found themselves separated by a sudden, unbridgeable gap.

Jacob had told a story about Earth's old class struggles that Culla failed to understand. He tried to illustrate the point of it with a Chinese proverb: "A peasant always hangs himself in his landlord's doorway."

The alien's eyes suddenly became bright and Jacob

for the first time heard an agitated clacking coming from Culla's mouth. Jacob had stared for a moment, then moved quickly to change the subject.

All things considered, however, Culla had the closest thing to a human sense of humor of any extraterrestrial he had met. Fagin excepted, of course.

Now, as they approached the landing, the Pring stood silently near his Patron—his expression, and Bubbacub's, once again unreadable.

Kepler tapped him gently on the arm. The scientist pointed at the port. "Pretty soon, now, the Captain will tighten up the Stasis Screens and begin to cut down the rate at which she lets space-time leak in. You'll find the effects interesting."

"I thought the ship sort of let the fabric of space slip past it, like riding a surfboard into a beach."

Kepler smiled.

"No, Mr. Demwa. That's a common fallacy. Space-surfing is just a phrase used by popularizers. When I speak of space-time I'm not talking about a 'fabric.' Space is not a material.

"Actually, as we approach a planetary singularity— a distortion in space caused by a planet—we must adopt a constantly changing metric, or set of parameters by which we measure space and time. It's as if nature wants us to gradually change the length of our meter sticks and the pace of our clocks whenever we get close to a mass."

"I take it the Captain is controlling our approach by allowing this change to take place slowly?"

"Exactly right! In the old days, of course, the adaptation was more violent. One adapted one's metric either by braking continuously with rockets until touchdown, or by crashing into the planet. Now we just roll up excess metric like a bolt of cloth in stasis. Ah! There goes that 'material' analogy again!"

Kepler grinned.

"One of the useful by-products of this is commercial grade neutronium, but the main purpose is to get us down safely."

"So when we finally start stuffing space into a bag, what will we see?"

Kepler pointed to the port.

"You can see it happening now."

Outside, the stars were going out. The tremendous spray of bright pinpoints which even the darkened screens had let through slowly faded as they watched. Soon only a few were left, weak and ochre colored against the blackness.

The planet below changed as well.

The light reflected from Mercury's surface was no longer hot and brittle. It took on an orange tint. The surface was quite dark now.

And it was getting closer, too. Slowly, but visibly, the horizon flattened. Surface objects only barely discerned earlier came into focus as the *Bradbury* settled lower.

Large craters opened up to show smaller craters within. As the ship descended past the ragged edge of one of these, Jacob saw it too was covered with still smaller pits, each similar in shape to the larger ones.

The tiny planet's horizon disappeared behind a range of mountains, and Jacob lost all perspective. With every minute of descent the ground below looked the same. How could you tell how high up you were? Is that thing just below us a mountain, or a boulder, or are we going to touch down in just a second or two and is it just a rock?

He sensed nearness. The gray shadows and orange outcrops seemed close enough to touch.

Expecting the ship to come to rest at any moment, he was surprised when a hole in the ground rushed up to engulf them.

As they prepared to disembark, Jacob remembered with a shock what he had been doing when he slipped into a light trance earlier, holding Kepler's jacket during the descent.

Surreptitiously, and with great skill, he had picked Kepler's pockets, taking a sample of every medication and removing a small pencil stub without smudging the fingerprints. They made a neat lump in Jacob's side pocket now, too small to stand out against the taper of his jacket.

So it's started already, he groaned.

Jacob's jaw tightened.

This time, he thought, I'm going to solve it myself!

I don't need help from my alter ego. I'm not going to go around breaking and entering!

He struck his balled fist against his thigh to drive out the itchy, *satisfied* feeling in his fingers.

PART III

The transition region between the corona and photosphere (the surface of the sun as seen in white light) appears during an eclipse as a bright red ring around the sun, and is therefore called the chromosphere. When the chromosphere is examined closely, it is seen to be not a homogeneous layer but a rapidly changing filamentary structure. The term "burning prairie" has been used to describe it. Numerous short-lived jets called "spicules" are continuously shooting up to heights of several thousand kilometers. The red color is due to the dominance of radiation in the H-alpha line of hydrogen. The problems of understanding what is going on in such a complex region are great. . . .

Harold Zirin

7.

INTERFERENCE

When Dr. Martine left her quarters and took service corridors to the E.T. Environments Section, she thought of herself as using discretion, not stealth. Pipes and communications cables clung, stapled, to the rough unfinished walls. The Hermetian stone glistened with condensation and gave off an odor of wet rock as her footsteps rang down the fused path ahead of her.

She arrived at a pressure-sealed door with a green overhead light, the back entrance to one alien's residence. When she pressed the sensing cell next to it, the door opened immediately.

A bright, greenish-tinted light spilled out—the reproduced sunshine of a star many parsecs distant. She shielded her eyes with one hand while with the other she took a pair of sunglasses from her hip pouch, and put them on to look into the room.

On the walls she saw spiderweb tapestries of hanging gardens and of an alien city set on the edge of a mountain scarp. The city clung to the jagged cliff, shimmering as if viewed through a waterfall. Dr. Martine thought she could almost hear high pitched music, keening just above her aural range. Could that explain the shortness of her breath? Her jittery nerves?

Bubbacub rose from a cushioned pallet to greet her. His gray fur shone as he waddled forward on stubby legs. In the actinic light and one point five g-field of his apartment, Bubbacub lost whatever "cuteness" Martine had seen in him before. The Pil's bowlegged stance spoke strength.

The alien's mouth moved in short snaps. His voice, coming from the Vodor which hung from his neck, was smooth and resonant, although the words came clipped and separated.

"Good. Glad you come."

Martine was relieved. The Library Representative sounded relaxed. She bowed slightly.

"Greeting, Pil Bubbacub. I came to ask if you have had any further word from the Branch Library."

Bubbacub displayed a mouth full of needle sharp teeth. "Come in and sit. Yes, good that you ask. I have a new fact. But come. Have food, drink first."

Martine grimaced as she passed through the g-transition field of the threshold—always a disconcerting experience. Inside the room she felt as though she weighed seventy kilos.

"No. Thank you, I just ate. I will sit." She selected a chair built for humans and carefully lowered herself into it. Seventy kilos was more than a person should weigh!

The Pil sprawled back on his cushion across from her, his ursine head barely above the level of his feet. He regarded her with small black eyes.

"I have heard from La Paz by ma-ser. They say no thing on Sun Ghosts. No thing at all. It may not be se-man-tics at all. It may be the Branch is too small. It is small, small branch, as I saided. But some Hu-man Off-ic-ials will make much of the lack of a re-fer-ence."

Martine shrugged. "I wouldn't worry about it. This will only go to show that too little effort has been spent on the Library project. A bigger branch, like my group has been lobbying for all along, would surely have had results."

"I sended for da-ta from Pil-a by time drop. There can be no con-fu-sion at a Main Branch!"

70

"That's good," Martine nodded. "What's bothering me, though, is what Dwayne is going to do during this delay. He's bubbling over with half cracked notions about how to communicate with the Ghosts. I'm afraid that in his stumbling around down there, he'll find some way of offending the psi-creatures so badly that all of the Library's wisdom won't patch things up. It's vital that Earth have good relations with its nearest neighbors!"

Bubbacub raised his head slightly and placed a short arm behind it. "You are mak-ing ef-forts to cure Dr. Kep-ler?"

"Of course," she replied, stiffly. "Actually, I'm hav-ing trouble seeing how he escaped Probation all of this time. Dwayne's mind is full of chaos, though I'll admit his P-score is within the acceptance curves. He had a tachisto test on Earth.

"I think I've got him pretty well stabilized, now. But what's driving me crazy is trying to figure out what his basic problem is. His manic depressive swings resemble the 'glare madness' of the late twentieth and early twenty-first centuries, when society was almost wrecked by the psychic effects of environmental noise. It nearly tore apart industrial culture when it was at its peak and led to the period of repression people today euphemistically call 'the Bureaucracy.' "

"Yes. I have readed of your race-es at-tempt at sui-cide. It seem to me that the time af-ter, of which you just spoke, was time of order and peace. But that not my af-fair. You are luck-y to be in-comp-e-tent even at sui-cide.

"But do not stray. What of Kep-ler?"

The Pil's voice did not rise at the end of his question, but there was something he did with his snout . . . a curling of the folds that served instead of lips . . . that told when he was asking, no, demanding an answer. It sent a shiver down Dr. Martine's spine.

He's so arrogant, she thought. And everyone else seems to think it's just a quirk of personality. Can they be blind to the power and the threat that this creature's presence on Earth represents?

In their culture shock, they see a little manlike bear. Cute, even! Are my boss and his friends on the

Confederacy Council the only ones who recognize a demon from outer space when they see one?

And somehow it's up to me to find out what it will take to propitiate the demon, while I keep Dwayne from shooting off his mouth, and try to be the one to come up with a *sensible* way to contact the Sun Ghosts! Ifni, help your sister!

Bubbacub was still waiting for an answer.

"W-well, I do know that Dwayne is determined to crack the Sun Ghost's secret without extraterrestrial help. Some of his crew are downright radical about it. I won't go so far as to say that any of them are Skins, but their pride is running pretty stiff."

"Can you keep him from do-ing rash things?" Bubbacub said. "He *has* broughted in ran-dom el-ements."

"Like inviting Fagin and his friend Demwa? They seem to be harmless. Demwa's experience with dolphins gives him a distant but plausible chance to be useful. And Fagin has a knack for getting along with alien races. The important thing is that Dwayne has someone to spill out his paranoid fantasies to. I'll talk to Demwa and ask him to be sympathetic."

Bubbacub sat up in a momentary writhing of arms and legs. He settled into a new position and looked straight into Martine's eyes.

"I do not care about them. Fa-gin is a pass-ive ro-man-tic. Dem-wa looks like a fool. Like any friend of Fa-gin's.

"No, I care more a-bout the two who now cause troub-le on the base. I did not know, when I came, that there was a chimp here who was made part of the staff. He and the journ-al-ist have been all claws since we hit dirt. The journ-al-ist is snubbed by the base crew and he makes lot of noise. And the Chip keeps at Cul-la all time . . . trying to 'lib-er-ate' him, so . . ."

"Has Culla been disobedient? I thought his indenture was only . . ."

Bubbacub leapt from his seat, pointy teeth bared in a hiss.

"Do not interrupt, human!" Bubbacub's real voice became audible for the first time in Martine's memory, a high pitched squeak, above the roar of the Vodor, that hurt her ears.

For a moment, Martine was too stunned to move.

Bubbacub's taut stance began to relax by degrees. In a minute the stiff brush of fur was almost smooth again.

"I apo-log-ize, human-Mar-tine. I should not fluff-up to such minor breach by one of mere in-fant race."

Martine let her breath out, trying not to make a sound.

Bubbacub sat once again. "To answer your question, no, Cul-la not out of place. He does know his species will be in-den-tured to mine by Paren-tal right for long time.

"Still, it bad that this Doc-tor Jeff-rey does push this myth of rights with-out duties. You humans must learn to keep your pets in line, for it on-ly by good grace of we old ones that they are called cli-ent soph-onts at all.

"And if they not be sophonts, where would you be, hu-man?"

Bubbacub's teeth shone brightly for a moment then he closed his mouth with a snap.

Martine felt very dry in the throat. She chose her words carefully. "I'm sorry about any offense you may have taken, Pil Bubbacub. I will speak to Dwayne and maybe he can get Jeffrey to ease off."

"And the journ-al-ist?"

"Yes, I'll talk to Pierre also. I'm sure he doesn't mean any harm. He won't cause any more trouble."

"That would be well," Bubbacub's voicebox said softly. He allowed his stocky body to settle once more into a slouch.

"We have great com-mon goals, you and I. I hope we can work as one. But know this: our means may dif-fer. Please do what you can or I be forced to, as you say, kill two birds with one stone."

Martine nodded again, weakly.

8.

REFLECTION

Jacob let his mind wander as LaRoque launched into one of his expositions. At any rate, the little man was now more interested in impressing Fagin than in winning any points with Jacob. Jacob wondered if it would be sinful anthropomorphizing to pity the E.T. for having to listen.

The three rode in a small car that moved through tunnels laterally as well as up and down. Two of Fagin's root-pods gripped a low rail that ran a few centimeters off the floor. The two humans held onto another that circuited the car higher up.

Jacob listened with half an ear as the car glided on. LaRoque still bearded a topic he started back aboard the *Bradbury*: that the missing Patrons of Earth . . . those mythical beings who supposedly began the Uplift of man thousands of years ago, and then gave it up halfway finished . . . were somehow associated with the Sun. LaRoque thought the Sun Ghosts themselves might be that race.

"Then you have all of the references in the religions of Earth. Almost in every one the Sun is something holy! It is one of the common threads that runs through all cultures!"

LaRoque made an expansive gesture with his arms, as if to encompass the scope of his idea.

"It makes so much *sense*," he said. "It would also explain why it is so difficult for the Library to trace our ancestry. Surely solar-type races have been known before. . . . That is why this 'research' is so stupid. But they *are* undoubtedly rare and no one has yet thought to feed the Library this correlation which could solve two problems at once!"

The trouble was that the idea was so damned hard to refute. Jacob sighed inwardly. Of *course* many primitive Earth civilizations once had Sun cults. The Sun was so obviously the source of heat and light and life, a thing of miraculous power! It must be a common stage for a primitive people to pass through, to see animate properties in their star.

And there was the problem. The galaxy had few "primitive peoples" to compare to the human experience; mostly animals, pre-sentient hunter-gatherers (or analogous types), and fully uplifted sophont races. Hardly ever did an "in-between" case like man show up—apparently abandoned by its patron without the training to make its new sapiency work.

In such rare cases the newly potent minds were known to burst free of their ecological niche. They invented strange mockeries of science—bizarre rules of cause and effect, superstition and myth. Without the guiding hand of a patron, such "wolfling" races seldom lasted long. Humanity's current notoriety was partly due to its survival.

The very lack of any other species with similar experience to compare with made generalizations easy to form and hard to refute. Since there were no other examples of species-wide indulgence in Sun-worship known to the small Branch in La Paz. LaRoque could maintain that those traditions of humanity recalled the Uplift that was never finished.

Jacob half listened for a moment longer just in case LaRoque said anything new. But mostly he let his mind drift.

It had been a long two days since the landing. He had had to get used to traversing from parts of the base that were gravity tuned to others in which the feathery pull of Mercury prevailed. There were many introductions to Base personnel, most of whose names he immediately forgot. Then Kepler had assigned someone to take him to his quarters.

The chief physician at Hermes Base turned out to be a Dolphin-Uplift bug. He was only too happy to examine Kepler's prescriptions, expressing mystification that there were so many. Afterwards he insisted on throwing a party at which everyone in the medical department, it seemed, wanted to ask questions about Makakai. Between toasts, that is. For that matter there weren't all that many questions after all.

Jacob's mind moved a little slowly as the car came to rest and the doors slid open to the huge underground cavern where the Sunships were serviced and stored. Then, for a fleeting moment, it seemed that space itself was bending out of shape, and, worse yet, there was two of everybody!

The opposite wall of the Cavern seemed to bulge forward, up to a rounded bulb only a few meters away, directly across from him. There, where it was closest, stood a Kanten two and a half meters high, a small red-faced human, and a tall, stocky, dark complexioned man who stared back at him with one of the stupidest expressions he'd ever seen.

Jacob suddenly realized that he was looking at the hull of a Sunship, the most perfect mirror in the solar system. The amazed man opposite him, with the obvious hangover, was his own reflection.

The twenty-meter spherical ship was so good a mirror that it was difficult to define its shape. Only by noting the sharp discontinuity of the edge and the way reflected images swept away in an arc could he focus his eyes on something to be interpreted as a real object at all.

"Very pretty," LaRoque admitted grudgingly. "Lovely, brave, misguided crystal." He lifted his tiny camera-recorder and scanned it left to right.

"Most impressive," Fagin added.

Yeah, Jacob thought. And big as houses, also.

Large as the ship was, the Cavern made it seem insignificant. The rough, rocky ceiling arched high overhead, disappearing in a misty fog of condensation.

Where they stood it was rather narrow, but it stretched to the right for a kilometer, at least, before curving out of sight.

They stood on a platform which brought them even with the equator of the ship, above the working floor of the hangar. A small crowd stood down below, dwarfed by the silvery sphere.

Two hundred meters to the left stood a pair of massive vacuum doors, easily a hundred and fifty meters broad. Those, Jacob supposed, were part of the airlock that led, by tunnel, to the unfriendly surface of Mercury, where the giant interplanetary ships, such as the *Bradbury*, rested in huge natural caves.

A ramp led down from the platform to the cavern floor below. At the bottom Kepler spoke with three men in overalls. Culla stood not far away. His companion was a well-dressed chimpanzee who sported a monocle and stood on a chair to get even with Culla's eyes.

The chimp jumped up and down with flexed knees and set the chair shivering. He tapped furiously at an instrument on his chest. The Pring diplomat watched with an expression that Jacob had learned to interpret as one of friendly respect. But there was something else in Culla's stance that surprised him . . . an indolence, a looseness of posture, before the chimpanzee, that he had never seen the E.T. display in talking to a human or Kanten or Cynthian or, especially, a Pil.

Kepler greeted Fagin first then turned to Jacob.

"Glad you could make the tour, Mr. Demwa." Kepler shook his hand with a firmness that surprised Jacob, then called the chimpanzee over to his side.

"This is Dr. Jeffrey, the first of his species to become a full member of a space research team, and one helluva fine worker. It's his ship that we'll be touring."

Jeffrey smiled with the wry, unhinged grin characteristic of the superchimp species. Two centuries of genetic engineering had wrought changes in the skull and pelvic arch, changes modeled on the human form, as it was the easiest to duplicate. He looked like a very fuzzy, short brown man with long arms and huge buck teeth.

Another bit of engineering became evident when Jacob shook his hand. The chimpanzee's fully opposable thumb pressed hard, as if to remind Jacob that it was there, the Mark of a man.

Where Bubbacub carried his Vodor, Jeffrey wore a device with black horizontal keys left and right. In the middle was a blank screen about twenty centimeters by ten.

The superchimp bowed and his fingers flew over the keys. Bright letters appeared on the screen.

I AM HAPPY TO MEET YOU. DOCTOR KEPLER TELLS ME YOU'RE ONE OF THE GOOD GUYS.

Jacob laughed. "Well thanks a lot, Jeff. I try to be, though I still don't know what it is I'm going to be asked to do!"

Jeffrey gave the familiar shrieking chimpanzee laugh; then, for the first time, he spoke. "You will find out ssooon!"

It was almost a croak, but Jacob was amazed. Speech was still almost impossibly painful for this generation of superchimp, but Jeff's words came out very clear.

"Dr. Jeffrey will take this, our newest Sunship, out on a dive shortly after we finish our tour," Kepler said. "Just as soon as Commandant deSilva returns from reconnaissance in our other ship.

"I'm sorry the Commandant wasn't here to meet us when we arrived on the *Bradbury*. And now it seems that Jeff will be gone while we hold our briefings. It'll add a dramatic touch, though, to get his first report just about the time we finish tomorrow afternoon."

Kepler started to turn toward the ship. "Any introductions I've forgotten? Jeff, I know you've met Kant Fagin earlier. Pil Bubbacub appears to have declined our invitation. Have you met Mr. LaRoque?"

The chimp's lips curled back in an expression of disgust. He snorted once and turned away to look at his own reflection in the Sunship.

LaRoque glared with hot-faced embarrassment.

Jacob had to hold back a laugh. No wonder the superchimps were called chips! For once, someone with less tact than LaRoque! The encounter between the two in the Refectory last night was already legend. He was sorry he'd missed it.

Culla laid a slender, six-fingered hand on Jeffrey's sleeve. "Come, Friend-Jeffrey. Let ush show Mishter Demwa and hish friends your ship." The chimp glanced sullenly at LaRoque then looked back at Culla and Jacob, and broke into a wide grin. He took one of Jacob's hands and one of Culla's and pulled them toward the entrance to the ship.

When the party reached the top of the other ramp they came to a short bridge that crossed a gap into the interior of the mirrored globe. It took a moment for Jacob's eyes to adjust to the dark. Then he saw a flat deck which stretched from one end of the ship to the other.

It floated, a circular disk of dark springy material, at the equator of the ship. The only breaks in the flat surface were a half dozen or so acceleration couches, set flush with the deck at intervals around its perimeter, some with modest instrument panels, and a dome of seven meters diameter at the exact center.

Kepler knelt by a control panel and touched a switch. The wall of the ship became semi-transparent. Dimly, light from the cavern came in from all sides to illuminate the interior. Kepler explained that interior lighting was kept to a minimum to prevent internal reflections along the inner surface of the spherical shell, which might confuse both equipment and crew.

Inside the nearly perfect shell, the Sunship was like a solid model of the planet Saturn. The wide deck made up the "ring." The "planet" protruded above and below the deck in two hemispheres. The upper hemisphere, which Jacob could see now, had several hatches and cabinets breaking its surface. He knew from his reading that the central sphere contained all of the machinery that ran the ship, including the timeflow controller, the gravity generator, and the refrigerator laser.

Jacob walked to the edge of the deck. It floated on a field of force, four or five feet away from the curving hull, which arched high overhead with a curious lack of highlights or shadows.

He turned as his name was called. The tour group stood by a door in the side of the dome. Kepler waved for him to join them.

"We'll inspect the instrument hemisphere now. We

call it 'flip-side.' Watch your step, it's a gravity arc so don't be too surprised."

At the doorway, Jacob stood aside to let Fagin pass, but the E.T. indicated that he would rather stay above. A seven-foot tall Kanten in a seven-foot hatch wouldn't be too comfortable at that. He followed Kepler inside.

And tried to duck out of the way! Kepler was above him, climbing a path that mounded just ahead, like part of a hill enclosed in bulkheads. He looked like he was about to fall over, judging from the angle of his body. Jacob couldn't see how the scientist could keep his balance!

But Kepler kept walking up and over the elliptical path and disappeared over the short horizon. Jacob put his hand on the bulkheads to either side and took a tentative step.

He felt no lack of balance. His other foot moved forward again. Still perfectly upright. Another step. He looked back.

The doorway tilted toward him. Apparently the dome enclosed a pseudo-gravity field so tight that it could be wrapped around a mere few yards. The field was so smooth and complete that it fooled his inner ear. One of the workmen stood in the hatch grinning.

Jacob set his jaw and continued over the loop, trying not to think of himself as slowly turning upside down. He examined the signs on access plates on the walls and floor of his path. Halfway around he passed over a hatch with the words TIME-COMPRESSION ACCESS inscribed on it.

The ellipse ended in a gentle slope. Jacob felt right-side-up when he got to the doorway and he knew what to expect, but even so he groaned.

"Oh no!" He brought his hands to his eyes.

A few meters over his head the floor of the hangar stretched away in all directions. Men walked around the ship's cradle like flies on a ceiling.

With a resigned sigh he walked out to join Kepler where the scientist stood at the edge of the deck, peering into the guts of a complicated machine. Kepler looked up and smiled.

"I was just exercising a boss's privilege to poke and

pry. Of course the ship has been fully checked out by now, but I like to look things over." He patted the machine affectionately.

Kepler led Jacob to the edge of the deck, where the upside-down effect was even more pronounced. The foggy ceiling of the cavern was visible far "below" their feet.

"This is one of the multi-polarization cameras we set up soon after we first saw the Coherent Light Ghosts." Kepler pointed to one of several identical machines that stood at intervals along the rim. "We were able to pick the Ghosts out from the jumbled light levels in the chromosphere because, no matter how the plane of polarization migrated, we were able to track it and show that the coherency of the light was real and stable with time."

"Why are all of the cameras down here? I didn't see any up above."

"We found that live observers and machines interfered with each other when they rode on the same plane. For this and other reasons the instruments line the edge of the plane down here, and us chickens ride on the other half.

"We can accommodate both, you see, by orienting the ship so the edge of the deck is aligned toward the phenomenon we wish to observe. It turned out to be an excellent compromise; since gravity is no problem, we can tilt in any angle and we can arrange for the point-of-view of both sentient and mechanical observers to be the same for later comparison."

Jacob tried to imagine the ship, tipped at some angle and tossed about in the storms of the Sun's atmosphere, while passengers and crew calmly watched.

"We've had a bit of trouble with this arrangement lately," Kepler went on. "This newer, smaller ship Jeff will take down has had some modifications, so soon we hope. . . . Ah! here come some friends . . ."

Culla and Jeffrey emerged from the doorway, the chimp's half simian, half human face contorted in disdain.

He tapped at the chest display.

"LR SICK. NAUSEOUS GOING OVER RAMP. SHIRTED BASTARD."

Culla spoke softly to the chimp. Jacob could barely overhear. "Shpeak with reshpect, Friend-Jeff. Mr. La-Roque ish human."

Incensed, Jeffrey tapped out with frequent misspellings, that he had as much respect as the next chimp, but that he wasn't about to toady up to any particular human, especially one who had no part in his species' Uplift.

DO YOU REALLY HAV TO TAKE CRAP FROM BUBBACUB JUST BECAUS HIS ANCESTORS DID YOURS A FAVOR HALF A MILLION YEARS AGO?

The Pring's eyes glowed. There was a flash of white between the thick lips. "Please, Friend-Jeff, I know you mean well, but Bubbacub ish my Patron. Humansh have given your race freedom. My race must sherve. It ish the way of the world."

Jeffrey sniffed. "We'll see," he croaked.

Kepler took Jeffrey aside, asking Culla to show Jacob around. Culla led Jacob to the other side of the hemisphere to show him the machine that allowed the ship to navigate like a bathysphere in the semi-fluid plasma of the solar atmosphere. He removed several panels to show Jacob the holographic memory units.

The Stasis Generator controlled the flow of time and space through the body of the Sunship, so that the violent tossing of the chromosphere would seem a gentle rocking to those inside. The fundamental physics of the generator was still only partly understood by the scientists of Earth, though the government insisted that it be built by human hands.

Culla's eyes glowed and his lisping voice revealed pride in the new technologies brought to Earth by the Library.

The logic banks controlling the generator looked like a jumble of glassy filaments. Culla explained that the rods and fibers stored optical information far more densely than any previous Earth technology, and responded more quickly. Blue interference patterns ran up and down the nearest rod, as they watched, flickering packets of lambient data. It seemed to Jacob that there was something almost alive in the machine. The laser input-output swung aside under Culla's touch and they both stared for minutes at the raw pulsing information that was the machine's blood.

Though he must have seen the computer's bowels hundreds of times, Culla seemed as enthralled as Jacob, meditating fixedly with those bright, unblinking eyes.

Finally, Culla replaced the cover. Jacob noticed that the E.T. looked tired. Must be working too hard, he thought. They spoke little as they walked slowly back around the dome to rejoin Jeffrey and Kepler.

Jacob listened with interest, but little comprehension, as the chimpanzee and his boss argued about some minor calibration of one of the cameras.

Jeffrey left then, claiming business on the Cavern floor, and Culla followed soon after. The two men remained for a few minutes, talking about the machinery, then Kepler motioned for Jacob to walk ahead as they made their way back around the loop.

When Jacob was about halfway around he heard a sudden commotion up ahead. Someone was shouting in anger. He tried to ignore what his eyes were telling him about the curving gravity-loop and quickened his pace. The path wasn't meant to be taken quickly, though. For the first time he felt a confusing mixture of pulling sensations as different portions of the complicated field tugged at him.

At the top of the arc Jacob's foot caught on a loose floor plate, scattering the plate and several bolts along the curving deck. He fought to keep his balance, but the unnerving perspective, midway around the curving path, made him stagger. By the time he made it gratefully to the hatch on the upper side of the deck, Kepler had caught up with him.

The shouting came from outside the ship.

At the base of the ramp Fagin waved his branches about in agitation. A number of base personnel ran toward LaRoque and Jeffrey, who stood locked in a wrestler's embrace.

His face a deep red, LaRoque puffed and strained as he tried to pry Jeffrey's hands off of his head. He made a fist and struck out to no apparent effect. The chimp screamed repeatedly and bared his teeth as he fought for a better grip to bring LaRoque's head down to the level of his own. Neither noticed that a crowd had gathered. They ignored the arms that tried to pull them apart.

Hurrying to the bottom, Jacob saw LaRoque free one hand and reach for the camera that hung from a cord at his belt.

Jacob shoved through to the combatants. Without a pause he struck LaRoque's grip free of the camera with the hard side of his hand and reached down with the other to grab the fur at the back of the chimpanzee's head. He yanked back with all of his might and threw Jeffrey into the arms of Kepler and Culla.

Jeffrey struggled. The long powerful simian arms heaved against the grip of his captors. He tossed his head back and shrieked.

Jacob felt movement behind him. He swiveled and planted a palm on LaRoque's chest as the man came rushing forward. The journalist's feet flew out from beneath him and he landed with an "Oof!"

Jacob reached for the camera at LaRoque's belt, just as the man grabbed for it. The cord parted with a snap. The men hauled LaRoque back as he struggled to his feet.

Jacob's hands went up.

"Now stop it!" he shouted. He placed himself so that neither LaRoque nor Jeffrey could easily see the other. LaRoque nursed his hand, ignoring the crewmen who held his shoulders, and glared angrily.

Jeffrey still strained to get loose. Culla and Kepler held onto him tightly. Behind them Fagin whistled helplessly.

Jacob took the chimp's face in his hands. Jeffrey snarled at him.

"Chimpanzee-Jeffrey, listen to me! I am Jacob Demwa. I am a human being. I am a supervisor with Project Uplift. I tell you now that you are behaving in an unseemly manner . . . you are acting like an animal!"

Jeffrey's head jerked back as if slapped. He looked at Jacob dazedly for a moment, a snarl half formed, then the deep brown eyes unfocused. He sagged limp in the grip of Culla and Kepler.

Jacob held onto the furry head. With his other hand he stroked the ruffled fur back into place. Jeffrey shuddered.

"Now just relax," he said gently. "Just try to collect yourself. We'll all listen when you tell us what happened."

Trembling, Jeffrey brought a hand to his speech display. It took him a few moments to slowly type, SORRY. He looked up at Jacob, meaning it.

"That's fine," Jacob said. "It takes a real man to apologize."

Jeffrey straightened. With elaborate calmness he nodded to Kepler and to Culla. They released him and Jacob stepped back.

For all of his success in dealing with both dolphins and chimps at the Project, Jacob felt somewhat ashamed of the patronizing way in which he had spoken to Jeffrey. It had been a gamble that worked, to use Patronomy on the chimp-scientist. From what Jeffrey had said earlier, Jacob guessed that he kept a great deal of patron-esteem inside, but reserved it for some humans and not others. Jacob was glad he'd been able to tap that reserve, but not particularly proud of it.

Kepler took charge as soon as he saw that Jeffrey was calm.

"What the hell was going on here!" he shouted, glaring at LaRoque.

"The animal attacked me!" LaRoque cried. "I had just managed to conquer my fears and get out of that terrible place and I was talking to the honorable Fagin, when the beast leapt at me, lithe like a tiger, and I had to fight for my life!"

LIAR. HE WAS DOING SABOTAGE. I FOUND T.C. ACCESS PLATE LOOSE. FAGIN SAID THE CREEP ONLY CAME OUT WHEN HE HEARD US COMING.

"Apologies for my contradiction!" Fagin fluted. "I did not say the pejorative 'Creep,' I merely answered a query to state . . ."

"He sspent an hour in there!" Jeffrey interrupted aloud, grimacing at the effort.

Poor Fagin, Jacob thought.

"I told you before," LaRoque shouted back. "That crazy place scared me! I spent half the time clutching the floor! Listen, you little ape, don't cast your slurs on me. Save them for your tree-mates!"

The chip shrieked, and Culla and Kepler rushed forward to hold the two apart. Jacob walked over to Fagin, uncertain what to say.

Over the tumult the Kanten said to him, gently,

"It appears that your patrons, whoever they might have been, Friend-Jacob, must have been unique, indeed."

Jacob nodded numbly.

9.

REMEMBERING THE GREAT AUK

Jacob studied the group at the foot of the ramp. Culla and Jeffrey, each in his own fashion, spoke earnestly with Fagin. A small group of base personnel gathered nearby . . . perhaps to escape LaRoque's persistent questioning.

The man had stalked the Cavern ever since the altercation broke up, shooting questions at those at work and complaining to those who weren't. For a while his rage at being deprived of his camera was awesome, only slowly declining to a state Jacob would call just short of apoplexy.

"I'm not sure why I took it from LaRoque," Jacob said to Kepler, taking it out of his pocket. The slim black camera-recorder had a maze of tiny knobs and attachments. It looked like a perfect reporter's tool, compact and flexible and obviously very expensive.

He handed it to Kepler. "I guess I thought he was reaching for a weapon."

Kepler put the camera in his own pocket. "We'll check that out anyway, just in case. In the meantime

I'd like to thank you for the way you handled things."

Jacob shrugged. "Don't make much of it. I'm sorry I stepped on your authority."

Kepler laughed. "I'm glad as hell you did! *I* sure wouldn't have known what to do!"

Jacob smiled, but he still felt troubled.

"What are you going to do now?" he asked.

"Well, now I'm going to inspect Jeff's T.C. system, to make certain nothing's wrong, not that I think there is. Even if LaRoque poked around in the machine, what could he do? The circuits are all worked with special tools. He had none."

"But the panel *was* loose when we came over the gravity arc."

"Yes, but maybe LaRoque was just curious. In fact, I wouldn't be too surprised to find out that *Jeff* loosened the plate to have an excuse to pick a fight with him!"

The scientist laughed. "Don't look so shocked. Boys will be boys. And you know that even the most advanced chimp oscillates between extreme priggishness and schoolboy pranksterism."

Jacob knew the truth of that. But still he wondered why Kepler was so generous in his attitude toward LaRoque, whom he undoubtedly despised. Was he that anxious for a good press?

Kepler repeated his thanks and left, picking up Culla and Jeffrey on his way back to the entrance of the Sunship. Jacob found a place where he wouldn't be in the way and sat down on a shipping crate.

He drew a sheaf of papers from his inside jacket pocket.

Masergrams had arrived from Earth for many of the *Bradbury* passengers earlier in the day. Jacob had been hard put not to laugh when he caught the conspiratorial glances that passed between Bubbacub and Millie Martine when the Pil went to pick up his own coded message.

During breakfast she had sat between Bubbacub and LaRoque, trying to mediate the Earthman's embarrassing Xenophilia with the Library Representative's aloof suspicion. She appeared anxious to bridge the gap between them. But when the messages came

LaRoque was left alone as she and Bubbacub hurried upstairs.

It probably hadn't helped the journalist's temper.

Jacob had finished his own meal and considered a visit to the Medical Lab, but instead went to pick up his own masergrams. Back in his rooms the Library material made a pile over a foot deep, which he placed on his desk before settling into a reading trance.

The reading trance was a technique for absorbing a lot of information in a short time. It had been useful many times in the past, the only disadvantage being that it cut off the critical faculties. The information would be stored, but the material would have to be read again normally for it all to be brought to mind.

When he came to, the papers were all stacked on the left. He was certain that they had all been read. The data he'd absorbed stalked at the edge of consciousness, isolated bits capriciously leaping to mind unbidden and as yet unconnected to a whole. For at least a week he would relearn, with a sense of *déjà vu*, things read in the trance. If he didn't want to be disoriented too long he'd better start wading through the stuff normally, soon.

Now, perched on the plastic packing crate in the Sunship Cavern, Jacob poked at random through the papers he'd bought. Teasing fragments of information read familiarly.

. . . The Kisa race, newly free from indenture to the Soro, discovered the planet Pila shortly after the recent migration of galactic culture to this quadrant. Traces were evident that the planet had been occupied by another transient race some two hundred million years before. Thus Pila was verified in Galactic Archives as having once been a residence, for six hundred millenia, of the Mellin Species, (see listing; Mellin-extinct).

The planet Pila, having lain fallow for greater than the required period, was surveyed and routinely registered as a Kisa colony, Class C (temporary occupancy, no more than three million years, minimal impact on contemporary biosphere allowed).

On Pila, the Kisa found a pre-sophont species whose name is taken from the planet of their origin...

Jacob tried to picture the Pil race as it had been before the arrival of the Kisa and the beginning of their uplift. Primitive hunter-gatherers, no doubt. Would they have been the same today, after half a million years, if the Kisa had never come? Or would they have evolved, as some Earth anthropologists still insisted was possible, into a different kind of intelligent culture, without the influence of their patrons?

The cryptic reference to the extinct "Mellin" species brought home the time scale covered by the ancient civilization of the Galactics and their incredible Library. Two hundred million years! That long ago the planet Pila had been held by a spacefaring race, who had resided there for six thousand centuries while Bubbacub's ancestors were insignificant little burrowing animals.

Presumably the Mellin paid their dues and had a Branch Library of their own. They offered proper respect (though perhaps more in word than in deed) to the patron race that had uplifted them long before they colonized Pila, and perhaps they, in turn, uplifted some promising species they found when they arrived . . . biological cousins to Bubbacub's people . . . which by now had probably gone extinct as well.

Suddenly the strange Galactic Laws of Residence and Migration made sense to Jacob. They forced species to look upon their planets as temporary homes, to be held in trust for future races whose present form might be small and silly. Small wonder many of the Galactics frowned at humanity's record on Earth. Only the influence of the Tymbrimi, and other friendly races had enabled humanity to purchase its own three colonies in Cygnus from the stodgy and environmentally fanatic Institute of Migration. And at that it had been fortunate that the Vesarius had returned with enough warning for human beings to bury the evidence of some of their crimes! Jacob was one of less than a hundred thousand human beings who knew that there had ever been such a thing as a Manatee, or a giant ground sloth, or an orangutang.

That Man's victims might have someday become thinking species was something that he, more than most, was in a position to appreciate, and regret. Jacob thought of Makakai, of the whales, and how narrowly they were saved.

He brought up the papers and resumed his skimming. Another piece leapt into recognition as he read it. It had to do with Calla's species.

> . . . colonized by an expedition from Pila. (The Pila, having threatened their Kisa patrons with an appeal to Soro for a Jihad, had won release from their indenture.] Upon receiving their license to the planet Pring, the Pila undertook their occupancy with more than perfunctory attention to the minimal-impact provisions of their contract. Since the Pila arrival on Pring, inspectors from the Institute of Migration have observed that the Pila have taken greater than average safeguards to protect indigenous species whose pre-sophont potential seemed realistic. Among those in danger of extinction upon the establishment of the colony were the genetic ancestors of the Pring race whose species name is also that of the planet of their origin . . .

Jacob made a mental note to learn more about the Pilan Jihads. The Pila were aggressive conservatives in galactic politics. The Jihads, or "Holy Wars" were supposedly the last resort used to enforce tradition among the races of the galaxy. The Institutes served the traditions, but left enforcement to the opinion of the majority, or to the strongest.

Jacob felt sure that the Library references would be full of justified Holy Wars, with few "regrettable" cases of species using tradition as an excuse to wage war for power or for hate.

History is usually written by the winners.

He wondered on which grievance the Pila had won free of their indenture to the Kisa. He wondered what a Kisa looked like.

Jacob started as a loud bell rang, sending reverberations throughout the Cavern. Three more times it pealed, echoing off stone walls and bringing him to his feet.

All the workmen in sight downed tools and turned to look at the mammoth doors which led, by airlock and tunnel, to the surface of the planet.

With a low rumbling, the doors slowly parted. At first only blackness could be seen in the widening crack. Then something big and bright came up and nudged the separation from the other side, like a puppy bumping impatiently with its nose to hurry the opening and get inside.

It was another shiny mirrored bubble, like the one he had just toured, only larger. It floated above the tunnel floor as though insubstantial. The ship bobbed slightly in the air and, when the way was open, entered the lofty hangar as if blown in by a breeze from the outside. Reflections of rockwall, machinery, and people swam along its sides brightly.

As the ship approached, it emitted a faint humming and crackling sound. Workmen gathered at a nearby cradle.

Culla and Jeffrey rushed past Jacob as he watched, the chimpanzee flashing him a grin and waving for him to come along. Jacob smiled back and started to follow folding his papers and slipping them into his pocket. He looked for Kepler. The Sundiver chief must have stayed aboard Jeffrey's ship to finish the inspection, for he was nowhere in sight. The ship crackled and hissed as it maneuvered over its nest, and then began to descend slowly. It was hard to believe that it didn't shine with light of its own, its mirrored surface gleamed so. Jacob stood near Fagin, at the edge of the crowd. They watched together as the ship came to rest.

"You appear to be deep within your thoughts," Fagin fluted. "Please forgive the intrusion, but I judge that it is acceptable to inquire informally concerning their nature."

Jacob was close enough to Fagin to pick up a faint odor, somewhat like oregano. The alien's foliage rippled gently nearby.

"I suppose I was thinking about where this ship has just been," he answered. "I was trying to imagine what it must be like, down there. I—I just can't."

"Do not feel frustrated, Jacob. I am similarly in awe,

and incapable of comprehending what you of Earth have accomplished here. I await my first descent with humble anticipation."

And so put me to shame again, you green bastard, Jacob thought. I'm still trying to find a way not to have to go on one of these crazy dives. And you blather about being anxious to go!

"I don't want to call you a liar, Fagin, but I think you're stretching diplomacy a bit by saying you're impressed by this project. The technology is early stone age by galactic standards. And you can't tell me no one has ever dived into a star before! There have been sophonts loose in the galaxy for almost a billion years. Everything worth doing has been done at least a trillion times!"

There was a vague bitterness in his voice as he spoke. The strength of his own feelings surprised Jacob.

"That is no doubt quite true, Friend-Jacob. I do not pretend that Sundiver is unique. Only that it is unique in my experience. The sentient races with whom I have contact have been satisfied to study their suns from a distance and to compare the results with Library standards. For me this is adventure in its truest form."

A rectangular slice of the Sunship started to slide downward, to form a ramp to the cradle's rim.

Jacob frowned.

"But manned dives *have* to have been performed before! It's such an obvious thing to try at some time or another if it's proven possible! I can't believe that we're the first!"

"There is very little doubt, of course," Fagin said slowly. "If no one else, then surely the Progenitors did this. For they did all things, it is said, before they departed. But so many things have been done, by so many peoples, it is very hard to ever know for certain."

Jacob mulled over this in silence.

As the section of the Sunship neared the ramp, Kepler approached, smiling at Jacob and Fagin.

"Ah! There you are. Exciting, isn't it? Everyone's here! It's this way every time someone gets back from the Sun, even for a short scout dive like this one was!"

"Yes," Jacob said. "It's very exciting. Um, there's

93

something I want to ask you, Doctor Kepler, if you have a moment. I was wondering if you've asked the Branch Library at La Paz for a reference on your Sun Ghosts. Surely someone else has encountered a similar phenomenon, and I'm sure it would be a big help to have ..."

His voice fell away as he saw Kepler's smile fade.

"That was the reason Culla was assigned to us in the first place, Mr. Demwa. This was going to be a prototype project to see how well we could mix independent research with limited help from the Library. The plan worked well when we were building the ships, I have to confess that the Galactic technology is something astounding. But since then the Library hasn't been much help at all.

"It's really very complicated. I was hoping to get into it tomorrow, after you've had a complete briefing, but you see ..."

A loud cheer came from all around as the crowd surged forward. Kepler smiled resignedly.

"Later!" he shouted.

At the top of the cradle three men and two women waved at the cheering crowd. One of the women, tall and slender with a close cut of straight blonde hair, caught sight of Kepler and grinned. She started down and the rest of the crew followed.

This was apparently the Hermes Base commander Jacob had heard about from time to time during the last two days. One of the physicians at the party last night had called her the best Commandant the Confederacy outpost on Mercury ever had. A younger man had then interrupted the old-timer with a comment that she was also ". . . a fox." Jacob had assumed that the med-tech was referring to the commander's mental skill. As he watched the woman (she seemed hardly older than a girl) lithely stride down the steep ramp, he realized that the remark could easily have another complimentary meaning.

The crowd parted and the woman approached the Sundiver chief, hand outstretched.

"They're there all right!" she said. "We went down to tau point two, in the first active region, and there they were! We got within eight hundred meters of one!

Jeff won't have any trouble. It was the biggest herd of magnetovores I've ever seen!"

Jacob found her voice low and melodious. Confident. Her accent, though, was hard to place. Her pronunciation seemed quaint, old fashioned.

"Wonderful! Wonderful!" Kepler nodded. "Where there are sheep, there must be shepherds, eh?"

He took her arm and turned to introduce her to Fagin and Jacob.

"Sophonts, this is Helene deSilva, Confederacy Commandant here on Mercury, and my right-hand man. Couldn't get along without her. Helene, this is Mr. Jacob Alvarez Demwa, the gentleman I told you about by maser. The Kanten Fagin, of course, you met some months back, on Earth. I understand you've exchanged a few masergrams since."

Kepler touched the young woman's arm. "I must run now, Helene. There are a few messages from Earth that have to be handled. I already put them off too long to be here for your arrival, so I'd better go now. You're sure everything went smoothly and the crew is well rested?"

"Sure, Dr. Kepler, everything's great. We slept on the way back. I'll meet you back here when it's time to see Jeff off."

The Sundiver chief made his salutations to Jacob and Fagin, and nodded curtly to LaRoque, who stood just close enough to overhear but not close enough to be civil. Kepler left in the direction of the elevators.

Helene deSilva had a way of bowing respectfully to Fagin that was warmer than most people could hug. She radiated delight at seeing the E.T. again, and redundantly said so as well.

"And this is Mr. Demwa," she said as she shook Jacob's hand. "Kant Fagin spoke of you. You're the intrepid young fellow who dove the entire height of the Ecuador Needle to save it. That's a story I insist on hearing from the hero himself!"

A part of Jacob winced, as always when the Needle was mentioned. He hid it behind a laugh.

"Believe me, that jump wasn't made on purpose! In fact, I think I'd rather go on one of your little solar, toe-frying junkets than ever do that again!"

The woman laughed, but at the same time she looked at him strangely, with a certain *appraising* expression that Jacob found himself liking, although it confused him. He felt oddly at a loss for words.

"Um . . . anyway it's a bit odd being called a 'young fellow' by someone as young as you appear to be. You must be a very competent person to have been offered a command like this before any worry lines have shown."

DeSilva laughed again. "How gallant! That's very sweet of you, sir, but actually I have sixty-five years worth of invisible worry lines. I was a junior officer on Calypso. You may recall we got back in system a couple of years ago. I'm over ninety years old!"

"Oh!"

Starship crewmen were a very special breed. No matter what their subjective ages, they could pick their jobs when they came home . . . when they chose to keep working, that is.

"Well in that case, I really must treat you with the respect you're due, Granny."

DeSilva took a step back and cocked her head, looking at him through wryly narrowed eyes. "Just don't go too far the other way! I've worked too hard at becoming a woman, as well as an officer and a gentleman, to want to jump from 'jail bait' straight into social security. If the first attractive male to arrive in months who isn't under my command starts thinking of me as unapproachable, I just might be persuaded to throw him in irons!"

Half of the woman's referents were indecipherably archaic (what the devil was 'jail bait'?), but somehow the meaning was clear. Jacob grinned and put up his hands in surrender—willingly enough. Somehow, Helene deSilva reminded him a lot of Tania. The comparison was vague. There was an answering tremor, also vague and hard to identify. But it felt worth following.

Jacob shook aside the image. Philosophical-emotional bullshit. He was very good at that when he allowed himself. The plain fact was that the Base Commandant was an awful damned attractive fem.

"So be it," he said. "And dammed be he who first says, 'Hold, enough!' "

DeSilva laughed. She took him lightly by the arm and turned to Fagin.

"Come, I want you both to meet the dive crew.

Then we'll be busy getting Jeffrey ready to leave. He's terrible about good-byes. Even when going on a short dive like this one will be, he always bawls and hugs everyone who's staying behind as if he's never going to see them again!"

PART IV

Only with the Solar Probe is it possible to obtain data on the distribution of mass and angular momentum in the solar interior . . . obtain high resolution pictures . . . detect neutrons released in nuclear processes occurring at or near the solar surface . . . (or) determine how the solar wind is accelerated.

Finally, given the communications and tracking systems and, perhaps, the on-board hydrogen maser . . . the Solar Probe will be by far the best platform to use in the search for low frequency gravity waves from cosmological sources.

Excerpted from the report of the NASA preliminary Solar Probe Workshop

10.

HEAT

Like taffy twists and feather boas, the ochre shapes drooped in a pink misty background, as if suspended from invisible strings. The row of wispy dark arches, each a fluffy rope of gaseous tendrils, led off into the distance, each farther arch smaller in perspective than the one before, until the last faded into the swirling red miasma.

Jacob found it difficult to focus on any one detail of the recorded holographic image. The dark filaments and streamers that made up the visible topography of the middle chromosphere were deceptive in both shape and texture.

The closest filament almost filled the left forward corner of the tank. Wispy strands of darker gas coiled about an invisible magnetic field which arched over a sunspot almost a thousand kilometers below.

High above the place where most of the Sun's energy production leaked out into space as light, an observer could make out details for tens of thousands of miles. Even so it was still hard to get used to the idea that the magnetic arch he now looked at was about the size of Norway. It was merely one filigree in a chain that arched for 200,000 kilometers over a sunspot group below.

And this one was a wimp, compared to many they'd seen.

One arching spectacle had stretched a quarter of a million kilometers from end to end. The image had been recorded several months back, over an active region that had long since vanished, and the ship that recorded it had kept its distance. The reason became clear when the top of the gigantic, twisted faerie arch erupted into the most awesome of Solar events, a flare.

The flare was beautiful and terrible—a churning, boiling maelstrom of brightness representing an electrical short circuit of imcomprehensible magnitude. Even a Sunship would not have survived the sudden surge of high energy neutrons from the nuclear reactions driven by the flare, particles immune to the ship's electromagnetic shields, too many neutrons to damp away using time compression. The Sundiver Project chief emphasized, for that reason, that flares were usually predictable and avoidable.

Jacob would have found the assurance more comforting without the proviso, "usually."

The briefing had been rather routine otherwise, as Kepler led his audience through a quick review of solar physics. Jacob had learned most of the material earlier in his studies aboard the *Bradbury*, but the projections of actual dives into the chromosphere were, he had to admit, fantastic visual aids. If it was hard to comprehend the sizes of the things he saw, Jacob could blame no one but himself.

Kepler had briefly covered the basic dynamics of the Sun's interior, the real star, to which the chromosphere was just a thin skin.

In the deep core the unimaginable weight of the Sun's mass drives the nuclear reactions, producing heat and pressure and preventing the giant ball of plasma from contracting under its own gravitational pull. Pressure keeps the body "inflated."

The energy given off by the fires at the core works slowly outward, sometimes as light, and sometimes as a convective exchange of hot material from below for cooler stuff returning from above. By radiation, then convection, then radiation again, the energy reaches the kilometers-thick layer known as the photosphere —the "sphere of light" where it finally finds freedom and leaves home forever, for space.

So dense is matter inside a star, that a sudden cataclysm in the interior would take a million years to show up in a change in the amount of light leaving the surface.

But the sun doesn't stop at the photosphere; the density of matter falls off slowly with height. If one included the ions and electrons that forever stream out into space in the solar wind—to cause auroras on Earth and to shape the plasma tails of comets—one might say that there was no real boundary to the Sun. It truly reaches out to touch the other stars.

The halo of the *corona* shimmers around the rim of the Moon during a Solar eclipse. The tendrils that seem so soft on a photographic plate are comprised of electrons heated to millions of degrees, but they are diffuse, almost as thin (and harmless to Sunships) as the Solar wind.

Between the photosphere and the corona lies the *chromosphere,* the "sphere of color" . . . the place where old Sol makes the final alterations to his light show, where he places his spectral signature on the sunshine Earthmen see.

Here the temperature suddenly plummets to its minimum, a "mere" few thousand degrees. The pulsing of the photospheric cells sends ripples of gravitation upwards through the chromosphere, subtly strumming chords of space-time across millions of kilometers, and charged particles, riding the crests of Alfven waves, sweep outward in a mighty wind.

This was the domain of Sundiver. In the chromosphere, the Sun's magnetic fields play games of tag, and simple chemical compounds ephemerally brew. One can see, if the right bands are chosen, for tremendous distances. And there is a lot to see.

Kepler was in his element, now. In the darkened room his hair and moustache glowed reddish in the light given off by the tank. His voice was confident as he used a slender rod to point out features of the chromosphere for his audience.

He told the story of the sunspot cycle, the alternating rhythm of high and low magnetic activity that flips polarity every eleven years. Magnetic fields "pop out" of the Sun to form complicated loops in the chromosphere—loops which could sometimes be traced by looking at the paths of the dark filaments in hydrogen light.

The filaments twisted around the field lines and glowed with complex induced electric currents. In close-up they looked less feathery than Jacob had at first thought. Bright and dark red strips knotted around one another all along the length of the arch, sometimes swirling in complicated patterns until some tightening knot squeezed closed and splattered bright droplets away like hot grease from a skillet.

It was numbingly beautiful, although the red monochrome eventually made Jacob's eyes hurt. He looked away from the tank and rested by staring at the wall of the viewing room.

The two days since Jeffrey had waved good-bye and taken his ship off to the Sun were mixed pleasure and frustration for Jacob. They had certainly been busy.

He saw the Hermetian mines yesterday. The great layered flows that filled huge hollowed caverns north of the base with smooth rainbowed crusts of pure metal startled Jacob with their beauty, and he stared in awe at the dwarfed machines and men that ate at their flanks. He would carry with him always the amazement he felt . . . at both the loveliness of the giant field of frozen melt and at the temerity of the tiny men who dared to disturb it for its treasure.

Also enjoyable was an afternoon spent in the company of Helene deSilva. In the lounge of her apartment she broke the seal on a bottle of alien brandy whose worth Jacob didn't dare to calculate, and shared it all with him.

In a few hours he came to like the Base Commandant for her wit and the range of her interests, as well as for her pleasantly archaic flirtatious charm. They exchanged stories of peripheral interest, saving, by mute agreement, the best for later. He told her about his work with Makakai, to her delight, explaining how he persuaded the young dolphin—by means of hypnosis, brib-

104

ery (letting her play with "toys" such as the waldo-whales), and love—to concentrate on the kind of abstract thought that humans used, instead of (or in addition to) the cetacean Dreaming.

He described how the whale dream, in turn, was slowly becoming understood . . . using Hopi and Australian Aborigine philosophies to help translate that totally alien world view into something vaguely accessible to a human mind.

Helene deSilva had a way of listening that drew the words out of Jacob. When he finished his story she radiated satisfaction, then reciprocated with a tale about a dark star that nearly stood his hair on end.

She spoke of the Calypso as if it were mother, child, and lover all in one. The ship and its crew had been her world for only three years, subjective time, but on the return to Earth they became a link with the past. Of those she had left behind on Earth, on her first voyage out, only the youngest had lived to see Calypso's return. And they were now old.

When an interim assignment with Sundiver had been offered, she had jumped at the opportunity. While the scientific adventure of the solar expedition, plus a chance to gain some command experience, were probably reasons enough, Jacob thought he could sense another reason behind her choice.

Although she tried not to show it, Helene apparently disapproved of both extremes of behavior for which returning starship crewmen were famous:—cloistered insularity or boisterous hedonism. There was a core of . . . "shyness" could be the only word to describe it . . . which peeked out from beneath both the articulate and competent outer persona and the laughing, playful inner woman. Jacob looked forward to finding out more about her during his stay on Mercury.

But the dinner was postponed. Dr. Kepler had called a formal banquet and, in the manner of such things, Jacob had little to think about all evening, while everyone bent over backwards being polite and flattering.

But the biggest frustration came from Sundiver itself.

Jacob tried questioning deSilva, Culla, and perhaps a dozen base engineers, getting about the same answer each time.

"Of course, Mr. Demwa, but wouldn't it be better to talk about it after Dr. Kepler's presentation? It'll be so much clearer then . . ."

It became very suspicious.

The stack of Library documents still sat in his room. He read from the pile for an hour at a time, in a normal state of consciousness. While he slogged through the pile, isolated fragments jumped into familiarity as soon as he read them.

. . . nor is it understood why the Pring are a binocular species, since no other indigenous life form on their planet has more than one eye. It is generally assumed that these and other differences are the result of genetic manipulation by the Pila colonists. Although the Pila are reluctant to answer questions from any but officials from the Institutes, they do admit to having altered the Pring from a brachiating, arboreal animal to a sophont capable of walking and serving in their farms and cities.

The unique Pring dental arrangement had its origin in their previous state as tree grazers. It evolved as a method for scraping off the high-nutrient outer bark of their planet's trees; that bark serving in the place of fruit as a fertilization-spore spreading organ for many of the plants on Pring . . .

So that was the background behind Culla's weird dentation! Knowing their purpose somehow made a mental image of the Pring's mashies less disgusting. The fact that their function was vegetarian was downright reassuring.

It was interesting to note, while re-reading the article, how good a job the Branch Library had done with this report. The original had probably been written scores, if not hundreds of light years away from Earth, and long before Contact. The semantics machines at the Branch in La Paz were obviously getting the knack of converting alien words and meanings into English sentences that made sense, though, of course, something might have been lost in the translation.

The fact that the Institute of the Libraries had been

forced to ask for human help in programming those machines, after those first disastrous attempts just after Contact, was a source of some small satisfaction. Used to translating for species whose languages all derived from the same general Tradition, the E.T.'s had been boggled, at first, by the "flighty and imprecise" structure of all human languages.

They had moaned (or chirped or zithered or flapped) in despair at the extent to which English, in particular, had declined into a state of sublime, contextually discursive, disorder. Latin, or even better, late Neolithic Indo-European, with its highly organized structure of declensions and cases, would have been preferred. Humans obstinately refused to change their *lingua franca* for the sake of the Library, (though both Skins and Shirts began studying Indo-European for fun—each for their own reasons) and instead sent their brightest mels and fems to help the helpful aliens adjust.

The Pring serve in the cities and farms of nearly all Pil planets, except for the home planet, Pila. The sun of Pila, an F3 dwarf, is apparently too bright for this generation of uplifted Pring. (The Pring sun is F7.) This is the reason given for continuing genetic research on the Pring visual system by the Pila, long after their Uplift license would normally have expired . . .

. . . have only allowed the Pring to colonize class A worlds, devoid of life and requiring terraforming, but free of use restrictions by the Institutes of Tradition and Migration. Having taken leadership in several Jihads, the Pila apparently don't wish to have their Clients in a position to embarrass them by mishandling an older, living world . . .

The data on Culla's race spoke volumes about Galactic Civilization. It was fascinating, but the manipulation it told of made him uncomfortable. Inexplicably, he felt personally responsible.

It was at this stage in the re-reading that the summons to Dr. Kepler's long awaited talk arrived.

Now he sat in the viewing room, and wondered when the man would get to the point. What were the magnetovores? And what did people mean when they mentioned a "second type" of Solarian . . . that played tag with Sunships and made threatening gestures to their crews in anthropomorphic shapes?

Jacob looked back at the holo-tank.

The filament Kepler chose had grown to fill the tank and then expanded until the viewer felt himself visually immersed in the feathery, fiery mass. Details became clearer—twisted clumps that meant a tightening of magnetic field lines, wisps that came and went like vapor as movement dopplered the hot gasses into and out of the camera's visible band, and clusters of bright pinpoints that danced at the distant edge of vision.

Kepler kept up a running monologue, sometimes getting too technical for Jacob, but always returning to simple metaphors. His voice had become firm and confident, and he clearly enjoyed giving the show.

Kepler gestured at one of the nearby plasma streamers: a thick, twisted strand of dark red, coiling around a few painfully bright pinpoints.

"These were first thought to be your usual compressional hot spots," he said. "Until we took a second look at them. Then we found that the spectrum was all wrong."

Kepler used a control at the base of his pointer to zoom in on the center of the sub-filament.

The bright points grew. Smaller dots became visible as the image expanded.

"Now you'll recall," Kepler said, "that the hot spots we saw earlier still looked red, albeit a very bright red. That's because the ship's filters, at the time these pix were taken, were tuned only to let in a very narrow spectral band, centered on hydrogen alpha. You can see, even now, the thing that caught our interest."

Indeed I do, Jacob thought.

The bright points were a brilliant shade of green!

They flickered like blinkers and they had the color of emeralds.

"Now there are a couple of bands in the green and blue that are cut out less efficiently than most, by the filter. But the alpha line usually washes these out entirely with distance. Besides, this green isn't even one of those bands!

"You can imagine our consternation, of course. No thermal light source could have sent that color through these screens. In order to get through, the light from these objects had to be not only incredibly bright, but totally monochromatic as well, with a brightness temperature of millions of degrees!"

Jacob straightened up from the slumped posture he had assumed during the talk, interested at last.

"In other words," Kepler went on. "They had to be lasers."

"There are ways in which lasing action can occur naturally in a star," Kepler said. "But no one had ever seen it happen in our Sun before, so we went in to investigate. And what we found was the most incredible form of life anyone could imagine!"

The scientist twisted the control on his pointer and the field of view began to shift.

A soft chime sounded from the front row of the audience. Helene deSilva could be seen picking up a telephone receiver. She spoke softly into the instrument.

Kepler concentrated on his demonstration. Slowly the bright points grew in the tank until they resolved into tiny rings of light, still too small to make out in detail.

Suddenly Jacob could make out the murmur of deSilva's voice as she spoke into the phone.

Even Kepler stopped what he was doing and waited as she shot hushed questions to the person on the other end.

She put the phone down, then, her face frozen in a mask of steel control. Jacob watched her rise and walk to where Kepler stood, nervously twisting his baton in his hands. The woman bent over slightly to whisper in Kepler's ear, and the Sundiver director's eyes closed once. When they reopened his expression was totally blank.

Suddenly everyone was talking at once. Culla left his seat in the front row to join deSilva. Jacob felt air rush by as Dr. Martine sped down the aisle to Kepler's side.

Jacob rose to his feet and turned to Fagin, who stood in the aisle nearby. "Fagin, I'm going to find out what's going on. Why don't you wait here."

"That will not be necessary," the Kanten philosopher fluted.

"What do you mean?"

"I could overhear what was said to Commandant

109

Human Helene deSilva over the telephone, Friend-Jacob. It is not good news."

Jacob shouted inside. Always deadpan, you damn leafy eggplant egghead, of course it's not good news!

"So what the hell is happening!" he asked.

"I grieve most sincerely, Friend-Jacob. It appears that Scientist-Chimpanzee Jeffrey's Sunship has been destroyed in the chromosphere of your Sun!"

11.

TURBULENCE

In the ochre light of the holo-tank, Dr. Martine stood by Kepler's side, speaking his name over and over and passing her hand in front of his empty eyes. The audience milled onto the stage, jabbering. The alien Culla stood alone, facing Kepler, his great round head rolling slightly on his slender shoulders.

Jacob spoke to him.

"Culla . . ." The Pring didn't seem to hear him. The huge eyes were dull and Jacob could hear a buzzing sound, like teeth chattering coming from behind Culla's thick lips.

Jacob frowned at the grim red light pouring out of the holo-tank. He went to where Kepler stood in shock, to pry the controller rod gently from the man's hands. Martine took no notice of him as she vainly tried to get Kepler's attention.

After a couple of tentative twists on the controller, Jacob got the image to fade and brought the room lights back on. The situation seemed much easier to deal with now. The others must have sensed this as well, because the cacophony of voices subsided.

DeSilva looked up from the telephone and saw Jacob holding the controller. She smiled her thanks. Then she was back on the line shooting terse questions to the person at the other end.

A medical team arrived on the run with a stretcher. Under Dr. Martine's guidance they laid Kepler in the fabric frame and gently bore him off through the crowd gathered at the door.

Jacob turned back to Culla. Fagin had managed to push a chair up behind the Library Representative and was trying to get him to sit down. The rustling of branches and high pitched flutings subsided when Jacob approached.

"He is, I believe, all right," the Kanten said in a sing-song voice. "He is a highly empathic individual, and I fear that he will grieve excessively over the loss of his friend Jeffrey. It is often the reaction of younger species to the death of another with whom one has become close."

"Is there anything we should do? Can he hear us?"

Culla's eyes didn't appear to be focused. But then Culla's eyes never did tell Jacob anything. The chattering from inside the alien's mouth went on.

"I believe he can hear us," Fagin answered.

Jacob took hold of Culla's arm. It felt very thin and soft. There didn't appear to be any bone.

"Come on, Culla," he said. "There's a chair right behind you. You'd make us all feel a lot better if you'd sit down now."

The alien tried to answer. The huge lips parted and suddenly the chattering was very loud. The coloration of his eyes changed slightly and the lips closed again. He nodded shakily and allowed himself to be guided to the chair. Slowly the round head came down into his slender hands.

Empathic or no, there was something eerie about the alien feeling this strongly about the death of a man —a chimpanzee—who would be, down to his fundamental body chemistry, always an alien; a being whose fishlike far ancestors swam in different seas than his, and gaped in anaerobic surprise at the sunshine of a totally different star.

"May I have your attention please!" deSilva stood on the dais.

"For those of you who haven't yet heard, preliminary

reports indicate that we may have lost Dr. Jeffrey's ship in active region J-12, near Sunspot Jane. This is only a preliminary report, and further confirmation will have to wait until we can go over the telemetry we received up to the mishap."

LaRoque waved from the far side of the room to attract the Commandant's attention. In one hand he held a small steno-camera, a different model from the one taken from him in the Sunship Cavern. Jacob wondered why Kepler hadn't returned the other one yet.

"Miss deSilva," LaRoque cut in. "Will it be possible for the press to attend the telemetry review? There should be a public record." In his excitement, LaRoque's accent had virtually disappeared. Without it, the anachronistic appelation, "Miss deSilva," sounded very odd.

She paused without looking directly at the man. The Witness Laws were very clear about denying access to a public record at news events without a "Seal" from the Agency for Secrets Registration. Even the ASR people, responsible for enforcing honesty above the law, were reluctant to allow it. LaRoque obviously had her cornered, but he wasn't pushing. Yet.

"All right. The observing gallery above the Control Center can hold just about everybody who wants to come . . . *except*," she glared at a cluster of base crewmen who had gathered near the door, "for people who have work to do." She ended with a raised eyebrow. There was an immediate bustle of motion by the exit.

"We'll gather in twenty minutes," she concluded and stepped down.

Members of the Hermes Colony Staff started leaving right away. Those wearing Earth clothing, recent arrivals and visitors, left more slowly.

LaRoque was already gone, no doubt on his way to the maser station to send his story to Earth.

That left Bubbacub. He had been talking to Dr. Martine before the meeting began, but the little bearlike alien hadn't come in. Jacob wondered where Bubbacub had been during the meeting.

Helene deSilva joined him and Fagin.

"Culla's quite a little Eatee," she said to Jacob, softly. "He used to joke that he got along with Jeffrey so well

113

because they were both low men on the status pole, and because they'd both come down so recently from the trees." She looked at Culla with pity, and put out one hand to the side of the alien's head.

I'll bet that's comforting, Jacob thought.

"Sadness is the primary perquisite of youth." Fagin rustled his leaves, like a tinkling of sand dollars in a breeze.

DeSilva let her hand fall. "Jacob, Dr. Kepler left written instructions that I was to consult with you and Kant Fagin if anything ever happened to him."

"Oh?"

"Yessir. Of course the directive has very little legal weight. All I really have to do is let you in on our staff meetings. But it's obvious anything you'd offer would be useful. I was hoping that the two of you, in particular, wouldn't miss the telemetry replay."

Jacob appreciated her position. As Base Commandant she would bear the onus of any decision made today. Yet of those with substantial reputations now on Mercury, LaRoque was hostile, Martine was barely friendly to the project, and Bubbacub was an enigma. If Earth should hear many accounts of what went on here, it would be in her interest to have some friends as well.

"Of course," Fagin whistled. "We will both be honored to aid your staff."

DeSilva turned back to Culla and asked softly if the alien would be all right. After a pause, he lifted his head from his hands and nodded slowly. The chattering had stopped, but Culla's eyes were still dull, with bright pinpoints flickering randomly at the edge. He looked exhausted, as well as miserable.

DeSilva departed to help prepare the telemetry replay. Shortly afterwards Pil Bubbacub puffed importantly into the room, his sleek fur ruffled in a collar around his short fat neck. When he spoke his mouth moved in quick snaps and the Vodor on his chest boomed out the words in audible range.

"I have heard the news. It vital that all be at the Tel-e-me-try Review, so I es-cort you there."

Bubbacub moved to look behind Jacob. He saw Culla sitting absently on the flimsy folding chair.

"Culla!" he called. The Pring looked up, hesitated

than made a gesture that Jacob didn't understand. It seemed to imply supplication, negation.

Bubbacub bristled. He emitted a series of clicks and high pitched squeaks at a rapid clip. Culla stumbled to his feet quickly. Immediately Bubbacub turned his back on them all to start in short powerful steps down the hallway . . .

Behind him, Jacob and Fagin walked with Culla. From somewhere at the top of Fagin's "head" there came a strange music.

12.

GRAVITY

Automation kept the Telemetry Room small. A mere dozen consoles made two rows below a large viewing screen. Behind a railing, on a raised dais, the invited guests watched as the operators carefully rechecked the recorded data.

Occasionally a man, male or female, would lean forward and peer at some detail on a screen, in vain hope for a clue that a Sunship still existed down there.

Helene deSilva stood near the pair of consoles closest to the dais. From there the recording of Jeffrey's last remarks played on a visual display.

A row of words appeared, representing fingerstrokes on a keyboard forty million kilometers away, hours before.

RIDE IS SMOOTH ON AUTOMATICS . . . HAD TO DAMP TIME FACTOR OF TEN DURING TURBULENCE . . . I JUST HAD LUNCH IN TWENTY SECONDS HA HA . . .

Jacob smiled. He could imagine the little chimpanzee getting a kick out of the time differential.

DOWN PAST TAU POINT ONE NOW . . . FIELD LINES CONVERGING AHEAD . . . INSTRUMENTS

SAY THERE'S A HERD THERE JUST LIKE HELENE
SAID . . . ABOUT A HUNDRED . . . CLOSING
NOW . . .

Then Jeffrey's simian voice came on, gruff, abrupt,
over a loudspeaker.

"Wait 'til I tell em inna trees, boys! First solo onna
Sun! Eat yer heart out, Tarzan!" one of the controllers
started to laugh, then cut it off. It finished sounding
like a sob.

Jacob started. "You mean he was all alone down
there?"

"I thought you knew!" deSilva looked surprised.
"The dives are pretty well automatic nowadays. Only a
computer can adjust the stasis fields fast enough to
keep the turbulence from pounding a passenger to
jelly. Jeff . . . had two: one onboard and also a laser
remote from the big machine here on Mercury. What
can a man do anyway, besides add a touch here or
there?"

"But why add any risk?"

"It was Dr. Kepler's idea," she answered, a little de-
fensively. "He wanted to see if it was only human psi
patterns that were causing the Ghosts to run away or
make threatening gestures."

"We never got to that part of the briefing."

She brushed a lock of blonde hair back.

"Yes, well in our first few encounters with the magnetovores, we never saw any of the herdsmen. Then
when we did, we watched from a distance to determine
their relationship to the other creatures.

"When we finally approached, the herdsmen just ran
away at first. Then their behavior changed radically.
While most of them fled, one or two would arc up over
the ship, out of the plane of the instrument platform,
and come down close to the ship!"

Jacob shook his head, "I'm not sure I understand . . ."

DeSilva glanced at the nearest console but there
was no change. The only reports from Jeff's ship were
solonomic data—routine reports of solar conditions.

"Well, Jacob, the ship is a flat deck inside an almost
perfectly reflecting shell. The Gravity Engines, Stasis
Field Generators and the Refrigerator Laser are all in
the smaller sphere that sits in the middle of the deck.
The recording instruments line the rim of the deck on

the "bottom" side, and the people occupy the "top" side, so both will have an unobstructed view to anything looked at edge on. But we hadn't counted on anything purposely dodging our cameras!"

"If the Ghost went out of view of your instruments by coming up overhead, why didn't you just turn the ship? You have complete gravity control."

"We tried. They just disappeared! Or worse, they stayed overhead however fast we'd turn. They'd just hover! That's when some of the crew started seeing some of the most damnable anthropoid shapes!"

Suddenly Jeffrey's raspy voice filled the room again.

"Hey! There's a whole pack of sheep dogs pushin' those toroids around! Goin' in to give em a pet! Nice Doggies!"

Helene shrugged.

"Jeff was always a skeptic. He never saw any shapes-in-the-ceiling and he always called the herdsmen 'sheep dogs' because he saw nothing in their behavior to imply intelligence."

Jacob smiled wryly. The condescension of super-chimp toward the canine race was one of the more humorous aspects of their me-too obsession. Also perhaps it diluted their sensitivity over the special relationship, of dog with human being, that antedated their own. Many chimps kept dogs as pets.

"He called the magnetovores toroids?"

"Yes, they're shaped like huge doughnuts. You would have seen that if the briefing hadn't . . . been interrupted." She shook her head sadly and looked down.

Jacob shifted his feet. "I'm sure there's nothing anyone could have done . . ." he began. Then he realized that he was sounding foolish. DeSilva nodded once and turned back to the console; busy, or pretending to be, with technical readouts.

Bubbacub lay sprawled on a cushion to the left, near the barrier. He had a book play-back in his hands and had been reading, in total absorption, the alien characters that flashed from top to bottom on the tiny screen. The Pil had raised his head and listened when Jeffrey's voice came on, and then gazed enigmatically at Pierre LaRoque.

LaRoque's eyes flashed as he recorded an "historic

moment." Occasionally he spoke in a low excited voice into the microphone of his borrowed steno-camera.

"Three minutes," deSilva said thickly.

For a minute, nothing happened. Then, the big letters came on the screen again.

THE BIG BOYS ARE HEADING TOWARD ME FOR ONCE! OR AT LEAST A COUPLE OF 'EM ARE. I JUST TURNED ON THE CLOSEUP CAMERAS . . . HEY! I'M GETTIN A T-T-TILT IN HERE! TIME-COMPRESSION JAMMED!!

"Gonna abort!" came the deep, croaking voice, suddenly. "Ridin' up fast. . . . More tilt! 'S' falling! . . . The Eatees! They . . ."

There came a very brief burst of static, then silence followed by a loud hiss as the console operator turned up his gain. Then, nothing.

For a long moment nobody said a word. Then one of the console operators rose from his station.

"Implosion confirmed," he said.

She nodded once. "Thank you. Please prepare a summary of the data for transmission to Earth."

Strangely, the strongest emotion Jacob felt was a poignant pride. As a staff member of the Center for Uplift, he'd noticed that Jeffrey spurned his keyboard in the last moments of his life. Instead of retreating before fear, he made a proud, difficult gesture. Jeff the Earthman spoke aloud.

Jacob wanted to mention this to somebody. If anyone could, Fagin would understand. He started over to where the Kanten stood, but Pierre LaRoque hissed sharply before he got there.

"Fools!" The journalist stared about with an expression of disbelief.

"And I am the biggest fool of all! Of any here I should have seen the danger in sending a chimpanzee down to the Sun alone!"

The room was silent. Blank expressions of surprise turned to LaRoque, who waved his arms in an expansive gesture.

"Can you not see? Are you all blind? If the Solarians are our Ancestrals, and there can be little doubt of that, then they have obviously gone to great pains to

119

avoid us for millennia. Yet perhaps some distant affection for us has kept them from destroying us so far!

"They have tried to warn you and your Sunships off in ways that you could not ignore, and yet you persist in trespassing. How are these mighty beings to react, then, if they are burst upon by a Client race of the race they have abandoned? What is it you expect them to do when they are invaded by a monkey . . . !"

Several crewmen rose to their feet in anger. DeSilva had to raise her voice to get them to subside. She faced LaRoque, an expression of iron control on her features.

"Sir, if you will please put your interesting hypothesis down on paper, with a minimum of invective, the staff will be only too happy to consider it."

"But . . ."

"And that will be enough on the subject now! We'll have plenty of time to talk about it later!"

"No, we don't have any time at all."

Everyone turned. Dr. Martine stood at the back of the Gallery, in the doorway. "I think we'd better discuss this right now," she said.

"Is Dr. Kepler all right?" Jacob asked.

She nodded. "I've just come from his bedside. I managed to break him out of his shock and he's sleeping now. But before he fell asleep he spoke rather urgently about making another dive right away."

"Right away? Why? Shouldn't we wait until we know for certain what happened to Jeffrey's ship?"

"We know what happened to Jeff's ship!" she answered sharply. "I overheard what Mr. LaRoque said just as I came in, and I'm not at all happy with the way you all received his idea! You're all so hidebound and sure of yourselves that you can't listen to a fresh approach!"

"You mean you really think that the Ghosts are our Ancestral Patrons?" DeSilva was incredulous.

"Perhaps, and perhaps not. But the rest of his explanation makes sense! After all, did the Solarians ever do more than threaten before this? And now they suddenly became violent. Why? Could it be that they felt no compunctions over killing a member of a species as immature as Jeff's?"

She shook her head sadly.

"You know, it's only a matter of time before human

beings begin to realize just how much we're going to have to adapt! The fact is that every other oxygen-breathing race subscribes to a status system . . . a pecking order based on seniority, strength, and parentage. Many of you don't find this nice. But it's the way things are! And if we don't want to go the way of the non-European races in the nineteenth century, we'll just have to learn the way other, stronger species like to be treated!"

Jacob frowned.

"You're saying that if a chimpanzee is killed, and human beings are threatened or snubbed, then . . ."

"Then perhaps the Solarians don't want to mess around with children and pets . . ." One of the operators pounded his fist onto his console. A glare from deSilva cut him off. ". . . but might be willing to speak with a delegation with members of older, more experienced species. After all, how do we even know until we try?"

"Culla's been down there with us on most of our dives," the console operator muttered. "And he's a trained ambassador!"

"With all due respect to Pring Culla," Martine bowed slightly toward the tall alien. "He is from a very young race. Almost as young as ours. It's apparent that the Solarians don't think he's any more worthy than us of their attention.

"No, I propose that we take advantage of the unprecedented presence here on Mercury of two members of ancient and honored races. We should humbly ask the Pil Bubbacub and Kant Fagin to join us, down in the Sun, in one last attempt to make contact!"

Bubbacub rose slowly. He looked around deliberately, aware that Fagin would wait for him to speak first. "If human beings say they need me down on Sol, then despite the seen dangers of prim-it-ive Sunships, I be inc-lined to ac-cept."

He returned complacently to his cushion.

Fagin rustled and his voice sighed. "I too shall be pleased to go. Indeed, I would perform any labor to earn the lowest berth on such a craft. I cannot imagine what help I could be. But I will happily go along."

"Well I object, damnit!" deSilva shouted. "I refuse to accept the political implications of taking Pil Babbacub

121

and Kant Fagin down, particularly after the accident! You talk of good relations with powerful alien races, Dr. Martine, but can you imagine what would happen if they died down there in an Earth ship?"

"Oh fish and falafal!" Martine said. "If anyone can handle things so no blame falls on Earth, it's these sophonts. The galaxy is a dangerous place, after all. I'm sure they could leave depositions or something."

"Such documents are already recorded in my case." Fagin said.

Bubbacub, as well, stated his magnanimous willingness to risk his life in a primitive craft, absolving all of responsibility. The Pil turned away as LaRoque began to thank him. Even Martine joined in asking the man to please shut up.

DeSilva looked to Jacob. He shrugged.

"Well, we've got time. Let's give the crew here a chance to check the data from Jeff's dive, and let Dr. Kepler recover. Meanwhile we can refer this idea to Earth for suggestions."

Martine sighed. "I wish it were that simple, but you just haven't thought this out. Consider, if we were to try to make peace with the Solarians, shouldn't we return to the same group that was offended by Jeff's visit?"

"Well, I'm not sure that necessarily follows, but it sounds right."

"And how do you plan to find the same group, down in the solar atmosphere?"

"I suppose you'd just have to return to the same active region, where the grazers are feeding. . . . Oh, I see what you mean."

"I'll bet you do," she smiled. "There is no permanent 'Solography' down there to make a map from. The active regions, and sunspots themselves, fade away in a matter of weeks! The Sun has no surface, per se, only different levels and densities of gas. Why, the equator even rotates faster than the other latitudes! How are you ever going to find the same group if you don't leave right away, before the damage done by Jeff's visit spreads over the entire star?"

Jacob turned to deSilva, puzzled. "Do you think she might be right, Helene?"

She rolled her eyes upward. "Who knows? Maybe.

It's something to think about. I do know that we aren't going to do a damn thing until Dr. Kepler is well enough to be heard."

Dr. Martine frowned. "I told you before! Dwayne agreed that another expedition should leave right away!"

"And I'll hear from him personally!" deSilva answered hotly.

"Well, here I am, Helene."

Dwayne Kepler stood in the doorway, leaning against the jamb. Beside him, supporting his arm, Chief Physician Laird glared across the room at Dr. Martine.

"Dwayne! What are you doing out of bed! Do you want a heart attack?" Martine strode toward him, furious and concerned, but Kepler waved her back.

"I'm fine, Millie. I've just diluted that prescription you gave me, that's all. In a smaller dose it really is useful, so I know you meant well. It's just that it wasn't helping to knock me out like that!"

Kepler chuckled weakly. "Anyway, I'm glad I wasn't too doped up to hear your brilliant speech. I caught most of it from the doorway."

Martine reddened.

Jacob felt relieved that Kepler didn't mention the part he had played. After landing and obtaining Laboratory space, it had seemed a waste not to go ahead and analyze the samples he'd pilfered, back on the *Bradbury*, of Kepler's pharmacopoeia.

No one asked where he got his samples, fortunately. Although the base surgeon, when consulted, thought that some of the doses seemed a bit high, all but one of the drugs turned out to be standard for treatment of mild manic states.

The unknown drug stayed at the back of Jacob's mind; one more mystery to solve. What sort of physical problem did Kepler have that required large doses of a powerful anticoagulant? Physician Laird had been incensed. Why had Martine prescribed Warfarin?

"Are you sure you're well enough to be up here now?" deSilva asked Kepler. She helped the physician guide him to a chair.

"I'm all right," he answered. "Besides, there are things that just won't wait.

"First of all, I'm not at all sure about Millie's theory that the Ghosts would greet Pil Bubbacub or Kant Fagin with more enthusiasm than they've shown to the rest of us. I do know that I'm definitely not taking responsibility for taking them down on a dive! The reason is that if they were killed down there it wouldn't be at the hands of the Solarians . . . it would be caused by human beings! There should be another dive right away . . . *without* our distinguished extraterrestrial friends, of course . . . but it should leave immediately to go to the same region, as Millie suggested."

DeSilva shook her head emphatically. "I don't agree at all, sir! Either Jeff was killed by the Ghosts, or something went wrong with his ship. And I think it was the latter, much as I hate to admit it . . . . We should check everything out before . . ."

"Oh, there's no doubt it was the ship," Kepler interrupted. "The Ghosts didn't kill anybody."

"What is it you say?" LaRoque shouted. "Are you a blind man? How can you deny the obvious facts!"

"Dwayne," Martine said smoothly. "You're much too tired to think about this now."

Kepler just waved her away.

"Excuse me, Dr. Kepler," Jacob said. "You mentioned something about the danger coming from human beings? Commandant deSilva probably thinks you meant an error in prepping Jeff's ship caused his death. Are you talking about something else?"

"I just want to know one thing," Kepler said slowly. "Did the telemetry show that Jeff's ship was destroyed by a collapse of his stasis field?"

The console operator who had spoken earlier stepped forward. "Why . . . yessir. How did you know?"

"I didn't know," he smiled. "But I guessed pretty well, once I thought of sabotage."

"What!?" Martine, deSilva and LaRoque shouted almost at once.

And suddenly Jacob saw it. "You mean during the tour . . . ?" He turned to look at LaRoque. Martine followed his eyes and gasped.

LaRoque stepped back as if he had been struck. "You are an insane man!" he cried. "And you are as well!" He shook a finger at Kepler. "How could I have sabotaged the engines when I was sick all of the time I was in that crazy place?"

"Hey look, LaRoque," Jacob said. "I didn't say anything, and I'm sure Dr. Kepler is only speculating." He ended in a question and raised an eyebrow to Kepler.

Kepler shook his head. "I'm afraid I'm serious. LaRoque spent an hour next to Jeff's Gravity Generators, with no one else around. We checked the Grav Generator for any damage that might have been caused by anyone fumbling around with their bare hands, and we didn't find any. It didn't occur to me until later to check Mr. LaRoque's camera.

"When I did, I found that one of its little attachments is a small sonic stunner!" From one of the pockets of his tunic he pulled out the small recording device. "This is how the kiss of Judas was delivered!"

LaRoque reddened. "The stunner is a standard self-defense device for journalists. I had even forgotten about it. And it could never have harmed so big a machine!

"And all of that is beside the point! This terra-chauvinist, archaeo-religious lunatic, who has nearly destroyed all chance of meeting our Patrons as friends, dares to accuse me of a crime for which there is no motive! He murdered that poor monkey, and he wishes to throw the blame on someone else!"

"Shut up, LaRoque," deSilva said evenly. She turned back to Kepler.

"Are you aware of what you're saying, sir? A Citizen wouldn't commit murder, simply out of dislike for an individual. Only a Probationary Personality could kill without dire cause. Can you think of any reason Mr. LaRoque might have had to do such a drastic thing?"

"I don't know," Kepler shrugged. He peered at LaRoque. "A Citizen who feels justified in killing still feels remorse afterward. Mr. LaRoque doesn't look like he regrets anything, so either he's innocent, or a good actor . . . or he is a Probationer after all!"

"In space!" Martine cried. "That's impossible, Dwayne. And you know it. Every spaceport is loaded with P-receivers. And every ship is equipped with detectors also! Now you should apologize to Mr. LaRoque!"

Kepler grinned.

"Apologize? At the very least I know LaRoque lied about being 'dizzy' in the gravity loop. I sent a maser-gram to Earth. I wanted a dossier on him from his paper. They were only too happy to oblige.

"It seems that Mr. LaRoque is a trained astronaut! He was separated from the Service for 'medical reasons'— a phrase that's often used when a person's P-test scores rise to probation levels and he's forced to give up a sensitive job!

"That may not prove anything, but it does mean that LaRoque has had too much experience in spaceships to have been 'scared to death' in Jeffrey's gravity loop. I only wish I realized this conflict in time to warn Jeff."

LaRoque protested and Martine objected, but Jacob could see the tide of opinion in the room turn against them. DeSilva eyed LaRoque with a cold feral gleam that startled Jacob somewhat.

"Wait a minute," he held up a hand. "Why don't we check if there are any Probationers without transmitters here on Mercury. I suggest we all have our retina patterns sent back to Earth for verification. If Mr. La-Roque isn't listed as a Probationer, it will be up to Dr. Kepler to show why a Citizen might have thought he had reason to murder."

"All right, then, for Kukulkan's sake, let us do it now!" LaRoque said. "But only on the condition that I not be singled out!" For the first time Kepler began to look unsure.

For Kepler's benefit, deSilva ordered the entire base reduced to Mercurian gravity. The Control Center answered that the conversion would take about five minutes. She went on the intercom and announced the identity test to the crew and visitors, then left to supervise the preparations.

Those in the Telemetry Room began to drift out, on their way to the elevators. LaRoque kept close to Kepler and Martine, as if to demonstrate his eagerness to disprove the charges against him, his chin raised in an expression of high martyrdom.

The three of them, plus Jacob and two crewmen, were waiting for an elevator car when the gravity change happened. It was an ironic place for it to occur for it felt as if the floor had suddenly started to drop.

They were all used to changes in gravity—many places in Hermes Base were kept off Earth Gee. But usually the transition was through a stasis-controlled doorway, itself no more pleasant than this but, from familiarity, less disconcerting. Jacob swallowed hard and one of the crewmen staggered slightly.

In a sudden violent motion LaRoque dove for the camera in Kepler's hand. Martine gasped and Kepler grunted in surprise. The crewman who grabbed after the journalist got a fist in the face as LaRoque twisted like an acrobat and began to run backward down the hall, bringing up his recaptured camera. Jacob and the other crewman gave chase, instinctively.

There was a flash and a shooting pain in Jacob's shoulder. Something in his mind spoke as he dove to avoid another stunner bolt. It said, "Okay, this is my job. I'm taking over now."

He was standing in a hallway, waiting. It had been exciting, but now it was sheer hell. The passageway dimmed for a moment. He gasped and reached to steady himself on the rough wall as his vision cleared.

He was alone in a service corridor with a pain in his shoulder and the remnants of a deep, almost smug sense of satisfaction dissipating like a fading dream. He looked carefully around himself, then sighed.

"So you took over and thought you could handle it without me, didn't you?" he grunted. The shoulder tingled as if it was just now coming awake.

How his other half had got loose Jacob had no idea, nor why it had tried to handle things without the main persona's help. But it must have run into trouble to have given up now.

A sensation of resentment answered that thought. Mr. Hyde was sensitive about his limitations, but capitulation came at last.

Is that all? Full memory of the last ten minutes flooded back. He laughed. His amoral Self had been confronted by an insurmountable barrier.

Pierre LaRoque was in a room at the end of the hallway. Amid the chaos that followed his seizure of the camera-stunner only Jacob had been able to stay on a man's trail, and he'd selfishly kept the stalk to himself.

He had played LaRoque like a trout, letting him think he'd eluded all pursuit. Once he even diverted a posse of base crewmen when they were getting too close.

Now LaRoque was putting on a spacesuit in a tool closet twenty meters from an outer airlock. He'd been in there five minutes and it would take at least another ten for him to finish. That was the insurmountable barrier. Mr. Hyde couldn't wait. He was only a collection of drives, not a person, and Jacob had all of the patience. He'd planned it that way.

Jacob snorted his disgust but not without a twinge. Not too long ago that drive had been a daily part of him. He could understand the pain that waiting caused the small artificial personality that demanded instant gratification.

Minutes passed. He watched the door silently. Even in his full awareness he began to get impatient. It took a serious effort of will to keep his hand off the door latch.

The latch started to turn. Jacob stepped back with his hands at his sides.

The glassy bubble of a spacesuit helmet poked through the opening as the door swung outward. LaRoque looked to the left and then to the right. His teeth made a hissing shape when he saw Jacob. The door swung wide and the man came forward with a bar of plastic bracing material in his hand.

Jacob held up a hand. "Stop, LaRoque! I want to talk to you. You can't get away anyway."

"I don't want to hurt you, Demwa. Run!" LaRoque's voice twanged nervously from a speaker on his chest. He flexed the plastic cudgel menacingly.

Jacob shook his head. "Sorry. I jimmied the airlock down the hall before waiting here. You'll find it a long walk in a spacesuit to the next one."

LaRoque's face twisted. "Why?! I did nothing! Particularly to you!"

"We'll see about that. Meanwhile, let's talk. There isn't much time."

"I'll talk!" LaRoque screamed. "I'll talk with this!" He came forward with the bar, swinging.

Jacob dropped into a deflection stance and tried to raise both hands to seize LaRoque's wrist. But he'd forgotten about the numb left shoulder. His left hand just fluttered weakly, halfway to its assigned position. The right shot out to block and got a piece of the bar coming around instead. Desperately, he fell forward and tucked his head in as the club whistled inches above.

The roll, at least, was perfect. The lesser gravity helped as he came up and around effortlessly in a crouch. But his right hand was numb now, as he automatically shut off the pain from an ugly bruise. In his suit LaRoque swiveled more lightly than Jacob expected. What was it that Kepler said about LaRoque having been an astronaut? No time. Here he comes again.

The bar came down in a vicious overhead cut. LaRoque held it in a two-handed kendo grip; easy to block if only Jacob had his hands. Jacob dove under the cut and buried his head in LaRoque's midriff. He kept driving forward until together they slammed into the corridor wall. LaRoque said "Oof!" and dropped the bar.

Jacob kicked it away and jumped back.

"Stop this, LaRoque!" He gulped for breath. "I just want to talk to you. . . . Nobody has enough evidence to convict you of anything, so why run? There's no place to run to anyway!"

LaRoque shook his head sadly. "I'm sorry, Demwa." The affected accent was completely gone. He lunged forward, arms outstretched.

Jacob hopped backward until the distance was right, counting slowly. At the count of five his eyelids fell and locked into slits. For an instant Jacob Demwa was whole. He dropped back and traced a geodesic in his mind from the toe of his shoe to his opponent's chin. The toe followed the arc in a snap that seemed to expand to minutes. The impact felt feather soft.

LaRoque rose into the air. In his plentitude, Jacob Demwa watched the space-suited figure fly backward in slow motion. He empathized, and it was he, it seemed, who went horizontal in midair and then drifted down in shame and hurt until the hard floor slammed into his back through the utility pack.

Then the trance ended and he was loosening La-Roque's helmet . . . pulling it off and helping him to sit up against the wall. LaRoque was crying softly.

Jacob noticed a package attached to LaRoque's waist. He cut the attachment and started to unwrap it, pushing LaRoque's hands aside when he resisted.

"So," Jacob pursed his lips. "You didn't try to use the stunner on me because the camera was too valuable. Why, I wonder? I might find out if we play this thing back.

"Come on, LaRoque," he rose and pulled the man to his feet. "We're going to stop where there's a readout machine. That is unless you have something to say first?"

LaRoque shook his head. He followed meekly with Jacob's hand on his arm.

At the main corridor, as Jacob was about to turn to the photo lab, a posse led by Dwayne Kepler found them. Even in the reduced gravity the scientist leaned heavily on the arm of a med-aid.

"Aha! You caught him! Wonderful! This proves everything I said! The man was fleeing a righteous punishment! He's a murderer!"

"We'll see about that," Jacob said. "The only thing this adventure proves is that he got scared. Even a Citizen can be violent when he panics. The thing I'd like to know is where he thought he was going. There's nothing out there but blasted rock! Maybe you should have some men go out and search the area around the base to be sure."

Kepler laughed.

"I don't think he was going anywhere. Probationers never do know where they're going. They act on basic instinct. He simply wanted to get out of an enclosed place, like any hunted animal."

LaRoque's face remained blank. But Jacob felt his arm tense when a surface search was mentioned, then relax when Kepler shrugged the idea aside.

"Then you're giving up the idea of an adult-murder," Jacob said to Kepler as they turned toward the elevators. Kepler walked slowly.

"On what motive? Poor Jeff never harmed a fly! A decent, god-fearing chimpanzee! Besides, there hasn't

130

been a murder by a Citizen in the System for ten years! They're about as common as gold meteors!"

Jacob had his doubts about that. The statistics were more a comment on police methods than anything else. But he remained silent.

By the elevators Kepler spoke briefly into a wall communicator. Several more men arrived almost immediately and took LaRoque from Jacob.

"Did you find the camera, by the way?" Kepler asked.

Jacob dissembled briefly. For a moment he considered hiding it and then pretending to discover it later.

"Ma camera a votre oncle!" LaRoque cried. He thrust out a hand and reached for Jacob's back pocket. The crewmen pulled him back. Another came forward and held out his hand. Jacob reluctantly handed over the camera.

"What did he say?" Kepler asked. "What language was that?"

Jacob shrugged. An elevator came and more people spilled out, including Martine and deSilva.

"It was just a curse," he said. "I don't think he approves of your ancestry."

Kepler laughed out loud.

13.

UNDER THE SUN

To Jacob the Communications Dome seemed like a bubble stuck in tar. All around the hemisphere of glass and stasis, the surface of Mercury gave off a dull, lambent shine. The liquid quality of the reflected sunlight enhanced the feeling of being inside a crystal ball that was trapped in mire, unable to escape into the cleanliness of space.

In the near distance, the rocks themselves looked strange. Unusual minerals formed in that heat and under constant bombardment of particles from the solar wind. The eye puzzled without quite knowing why, at powders and odd crystal shapes. And there were puddles as well. One shied away from thinking about those.

And something else near the horizon demanded attention.

The Sun. It was very dim, cut down by the powerful screens. But the whitish yellow ball seemed like a golden dandelion near enough to touch, an incandescent coin. Dark sunspots ran in clusters, fanning north-and south-eastward, away from the equator. The surface had a fineness of texture that just escaped focus.

Looking directly at the Sun brought a strange detachment in Jacob. Dimmed, but not red tuned, its light bathed those inside the dome in an energizing glow. Streamers of sunshine seemed to caress Jacob's forehead.

It was as if he had, like some ancient lizard seeking more than warmth, exposed every part of his self to the Lord of Space and, under those fires, felt a pulling force, a need to go.

He felt an uneasy certainty. Something lived in that furnace. Something terribly old, and terribly aloof.

Beneath the dome, men and machines stood on a fused plate of iron silicate. Jacob craned his head back to look at the huge pylon that filled the center of the chamber and protruded from the top of the stasis shield, into the hot Mercurial sunshine.

At its tip were the masers and laser which kept Hermes Base in touch with Earth, and, via a net of synchronous satellites, orbiting 15 million kilometers above the surface, followed the Sunships down into the Maelstrom of Helios.

The maser beam was busy now. One retinal pattern after another flew at lightspeed to the computers at home. It was tempting to imagine riding that beam back to Earth, to blue skies and waters.

The Retinal Reader was a small machine attached to the laser optics of the Library-designed computer system. The reader was essentially a large eyepiece against which a human user could press cheek and forehead. The optical input did the rest.

Although the E.T.'s were exempted from the search for Probationers (there was no way they could qualify, and there certainly weren't any retinal codes on file for the few thousand galactics in the solar system) Culla insisted on being included. As Jeffrey's friend he claimed a right to participate, however symbolically, in the investigation of the chimpanzee scientist's death.

Culla had trouble fitting his huge oculars one at a time into the pieces. He was very still for a long time. Finally, at a musical tone, the alien walked away from the machine.

The operator adjusted the height of the eyepiece for Helene deSilva.

133

Jacob's turn came then. He waited until the eyepiece was adjusted, then pressed his nose, cheek, and forehead against the stops and opened his eyes.

A blue dot shone inside. Nothing else. It reminded Jacob of something, but he couldn't focus on what. It seemed to turn around and sparkle as he looked, eluding analysis, like the shining of somebody's soul.

Then the musical tone told him his turn was over. He stepped back and made room, as Kepler came forward, leaning on Millie Martine's arm. The scientist smiled as he passed Jacob.

Now that's what it reminded me of! he thought. The dot had been like a twinkle in a man's eye.

Oh well, it fits. Computers can just about think today. There are some that are supposed to have a sense of humor, even. Why not this as well? Give the computers eyes to flash, and arms to put akimbo. Let them cast meaningful glances or stares that would kill if only stares could. Why should they not, the machines, begin to take on the aspect of those whom they absorb?

LaRoque submitted to the Reader, looking confident. When he finished, he sat aloof and silent under the gaze of Helene deSilva and several of her crew.

The Base Commandant had refreshments brought in, as everyone connected with the Sundiver ships took his or her turn at the Reader. Many of the technicians grumbled at the interruption of their work. Jacob had to admit, as he watched the procession pass, that it was an awful lot of effort to go through. He had never thought Helene would want to check on everybody.

DeSilva had offered a partial explanation in the elevator on the way up. After putting Kepler and LaRoque in separate cars, she had ridden with Jacob.

"One thing confuses me," he had said.

"Only one thing?" she smiled grimly.

"Well, one thing stands out. If Dr. Kepler accuses LaRoque of sabotaging Jeff's ship, why does he object to taking Bubbacub and Fagin on a followup dive, whatever the result of this investigation? If LaRoque is guilty that would mean that the next dive will be perfectly safe with him out of the way."

DeSilva looked at him for a moment, pondering.

"I guess if there's anyone on this base I can confide in it's you, Jacob. So I'll tell you what I think.

"Dr. Kepler never did want any E.T. help on this program. You'll understand that I'm telling you this in strict confidence, but I'm afraid the usual balance between humanism and xenophilia that most spacemen get might have swung a bit too far in his case. His background makes him bitterly opposed to the Danikenite philosophy, and I suppose that converts into a partial distrust of aliens. Also, a lot of his colleagues have been thrown out of work by the Library. For a man who loves research as much as he, it must have been hard.

"I'm not saying he's a Skin or anything like that! He gets along with Fagin pretty well and manages to hide his feelings around other Eatees. But he might say that if one dangerous man got on Mercury, another could, and use our guests' safety as an excuse to keep them off his ships."

"But Culla's been on almost every dive."

DeSilva shrugged.

"Culla doesn't count. He's a Client.

"I do know one thing, though; I'm going to have to go over Dr. Kepler's head if this proves out. Every man on this base is having his identity checked and Bubbacub and Fagin go on the next dive if I have to shanghai them! I'm not going to let the slightest rumor get around that human crews are unreliable!"

She nodded with her jaw set. At the time Jacob thought her grimness was excessive. Though he could understand her feelings, it was a shame to masculinize those lovely features. At the same time he wondered if Helene was being totally candid on her own motivations.

A man who stood waiting by the maser link tore off a slip of message tape and carried it to deSilva. There was a tense silence as everyone watched her read. Then, grimly, she motioned to several of the husky crewmen who stood by.

"Place Mr. LaRoque under detention. He's to be returned on the next ship out."

"On what charge!" LaRoque shouted. "You cannot do this, you, you Neanderthaler woman! I will see that you pay for this insult!"

DeSilva looked down at him as if he were a form of insect. "For now the charge is illegal removal of a probationary transmitter. Other charges may be added later."

"Lies, lies!" LaRoque shrieked as he leapt up. A crewman siezed his arm and pulled him, choking with rage, toward the elevators.

DeSilva ignored them and turned to Jacob. "Mr. Demwa, the other ship will be ready in three hours. I'll go tell the others.

"We can sleep en route. Thanks again for the way you handled things downstairs."

She turned away before he could answer, giving orders in a low voice to crewmen who clustered about, efficiency masking her anger at the news: a Probationer in space!

Jacob watched for a few minutes as the dome slowly emptied. A death, a wild chase, and now a felony. So what, he thought, if the only felony proven so far is one I'd probably commit if I ever became a P.P. . . . it does mean that there's a good chance that LaRoque caused the death as well.

As much as he disliked the man, he had never thought him capable of cold-blooded murder, in spite of those wicked swipes with the plastic cudgel.

At the back of his mind Jacob could feel his other half rubbing hands gleefully . . . amorally delighted at the mysterious twists and turns the Sundiver case had taken and clamoring now to be set loose.

Forget it.

Dr. Martine approached him near the elevator. She appeared to be in shock.

"Jacob . . . you, you don't think Pierre could kill that silly little fellow, do you? I mean, he *likes* chimpanzees!"

"I'm sorry, but the evidence seems to point that way. I don't like the Probation Laws any more than you do. But people who are assigned that status *are* capable of easy violence, and for Mr. LaRoque to remove his transmitter *is* against the law.

"But don't worry, they'll work it all out on Earth. LaRoque is sure to get a fair hearing."

"But . . . he's already being unfairly accused!" she blurted. "He's not a Probationer, and he's not a murderer! I can prove it!"

"That's great! Do you have evidence here?"

He frowned suddenly. "But the transmission from Earth said he *was* a Probationer!"

She bit her lip, looking away from his eyes. "The transmission was a forgery."

Jacob felt pity for her. Now the supremely confident psychologist was stammering and grasping at far-fetched ideas in her shock. It was degrading and he wished he was elsewhere.

"You have proof that the maser message was a lie? Can I see it?"

Martine looked up at him. Suddenly she seemed very unsure, as if wondering whether to say more.

"The . . . the crew here. Did you actually see the message? That woman . . . she only read it to us. She and the others hate Pierre . . ."

Her voice trailed off weakly, as if she knew her argument was thin. After all, Jacob thought, could the Commandant have faked reading from a piece of tape and known for certain that no one would ask to see it? Or, for that matter, would she place LaRoque in a position to sue her for every penny she'd earned in seventy years, just for a grudge?

Or had Martine been about to say something else?

"Why don't you go down to your quarters and get some rest," he said gently, "and don't worry about Mr. LaRoque. They'll need more evidence than they have now to convict him of a murder in a court on Earth."

Martine let him lead her into the elevator. There, Jacob looked back. DeSilva was busy with her crew, Kepler had been taken below. Culla stood morosely near Fagin, the two of them towering over everyone else in the chamber, under the great yellow disc of the Sun.

He wondered, as the door closed, whether this was really a good way to begin a journey.

PART V

Life is an extension of the
physical world. Biological systems
have unique properties, but they
nevertheless must obey the constraints
imposed by the physical and chemical
properties of the environment and
of the organisms themselves . . .
evolutionary solutions to biological
problems are . . . influenced by the
physico-chemical environment.

Robert E. Ricklefs
Ecology
Chiron Press

14.

THE DEEPEST OCEAN

Project Icarus it was called, the fourth space program of that name and the first for which it was appropriate. Long before Jacob's parents were born—before the Overturn and the Covenant, before the Power Satellite League, before even the full flower of the old Bureaucracy—old grandfather NASA decided that it would be interesting to drop expendible probes into the Sun to see what happened.

They discovered that the probes did a quaint thing when they got close. They burned up.

In America's "Indian Summer" nothing was thought impossible. Americans were building *cities* in space—a more durable probe couldn't be much of a challenge!

Shells were made, with materials that could take unheard of stress and whose surfaces reflected almost anything. Magnetic fields guided the diffuse but tremendously hot plasmas of corona and chromosphere around and away from those hulls. Powerful communications lasers pierced the solar atmosphere with two-way streams of commands and data.

Still, the robot ships burned. However good the mirrors and insulation, however evenly the superconductors distributed heat, the laws of thermodynamics still held. Heat will pass from a higher temperature to a zone where the temperature is lower, sooner or later.

The solar physicists might have gone on resignedly burning up probes in exchange for fleeting bursts of information had Tina Merchant not offered another way.

"Why don't you refrigerate?" she asked. "You have all the power you want. You can run refrigerators to push heat from one part of the probe to another."

Her colleagues answered that, with superconductors, equilizing heat throughout was no problem.

"Who said anything about equalizing?" the Belle of Cambridge replied. "You should take all excess heat from the part of the ship were the instruments *are* and pump it into another part where the instruments *aren't*."

"And that part will burn up!" one colleague said.

"Yes, but we can make a chain of these 'heat dumps,'" said another engineer, slightly more bright. "And then we can drop them off, one by one . . ."

"No, no you don't quite understand." The triple Nobel Laureate strode to the chalkboard and drew a circle, then another circle within.

"Here!" She pointed to the inner circle. "You pump your heat into here until it is, for a short time, *hotter* than the ambient plasma outside of the ship. Then, before it can do harm there, you dump it out into the chromosphere."

"And how," asked a renowned physicist, "do you expect to do that?"

Tina Merchant had smiled as if she could almost see the Astronautics Prize held out to her. "Why I'm surprised at all of you!" she said. "You have onboard a communications laser with a brightness temperature of millions of degrees! Use it!"

Enter the age of the Solar Bathysphere. Floating in part by buoyancy and also by balancing atop the thrust of their refrigerator lasers, probes lingered for days, weeks, monitoring the subtle variations at the Sun, that wrought weather on the Earth.

That era came to an end with Contact. But soon a new type of Sunship was born.

Jacob thought about Tina Merchant. He wondered if the great lady would have been proud, or merely bemused, to stand on the deck of a Sunship and cruise calmly through the worst tempests of this irascible star. She might have said "Of course!" But how could she have known that an alien science would have to be added to her own for men to ride those storms?

To Jacob the mixture didn't inspire confidence.

He knew, of course, that a couple of dozen successful descents had been made in this ship. There was no reason to think that this trip would be dangerous.

Except that another ship, the scaled-down replica of this one, had mysteriously failed just three days before.

Jeff's ship was probably now a drifting cloud of dissolving cermet fragments and ionized gases, scattered through millions of cubic miles in the solar maelstrom. Jacob tried to imagine the storms of the chromosphere the way the chimp scientist saw them in the last instant of his life, unprotected by the space-time fields.

He closed his eyes and rubbed them gently. He had been staring at the Sun, blinking too seldom.

From his point of view, on one of the observation couches flush with the deck, he could see almost an entire hemisphere of the Sun. Half of the sky was filled by a feathery, slowly shifting ball of soft reds and blacks and whites. In hydrogen light, everything glowed in shades of crimson; the faint, delicate arch of a prominence, standing out against space at the star's rim; the dark, twisting bands of filaments; and the sunken, blackish sunspots with their umbral depths and penumbral flows.

The topography of the Sun had almost infinite variety and texture. From flickers too fast to follow with the eye, to slow majestic turnings, all he could see was in motion.

Although the major features changed little from one hour to the next, Jacob could now make out countless lesser movements. The quickest were the pulsations of forests of tall slender "spicules" around the edges of great mottled cells. The pulses took place within seconds. Each spicule, he knew, covered thousands of square miles.

Jacob had spent time at the telescope on the Flipside of the Sunship, watching the flickering spikes of superheated plasma jetting up out of the photosphere like quick waving fountains, flinging free of the Sun's gravity great rolling waves of sound and matter that became the corona and the solar wind.

Within the spicule fences, the huge granulation cells pulsed in complicated rhythm as heat from below finished its million-year journey of convection to escape suddenly as light.

These, in turn, bunched together in gigantic cells, whose oscillations were the basic modes of the almost perfectly spherical Sun—the ringing of a stellar bell.

Above all this, like a broad deep sea rolling over the ocean floor, flowed the chromosphere.

The analogy could be overstated, but one could think of the turbulent areas above the spicules as coral reefs, and of the rows of stately, feathery filaments, tracing everywhere the paths of magnetic fields, as beds of kelp, gently swaying with the tide. No matter that each pink arch was many times the size of Earth!

Once more Jacob tore his eyes away from the boiling sphere. I'm going to be useless for anything if I keep staring like this, he thought. I wonder how the others resist it?

The entire observation floor was visible from his position, except for a small section on the other side of the forty-foot dome at the Center.

An opening grew in the side of the central dome and light spilled out into the deck. Silhouetted, a man emerged, followed by a tall woman. Jacob didn't have to wait for his eyes to adapt to know the outline of Commandant deSilva.

Helene smiled as she walked over and sat cross-legged next to his couch.

"Good morning, Mr. Demwa. I hope you had a good night's sleep. It'll be a busy day."

Jacob laughed. "That's three times in one breath you've talked as if there was anything called night here. You don't have to keep up the fiction, like providing this sunrise here." He nodded to where the Sun covered half of the sky.

"Rotation of the ship to make eight hours of night allows groundlubbers a chance to sleep," she said.

"You needn't have worried," Jacob said. "I can catch Zee's anytime. It's my most valuable talent."

Helene's smile widened. "It was no inconvenience. But, now that you mention it, it's always been a tradition of Helionauts to rotate the ship once before final descent and call it night."

"You have traditions already? After only two years?"

"Oh this tradition is much older than that! It dates back to when nobody could imagine any other way to visit the Sun but . . ." She paused.

Jacob groaned out loud.

"But to go at night, when it isn't so hot!"

"You figured it out!"

"Filamentary, my dear Watson."

It was her turn to groan. "Actually, we are building up some feeling of tradition among those who have gone down to Helios. We make up the Fire-Eaters Club. You'll be initiated back on Mercury. Unfortunately, I can't tell you what the initiation consists of . . . but I hope you can swim!"

"I don't see any place to hide, Commandant. I'll be proud to be a Fire-Eater."

"Good! And don't forget, you still owe me that story about how you saved the Finnila Needle. I never did tell you how glad I was to see that old monstrosity when the Calypso returned, and I want to hear about it from the man who preserved it."

Jacob stared past the Sunship Commandant. For a moment he thought he could hear a wind whistling, and someone calling . . . a voice crying out indecipherable words as somebody fell. . . . He shook himself.

"Oh, I'll save it for you. It's much too personal to talk about in one of those story-swaps. There was someone else involved in saving the needles, someone you might like to hear about."

There was something in Helene deSilva's expression, something compassionate, that implied she already knew about what had happened to him at Ecuador, and would let him tell about it in his own good time.

"I'm looking forward to it. And I've finally thought of one for you. It's about the 'song-birds' of Omnivarium. It seems the planet is so silent that the human settlers have to be very careful lest the birds start mimicking any noise they make. This has an interesting effect on the settler's lovemaking behavior, particularly among the women, depending on whether they want to advertise their partner's 'abilities' in the age-old fashion or remain discreet!

"But I must go back to my duties now. And I certainly don't want to give away the whole story. I'll let you know when we reach the first turbulence."

Jacob rose to his feet with her and watched as she walked toward the command station. Partway into the solar chromosphere was probably an odd place to be enthralled by the way a fem walked, but until she went out of sight he felt no inclination to turn his eyes away. He admired the limberness that members of the interstellar corps inculcated into their extremities.

Hell, she was probably doing it on purpose. Where it didn't interfere with her job, Helene deSilva obviously pursued libido as a hobby.

There was something strange, though, in her behavior towards him. She appeared to trust him more than would normally be warranted by the small contributions he'd made on Mercury and their few friendly conversations. Perhaps she was after something. If so he couldn't figure out what.

On the other hand, maybe people were more naturally intimate when she'd left Earth for the long Jump on Calypso. Someone brought up on an O'Niel Colony, in a period of introspection caused by political stultification, might be more willing to trust her instincts than a child of the highly individualistic Confederacy.

He wondered what Fagin had told her about him.

Jacob went to the central dome, the outside wall of which contained a little boxlike head.

When he came out, Jacob felt much more awake. On the other side of the dome, by the food and beverage machines, he found Dr. Martine standing with the two bipedal aliens. She smiled at him, and Culla's eyes brightened with friendliness. Even Bubbacub grunted a greeting through his Vodor.

He pressed buttons for orange juice and an omelette.

"You know, Jacob, you turned in too early last night. Pil Bubbacub was telling us some more incredible stories after you went to bed. They were astounding, really!"

Jacob bowed slightly at Bubbacub.

"I apologize, Pil Bubbacub. I was very tired, otherwise I would have been thrilled to hear more about the great Galactics, particularly of the glorious Pila. I'm sure the stories are inexhaustible."

Martine stiffened next to him, but Bubbacub showed his pleasure by preening. Jacob knew it would be dangerous to insult the little alien. But by now he'd guessed the Ambassador wouldn't know any accusation of hubris as an insult. Jacob couldn't resist the harmless dig.

Martine insisted that he come over to eat with them, where the couches had already been raised for dining. Two of deSilva's four crewmen ate nearby.

"Has anyone seen Fagin?" Jacob asked.

Dr. Martine shook her head. "No, I'm afraid he's been on Flip-side for over twelve hours. I don't know why he doesn't join us here."

It wasn't like Fagin to be reticent. When Jacob had gone to the instrument hemisphere to use the telescope, and found the Kanten there, Fagin had hardly said a word. Now the Commandant had put the other side of the ship off limits to everyone except the E.T., who occupied it alone.

If I don't hear from Fagin by lunchtime, I'm going to demand an explanation, Jacob thought.

Nearby, Martine and Bubbacub talked. Occasionally Culla said a word or two, always with the most unctuous respect. The Pring seemed always to have a liquitube between his giant lips. He sipped slowly, steadily consuming the contents of several tubes while Jacob ate his meal.

Bubbacub launched into a story about an Ancestral of his, a member of the Soro race who had, some million or so years ago, taken part in one of the few peaceful contacts between the loose civilization of oxygen breathers and the mysterious parallel culture of hydrogen-breathing races which coexisted in the galaxy.

For aeons there had been little or no understanding between hydrogen and oxygen. Whenever conflict arose between the two a planet died. Sometimes more. It was fortunate that they had almost nothing in common, so conflicts were rare.

The story was long and involved, but Jacob ad-

147

mitted to himself that Bubbacub was a master story-teller. Bubbacub could be charming and witty, as long as he controlled the center of attention.

Jacob allowed his imagination to drift along as the Pil vividly described those things which only a handful of men had ever even sampled: the infinite strangeness and beauty of the stars, and the variety of things which dwelt on a multitude of planets. He began to envy Helene deSilva.

Bubbacub felt the cause of the Library intensely. It was the vehicle of knowledge and of a tradition which unified all of those who took in oxygen as breath. It provided continuity and more, for without the Library, there would be no bridges between species. Wars would not be fought with restraint but to extinction. Planets would be ruined by over-use.

The Library, and the other loosely-knit Institutes, helped to prevent genocide among its members.

Bubbacub's story reached its climax and he allowed his awed audience a few moments of silence. Finally, he good-naturedly asked Jacob if he would care to honor them with a story of his own.

Jacob was taken aback. By human standards, perhaps, he had led an interesting life, but certainly not remarkable! What could he talk about from history? Apparently the rules were that it had to either be a personal experience, or an adventure of an Ancestor or Ancestral.

Perspiring in his chair, Jacob considered telling a story about some historical figure; perhaps Marco Polo or Mark Twain. But Martine would probably not be interested.

Then there was the part his grandfather Alvarez had played in the Overturn. But that story was rather heavily political and Bubbacub would think its moral downright subversive. His best story had to do with his own adventure at the Vanilla Needle, but that was too personal, too filled with painful memories to share here and now. Besides he'd promised it to Helene deSilva.

It was too bad LaRoque wasn't here. The feisty little man would probably have been able to talk until the fires below burned out.

An impish thought struck Jacob. There *was* a character out of history, who was a direct Ancestor of his and whose story might be sufficiently relevent. The amusing part was that the story could be interpreted on two levels. He wondered how obvious he could get without certain listeners catching on.

"Well, as a matter of fact," he began slowly. "There's a male from the history of Earth who I would like to talk about. He is of interest because he was involved in a contact between a 'primitive' culture and technology and another that could overpower it in almost every respect. Naturally, you're all familiar with the premise. Since Contact, it's been almost all historians talk about.

"The fate of the Amerind is this era's morality play. Old twentieth-century movies glorifying the 'Noble Red Man' are shown today strictly for laughs. As Millie reminded us, back on Mercury, and as everyone back home knows, the Red Man did just about the poorest job of any of the impacted cultures at adapting to the arrival of Europeans. His vaunted pride kept him from studying the white man's powerful ways until it was too late, exactly opposite to the successful "co-opting" made by Japan in the late nineteenth century . . . the example that the 'Adapt and Survive' faction keeps pointing out to all who will listen these days."

He had them. The humans were watching him silently. Culla's eyes were bright. Even Bubbacub, usually inattentive, kept his beady little eyes on Jacob. Martine had winced when he mentioned the A & S faction, though. A datum.

If LaRoque were here, he wouldn't care for what I'm saying, Jacob thought. But LaRoque's distress would be nothing next to that of his Alverez kin, should they ever hear him talk like this!

"Of course, the failure of the Amerinds to adapt wasn't entirely their fault," Jacob continued. "Many scholars think that western hemisphere cultures were in a periodic slump that happened, unfortunately, to coincide with the arrival of Europeans. Indeed, the poor Mayans had just finished a civil war in which they'd all moved out to the country and left their cities, and princes and priests, to rot. When Columbus arrived the temples were mostly deserted. Of course, the population had doubled and wealth and trade had quadrupled over the 'Golden Age of the Maya,' but those are hardly valid measures of cultures."

Careful, boy. Don't go too heavy on the irony.

Jacob noticed that one of the crewmen, a fellow he'd met named Dubrowsky, had backed away from the others. Only Jacob could see the sardonic grin on the man's face. Everyone else appeared to be listening with unsuspicious interest, though it was hard to tell with Culla and Bubbacub.

"Now this ancestor of mine was an Amerind. His name was Se-quo-yi, and he was a member of the Cherokee nation.

"At the time, the Cherokee lived mostly in the state of Georgia. Since that was the East Coast of America, they had even less time than the other Amerinds to prepare to deal with the white man. Still, they tried, after their own fashion. Their attempt was nowhere near as grand or complete as the Japanese, but they tried.

"They were quick to pick up on the technology of their new neighbors. Log cabins replaced lodge houses and iron tools and blacksmithing became a part of Cherokee life. They learned about gunpowder early, as well as European methods of farming. Though many didn't like the idea, the tribe even became a slaveholding enterprise at one point.

"That was after they'd been whipped in two wars. They'd made the mistake of supporting the French in 1765, and then backed the Crown during the first American Revolution. Even so, they had a fair-sized little republic in the first part of the nineteenth century, partly because several young Cherokee had picked up enough of the white man's knowledge to become lawyers. Along with their Iroquois speaking cousins to the north, they did a fair job of playing the treaty game.

"For a while.

"Enter my ancestor. Se-quo-yi was a man who didn't like either of the choices offered his people, either staying noble savages and getting wiped out, or coopting the settlers' ways completely and disappearing as a people. In particular, he saw the power of the

150

written word but thought the Indian would forever be at a disadvantage if he had to learn English to become literate."

Jacob wondered if anyone would make the connection, comparing the situation that faced Se-quo-yi and the Cherokee with humanity's present predicament, vis-à-vis the Library.

Judging by the look on Martine's face, at least one person was surprised to hear such a long historical tale from the normally quiet Jacob Demwa. There was no way she could, or ever would, know about the long lessons, after school, in history and oratory that he and the other Alvarez children had endured. Though he had turned away from politics, a family black sheep, he still had some of the skills.

"Well, Se-quo-yi solved his problem to his own satisfaction by inventing a written form of the Cherokee language. It was a Herculean task, accomplished at cost of episodes of torture and exile, for many in his own tribe resisted his efforts. But when he finished all of the world of literature and technology was available, not just to the intellectual who could study English for years, but to the Cherokee of average intelligence, as well.

"Soon even the assimilationists accepted the work of Se-quo-yi's genius. His victory set the tone for all succeeding generations of Cherokee. These people, the only Amerinds whose principle hero was an intellectual, and not a warrior, chose to be selective.

"And that was their big mistake. If they'd let the local missionaries change them over into imitation settlers they would have been able, probably, to merge into the yeoman class and be looked upon by the Europeans as a slightly lower type of white man.

"Instead, they thought they could become modern Indians, retaining the essential elements of their old culture . . . obviously a contradiction in terms.

"Still, there are some scholars who think they might have made it. Things were going well until a group of white men discovered gold on Cherokee land. That got the settlers fairly excited. They got a bill through the Georgia legislature to declare the land up for grabs.

"Then the Cherokee did a strange thing, something

151

that wasn't adequately duplicated for about a hundred years after. That Indian nation took the Georgia state legislature to court over the land seizure! They had some help from some sympathetic white men and managed to bring the case before the United States Supreme Court.

"The Court ruled that the seizure was illegal. The Cherokee could keep their land.

"But here is where the incompleteness of their adjustment let them down. Because they'd made no major attempt to fit themselves into the basic structure of settler society, the Cherokee had no *political power* to back up the rightness of their cause. They trusted, and cleverly used, the high and honorable *laws* of the new nation, but didn't realize that public opinion has every bit as much force as law.

"To most of their white neighbors they were just another tribe of Indians. When Andy Jackson told the Court to go to hell, and sent the Army in to evict the Cherokee *anyway*, there was nowhere for them to turn.

"So Se-quo-yi's people had to pack a few belongings and march the tragic Trail of Tears to a new 'Indian Territory,' in western lands none of them had ever seen.

"The story of the Trail of Tears was an epic of human courage and endurance. The sufferings of the Cherokee on that long march were deep and sad. Some very moving literature came out of it, as well as a tradition of strength in privation that has affected the spirit of that people ever since, even down to today.

"That eviction wasn't the last trauma to fall on the Cherokee.

"When the United States had a Civil War, the Cherokee did as well. Brother killed brother when the Confederate Indian Volunteers met the Union Indian Brigade. They fought as passionately as did the white troops, and usually with more discipline. And in the process their new homes were ravaged.

"Later there were troubles with bandit gangs, diseases, and more land seizures. In their stoicism they came to be known by some as the 'Amerind Jews.' While some other tribes dissolved in despair and apathy in the face of the crimes committed against them, the Cherokee maintained their tradition of self reliance.

"Se-quo-yi was remembered. Perhaps in symbolism of the pride of the Cherokee, his name was given to a certain type of tree, one that grows in the misty forests of California. The tallest tree in the world.

"But all of this leads us away from the folly of the Cherokee. For while their pride helped them survive the depredations of the nineteenth century and the neglect of the twentieth, it held them back from participating in the Indian Consolation of the twenty-first. They refused the 'cultural reparations' offered by the American governments just before the beginning of the Bureaucracy; riches heaped on the remnants of the Indian Nations to salve the delicate consciences of the enlightened, educated public in that era that is today, ironically, referred to as America's 'Indian Summer.'

"They refused to set up Cultural Centers to perform ancient dances and rituals. While other Amerind revivalists resurrected pre-Columbian crafts to 'regain contact with their heritage,' the Cherokee asked why they should dig up 'Model T's' when they could be building their own specially-flavored version of twenty-first-century American culture.

"Along with the Mohawks and scattered groups from other tribes, they traded their 'Consolation' and half of their tribal wealth to buy into the Power Satellite League. The pride of their youth went up to help build the cities in space, as their grandfathers had helped build the great cities of America. The Cherokee gave away a chance to be rich in exchange for a share of the sky.

"And once again they paid terribly for their pride. When the Bureaucracy began its suppression, the League rebelled. Those bright young males and fems, the treasure of their nation, died by the thousands alongside their space-brothers, descendants of Andy Jackson and of Andy Jackson's slaves. The League cities they built were decimated. The survivors were allowed to remain in space only because someone had to be there to show the Bureaucracy's carefully selected replacements how to live.

"On Earth the Cherokee suffered, too. Many took part in the Constitutionalist Revolt. Alone of the Indian

153

nations, they were punished by the victors *as a group*, along with the VietAms, and the Minnesotans. The Second Trail of Tears was as sad as the first. This time, though, they had company.

"Of course, the first ruthless generation of Bureaucracy leaders passed, and the era of the *true* bureaucrats arrived. The Hegemony cared more about productivity than vengeance. The League rebuilt, under supervision, and a rich new culture developed in the O'Niel Colonies, influenced by the survivors of the original builders.

"On Earth, the Cherokee *still* meet, long after many tribes have been absorbed into cosmopolitan culture or into quaintness. They still haven't learned their lesson. I hear that their latest crackpot scheme is a joint project with the VietAms and Israel-APU to try to terraform Venus. Ridiculous, of course.

"But all of that is beside the point. If my Ancestor, Se-quo-yi, and his kin, had adapted *completely* to the ways of the white man they could have won a small place in his culture and been absorbed in peace, without suffering. If they had resisted with indiscriminate stubbornness, along with many of their Amerind neighbors, they would have suffered still, but finally been given a place, through the 'kindness' of a later generation of white man.

"Instead, they tried to find a synthesis between those obvious good and powerful aspects of western civilization, and their own heritage. They experimented and were choosy. They picked and fussed over the meal for six hundred years and suffered, because of it, more than any other tribe.

"The moral of this story I have told, should be obvious. We humans are faced with a choice similar to that faced by the Amerinds, whether to be picky or to accept wholeheartedly all of the billion-year-old culture offered us through the Library. Let anyone who urges choosiness remember the story of the Cherokee. Their trail has been long, and it isn't over yet."

There was a long silence after Jacob finished. Bubbacub still watched him with little black eyes. Culla stared fixedly. Dr. Martine looked down at the deck, her eyebrows knotted in thought.

154

The crewman, Dubrowsky, stood well back. One arm was crossed in front of him. His other hand covered his mouth. Crinkles around his eyes; did they betray silent laughter?

Must be a League-man. Space is infested with them. I hope he keeps his mouth shut about this. I took enough of a chance as it is.

His throat felt parched. He took a long drink from the liquitube of orange juice he had saved from breakfast.

Bubbacub finally placed both little hands behind his neck and sat up. He looked at Jacob for a moment.

"Good sto-ry," he snapped, finally. "I will ask you to rec-ord it for me, when we get back. It has good les-son for Earth folk.

"There are some ques-tions I would ask, though. Now or la-ter. Some things I do not un-der-stand."

"As you wish, Pil-Bubbacub," Jacob bowed, trying to hide his grin. Now to change the subject *quick*, before Bubbacub could get started asking about pesky details! But how?

"I too, enjoyed my friend Jacob's story," a whistling voice fluted from behind them. "I approached as silently as I could, when I came into range to hear it. I am pleased that my presence did not disturb the telling."

Jacob shot to his feet with relief.

"Fagin!" Everyone rose as the Kanten slithered toward them. In the ruby light, he looked jet black. His movements were slow.

"I wish to offer apologies! My absence was unavoidable. The Commandant graciously assented to allow more radiation through the screens so that I could take nourishment. But, understandably, it was necessary that she do so only on the unoccupied reverse side of the ship."

"That's true," Martine laughed. "We wouldn't want any sunburn here!"

"Quite so. And yet it was lonely there, I am glad to have company again."

The bipeds sat down and Fagin settled himself onto the deck. Jacob seized the opportunity to get out of his fix.

"Fagin, we've been exchanging some stories here,

155

waiting for the surfing to start. Maybe you can tell us one about the Institute of Progress?"

The Kanten rustled its foliage. There was a pause. "Alas, Friend-Jacob. Unlike that of the Library, the Institute of Progress is not an important society. The very name is poorly translated into English. There are no words in your language to represent it properly.

"Our small order was founded to fulfill one of the least of the Injunctions that the Progenitors placed upon the oldest of races when they left the galaxy so long ago. Crudely stated, it imposed upon us the duty to respect 'Newness.'

"It may be hard for a species such as your own, orphans so to speak, who have until recently never felt the bittersweet bonds of kinship and patron-client obligation, to understand the inherent conservatism of our Galactic culture. This conservatism is not bad. For admidst so much diversity a belief in the Tradition and in a common heritage is a good influence. Young races heed the words of those older, who have learned wisdom and patience with years.

"You might say, to borrow an English expression, that we hold a deep regard for our roots."

Only Jacob noticed that Fagin shifted his weight slightly at that point. The Kanten was folding and unfolding the short knotty tentacles that served as his feet. Jacob tried not to choke as a swallow of orange juice went down wrong.

"But there remains a need to face the future, as well," Fagin continued. "And in their wisdom, the Progenitors warned the Oldest not to scorn that which is new under the Sun."

Fagin was silhouetted against the giant red orb, their destination. Jacob shook his head helplessly.

"So when word got out that somebody'd found a bunch of savages sucking at a wolf's teat, you came running, right?"

More rustling foliage. "Very graphic, Friend-Jacob. But your surmise is essentially correct. The Library has the important task of teaching the races of Earth what they need to know to survive. My Institute has the humbler mission of appreciating your Newness."

Dr. Martine spoke.

"Kant Fagin, to your knowledge, has this ever happened before? I mean, has there ever been a case of a species which has no memory of Ancestral Upbringing, bursting into the galaxy on their own like we did?"

"Yes, respected Doctor Martine. It has happened a number of times. Space is large beyond all imagining. The periodic migrations of oxygen and hydrogen civilizations cover great distance, and rarely is even a settled area ever full explored. Often, in these great movements, a tiny fragment of a race, barely raised from bestiality, has been abandoned by its patrons to find its way alone. Such abandonments are usually avenged by civilized peoples . . ." The Kanten hesitated. Suddenly Jacob realized why with a shock as Fagin hurried on.

"But since it is usually at a time of migration that these rare cases occur, there is an added problem. The wolfling race may develop a crude spacedrive from the dregs of its patron's technology, but by the time it enters interstellar space, its part of the galaxy might be under Interdict. Unknowingly it might fall prey to hydrogen breathers whose turn it may be to occupy that cluster or spiral arm.

"Nevertheless, such species are found occasionally. Usually the orphans retain vivid memories of their patrons. In some cases, myth and legend have taken the place of fact. But the Library is almost always able to trace the truth, for that is where our truths are stored."

Fagin lowered several branches in Bubbacub's direction. The Pil acknowledged with a friendly bow.

"That is why," Fagin went on, "we await with great expectation the discovery of the reason why there is no mention of your Earth in that great archive. There is no listing, no record of previous occupation, in spite of five full migrations through this region since the Progenitors departed."

Bubbacub froze in his bow. The small black eyes snapped up to bear on the Kanten with narrowly focused ferocity, but Fagin appeared not to notice as he continued.

"To my knowledge, mankind is the first case in which there exists the intriguing possibility of *evolved* intelligence. As I am sure you know, this idea violates several well-established principles of our biological science. Yet some of your anthropologists' arguments possess startling self-consistency."

"It is quaint idea," Bubbacub sniffed. "Like per-pet-ual motion, these boast-ings by those you call 'Skins.' The theories of 'natural' growth of full sent-ience, are great source of good-natured jokes, human-Jacob-Dem-wa. But soon the Lib-rar-y give your troub-led race what it needs; the com-fort of knowing where you came from!"

The low hum of the ship's engines grew louder, and for a second Jacob felt a slight disorientation.

"Attention everybody," the amplified voice of Com-mandant deSilva carried throughout the ship. "We've just crossed over the first reef. From now on there will be momentary shocks like that one. I'll inform you when we near our target area. That is all."

The Sun's horizon was now nearly flat. On all sides of the ship, a sparse red and black tangle of curling shapes stretched away to infinity. More and more of the highest filaments were coming even with the vessel to become prominences against what remained of the blackness of space, and then to disappear into the red-dish haze that grew over their heads.

The group moved, by mutual consent, to the edge of the deck where they could look straight into the lower chromosphere. They were quiet, for a while, watching as the deck quivered from time to time.

"Dr. Martine," Jacob said. "Are you and Pil Bub-bacub ready with your experiments?"

She pointed to a pair of stout space-trunks on the deck next to Bubbacub's station and her own.

"We have all we need right here. I'm bringing along some psi equipment I used on earlier dives, but most-ly I'm going to help Pil Bubbacub in any way I can. My brain wave amplifiers and Q-devices are like knuckle-bones and tea leaves next to what he's got in his case. But I'll try to be of assistance."

"Your help be take-en with glad-ness," Bubbacub said. But when Jacob asked to see the Pil's psi-testing apparatus he held up his four-fingered hand. "Later, when we are ready."

The old itchiness returned to Jacob's hands. What

does Bubbacub have in those trunks? The Branch Library had next to nothing on psi. Some phenomenology, but very little on methodology.

What does a billion-year-old galactic culture know, he thought, about the deep fundamental levels that all sentient species seem to have in common? Apparently they don't know everything, for the Galactics still operate on this plane of reality. And I know for a fact that at least some of them don't have any more telepathy than I do.

There were rumors that older species periodically faded away from the galaxy; sometimes from natural attrition or war or apathy, but also occasionally by simply "stepping off" . . . disappearing into interests and behavior that have no meaning to their clients or neighbors.

Why does our Branch Library have nothing on these events, or even on the practical aspects of psi?

Jacob frowned and locked his two hands together. No, he decided. I'm going to leave Bubbacub's trunk alone!

Helene deSilva's voice came on again over the intercom.

"We will be approaching the target area in thirty minutes. Those who wish may now approach the Pilot Board to get a good view of our destination."

The rest of the Sun seemed to dim slightly as their eyes adapted to the added brightness of the area. The faculae were bright pinpoints, flashing on and off far below in sudden brilliance. At some indeterminable distance, a great sunspot group stretched away. The nearest spot looked like an open pit mine, a sunken recess in the grainy "surface" of the photosphere. The dark Umbra was very still, but the penumbral regions around the sunspot's rim rippled incessantly outward, like wavelets spreading from a pebble thrown into a lake. The border was vague, like a plucked piano string, vibrating.

Above and all around, the huge shape of a filament tangle loomed. It had to be one of the biggest things that Jacob had ever seen. Following the lines of magnetic fields that merged, twisted, and looped around one another, giant clouds swirled and flowed. A strand emerged from nothingness, rose, twisted around another, and then disappeared into "thin air."

All around them now was a swirl of smaller shapes; almost invisible, but excluding the comforting black of space in an overall pink haze.

Jacob wondered what a literary man would make of this scene. For all of his egregious—perhaps murderous faults—LaRoque had a reputation built on a beautiful facility with words. Jacob had read several of his articles and enjoyed the flowing prose, while perhaps laughing at the man's conclusions. Here was a scene that demanded a poet, whatever his politics. He thought it a pity that LaRoque wasn't here . . . for more than one reason.

"Our instruments have picked up a source of anomalous polarized light. That's where we start our search."

Culla stepped up to the lip of the deck and stared intently at a position pointed out to him by a crewman.

Jacob asked the Commandant what he was doing.

"Culla can detect color far more accurately than we," deSilva said. "He can see differences in wave length down to about an angstrom or so. Also he's somehow able to retain the phase of the light he sees. Some interference phenomenon, I suppose. But it makes him really handy at spotting the coherent light these laser beasties put out. He's almost always the first one to see them."

Culla's mashies clacked together once. He pointed with a slender hand.

"It ish there," he stated. "There are many points of light. It ish a large herd, and I believe that there are sheperdsh there ash well."

DeSilva smiled, as the ship hastened its approach.

15.

OF LIFE
AND DEATH . . .

In the center of the filament, the Sunship moved like
a fish caught in a swift current. The current was electrical, and the tide that swept the mirrored sphere along
was a magnetized plasma of incredible complexity.

Lumps and streaming shreds of ionized gas seared
thither and back, twisted by the forces that their very
passage created. Flows of glowing matter popped suddenly in and out of visibility, as the Doppler effect
took the emission lines of the gas into and then out of
coincidence with the spectral line being used for observation.

The ship swooped through the turbulent chromospheric crosswinds, tacking on the plasma forces by
subtle shifts in its own magnetic shields . . . sailing
with sheets made of almost corporeal mathematics.
Lightning fast furling and thickening of those shields of
force—allowing the tug of the conflicting eddies to be
felt in one direction and not another—helped to cut
down the buffeting dealt out by the storm.

Those same shields kept out most of the screaming

heat, diverting the rest into tolerable forms. What got through was sucked up into a chamber to drive the Refrigerator Laser, the kidney whose filtered waste-flow was a stream of x-rays which clove aside even the plasma in its path.

Still, these were mere inventions of Earthmen. It was the science of the Galactics that made the Sun-ship graceful and safe. Gravity fields held back the amorous, crushing pull of the Sun so the ship fell or flew at will. The pounding forces of the center of the filament were absorbed or neutralized, and duration itself was altered by time-compression.

In relation to a fixed position on the Sun (if such a thing existed), it was swept along the magnetic arch at thousands of miles per hour. But relative to the surrounding clouds, the ship seemed to poke its way slowly, pursuing a quarry seen in glimpses.

Jacob watched the chase with half an eye, and kept Culla in sight the rest of the time. The slender alien was the ship's lookout. He stood by the helmsman, eyes glowing and arm pointing into the murk.

Culla's directions were only a little better than those given by the ship's own instruments, but the instruments were difficult for Jacob to read. He appreciated having someone there to show passengers, as well as crew, the way to look.

For an hour they'd chased after specks that glowed in the distant haze. The specks were extremely faint, in the blue and green lines deSilva had ordered opened, but occasionally a burst of greenish light stabbed out from one or another, like a searchlight that suddenly took in the ship and then swept past.

Now the glimpses occurred more frequently. There were at least a hundred of the objects, all about the same size. Jacob looked at the Proximity Meter. Seven hundred kilometers.

At two hundred their shape became clear. Each of the "magnetic grazers" was a torus. At this range the colony looked like a large collection of tiny blue wedding rings. Every little ring was aligned the same way, along the filamentary arch.

"They line up along the magnetic field where it's most intense," deSilva said. "And spin on their axes to generate an electric current. Heaven knows how they get from one active region to another when the fields shift. We're still trying to figure out what keeps them together."

Toward the edge of the crowd a few toruses wobbled slowly as they spun. Precessing.

Suddenly, for an instant, the ship was bathed by a sharp green glow. Then the ochre hue returned. The pilot looked up at Jacob.

"We just passed through the laser tail of one torus. An occasional shot like that doesn't do any harm," he said. "But if we were coming up from behind and below the main herd we might have had trouble!"

A clump of dark plasma, either cooler or moving much faster than the surrounding gas, passed in front of the ship, blocking their view.

"What purpose does the laser serve?" Jacob asked.

DeSilva shrugged. "Dynamic stability? Propulsion? Possibly they use it for cooling like we do. I suppose there might even be solid matter in their makeup, if that were true.

"Whatever the purpose, it sure is powerful to punch green light through these red-tuned screens. That's the only reason we discovered them. Big as they are, they're like pollen blowing in the wind down here. We could search for a million years and never find a toroid, without the laser for a trace. They're invisible in the hydrogen alpha, so to observe them better, we opened up a couple of bands in the green and blue. Naturally we won't be opening the wavelength that laser's tuned to! The lines we choose are quiet and optically thick, so whatever you see that's green or blue comes from a beastie. It should come as a pleasant change."

"Anything would be welcome but this damned red."

The ship passed through the dark matter and suddenly they were almost among the creatures.

Jacob gulped and closed his eyes momentarily. When he looked again, he found that he couldn't swallow. On top of three days of unbelievable sights, what he saw left him helpless before a powerful tremor of emotion.

If a group of fish is called a "school" for its discipline, and several lions comprise a "pride," named for

163

their attitude, Jacob decided that the cluster of solar-beings could only be called a "flare." So intense was its brilliance that its members seemed to shine against black space.

The nearer toroids shone with the colors of an Earth spring. Only with distance did the colors fade. Pale green shimmered below their axes, where laser light scattered in the plasma.

Around all of them sparkled a diffuse halo of white light.

"Synchrotron radiation," a crewman said. "Those babies must really be spinning! I'm picking up a big flux at 100KeV!"

Four hundred meters across and more than 2,000 distant, the nearest toroid spun madly. Around its rim geometric shapes flew past like beads on a necklace, changing, so that deep blue diamonds became purple sinuous bands, circuiting a brilliant emerald ring, all within seconds.

The Sunship captain stood by the Pilot Board, eyes darting from indicator to gauge and alert to every detail. To glance at her was to watch a softened version of the show outside the ship, for the fluxious, iridescent colors of the nearest toroid bathed her face and her white uniform and were thereby tamed and diffused for the second half of the trip to Jacob's eye. First faintly, then more brightly as green and blue mixed with and drove out the pink, the colors sparkled each time she looked up and smiled.

Suddenly, the blueness swelled as a burst of exuberance from the toroid coincided with an intricate display of patterns, like a weaving of ganglia around the ring-beast's rim.

The performance was peerless. Arteries erupted in green and twined with veins drawn in pulsing, chaste blue. These throbbed in counterpoint, then grew like gravid vines, peeling back to release clouds of tiny triangles—sprays of two dimensional pollen that scattered in a multitude of miniscule three-point collisions around the non-Euclidian body of the torus. At once the motif became isosceles, and the doughnut-rim became a cacophote of sides and angles.

The display reached a peak of intensity, then receded. The rim patterns became less bright and the torus backed away, finding a place to spin among its fellows as the red started to return, pushing out greens and blues from the deck of the ship and from the faces of the watchers.

"That was a greeting," Helene deSilva said finally. "There are skeptics back on Earth who still think that the magnetovores are just some form of magnetic aberration. Let them come and see for themselves, then. We are witnessing life. Clearly the Creator accepts few limits to the range of his handiwork."

She touched the pilot's shoulder lightly. His hands moved on his controls and the ship began to bank away.

Jacob agreed with Helene, though her logic was unscientific. He had no doubts that the toroids were alive. The creature's display, whether it was a greeting or simply a territorial response to the presence of the ship, had been a sign of something vital, if not sentient.

The anachronistic reference to a supreme deity had sounded oddly fitting to the beauty of the moment.

The Commandant spoke again into her microphone as the flare of magnetovores fell back and the deck turned.

"Now we go hunting ghosts.

"Remember, we aren't really here to study the magnetovores but their predators. A constant watch is to be maintained by the crew for any sign of these elusive creatures. Since they have been sighted as often by accident as not, it would be appreciated if everyone helped. Please report anything extraordinary to me.

DeSilva and Culla held a conference. The alien nodded slowly, an occasional flash of white between huge gums betraying his excitement. Finally, he set off around the curve of the central dome.

DeSilva explained that she had sent Culla to the other side of the deck, flip-side, where normally only instruments stood, to act as a lookout in case the laser beings should appear from the nadir, where the rim-mounted detectors could not reach them.

"We've had a number of zenith sightings," deSilva

repeated. "And these have often been the most interesting cases, such as when we saw anthropomorphic shapes.".

"And the shapes always disappeared before the ship could be turned?" Jacob asked.

"Or the beasts would turn with us to stay overhead. It was infuriating! But that gave us the first clue that psi might be involved. After all, whatever their motives, how could they know about our way of placing instruments at the rim of a disc and follow our movements so precisely, without knowing what we intended to do?"

Jacob frowned in thought. "But why not put a few cameras up here? Certainly it wouldn't be much of a chore?"

"No, not much of a chore," deSilva agreed. "But the support and dive crews didn't want to disturb the ship's original symmetry. We would have to put another conduit through the deck to the main recording computer, and Culla assured us that this would eliminate whatever small ability we might have to maneuver in a stasis-failure . . . though that ability is probably negligible anyway. Witness what happened to poor Jeff.

"Jeffrey's ship, the small one you toured on Mercury, was designed from the start to carry recorders aimed at zenith and nadir. His was the only one with this modification. We'll have to make do with the rim instruments, our eyes, and a few hand-held cameras."

"And the psi experiments," Jacob pointed out.

DeSilva nodded expressionlessly.

"Yes, we are all hoping to make friendly contact, of course."

"Excuse me, Captain."

The pilot looked up from his instruments. He held a button speaker to his ear. "Culla says there's a color difference at the upper north end of the herd. It might be a calving."

DeSilva nodded.

"Okay. Proceed along a north tangent to the field flux. Rise with the herd as you make your way around and don't get close enough to spook them."

The ship began to bank at a new angle. The Sun rose on the left until it became a wall that stretched up and ahead to infinity. A faint luminescence twisted away from them, down toward the photosphere below. The sparkling trail paralleled the alignment of the herd of toruses.

"That's the path of superionization our Refrigerator Laser left when we were pointed that way," deSilva said. "It must be a couple of hundred kilometers long."

"The laser is that strong?"

"Well, we have to get rid of a lot of heat. And the whole idea is to heat up a small part of the Sun. Otherwise the refrigerator wouldn't work. Incidentally, that's another reason why we're so careful not to let the herd get ahead of or behind us."

Jacob felt momentarily awed.

"When will we be in sight of . . . what was it he said? A calving?"

"Yes, a calving. We're very lucky. We've only seen this twice before. The shepherds were there both times. They appear to assist whenever a torus gives birth. It's a logical place to start looking for them.

"As for when we get there, that depends on how violent things are between here and there, and how much time-compression we need to get there comfortably. It could be a day. If we're lucky . . ." She glanced at the Pilot Board. ". . . we could be there in ten minutes."

A crewman stood nearby holding a chart, apparently waiting to see deSilva.

"I'd better go and warn Bubbacub and Dr. Martine to get ready," Jacob said.

"Yes, that would be a good idea. I'll make an announcement when I know how soon we'll arrive."

As he walked away, Jacob had a strange feeling that her eyes were still on him. It lasted until he passed around the side of the central dome.

Bubbacub and Martine took the news calmly. Jacob helped them pull their equipment boxes to a position near the Pilot Board.

Bubbacub's implements were incomprehensible, and astounding. Complex, shiny, and multifaceted, one of them took up half of the crate. Its curling spires and glassy windows hinted at mysteries.

Bubbacub laid out two other devices. One was a bulbous helmet apparently designed to fit over the head of a Pil. The other looked like a chunk off of a nickel iron meteoroid, with a glassy end.

"There is three ways to look at psi," Bubbacub said through his Vodor. He motioned with a four-fingered hand for Jacob to sit. "One is that the psi is just very fine sens-or-y power, to pick out brain waves at long range and de-cipher them. That the thing I will see ab-out with this." He pointed at the helmet.

"And this large machine?" Jacob moved to look clos-er.

"That sees if time and space are be-ing twisted here by the force of a soph-ont's will. The thing is done some-times. It sel-dom all-owed. The word is pi-ngrli. You have no word for it. Most, in-cluding hu-mans, do not need to know of it since it is rare.

"The Li-brar-y prov-ides these ka-ngrl," he stroked the side of the machine once, "to each Branch, in case out-laws try to use pi-ngrli."

"It can counteract that force?"

"Yes."

Jacob shook his head. It bothered him that there was a whole type of power to which man had no access. A deficiency in technology was one thing. It could be made up in time. But a qualitative lack made him feel vulnerable.

"The Confederacy knows about this . . . ka-ka . . . ?"

"Ka-ngrl. Yes. I have their leave to take it from Earth. If it is lost, it will be re-placed."

Jacob felt better then. The machine suddenly looked friendlier. "And this last item . . . ?" he began to move toward the lump of iron.

"That is a P-is." Bubbacub snatched it up and put it back in the trunk. He turned away from Jacob and be-gan to fiddle with the brain-wave helmet.

"He's pretty sensitive about that thing," Martine said when Jacob came near. "All I could get out of him was that it's a relic from the Lethani, his race's fifth high Ancestrals. It dates from just before they 'passed over' to another plane of reality."

The Perpetual Smile broadened. "Here, would you like to see ye olde alchemist's tools?"

Jacob laughed. "Well, our friend Pil has the Philoso-pher's Stone. What miraculous devices have you for mixing effluvium, and exorcising highly caloric ghosts?"

"Besides the normal run-of-the-mill psi detectors, such as they are, there's not much. A brain-wave device, an inertial movement sensor that's probably useless in a time-suppression field, a tachistoscopic 3-D camera and projector . . ."

"May I see that?"

"Sure, it's at the far end of the trunk."

Jacob reached in and removed the heavy machine. He laid it on the deck and examined the recording and projecting heads.

"You know," he said softly. "It's just possible . . ."

"What is?" Martine asked.

Jacob looked up at her. "This, plus the retinal pattern reader we used on Mercury, could make a perfect mental proclivities tester."

"You mean one of those devices used to determine Probation status?"

"Yes. If I had known this was available back at the base, we could have tested LaRoque then and there. We wouldn't have had to maser Earth and go through layers of fallible bureaucracy for an answer that might have been tampered. We could have found out his violence index on the spot!"

Martine sat still for a moment. Then she looked downward.

"I don't suppose it would have made any difference."

"But you were sure there was something wrong with the message from Earth!" Jacob said. "This could save LaRoque from two months in a brig if you were right. Hell, it's possible he would have been with us right now. We'd be less unsure about the possible danger from the Ghosts, too!"

"But his escape attempt on Mercury! You said he was violent!"

"Panicky violence does not a Probationer make. What's the matter with you anyway? I thought you were sure LaRoque was framed!"

Martine sighed. She avoided meeting his eyes.

"I'm afraid I was a little hysterical back at the base. Imagine, dreaming up a conspiracy, just to trap poor Peter!

"It's still hard to believe that he's a Probationer, and maybe some mistake *was* made. But I no longer think it was done purposely. After all, who would

169

want to saddle him with the blame for that poor little chimpanzee's death?"

Jacob stared for a moment, unsure what to make of her change of attitude. "Well, . . . the real murderer, for one," he said softly.

Immediately he regretted it.

"What are you talking about?" Martine whispered. She glanced quickly to both sides to be sure that no one was nearby. Both knew that Bubbacub, a few meters away, was deaf to whispered speech.

"I'm talking about the fact that Helene deSilva, much as she probably dislikes LaRoque, thinks it's unlikely the stunner could have damaged the stasis mechanism on Jeff's ship. She thinks the crew botched up, but . . ."

"Well then Peter will be released on insufficient evidence and he'll have another book to write! We'll find out the truth about the Solarians and everybody will be happy. Once good relations are established I'm sure it won't matter much that they killed poor Jeff in a fit of pique. He'll go down as a martyr to science and all this talk of murder can be ended once and for all. It's so distasteful anyway."

Jacob was beginning to find the conversation with Martine distasteful as well. Why did she squirm so? It was impossible to follow a logical argument with her.

"Maybe you're right," he shrugged.

"Sure I'm right." She patted his hand and then turned to the brain-wave apparatus. "Why don't you go look for Fagin. I'm going to be busy here for a while and it's possible he doesn't know about the calving yet."

Jacob nodded once and got to his feet. As he crossed the gently quivering deck he wondered what strange things his suspicious other half was thinking. The blurt about a "real murderer" worried him.

He met Fagin where the photosphere filled the sky in all directions, like a great wall. In front of the tree-like Kanten, the filament in which they rode spiraled down and away into red dissipation. To the left and right and far below, spicule forests wriggled like effervescent rows of elephant grass.

For a time they watched together in silence.

As a waving tendril of ionized gas drifted past the

ship, Jacob was reminded for the nth time of kelp floating in the tide.

Suddenly he had an image. It made him smile. He imagined Makakai, wearing a waldo-suit of cermet and stasis, plunging and leaping among these towering fountains of swirling flame, and diving, in her shell of gravity, to play among the children of this, the greatest ocean.

Do the Sun Ghosts while away the aeons as our cetaceans do? he wondered. By singing?

Neither have machines (or any of the neurotic hurry that machines bring—including the sickness of ambition?), because neither have the means. Whales have no hands and cannot use fire. Sun Ghosts have no solid matter and too much fire.

Has it been a blessing for them or a curse?

(Ask the humpback, as he moans in the stillness underwater. Probably, he won't bother to answer, but someday he may add the question to his song.)

"You're just in time. I was about to call," the Captain motioned ahead into the pink haze.

A dozen or more of the toroids spun in front of them colorfully.

This group was different. Instead of drifting passively they moved about, jostling for position around something deep in the middle of the crowd. One nearby torus, only a mile distant, moved aside and then Jacob could see the object of their attention.

The magnetovore was larger than the others. Instead of the changing, multifaceted geometric shapes, dark and light bands alternated around its circuit, and it wobbled lazily while its surface rippled. Its neighbors milled about on all sides but at a distance, as if held back by some deterrent.

DeSilva gave a command. The pilot touched a control and the ship turned, righting itself so the photosphere soon was beneath them once more. Jacob was relieved. Whatever the ship's fields told him, having the Sun on his left made him feel sideways.

The magnetovore Jacob thought of as "Big One" spun, apparently oblivious to its retinue. It moved sluggishly, with a pronounced wobble.

The white halo that bathed every other torus flickered dimly around the edges of this one, like a dying flame. The dark and light bands pulsed with an uneven undulation.

Each pulse evoked a response in the surrounding crowd of toroids. Rim patterns sharpened starkly in bright blue diamonds and spirals as each magnetovore kept its own backbeat to Big One's slowly strengthening rhythm.

Suddenly, the nearest of the attendant toruses rushed toward the banded Big One, sending bright green flashes of light along its spinning path.

From around the gravid torus, a score of brilliant blue dots flew up toward the intruder. They were in front of it in an instant, dancing, like shimmering drops of water on a hot skillet, next to its ponderous hulk. The bright dots began to push it back, nipping and teasing, it seemed, until it was almost below the ship.

The ship turned under the pilot's hand to present its edge to the nearest of the sparkling motes, only a kilometer away. Then, for the first time, Jacob could clearly see the life forms that were called Sun Ghosts.

It floated like a wraith, delicately, as if the chromospheric winds were a breeze to be taken with barely a flutter: as different from the firm, spinning, dervishlike toruses as a butterfly is from a whirling top.

It looked like a jellyfish, or like a brilliantly blue bath towel flapping in the wind as it hung on a clothesline. Possibly it was more an octopus, with ephemeral appendages that flickered in and out of existence along its ragged edges. Sometimes it looked to Jacob like a patch of the surface of the sea itself, somehow skimmed up and moved here; maintained in its liquid, tidal movement by a miracle.

The ghost rippled. It moved toward the Sunship, slowly, for a minute. Then it stopped.

It's looking at us too, Jacob thought.

For a moment they regarded one another, the crew of water beings, in their ship, and the Ghost.

Then the creature turned so that its flat surface was toward the Sunship. Suddenly, a flash of brilliant multicolored light washed the deck. The screens kept

172

the glare bearable, but the pale red of the chromosphere was banished.

Jacob put a hand out in front of his eyes and blinked in wonder. So this is what it's like, he thought somewhat irrelevently, inside a rainbow!

As suddenly as it came, the light show disappeared. The red Sun was back, and with it the filament, the sunspot far below, and the spinning toruses.

But the Ghosts were gone. They had returned to the giant magnetovore and once more danced as almost unseen dots about its rim.

"It . . . it blasted us with its laser!" the pilot said. "They never did *that* before!"

"One never came that close before in its normal shape, either," Helene deSilva said. "But I'm not sure what either action is supposed to mean."

"Do you think it meant to harm us?" Dr. Martine spoke hesitantly. "Maybe that's how they started with Jeffrey!"

"I don't know. Maybe it was a warning . . ."

"Or maybe it just wanted to get back to work," Jacob said. "We were in almost the opposite direction as the big magnetovore out there. You'll notice that all of its companions went back at the same time."

DeSilva shook her head.

"I don't know. I guess we'll be all right if we just stay here and watch. Let's see what they do when they finish with the calving."

Ahead of them, the big torus began to wobble more as it spun. The dark and light bands along its rim became more pronounced, the darker becoming narrow strictures and the lighter bands ballooning outward with each oscillation.

Twice Jacob saw groups of bright herdsmen jet away to head off a magnetovore that came too close, like sheepdogs at the heels of a wayward ram, as others stayed with the ewe.

The wobble deepened and the dark bands grew tighter. The green laser light, scattered below the big torus, dimmed. Finally it disappeared.

The Ghosts moved in. As the big one's nutation reached an almost horizontal pitch, they gathered at the rim to somehow seize it and complete the turnover with a sudden jerk.

The behemoth now spun lazily on an axis perpendicular to the magnetic field. For a moment the position held, until the creature suddenly began to fall apart.

Like a necklace with a broken string, the torus split where one of the dark bands tightened to nothing. One by one, as the parent body spun slowly, the light bands, now small individual doughnut shapes themselves, were flung free, each as it rotated to the place where the break occurred. One at a time, they were cast upwards, along the invisible lines of magnetic flux, until they ran like beads across the sky. Of the Big One, the parent, nothing remained.

About fifty of the little doughnut shapes spun dizzyingly in a protecting swarm of bright blue herdsmen. They precessed uncertainly and, from the center of each, a tiny green glow flickered tentatively.

In spite of their careful watch, the ghosts lost several of their erratic charges. Some of the infants, more active than their peers, jetted out of the queue. A brief burst of green brilliance took one baby magnetovore out of the protected area and toward one of the adults that lurked nearby. Jacob hoped it would continue toward the ship. If only the adult torus would get out of the way!

As if it heard his thoughts, the adult began to drop away below the oncoming path of the juvenile. Its rim pulsed with green-blue diamonds as the newborn passed overhead.

Suddenly the torus leaped upward on a column of green plasma. Too late, the juvenile tried to flee. It turned its feeble torch toward its pursuer's rim as it jetted away.

The adult was undeterred. In a moment the baby was overtaken, drawn down into its elder's pulsing central hole and consumed in a flash of vapor.

Jacob realized that he was holding his breath. He let it out and it felt like a sigh.

The babies were now arranged in orderly ranks by their mentors. They began to move away from the herd slowly, while a few herdsmen stayed to keep the adults in line. Jacob watched the brilliant little rings of light until a thick wisp of filament floated in to cut off his view.

"Now we start earning our pay," Helene deSilva

whispered. She turned to the pilot. "'Keep the remaining herdsmen aligned with the deck-plane. And ask Culla to please keep his eyes peeled. I want to know if anything comes in from the nadir.'"

Eyes peeled! Jacob suppressed an involuntary shudder, and firmly said no when his imagination tried to present an image. What kind of an era did this fem come from!

"Okay," the Commandant said. "Let's approach slowly."

"Do you think they'll notice we waited until they were through with the calving?" Jacob asked.

She shrugged. "Who knows? Maybe they thought we were just a timid form of adult torus. Perhaps they don't even remember our earlier visits."

"Or Jeff's?"

"Or even Jeff's. It wouldn't do to assume too much. Oh, I believe Dr. Martine when she says her machines register a basic intelligence. But what does that mean? In an environment like this . . . even more simple than an ocean on earth, what reason would a race have to develop a functioning semantic skill? Or memory? Those threatening gestures we saw on previous dives don't necessarily indicate a lot of brains.

"They might be like dolphins were before we started genetic experiments a few hundred years ago, lots of intelligence and no mental ambition at all. Hell, we should have brought in people like you, from the Center for Uplift, long ago!"

"You're talking as if evolved intelligence is the only route," he smiled. "Galactic opinion aside for the moment, shouldn't you at least consider another possibility?"

"You mean that the Ghosts might have once been uplifted!?" deSilva looked shocked for a moment. Then the idea soaked in and she leaped on the implications, her eyes sharp. "But if that were the case, then there'd have to have been . . ."

She was interrupted by the pilot.

"Sir, they're starting to move."

The Ghosts fluttered in the hot, wispy gas. Blue and green highlights rippled along the surface of each as it hovered lazily, a hundred thousand kilometers above the photosphere. They retreated from the ship slowly, allowing the separation to diminish, until a faint corona of white could be seen surrounding every one.

Jacob felt Fagin come up beside him on his left.

"It would be sad," the Kanten fluted softly, "if such beauty were found sullied by a crime. I could have great trouble sensing evil while struck in awe."

Jacob nodded slowly.

"Angels are bright . . ." he began. But of course, Fagin knew the rest.

Angels are bright, though the brightest fell.
Though all things foul would wear the brows of grace,
Still grace must look so.

"Culla says they're about to do something!" the pilot peered ahead with a hand over his ear.

A wisp of darker gas from the filament moved swiftly into the area, momentarily blocking off the view of the Ghosts. When it cleared, all but one had moved farther away.

That one waited as the ship edged slowly closer. It looked different, semi-transparent, bigger and bluer. And simpler. It looked stiff and did not ripple like the others. It moved more deliberately.

An ambassador, Jacob thought.

The Solarian rose slowly as they neared.

"Keep him edge-on," deSilva said. "Don't lose instrument contact!"

The pilot glanced up at her grimly, and turned back to his instruments with tight lips. The ship started to rotate.

The alien rose faster and drew near. The fan-shaped body seemed to beat against the plasma like a bird trying to gain altitude.

"It's toying with us," deSilva muttered.

"How do you know?"

"Because it doesn't have to work that hard to stay overhead." She asked the pilot to speed up the rotation.

The Sun rose on the right and crept toward the zenith. The Ghost continued to beat toward a position overhead, even though it had to be spinning upside down along with the ship. The Sun rolled overhead and then set. Then it rose and set again in less than a minute.

The alien stayed overhead.

The spin accelerated. Jacob gritted his teeth and resisted an urge to grab Fagin's trunk for balance as the ship experienced day and night in seconds. He felt hot, for the first time since the journey to the Sun began. The Ghost stayed maddeningly overhead and the photosphere blasted on and off like a flashing lamp.

"Okay, give it up," deSilva said.

The spinning slowed. Jacob swayed as they came to complete rest. He felt as if a cool breeze was washing his body. First heat, then chills: Am I going to be ill? he wondered.

"It won," deSilva said. "It always does, but it was worth a try. Just once I'd like to try that with the Refrigerator Laser operating though!" She glanced at the alien overhead. "I wonder what would happen when he got near a fraction of the speed of light."

"You mean you had our refrigerator turned off just then?" Now Jacob couldn't help it. He touched Fagin's trunk lightly.

"Sure," the Commander said. "You don't think we want to fry dozens of innocent toruses and herdsmen do you? That's why we were under a time limit. Otherwise we could have tried to line him up with the rim instruments till hell froze over!" She glared up at the Ghost.

Again, the touching turn of phrase. Jacob wasn't sure whether the woman's fascination lay in her more straightforward qualities or in this way she had with quaint expressions. In any event, the overheating and subsequent cool breezes were explained. For a time the heat of the Sun had been allowed to leak in.

I'm glad that's all it was, he thought.

16.

... AND APPARITIONS

"All we get is a dim picture," the crewman said. "The stasis screens must be bending the Ghost's image somehow because it looks warped . . . like it's refracted at an angle through a lens."

"Anyway," he shrugged as he passed the photos around. "This is the best we can do with a hand-held camera."

DeSilva looked at the picture in her hand. It showed a blue, streaky caricature of a man, a stick figure with spindly legs, long arms, and big, splayed hands. The photograph had been taken just before the hands had balled into fists, crude but identifiable.

When his turn came, Jacob concentrated on the face. The eyes were empty holes, as was the ragged mouth. In the photograph they looked black but Jacob recalled that the crimson of the chromosphere had been the real color. The eyes burned red and the maw worked as if mouthing vicious oaths, all in red.

"One thing, though," the crewman went on. "The

guy's transparent. The H-alpha passes right through. We only notice it in the eyes and mouth because the blue he's putting out doesn't swamp it there. But as far as we can tell, his body doesn't block any of it.'"

"Well, that's your definition of a Ghost if I ever heard one," Jacob said, and handed the picture back.

Glancing up again, for the hundredth time, he asked, "Are you sure the solarian is coming back?"

"It always has," deSilva said. "It was never satisfied with just one round of insults before."

Nearby, Martine and Bubbacub rested, ready to put on their helmets if the alien reappeared. Culla, relieved of his duties on the flip-side, lay in a couch, sucking slowly on a liquitube containing a blue beverage. The big eyes were glossy now, and he looked tired.

"I guess we all should lie down," deSilva said. "It won't do to break our necks looking up. That's where the Ghost will be when he shows."

Jacob chose a seat next to Culla, so he could watch Bubbacub and Martine at work.

The two had little time to do much during the first appearance. No sooner had the Sun Ghost taken a position near the zenith than it had changed into the man-like, threatening shape. Martine hardly got her head-set adjusted before the creature leered, shook a balled image of a fist, and then faded away.

But Bubbacub had time to check his ka-ngrl. He announced that the Solarian was not using the particularly potent type of psi the machine was designed to detect and counteract. Not then at least. The little Pil left it turned on anyway, just in case.

Jacob rested back in the seat, and touched the button that allowed it to recline slowly until he looked up at the pink, feathery sky overhead.

It was a relief to learn that the pi-ngrli power was not at work here. But if not, what *was* the reason for the Ghost's strange behavior? Idly, he wondered again if LaRoque might have been right . . . that the Solarians knew how to make themselves partly understood because they knew humans from days gone by. Surely men never visited the Sun in the past, but did plasma creatures once go to Earth, and even nurture civilization there? It sounded preposterous, but then, so did Sundiver.

Another thought: If LaRoque was not responsible for the destruction of Jeff's ship, then the Ghosts might be capable of killing them all at any time.

If so, Jacob hoped the journalist-astronaut was right about the rest of it; that the Solarians would feel more restraint in dealing with humans, Pila, and Kanten than they had toward a chimpanzee.

Jacob considered trying his own hand at telepathy when the creature next appeared. He'd been tested once and found to have no psi talent, despite extraordinary hypnotic and memory skills, but maybe he should try anyway.

A movement to his left caught his eye. Culla, staring at a point in front of him and forty-five degrees to zenith, lifted a deck-mike to his lips.

"Captain," he said, "I believe it ish coming back." The Pring's voice echoed around the ship. "Try angles 120 by 30 degrees."

Culla put the mike down. The flexible cord drew it back into a slot, next to his slender right hand and the now-empty beverage tube.

The red haze darkened briefly as a wisp of darker gas passed the ship. Then the Ghost was back, still small with distance but getting bigger as it approached.

It was brighter this time, and more crisp around the edges. Soon, its blueness was almost painful to look at.

It came once again as a stick figure of a man, the eyes and mouth glowing like coals as it hovered, half way up to zenith.

For several long minutes it stayed there, doing nothing. The figure was definitely malevolent. He could feel it! Dr. Martine's cursing brought him around, and he realized that he had been holding his breath.

"Damn it!" she tore off her helmet. "There's so much noise! One moment I think I'm onto something . . . a touch here and there . . . and then it's gone!"

"Do not bo-ther," Bubbacub said. The clipped voice came from the Vodor, now lying on the deck next to the little Pil. Bubbacub had his own helmet on and stared intently with small black eyes at the Ghost.

180

"Hu-mans do not have the psi they use. Your attempt, in fact, does cause them pain and some of their anger."

Jacob swallowed quickly. "You're in touch with them?" he and Martine asked almost at once.

"Yes," the mechanical voice said. "Do not bo-ther me." Bubbacub's eyes closed. "Tell me if it moves. Only if it moves!" After that they could get nothing from him.

What's he saying to it? Jacob wondered. He looked at the apparition. What can one say to a creature like that?

Suddenly, the Solarian began to wave its "hands" and move its "mouth." This time its features were more clear. There was none of the image warping they had seen at its first appearance. The creature must have learned to handle the stasis screens. One more example of its ability to adapt. Jacob didn't want to think about what that implied about the safety of the ship.

A flash of color drew Jacob's attention to the left. He groped on the panel next to him, then pulled up his deck-mike and switched it to personal.

"Helene, look at about one eight by sixty-five. I think we've got more company."

"Yes," deSilva's voice quietly filled the area of the couch occupied by his head. "I see it. It seems to be in its standard form. Let's see what it does."

The second Ghost approached, hesitantly, from the left. Its rippling, amorphous form was like a patch of oil on the surface of the ocean. Its shape was nothing like a man's.

Dr. Martine drew her breath in sharply when she saw the intruder and started to pull her helmet on.

"Do you think we should arouse Bubbacub?" he asked quickly.

She thought for a moment, then glanced up at the first Solarian. It still waved its "arms" but it hadn't changed positions. Nor had Bubbacub. "He said to tell him if it moves," she said.

She looked up eagerly at the newcomer. "Maybe I should work on this new one and let him go on with the first one undisturbed."

Jacob wasn't sure. So far Bubbacub was the only one to come up with anything positive. Martine's motive for not informing him of the second Solarian was suspect. Was she envious of the Pil's success?

Oh well, Jacob shrugged, E.T.'s hate to be interrupted anyway.

The newcomer approached cautiously, in short fits and starts, toward where its larger and brighter cousin performed its impersonation of an angry man.

Jacob glanced at Culla.

Should I tell him at least? He seems so intent on watching the first ghost. Why hasn't Helene made an announcement? And where's Fagin? I hope he's not missing this.

Somewhere above there was a flash. Culla stirred.

Jacob looked up. The newcomer was gone. The first Ghost slowly shrank back and faded away.

"What happened," Jacob asked. "I only turned away for a second . . ."

"I don't know, Friend-Jacob! I wash watching, to see if the being'sh visual behavior might betray some cluesh to itsh nature, when suddenly a shecond one came. The first one attacked the shecond with a bursht of light, and made it depart. Then it too shtarted to leave!"

"You should have told me when new one came," Bubbacub said. He was on his feet, the Vodor around his neck once more. "No mat-ter. I know all I need to know. I now re-port to hu-man deSilva."

He turned and left. Jacob scrambled to his feet to follow.

Fagin awaited them, near deSilva and the Pilot Board. "Did you see it?" Jacob whispered.

"Yes, I had a good view. I am eager to hear what our dear esteemed friend learned."

With a theatrical wave of his arm, Bubbacub asked everyone to listen in.

"It said that it is old. I be-lieve it. It is ver-y old race."

Yes, Jacob thought. That's the first thing Bubbacub would find out.

"The Sol-ar-ians say that they killed the chimp. LaRoque killed him too. They will start to kill hu-mans also, if they do not leave for-ever."

182

"What?" deSilva cried. "What are you talking about? How could LaRoque and the Ghosts be responsible!"

"Re-main calm, I urge you," the voice of the Pil, moderated by the Vodor, carried a tone of threat. "The Sol-ar-ian told me that they caused the man to do the thing. They gave him his rage. They gave him a need to kill. They gave him the truth as well."

Jacob finished summarizing Bubbacub's remarks to Dr. Martine.

". . . Then he finished by saying that there was only one way that the Ghosts could have influenced La-Roque from such a distance. And if they used that method it explained the lack of Library references. Anywhere anyone uses that power is taboo, closed off. Bubbacub wants us to stick around just long enough to check and then get the hell out of here."

"What power?" Martine asked. She sat with the crude Earth psi helmet in her lap. Nearby Culla listened in, another slender liquitube between his lips.

"It's not pi-ngrli. That's used sometimes legally. Besides, it can't reach that far and he couldn't find any trace of it anyway. No, I think Bubbacub plans to use that stonelike thing."

"The Lethani relic?"

"Yes."

Martine shook her head. She looked down and fiddled with a knob on her helmet.

"It's so complicated. I don't understood it at all. Nothing's gone right ever since we got back to Mercury. No one is what he appears to be."

"What do you mean?"

The parapsychologist paused, then shrugged.

"Never be sure about anyone . . . I was so sure that Peter's silly pique with Jeffrey was both genuine and harmless. Now I find that it was artificially induced and deadly. And he was right, I guess, about the Solarians, too. Only it wasn't his idea, it was theirs."

"Do you think they really are our long lost Patrons?"

"Who knows?" she said. "If it's true, it's a tragedy that we can't ever come back here again to talk to them."

"Then you accept Bubbacub's story without reservations?"

183

"Yes, of course! He's the only one who's ever made contact and besides, I know him. Bubbacub would never mislead us. Truth is his life's work!"

But Jacob knew, now, of whom she spoke when she said "never be sure you know anyone." Dr. Martine was terrified.

"Are you sure that Bubbacub was the only one to make any sort of contact?"

Her eyes widened, then she looked away. "He seems to be the only one with the ability."

"Then why did you stay behind with your helmet on, when Bubbacub called us together for his report?"

"I don't have to take a cross-examination from you!" she answered hotly. "If it's any of your business, I stayed to try once more. I was jealous of his success and wanted another go at it! I failed, of course."

Jacob was unconvinced. Martine's testiness seemed uncalled for and it was clear she knew more than she was saying.

"Dr. Martine," he said, "what do you know about a drug called 'Warfarin'?"

"You too!" she reddened. "I told the Base Physician I never heard of it, and I certainly don't know how any got into Dwayne Kepler's medicine. That is, if there ever was any in the first place!"

She turned away. "I think I'd better rest now, if you don't mind. I want to be awake when the Solarians come back."

Jacob ignored her hostility; a bit of the toughness of his other self must have leaked out with the suspicion. But it was obvious Martine wouldn't say any more. He rose to his feet. She pointedly ignored him as she lowered her couch.

Culla met him by the refreshment machines. "You are upshet, Friend-Jacob?"

"Why no, I don't think so. Why do you ask?"

The tall E.T. gazed down at him. He looked tired. The slender shoulders drooped, though the huge eyes were bright.

"I hope you are not taking thish too hard, thish news that Bubbacub hash announced."

Jacob turned fully from the machines and faced

184

Culla, "Take what too hard, Culla? His statements are data. That's all. I'd be disappointed if it turned out that Sundiver has to end. And I'll want some way to verify what he says before I'll agree that's necessary . . . like at least a Library reference. But other than that my strongest emotion is curiosity." Jacob shrugged, irritated at the question. His eyes smarted, probably from an overdose of red light.

Culla slowly shook his large round head. "I think it ish otherwise. Excuse my presumption, but I think you are very dishturbed."

Jacob felt an instant of hot anger. He almost spoke it, but managed to hold back. "Again, what are you talking about, Culla?" He spoke slowly.

"Jacob, you have done a good job in staying neutral in your species' remarkable internal conflict. But all sophontsh have opinionsh. You are badly hurt to find that Bubbacub made contact where humansh fail. Though you have never expreshed a position on the Origin Question, I know you are not happy to find that humanity did indeed have Patronsh."

Jacob shrugged again.

"It's true, I'm still not convinced by this story of Solarians uplifting mankind in the dim past and then abandoning us before the job's finished. Neither part makes any sense."

Jacob rubbed his right temple. He felt a headache coming on. "And people have been behaving very peculiarly everywhere in this project. Kepler's suffered from some sort of unexplained hysteria and was overly dependent on Martine. LaRoque was more than his usual abrasive self, sometimes self-destructively. And don't forget his alleged sabotage. Then Martine herself turns from an emotional defense of LaRoque to a very strange fear of saying anything that might undermine Bubbacub. It makes me wonder . . ." he paused.

"Perhapsh the Sholarians are responsible for all of thish. If they could make Mishter LaRoque do a murder from so far away, they might have caused other aberrationsh ash well."

Jacob's hands balled in fists. He looked up at Culla barely able to choke back his anger. The alien's bright eyes were oppressive. He didn't want to be under them.

"Don't interrupt," he said, tight-lipped, and as calmly as he could.

He could tell that something was wrong. A cloud seemed to surround him. Nothing was very clear but still there was a felt need to say something important. Anything.

He looked quickly around the deck.

Bubbacub and Martine were at their stations again. Both wore their helmets and looked his way. Martine was talking.

The bitch! Probably she's telling the gross arrogant little fool everything I said. Toady!

Helene deSilva stopped by the two while making her rounds, taking their attention away from Culla and Jacob. For a moment he felt better. He wished Culla would go away. It was too bad the fellow had to be put down but a Client must know his place!

DeSilva finished speaking to Bubbacub and Martine, and started to walk toward the refreshment machines. Once again Bubbacub's small black eyes were on him.

Jacob growled. He swiveled away from the beady stare and faced the beverage machine.

Fuck them all. I came here for a drink and that's what I'm going to get. They don't exist anyway!

The machine wavered in front of him. An internal voice was shouting about some sort of emergency but he decided that the voice didn't exist either.

Now this is a strange machine, he thought. I hope it isn't like that sneaky one aboard the *Bradbury*. That one hadn't been friendly at all.

No, this one has a bunch of transparent 3-D buttons that stand out from the others. In fact there are rows and rows of little buttons, all of them standing out in space.

He reached forward to press one at random, then caught himself. Uh-uh. We'll *read* the labels this time!

Now what do I want. Coffee?

The little internal voice was screaming for Gyroade. Yes, that's sensible. A wonderful drink, Gyroade. Not only is it delicious, but it also straightens you out. A perfect drink for a world full of hallucinations.

He had to admit that it might be a good idea to have some at that. Something *did* seem a little fishy. Why was everything going so slowly?

His hand moved like a snail toward the button he wanted. It shifted back and forth a few times but finally he was aimed right for it. He was about to press it when the little voice came back, this time begging him to stop!

Of all the nerve! You give me good advice and then you chicken out. Dammit, who needs you anyway?

He pressed. Time speeded up a little, and he heard the sound of liquid pouring.

Who the hell needs anybody! Damn upstart Culla. Snobby Bubbacub and his fish-cold human consort. Even crazy Fagin . . . dragging me away from Earth to this stupid place.

He bent over and pulled the liquitube out of its slot. It looked delicious.

Time speeded up now, almost back to normal. He already felt better, as if a great pressure was relieved. Antagonisms and hallucinations seemed to fade away. He smiled at Helene deSilva as she approached. Then he turned to smile at Culla.

Later, he thought, I'll apologize for being rude. He raised the tube in a toast.

". . . been hovering around out there, just at the edge of detection." deSilva was saying. "We're ready whenever it is so maybe you'd better . . ."

"Shtop, Jacob!" Culla shouted.

DeSilva cried out and leaped forward to grab his hand. Culla joined in, adding his own slight strength to pull the tube away from his lips.

Spoilsports, he thought amiably. Show a puny alien and a ninety-year old woman what a mal can do.

He pulled them off one by one, but they kept attacking. The Commandant even tried some nasty disabling shots but he parried them and brought the drink to his face slowly, triumphantly.

A wall broke and the sense of smell he hadn't known he'd lost returned like a steamroller. He coughed once and looked down at the vile concoction in his hand.

It steamed brown and poisonous with lumps and bubbles. He threw it away. Everyone was looking at him. Culla chattered from the floor where he'd been thrown. DeSilva stood up warily. The other humans were gathering around.

He could hear Fagin's concerned whistle coming from somewhere. Where *is* Fagin, he thought as he stumbled forward. He made it three steps and then collapsed onto the deck in front of Bubbacub.

He came around slowly. It was difficult because his forehead was so tight. The skin felt stretched like the leather on a drum. But it wasn't dry like leather. It kept getting wet, first with perspiration and then with something else, something cool.

He groaned and brought his hand up. It touched skin, someone else's hand, warm and soft. Female, he could tell by the smell.

Jacob opened his eyes. Dr. Martine sat nearby with a washcloth in her brown hand. She smiled and brought out a liquitube to hold to his lips.

For a moment he started, then he bent forward to take a sip. It was lemonade, and it tasted wonderful.

He finished it off while he looked around himself. The couches scattered on the deck were filled with recumbent figures.

He looked up. The sky was almost black!

"We're on our way back," Martine said.

"How . . ." he could feel his larynx hum from disuse. "How long have I been under?"

"About twelve hours."

"Was I sedated?"

She nodded. The Perpetual Professional Smile was back. But it didn't seem so put-on now. He brought a hand to his forehead. It still hurt.

"Then I guess I didn't dream it. What was it I tried to drink yesterday?"

"It was an ammonia compound that we brought along for Bubbacub. It probably wouldn't have killed you. But it would have hurt, a lot.

"Can you tell me why you did it?"

Jacob allowed his head to settle back against the cushion. "Well . . . it seemed like a pretty good idea at the time."

He shook his head. "Seriously, I guess something went wrong with me. But I'll be damned if I know what it was."

"I should have known something was wrong when

188

you started saying strange things about murders and conspiracies," she nodded. "It's partly my fault for not recognizing the signs. It's nothing to be ashamed of. I think it's just a case of orientation shock. A Sunship dive can be an awful disorienting experience, in so many ways!"

He rubbed the sleep out of his eyes.

"Well, you're right about that last part for sure. But it just occurred to me that some people are probably thinking I was influenced."

Martine started, as if surprised to find him so alert so soon.

"Yes," she said. "In fact Commandant deSilva thought it was the Ghost's work. She said they were probably demonstrating their psi powers to prove their point. She even started talking about shooting back. The theory has merits but I prefer my own."

"That I went crazy?"

"Oh no, not at all! Just disoriented and confused! Culla said you were behaving . . . abnormally in the minutes before your . . . accident. That, plus my own observations . . ."

"Yes," Jacob nodded. "I owe Culla a real apology . . . Ohmigosh! He wasn't hurt, was he? Or Helene?" He started to rise.

Martine pushed him back. "No, no, everyone is okay. Don't worry. I'm sure the only concern anyone had was for your welfare."

Jacob dropped back. He looked down at the empty liquitube. "May I have another?"

"Sure. I'll be right back."

Martine left him alone. He could hear her soft footsteps move toward the refreshment center . . . the place where the "accident" occurred. He winced as he thought about it. He felt shame mixed with disgust. But most of all there was the burning question, WHY?

Somewhere behind him two people spoke softly. Dr. Martine must have met somebody at the R.C.

Jacob knew that sooner or later he would have to make a dive that made Sundiver seem tame. That trance would be a lulu, but it would have to be taken if the truth was to come out. The only question was when? Now, when it might split his mind wide open?

189

Or back on Earth, in the presence of therapists at the Center, but where the answers might do him, Sundiver and his job no good at all?

Martine came back. She dropped down beside him and offered a full liquitube. Helene deSilva was with her. The Commandant sat next to the parapsychologist.

He spent several minutes assuring her that he was all right. She brushed his apologies aside.

"I had no idea you were so good at U.C., Jacob," she said.

"U.C.?"

"Unarmed combat. I'm pretty good, though I'm rusty I admit. But you're better. We found out in the surest way, a fight between parties each anxious to disable the other without pain or harm. It's awful hard to do but you're an expert."

He never would have thought it possible to blush at that sort of compliment, but Jacob could feel himself redden.

"Thanks. It's hard to remember but it seems you were pretty tricky, too."

They looked at each other in complete understanding and grinned.

Martine looked from one to the other. She cleared her throat. "I don't think Mr. Demwa should spend too much time talking. A shock like that calls for plenty of rest."

"I just want to know a few things, Doctor, then I'll cooperate. First of all, where's Fagin? I don't see him anywhere."

"Kant Fagin is on flip-side," deSilva said. "He's taking nourishment."

"He was very concerned about you. I'm sure he'll be glad to know you're okay," Martine said.

Jacob relaxed. For some reason he had been worried about Fagin's safety.

"Now tell me what happened after I passed out."

Martine and deSilva shared a glance. Then deSilva shrugged.

"We had another visitation," she said. "It took quite a while. For several hours the Solarian just fluttered around at the edge of visibility. We'd left the toroid herd far behind and with it all of its fellows.

"It's a good thing it waited though. We were in an uproar for a while because of, well . . ."

"Because of my attention-grabbing performance," Jacob sighed. "But did anyone try to make contact while it flittered out there?"

DeSilva looked at Martine. The doctor shook her head very slightly.

"Nothing much was done then," the Commandant went on hurriedly. "We were still pretty upset. But then, at about fourteen hundred, it disappeared. It came back a while later in its . . . 'threatening mode.' "

Jacob let the interchange between the two women pass. But a thought suddenly occurred to him.

"Say, are you all positive that they were the same Ghosts at all? Maybe the 'normal' and 'threatening' modes are actually two different species!"

Martine looked blank for a moment. "That *could* explain . . ." Then she shut up.

"Uh, we aren't calling them Ghosts anymore," deSilva said. "Bubbacub says they don't like it."

Jacob felt a moment of irritation, but he suppressed it quickly lest either woman notice it. This conversation wasn't getting them anywhere!

"So what happened when it came in its threatening mode?"

DeSilva frowned.

"Bubbacub talked with it for a while. Then he got angry and made it go away."

"He what?"

"He tried reasoning with it. Quoted the book on Patron-Client rights. Promised trade, even. It just kept making threats. Said it would send psi messages to Earth and cause disaster of some undescribed sort.

"Finally Bubbacub called it quits. He had everybody lie down. Then he pulled out that lump of iron and crystal he was so secretive about. He ordered everyone to cover their eyes, then said some mumbo jumbo and set the darn thing off!"

"What did it do?"

She shrugged again.

"The Progenitors only know, Jacob. There was a dazzling light, a feeling of pressure in the ears . . . and when we next looked, the Solarian was gone!

191

"Not only that! We went back to where we thought we'd left the toroid herd. It was gone too. There wasn't a living thing in sight!"

"Nothing at all?" He thought about the beautiful toruses and their bright multicolored masters.

"Nothing," Martine said. "Everything had been scared away. Bubbacub assured us that they hadn't been harmed."

Jacob felt numb. "Well, then at least there's protection now. We can bargain with the Solarians from a position of strength."

DeSilva shook her head sadly.

"Bubbacub says there can be no negotiation. They're evil, Jacob. They'll kill us now, if they can."

"But . . ."

"And we can't count on Bubbacub anymore. He told the Solarians there'd be vengeance if Earth was ever harmed. But other than that he won't help. The relic goes back to Pila."

She looked down at the deck. Her voice grew husky. "Sundiver is finished."

PART VI

The measure of (mental) health is
flexibility (not comparison to some 'norm'),
the freedom to learn from experience . . .
to be influenced by reasonable arguments . . .
and the appeal to the emotions . . . and
especially the freedom to cease when sated.
The essence of illness is the freezing of
behavior into unalterable and insatiable patterns.

Lawrence Kubie

17.

SHADOW

The workbench was bare, each tool of its accustomed clutter hanging in uncomfortable disuse from the appropriate hook on the wall. The tools were clean. The scored and pitted tabletop shone under a new layer of wax.

The stack of partly disassembled instruments which Jacob had shoved aside lay on the floor accusingly, like the chief mechanic, who had watched him in idle suspicion as he appropriated the workbench. Jacob didn't care. Despite, or perhaps because of the fiasco aboard the Sunship, no one objected when he decided to continue his own studies. The workbench was a large and convenient space for him to use, and nobody else wanted it right now. Besides, it made it less likely he'd be found by Millie Martine.

In an apse of the huge Sunship Cavern, Jacob could see a sliver of the giant silvery ship, only partly cut off from view by the rock wall. Far overhead the wall arched into a mist of condensation.

He sat on a high stool in front of the bench. Jacob drew "Zwicky Choiceboxes" on two sheets of paper and laid them out on the table. The pink sheets had a yes or no question written on each, representing alternate possible morphological realities.

The one on the left read: B IS RIGHT ABOUT S-GHOSTS, YES (I)/NO(II)

The other sheet was even more difficult to look at: I HAVE FLIPPED OUT, YES(III)/NO(IV).

Jacob couldn't let anyone else's judgment sway him on these questions. That was why he'd avoided Martine and the others since the return to Mercury. Other than paying a courtesy call on the recuperating Dr. Kepler, he had become a hermit.

The question on the left concerned Jacob's job, thought he couldn't exclude a linkage with the question on the right.

The question on the right would be difficult. All emotion would have to be put aside to arrive at the right answer to that one.

He placed a sheet with the Roman numeral I just below the question on the left, listing the evidence that Bubbacub's story was correct.

BOX I: B's STORY TRUE.

It made a tidy list. First of all there was the neat self-consistency of the Pil's explanation for the Sun Ghost's behavior. It had been known all along that the creatures used some type of psi. The threatening, man-shaped apparitions implied knowledge of man and an unfriendly inclination. "Only" a chimpanzee had been killed, and only Bubbacub could demonstrate successful communication with the Solarians. All this fit in with LaRoque's story—the one supposedly implanted in his mind by the creatures.

The most impressive achievement, one that took place while Jacob was unconscious aboard the Sunship, was Bubbacub's feat with the Lethani relic. It was proof that Bubbacub had some contact with the Sun Ghosts.

To drive one Ghost off with a flash of light might be plausible (although Jacob was at a loss as to how a being drifting in the brilliant chromosphere could detect anything from the dim interior of a Sunship), but the dispersal of the entire herd of magnetovores and herdsmen implied that some powerful force (psi?) must have been the Pil's means.

Every one of these elements would have to be re-examined in the course of Jacob's morphological analysis. But on the face of it, Jacob had to admit that box number I looked true.

Number II would be a headache, for it assumed the opposite of the proposition in Box I.

BOX II: B's STORY WRONG—(IIA) HE'S MISTAKEN/(IIB) HE'S LYING.

IIA didn't give Jacob any ideas, Bubbacub seemed too sure, too confident. Of course, he would have been fooled by the *Ghosts themselves* . . . Jacob scribbled a note to that effect and put it in position IIA. It was actually a very important possibility, but Jacob couldn't think of any way to prove or disprove it short of making more dives. And the political situation made more dives impossible.

Bubbacub, supported by Martine, insisted that any further expeditions would be pointless and probably fatal as well, without the Pil and his Lethani relic along. Oddly enough, Dr. Kepler didn't fight them. Indeed, it was at his orders that the Sunship was drydocked, normal maintenance suspended, and even data reduction halted while he conferred with Earth.

Kepler's motives puzzled Jacob. For several minutes he stared down at a sheet that said: SIDE ISSUE—KEPLER? Finally he tossed it over on the stack of disassembled equipment, with a curse. Kepler obviously had political reasons for wanting Sundiver's closure to be on Bubbacub's head. Jacob was disappointed in the man. He turned to sheet IIB.

It was appealing to think that Bubbacub was lying. Jacob could no longer pretend any affection for the little Library Representative. He recognized his own personal bias. Jacob wanted IIB to be true.

Certainly Bubbacub had a *motive* for lying. The failure of the Library to come up with a reference on solar-type life-forms was an embarrassment to him. The Pil also resented totally independent research by a "wolfling" race. Both problems would be eliminated if Sundiver was cut off in a manner that boosted the stature of ancient science.

But to hypothesize that Bubbacub lied brought up a whole raft of problems. First, how much of the story was a lie? Obviously the trick with the Lethani relic was genuine. But where *else* could one draw the line?

And if Bubbacub lied he had to be awfully sure that he wouldn't get caught. The Galactic Institutes, especially the Library, relied on a reputation of absolute honesty. They'd have to fry Bubbacub alive if he was found out.

Box IIB had all of the meat in it. It looked hopeless, but somehow Jacob would have to show that IIB was true or Sundiver was finished.

This was going to be complicated. Any theory that had Bubbacub lying would have to explain Jeffrey's death, LaRoque's anomalous status and behavior, the Sun Ghost's threatening behavior . . .

Jacob scribbled a note and tossed it onto sheet IIB.

SIDE NOTE: *TWO TYPES OF SUN GHOSTS?* He remembered the remark that no one had ever actually seen a "normal" Sun Ghost turn into the semi-transparent variety that did the threat pantomimes.

Another thought came to him.

SIDE NOTE: CULLA'S THEORY THAT SOLARIAN'S PSI EXPLAINS NOT ONLY LR BUT OTHER STRANGE BEHAVIOR AS WELL.

Jacob was thinking of Martine and Kepler when he wrote that down. But after thinking about it he carefully wrote a second copy of the same remark and tossed it over on the sheet labeled I HAVE FLIPPED OUT—NO(IV)

The question of his own personal sanity took courage to face. Methodically he listed the evidence that something was wrong, under sheet number III.

1. BLINDING "LIGHT" BACK AT BAJA. The trance he'd entered just before the meeting at the Information Center was the last deep one he'd had. He had been awakened from it by an apparent psychological artifact—a "blueness" that cut through his hypnotic state like a searchlight. But whatever warning his subconscious must have been sending was interrupted when Culla approached.

2. UNCONTROLLED USE OF MR. HYDE. Jacob knew that the bifurcation of his mind into normal and abnormal parts was a temporary solution at best to a long-range problem. A couple of hundred years ago his state would have been diagnosed schizophrenic. But hypnotic transaction, supposedly, would allow his divided halves to reassemble peacefully under the guidance of his dominant personality. The occasions in which his feral other half pushed through or took

control would logically be when it was needed . . . when Jacob *had* to revert to the cold, hard, supremely confident meddler he once had been.

Jacob hadn't been worried, earlier, about his other side's exploits, so much as embarrassed. For instance, it was logical enough to pilfer samples of Dr. Kepler's pharmacopoeia on the *Bradbury,* given what he'd seen so far, although other means to the same ends might have been preferable.

But some of the things he'd said aboard the Sunship to Dr. Martine—they implied either a great deal of justified suspicion churning around in his unconscious, or very deep problems down below.

3. BEHAVIOR ON SUNSHIP: ATTEMPTED SUICIDE? That one hurt less than he thought it would, when he wrote it. Jacob felt disconcerted by the episode. But strangely, he felt more angry than ashamed, as if he had been made to act like a fool by somebody else.

Of course that could mean anything, including frantic self-justification, but it didn't feel that way. Jacob felt no internal resistance when he probed that line of reasoning. Only negation.

Number three *could* have been part of an overall pattern of mental decay. Or it might have been an isolated case of disorientation, as diagnosed by Dr. Martine (who since landing had been chasing him all over the base in order to get him into therapy). Or it could have been induced by the something external, as he had already considered.

Jacob pushed back from the workbench. This would take time. The only way to get anything done would be to take frequent breaks and let ideas filter up from the unconscious, the very unconscious he was investigating.

Well, that wasn't the *only* way, but until he had solved the question of his own sanity he wasn't about to try the other means.

Jacob stepped back and began to move his body slowly in the pattern of relaxing positions known as Tai Chi Chuan. The vertebrae in his back crackled from sitting awkwardly on the stool. He stretched and allowed energy to return to parts of his body that had fallen asleep.

The light jacket he wore bound his shoulders. He stopped the routine and took it off.

There was a coat rack by the chief mechanic's office, across the maintenance shop and near the drinking fountain. Jacob walked over to the rack, lightly, on the balls of his feet, feeling taut and energized by the Tai Chi.

The chief mechanic nodded grumpily when Jacob passed by; the man was obviously unhappy. He sat behind his desk in the foam-paneled office, wearing an expression Jacob had seen a lot of since coming back, especially among the lower echelons. The reminder pricked Jacob's bubble.

As he bent over the drinking fountain, Jacob heard a clattering sound. He lifted his head as it repeated, coming from the direction of the ship. Half of the ship was now visible from where he stood. As he walked to the corner of the rock wall, the rest came slowly into view.

Slowly, the wedge-shaped door of the Sunship descended. Culla and Bubbacub waited at the bottom, holding a long cylindrical machine between them. Jacob ducked behind the rock wall. Now what are those two doing?

He heard the catwalk extend from the rim of the Sunship's deck, then the sound of the Pil and Pring pulling the machine up into the ship.

Jacob rested his back against the rock wall and shook his head. This was too much. If he was given just one more mystery he'd probably *really* flip out . . . that is if he hadn't already.

It sounded like an air compressor was being used inside the ship, or a vacuum cleaner. Clattering and sliding and occasional squeaky Pilan oaths implied that the machine was being dragged all over the interior of the ship.

Jacob gave in to temptation. Bubbacub and Culla were inside the ship and no one else was in sight.

In any event there was probably nothing to be lost by being caught spying but the rest of his reputation.

He bounded up the springy catwalk in a few powerful steps. Near the top of the ramp he flattened and looked inside.

The machine *was* a vacuum cleaner. Bubbacub

pulled it, his back to Jacob, as Culla manipulated the long rigid suction member at the end of its flexible hose. The Pring shook his head slowly, his dentures chattering softly. Bubbacub shot off a series of sharp yaps at his Client and the chattering incresed, but Culla worked faster.

This was most queer and disturbing. Culla was apparently vacuuming the space between the deck and the curving ship's wall! Nothing existed there but the force fields that held the deck in place!

Culla and Bubbacub disappeared around the central dome as they made their way around the rim. At any moment they'd be coming around the other side and facing him this time. Jacob slid back down the ramp a few feet, then descended the rest of the way on foot. He walked back to the apse and sat again on the stool in front of the slips of paper.

If there was only time! If the central dome had been bigger or Bubbacub's work slower, he might have found a way to get down into that force-field gap and get a sample of whatever they were collecting. Jacob shuddered at the thought, but it would have been worth a try.

Or even a picture of Culla and Bubbacub at work! But where could he get a camera in the few minutes he had left?

There was no way to prove that Bubbacub was up to mischief, but Jacob decided that theory IIB had received a big boost. On a piece of paper he scribbled: B'S DUST OR WHATEVER . . . HALLUCINOGEN RELEASED ON BOARD SHIP? He threw it on that pile, then hurried over to the chief mechanic's office.

The man grumbled when Jacob asked him to come along. He claimed that he had to sit by his phone and said he couldn't imagine where a regular still camera could be found nearby. Jacob thought the fellow was lying but he had no time to argue. He had to get to a phone.

There was one set on the wall near the corner where he watched Culla and Bubbacub climb the ramp. But as he raised it he wondered who he could call, and what he could say.

Hello, Dr. Kepler? Rember me, Jacob Demwa? The

guy who tried to kill himself on one of your Sunships? Yeah . . . well I'd like you to come down here and watch Pil Bubbacub do spring cleaning . . .

No, that wouldn't do. By the time anyone got down here Culla and Bubbacub would be gone and his call would be another item on his list of public aberrations.

That thought struck Jacob.

Did I just imagine the whole thing? There was no sound of a vacuum cleaner now. Only silence. The whole thing was so damnably symbolic anyway . . .

From around the corner came a squeal, Pilan curses, and a clattering of falling machinery. Jacob closed his eyes for a moment. The sound was beautiful. He risked a peek around the edge.

Bubbacub stood at the bottom of the ramp holding one end of the vacuum cleaner, the bristles around his eyes jutting starkly on end, and his fur stuck out in a ruff around his collar. The Pil glared at Culla, who fumbled with the catch of the machine's dust bag. A small pile of red powder leaked from the opening.

Bubbacub snorted in disgust as Culla scooped handfuls of powder together and then turned the reassembled machine on the pile. Jacob was sure a handful went, instead of to the pile, into the pocket of Culla's silvery tunic.

Bubbacub kicked the remaining dust around until it blended with the floor. Then, after a furtive glance on all sides that sent Jacob's head jetting back behind the wall, he barked a quick command and led Culla back to the elevators.

When he returned to the workbench, Jacob found the chief mechanic looking over the scattered sheets of his morphological analysis. The man looked up when he approached.

"What was that all about?" he pointed his chin toward the Sunship.

"Oh, nothing," Jacob answered. He chewed on his cheek gently for a moment. "Just some Eatees messing around with the ship."

"With the ship?" The chief mechanic came erect. "Is that what you were jabbering about before? Why the hell didn't you say so!?"

"Wait, hold up!" Jacob held the man's arm as he

turned to hurry to the Sunship cradle. "It's too late, they're gone. Besides, figuring out what they're up to will take more than just catching them in the act of doing something strange. Strangeness is what Eatees are best at anyway."

The engineer looked at Jacob as if for the first time. "Yeah," he said slowly. "You have a point. But maybe now you'd better tell me what you saw."

Jacob shrugged and told the whole story, from hearing the sound of the hatch opening to the comedy of the spilled powder.

"I don't get it," the chief mechanic scratched his head.

"Well, don't worry about it. Like I said, it'll take more than one clue to get this buttock-beeper placed."

Jacob sat again on the stool and began scribbling carefully on several sheets.

C. HAS SAMPLE OF PWDR . . . WHY? DANGEROUS TO ASK HIM TO SHARE?

IS C. WILLING ACCOMPLICE? FOR HOW LONG? GET A SAMPLE! ! !

"Hey, what are you doing here, anyway," the chief mechanic asked.

"I'm chasing clues."

After a moment of silence the man tapped the sheets at the far right of the table. "Boy I couldn't be so cold-blooded about it if I thought *I* was going nuts! What did it feel like? I mean when you went swacko and tried to drink poison?"

Jacob raised his eyes from his writing. There was an image. A gestalt. The smell of ammonia filled his nostrils and a powerful throbbing beat at his temples. It felt as if he had spent hours under the glare of an inquisitor's spotlight.

He remembered the image vividly. The last thing he saw before he collapsed was Bubbacub's face. The small black eyes stared at him below the brow of the psi helmet. Alone of those aboard, the Pil watched impassively as Jacob lurched forward and fell to the deck senseless, a few feet away.

The thought made Jacob grow cold. He started to write it down but then stopped. This was too big. He jotted a short note in pidgin dolphin-trinary and threw it on pile IV.

"Im sorry," he looked up at the chief engineer. "Were you saying something?"

The engineer shook his head.

"Oh, it was none of my business anyway. I shouldn't have butted my nose in. I was just curious what you were doing here."

The man paused for a moment.

"Y're trying to save the project, aren't you?" he finally asked.

"Yes, I am."

"Then you must be the only one of the hotshots who is," he said bitterly. "I'm sorry I growled at you earlier. I'll stay out of your way so you can work." He started to move away.

Jacob thought for a moment. "Would you like to help?" he asked.

The man turned. "What do you need?"

Jacob smiled. "Well, for starters I could use a broom and a dustpan."

"Coming right up!" The chief mechanic hurried away.

Jacob drummed his fingers on the tabletop for a moment. Then he gathered the scattered sheets and stuffed them back into his pocket.

18.

FOCUS

"The director said no one was supposed to go in there, you know."

Jacob looked up from his work. "Gosh, chief," he grinned savagely, "I didn't know that! I'm just trying to pick this lock for my health!"

The other man shifted nervously where he stood, and mumbled about never having expected to be involved in a burglary.

Jacob rocked back. The room swayed and he touched the plastic leg of the table next to him for balance. In the dim light of the photo lab it was hard to see straight, especially after twenty minutes of close work with tiny tools.

"I've told you before, Donaldson," he said slowly. "We have no choice. What have we that we can show anyone? A patch of dust and a cockeyed theory? Use your head. We're caught TwoTwo as it is. They won't let us near the evidence because we haven't the evidence to prove we need it!"

Jacob rubbed at the muscles at the back of his neck. "No, we're going to have to do this ourselves . . . that is, if you want to hang around . . ."

The chief mechanic grunted. "You know I'll stay." His tone was hurt.

"Okay, okay." Jacob nodded. "Apologies. Now will you please hand me that small tool over there? No, the one with the hook on the end. That's right.

"Now why don't you go over to the outer door and keep a lookout? Give me some time to clean up if someone comes. And watch out for that trip-fall!"

Donaldson moved away a small distance, but he stayed to watch as Jacob went back to work. He rested against the cool side of one of the doorjambs and wiped perspiration from his cheeks and eyebrows.

Demwa seemed rational and reasonable, but the wild path his imagination had taken in the last few hours left Donaldson dizzy.

The worst part was that it all hung together so well. It was exciting, this hunt for clues. And what he'd found out before meeting Demwa here supported the man's story. But it was also frightening. There was always the chance that the guy really *was* crazy, in spite of the consistency of his arguments.

Donaldson sighed. He turned away from the tiny sounds of scraping metal and the nodding of Jacob's bushy head, and walked slowly toward the outer door of the photo lab.

It didn't really matter. Something was rotten under Mercury. If someone didn't act soon there wouldn't be any more Sunships.

A simple tumbler lock for a ridged and slotted key. Nothing could be easier In fact, Jacob could not have helped noticing that Mercury had few modern locks. Electronics required shielding on a planet where the magnetosheath grazed across the bare unprotected surface. It wasn't very expensive to shield but still someone must have thought such an expenditure ridiculous for locks. Who would want to break into the Inner Photo Lab anyway? And who would know *how?*

Jacob knew how. But that didn't appear to be helping. Somehow it didn't feel right. The tools weren't speaking to him. He felt no continuity from his hands to the metal.

At this rate it could take all night.

Let me do it.

Jacob gritted his teeth and slowly pulled the rake out of the lock. He laid it down.

Stop personifying, he thought. You're nothing but a set of asocial habits I've put under hypnotic lock for a while. If you keep acting like a separate personality you'll get us . . . me into a full-blown schizophrenic state!

Now look who's personifying.

Jacob smiled.

I shouldn't be here. I should have stayed home for the full three years and finished my mental house-cleaning in peace and quiet. The behavior patterns I wanted . . . *needed* to keep submerged are now needed wide awake, by my job.

Then why not use them?

When this mental arrangement was set up it wasn't supposed to be rigid. *That* sort of suppression would *really* lead to trouble! The amoral, cold-blooded, savant qualities leaked out in a steady stream, though usually under complete control. It had been intended that they be available in an emergency.

The suppression and personification by which he'd reacted to that stream lately may have *caused* some of his problem. His sinister half was to *sleep* as he worked off the trauma of Tania . . . not be severed off at the wrist.

Then let me do it.

Jacob picked another rake and rolled it in his fingers. The light slip of tool steel felt smooth, cool.

Shut up. You're not a person, just a talent unfortunately linked to a neurosis . . . like a well-trained singing voice that can only be used while standing naked on a stage.

Fine. Use the talent. The door could be open by now!

Jacob carefully laid his tools down and shuffled forward until his forehead rested against the door. Should I? What if I *did* flip out on the Sunship? My theory could be wrong. And then there's that blue flash back at Baja. Can I risk opening up if something's gone loose inside?

Weak from indecision, he felt the trance begin to fall. With an effort he stopped it, but then, with a mental shrug, allowed it to proceed. At the count of seven a barrier of fear blocked him. It was a familiar barrier. It felt like the edge of a precipice. He consciously brushed it aside and continued down.

At twelve he commanded: This Shall Be Temporary. He felt assent.

The backcount was done in an instant. He opened his eyes. A tingle wandered down the length of his arms and entered his fingers, suspiciously, like a dog returning, sniffing, to an old home.

So far so good, Jacob thought. I feel no less ethical. No less "me." My hands don't feel as if they're controlled by an alien force . . . only more alive.

The lockpicking tools weren't cool when he picked them up. They felt warm, like extensions of his hands. The rake slid sensuously into the lock and caressed the tumblers as the torque bar pulled. One after another tiny click telegraphed along the metal. Then the door was open.

"You did it!" Donaldson's surprise hurt a little.

"Of course," was all he said. It was reassuringly easy to squelch the insulting reply that popped into his mind. So far so good. The genie seemed benign. Jacob swung the door wide and entered.

Filing cabinets lined the left wall of the narrow room. Along the other wall a low table supported a row of photoanalysis machines. At the far end an open door led to the unlit and seldom used chemical darkroom.

Jacob began at one end of the row of filing cabinets, bending to look at labels. Donaldson worked along the bench. It wasn't long before the chief mechanic said, "I found them!" He pointed to an open box, next to a viewing machine halfway down the table.

Each spool was held in a padded niche, its sides inscribed with the date and times covered and a code for the instrument that made the recording. At least a dozen niches were empty.

Jacob held several cassettes to the light. Then he turned to Donaldson.

"Someone's been here first and pilfered every cassette we wanted."

"Stolen? . . . But how!"

Jacob shrugged. "Maybe the way we did it, by breaking and entry. Or maybe they had a key. All we know is that the final spool for each recording device is missing."

They stood for a moment in dark silence.

"Then we haven't got any proof at all," Donaldson said.

"Not unless we can track down the missing spools."

"You mean we should bust into Bubbacub's rooms too? . . . I don't know. If you ask me, those data are burned by now. Why would he keep them around?

"No, I suggest we sneak out of here and let Dr. Kepler or Dr. deSilva discover the fact that they're missing by themselves. It's not much but they may see it as slight evidence to support our story."

Jacob hesitated. Then he nodded.

"Let me see your hands," Jacob said.

Donaldson presented his palms up. The thin coating of flex-plastic was intact. They were probably safe from chemical and fingerprint tracing, then.

"Okay," he said. "Let's put everything back in its place, as exactly as you can remember it. Don't disturb anything you haven't already touched. Then we'll leave."

Donaldson turned to comply but then there was a crash as something fell in the Outer Photo Lab. The sound carried, muffled through the door.

The trap Jacob had set by the hall door had gone off. Someone was in the outer lab. Their escape route was blocked!

The two men hurried back into the dim doorway of the darkroom. They made it around the corner of the light-trap maze just as the sound of a metal key scratching at the lock carried across the narrow room.

Jacob heard the door sigh open slowly, over the subjective roar of his own rapid breathing. He patted the pockets of his overalls. Half of his burglar tools were out there, on top of one of the filing cabinets.

Fortunately his dentist's mirror wasn't. It was still in his breast-pocket case.

The intruder's footsteps clicked softly in the room a few feet away. Jacob carefully weighed the hazards against the potential benefits and then slowly eased the mirror out. He knelt and poked the round, shiny working end into the threshold, a few inches above the floor.

Dr. Martine stooped in front of a filing cabinet, sorting through a ring of metal keys. Once, she shot a furtive glance toward the outer door. She looked agitated, though it was hard to tell from the image in the tiny mirror, jiggling on the floor two meters from her feet.

Jacob felt Chief Donaldson leaning over, above and behind him, trying to peek past the doorway. Irritated, he tried to wave the man back, but Donaldson overbalanced instead. His left hand shot out for support and landed on Jacob's back.

"Oof!" The air expelled from Jacob's lungs as the chief engineer's weight fell on him. His teeth jarred as he took the full force through his stiffened left arm. Somehow he kept them both from collapsing into the doorway, but the mirror fell out of his hand and onto the floor with a tiny clink.

Donaldson slid backward into the dimness, breathing heavily—pathetically trying to be quiet. Jacob smiled wryly. Anyone who hadn't heard *that* debacle had to be deaf.

"Who . . . who's there?"

Jacob stood and brushed himself off deliberately. He cast a brief, disdainful glance at Chief Donaldson, who sat glumly and avoided Jacob's eyes.

Quick footsteps receded in the outer room. Jacob stepped out into the doorway.

"Wait a minute, Millie."

Dr. Martine froze midstep at the door. Her shoulders hunched as she turned slowly, her face a mask of fear until she recognized Jacob. Then her dark, patrician features washed deep red.

"What the hell are you doing here!"

"Watching you, Millie. An enjoyable pastime usually, but now especially interesting."

"You were spying on me!" she gasped.

Jacob walked forward, hoping Donaldson would have enough sense to stay hidden. "Not just you, dear. On everybody. Something is fishy on Mercury, all right. Everyone's whistling a different tuna, and

210

they're all red herrings! I have a feeling you know more than you're telling."

"I don't know what you are talking about," Martine said coldly. "But that's not surprising. You're not rational and you need help . . ." She started to back away.

"Perhaps," Jacob nodded seriously. "But maybe you will need help explaining your presence here today."

Martine stiffened. "I got my key from Dwayne Kepler. What about you!"

"Did you get the key *with* his knowledge?"

Martine blushed and didn't answer.

"There are several data spools missing from the collection taken last dive . . . all covering the period when Bubbacub did his trick with the Lethani relic. You wouldn't happen to know where they are, would you?"

Martine stared at Jacob.

"You're kidding! But who . . . ? No . . ." she shook her head slowly, confused.

"Did you take them?"

"No!"

"Then who did?"

"I don't know. How should *I* know? What business have you questioning . . ."

"I could call Helene deSilva right now," Jacob rumbled ominously. "I could have just arrived to find this door open with you inside and the key with your prints on it in your pouch. She'd search and find the spools missing and there you'd be. You've been covering for someone and I have some independent evidence who. If you don't come out with all you know right now, I swear you're going to take the fall, with or without your friend. You know as well as I that the crew at this base is just itching for someone to burn."

Martine wavered. Her hand went to her head.

"I don't . . . I don't know . . ."

Jacob maneuvered her into a chair. Then he closed and locked the door.

Hey, take it easy, a part of him said. He closed his eyes for a moment and counted to ten. Slowly, a brutal itch in Jacob's hands ebbed.

Martine held her face in her hands. Jacob caught a glimpse of Donaldson, peeking around the darkroom door. He jerked his hand and the chief engineer's head darted out of sight.

Jacob pulled open the filing cabinet the woman had been examining.

Aha. Here it is.

He picked up the steno-camera and carried it back to the bench, plugged the readout jack into one of the viewers and turned both machines on.

Most of the material was quite uninteresting, LaRoque's notes on events between the landing on Mercury and the morning that he took the camera to the Sunship Cavern, just before the fateful tour of Jeffrey's ship. Jacob ignored the audio portion. LaRoque tended to be even more wordy in leaving notes to himself than he was in his published prose. But suddenly the character of the visual portion changed, just after a panorama shot of the exterior of the Sunship.

For a moment he was puzzled as the pictures moved past. Then he laughed out loud.

Millie Martine was so surprised by this that she raised her red eyes from her misery. Jacob nodded to her genially.

"Did you *know* what you were fetching down here?"

"Yes," her voice was husky. She nodded slowly. "I wanted to get Peter's camera back to him so he could write up his story. I thought that after the Solarians had been so cruel to him . . . using him so . . ."

"He's still in confinement, isn't he?"

"Yes. They figured it's safest that way. The Solarians manipulated him once before, you see. They could do it again."

"And whose idea was it to return his camera?"

"His, of course. He wanted the recordings and I didn't think it would hurt . . ."

"To let him get his hands on a weapon?"

"No! The stunner would be put out of comm . . . commission. Bubb . . ." Her eyes widened and her voice trailed off.

"Go ahead and say it. I already know."

Martine lowered her gaze.

"Bubbacub said he'd meet me at Peter's quarters and

put the stunner out of commission, as a favor and to prove he had no hard feelings."

Jacob sighed. "That tears it," he muttered.

"What . . . ?"

"Let me see your hands." He motioned peremptorily when she hesitated. The long slender fingers trembled as he examined them.

"What is it?"

Jacob ignored her. He paced slowly up and back down the narrow room.

The symmetry of the trap appealed to him. If it carried through there wouldn't be a human left on Mercury with an unsullied reputation. He couldn't have done better himself. The only question now was, when was it supposed to be sprung?

He turned and looked back at the darkroom entrance. Again, Donaldson's head flicked back out of sight.

"It's all right, Chief. Come on out. You're going to have to help Dr. Martine clean this place of her fingerprints."

Martine gasped as the portly chief engineer emerged, smiling sheepishly.

"What are you going to do?" he asked.

Instead of answering, Jacob picked up the voicephone by the inner door and dialed.

"Hello, Fagin? Yes. I'm ready for a 'parlor scene' now. Oh yeah . . . ? Well, don't be so sure yet. It will depend on how lucky I can get in the next few minutes.

"Would you please invite the core group down to LaRoque's detention quarters for a meeting in five minutes? Yes, right away, and please insist. Don't bother with Dr. Martine, she's right here."

Martine looked up from wiping the handle of a filing cabinet, amazed by the tone of Jacob Demwa's voice.

"That's right," Jacob went on. "And please invite Bubbacub first and Kepler as well. Get them moving the way we both know you can. I'll have to run as it is. Yeah, thanks."

"So now what?" Donaldson said on their way out the door.

"Now you two apprentices graduate to first-class

213

burglarhood. And you've got to make it snappy. Dr. Kepler will be leaving his rooms shortly and you'd better not be too long following him to the meeting."

Martine stopped in her tracks. "You're kidding. You don't seriously expect me to help ransack Dwayne's apartment!"

"Why not?" Donaldson growled. "You've been giving him rat poison! You stole his keys to break into the Photo Lab."

Martine's nostrils flared. "I have not been giving him rat poison! Who told you that?"

Jacob sighed. "Warfarin. It was used as a rat poison in the old days. Before the rats got immune to it and nearly everything else."

"I told you *before*, I never *heard* of Warfarin! First the Doctor and then you on the Sunship. Why does everybody think I'm a poisoner!"

"I don't. But I do think that you'd better cooperate if you want to help us get to the bottom of this. Now you've got the keys to Kepler's rooms, right?"

Martine bit her lip, then nodded once.

Jacob told Donaldson what to look for and what to do with it when he found it. Then he was off, running in the direction of the E.T. Quarters.

19.

IN THE PARLOR

"You mean Jacob called this meeting and he isn't even here?" Helene deSilva asked from the doorway.

"I should not be concerned, Commandant deSilva. He shall arrive. I have never known Mister Demwa to call a meeting that was not well worth the time of attending."

"Indeed!" LaRoque laughed from one end of the large sofa, with his feet propped up on an ottoman. He spoke sarcastically around the stem of his pipe, and through a haze of smoke. "And why not? What else have we to do here? The 'research' is over, and the studies are done. The Ivory Tower has collapsed in arrogance and it is the month of the long knives. Let Demwa take his time. Whatever he has to say will be more amusing than watching all these serious faces!"

Dwayne Kepler grimaced from the other end of the sofa. He sat as far from LaRoque as he possibly could. Nervously, he twitched aside the lap blanket a med-aid had just finished adjusting. The med-aid looked up to the physician, who just shrugged.

"Shut up, LaRoque," Kepler said.

LaRoque merely grinned and took out a tool to work

on his pipe. "I still think I should have a recording device. Knowing Demwa, this may be historic."

Bubbacub snorted and turned away. He had been pacing. Uncharacteristically he hadn't gone near any of the cushions scattered around the carpeted room. The Pil stopped in front of Culla, standing by the wall, and clicked his quadrilaterally symmetric fingers in a complicated pattern. Culla nodded.

"I am instructed to shay that enough tragedy has occurred because of Mishter LaRoquesh recording devishesh. Also Pil Bubbacub hash indicated that he will not remain pasht another five minutes."

Kepler ignored the statement. Methodically, he rubbed his neck as if searching for an itch. A lot of the fleshiness had departed in recent weeks.

LaRoque raised his shoulders once in a gallic shrug. Fagin was silent. Not even the silvery chimes moved at the ends of his blue-green branches.

"Come on in and sit down, Helene," the physician said. "I'm sure the others will be here soon." With his eyes he commiserated. Walking into this room was like wading into a pool of very cold and not very clean water.

She found a seat as far from the others as possible. Unhappily, she wondered what Jacob Demwa was up to.

I hope it's not the same thing, she thought. If this group in here has anything in common, it's the fact that they don't even want the word "Sundiver" mentioned. They're just on the edge of tearing each others' throats out, but all the same there's this conspiracy of silence.

She shook her head. I'm glad this tour is over soon. Maybe things will be better in another fifty years.

She didn't hold out much hope for that. Already the only place you could hear a Beatles tune performed was by a symphony orchestra, of all the monstrosities. And good jazz didn't exist outside of a library.

Why did I ever leave home?

Mildred Martine and Chief Donaldson entered. To Helene, their attempts to look nonchalant were pathetic, but no one else seemed to notice.

Interesting. I wonder what *those* two have in common?

They looked around the room and then edged toward

216

a corner behind the only sofa, where Kepler and La-
Roque and the tension between them occupied all of the
space. LaRoque looked up at Martine and smiled. Was
that a conspirational wink? Martine avoided his eye
and LaRoque looked disappointed. He returned to
lighting his pipe.

"I have had e-nough!" Bubbacub announced finally,
and he turned for the door. But before he got there it
swung open, apparently on its own. Then Jacob Demwa
appeared in the doorway, a white canvas sack over his
shoulder. He entered the room whistling softly. Helene
blinked unbelievingly. The tune sounded *awfully like*
"Santa Claus Is Coming to Town." But surely . . .

Jacob swung the bag into the air. It came down on
the coffee table with a bang that made Dr. Martine
jump halfway out of her chair. Kepler's frown deepened and he gripped the arm of the sofa.

Helene couldn't help it. The anachronistic, homely
old tune, the loud noise, and Jacob's demeanor broke
the wall of tension like a custard pie in the face of
someone you didn't particularly like. She laughed.

Jacob winked once. "Ho ho."

"Are you here to play?" Bubbacub demanded. "You
steal my time! Comp-en-sate!"

Jacob smiled. "Why certainly, Pil Bubbacub. I hope
that you will be edified by my demonstration. But first,
won't you please be seated?"

Bubbacub's jaws snapped together. The small black
eyes seemed to burn for a moment, then he snorted
and threw himself onto a nearby cushion.

Jacob studied the faces in the room. The expressions
were mostly confused or hostile, except for LaRoque,
who remained pompously aloof, and Helene, who
smiled uncertainly. And Fagin, of course. For the thou-
sandth time he wished the Kanten had eyes.

"When Dr. Kepler invited me to Mercury," he began,
"I had some doubts about the Sundiver Project, but
approved of the idea overall. After that first meeting I
expected to become involved in one of the most exciting events since Contact . . . a complex problem of
interspecies relations with our nearest and strangest
neighbors, the Sun Ghosts.

"Instead, the problem of the Solarians seems to have

217

taken back burner to a complicated web of interstellar intrigue and murder."

Kepler looked up sadly. "Jacob, please. We all know you've been under a strain. Millie thinks we should be kind to you and I agree. But there are limits."

Jacob spread his hands. "If kindness is humoring me, then please do so. I'm sick of being ignored. If you don't listen, I'm sure the Earth authorities will."

Kepler's smile froze. He sat back. "Go ahead, then. I'll listen."

Jacob stepped onto the broad throw rug in the center of the room.

"First: Pierre LaRoque has consistently denied killing Chimp Jeffrey or using his stunner to sabotage the smaller Sunship. He denies having ever been a Probationer and claims that the records on Earth have somehow been fouled up.

"Yet, since our return from the Sun he has consistently refused to take a P-test, which might go a long way toward proving his innocence. Presumably he expects that the results of the test would also be falsified."

"That's right," LaRoque nodded. "Just another lie."

"Even if Physician Laird, Dr. Martine and I jointly supervised?"

LaRoque grunted. "It might prejudice my trial, especially if I decide to sue."

"Why go to trial? You had no motive to kill Jeffrey when you opened the access plate to the R.Q. tuner . . ."

"Which I deny doing!"

". . . and only a Probie would kill a man in a fit of pique. So why stay in detention?"

"Maybe he's comfortable here," the med-aid commented. Helene frowned. Discipline had gone straight to hell lately, along with morale.

"He refuses the test because he knows he'll fail!" Kepler shouted.

"That is why the Sun-Men chose him to do their kill-ing," Bubbacub added. "That is what they told me."

"And am I a Probationer? Some people seem to think the Ghosts made me try to commit suicide."

"You were un-der stress. Doct-or Mar-tin says so.

218

Yes?" Bubbacub turned to Martine. Her hands gripped each other whitely but she said nothing.

"We'll get to that in a few minutes," Jacob said. "But before we start I'd like to have a private word with Dr. Kepler and Mr. LaRoque."

Dr. Laird and his assistant moved away politely. Bubbacub glared at being forced to move, but followed suit.

Jacob passed around the back of the sofa. As he bent over between the two men his hand went behind his back. Donaldson leaned forward and placed a small object there which Jacob held tightly.

Jacob looked alternately at Kepler and LaRoque.

"I think you two should cut it out. Especially you, Dr. Kepler."

Kepler hissed. "What in god's name are you talking about?"

"I think you have some property of Mr. LaRoque's. No matter that he got it illegally. He wants it badly. Badly enough to temporarily take a rap he knows won't stick. Maybe enough to change the tone of the articles he's certain to write about all this.

"I don't think the deal will hold anymore. You see, I have the item now."

"My camera!" LaRoque whispered harshly. His eyes shone.

"Quite a little camera, too. A complete little sonic spectrograph. Yes, I have it. I also have the copies of recordings you made that were hidden in Dr. Kepler's rooms."

"You t-traitor," Kepler stammered. "I thought you were a friend . . ."

"Shut up, you skinny bastard!" LaRoque almost shouted. "You are the one who is a traitor." Contempt seemed to boil from the little writer like steam overlong contained.

Jacob laid a hand on the back of each man. "Both of you will be on no-return orbits if you don't keep your voices down! LaRoque can be charged with espionage and Kepler for blackmail and complicity after the fact in espionage!

"In fact, since the evidence of LaRoque's espionage is also circumstantial evidence that he wouldn't have had time to sabotage Jeffrey's ship, the immediate suspicion would fall on the last person to inspect the ship's generators. Oh I don't think you did it, Dr. Kepler. But I'd be careful if I were you!"

LaRoque fell silent. Kepler chewed on the end of his moustache.

"What do you want?" he said finally.

Jacob tried to resist but the suppressed side was now too much awake. He couldn't help making a little dig.

"Why, I'm not sure yet. Maybe I'll think of something. Just don't let your imagination go wild. Friends of mine on Earth know everything by now."

It wasn't true. But Mr. Hyde did believe in caution.

Helene deSilva strained to overhear what the three men were saying to each other. If she had been one to believe in possession she would have been sure the familiar faces were moving at the command of invading spirits. Gentle Dr. Kepler, turned taciturn and secretive since their return from the Sun, muttered like a wrathful sage denied his will. LaRoque—thoughtful, cautious—behaved as if his whole world hinged on a careful assessment of affairs.

And Jacob Demwa . . . earlier glimpses hinted at a charisma beneath his quiet, sometimes watery thoughtfulness. It had drawn her even as it frustrated in its peek-a-boo appearances. But now, now it radiated. It compelled like a flame.

Jacob stood straight and announced, "For now, Dr. Kepler has kindly agreed to drop all charges against Pierre LaRoque."

Bubbacub rose from his cushion. "You are mad. If hu-mans condone the kill-ing of their cli-ents, that is their own prob-lem. But the Sun-Men may bend him to do harm a-gain!"

"The Sun-Men never bent him to do anything." Jacob said slowly.

Bubbacub snapped. "As I said, you are mad. I spoke with the Sun-Men. They did not lie."

"If you wish," Jacob bowed. "But I still would like to continue with my synopsis."

Bubbacub snorted loudly and threw himself again on the cushion. "Mad!" he snapped.

"First," Jacob said. "I would like to thank Dr. Kepler for his gracious permission for Chief Donaldson and Dr. Martine and myself to visit the Photo Labs and study the films from the last dive."

At the mention of Martine's name, Bubbacub's expression changed. So that's what chagrin looks like on a Pil, Jacob thought. He empathized with the little alien. It had been a beautiful trap, now entirely defused.

Jacob told an edited version of their discovery in the Photo Lab, that the flipside spools of the last third of the mission were missing. The only other sound in the room was the tinkling of Fagin's branches.

"For a while, I wondered where these spools could be. I had an idea who took them, but whether he had destroyed them or taken the chance of hiding them I wasn't sure. Finally, I decided to gamble that a 'data-packrat' never throws anything away. I searched a certain sophont's quarters and found the missing spools."

"You dared!" Bubbacub hissed. "If you had prop-er mas-ters I would have you nerve whipped! You dared!"

Helene shook away her surprise. "You mean you admit that you hid Sundiver datatapes, Pil Bubbacub? Why!"

Jacob grinned. "Oh that will become clear. In fact the way this case was going, I thought for sure it would be more complicated than it is. But it's actually quite simple. You see, these tapes make it very clear that Pil Bubbacub has lied."

A low rumbling rose in Bubbacub's throat. The little alien stood very still as if he didn't trust himself to move.

"Well, where are the tapes?" deSilva demanded.

Jacob picked up the sack from the table.

"I've got to give the devil his due, though. It was only luck that I figured the spools would just fit into an empty gas cannister." He pulled out an object and held it up.

"The Lethani relic!" DeSilva gasped. A small trill of surprise escaped Fagin. Mildred Martine stood up, her hand brought to her throat.

"Yes, the Lethani relic. I'm sure Bubbacub counted on a reaction like yours on the obscure chance that his rooms were searched. Naturally, no one would think of disturbing a semi-religious object-of-reverence of an old and powerful race; particularly one that looked like nothing but a slab of meteoric rock and glass!'"

He turned it over in his hands.

"Now watch!"

The relic opened with a twist. A can of some sort was imbedded in one of the halves. Jacob laid the other half down and tugged at the end of the can. Something inside rattled softly. The can suddenly came loose and a dozen small black objects came rolling out and fell to the floor. Culla's mashies clacked.

"The spools!" LaRoque nodded with satisfaction as he fumbled with his pipe.

"Yes," Jacob said. "And on the outer surface of this 'relic' you can find the button which released the previous contents of this now-empty cannister. There appear to be some traces left inside. I'll bet anything that they match the substance that Chief Donaldson and I gave Dr. Kepler yesterday when we failed to convince ..." Jacob stopped himself. Then he shrugged.

"... Traces of an unstable monomolecule which, under a certain sophont's skillful control, spread out in a 'burst of light and sound' to coat the inner surface of the upper hemisphere of the shell of the Sunship ..."

DeSilva rose to her feet. Jacob had to speak louder to overcome the rising chatter coming from Culla.

"... and to effectively block out all green and blue light—the only wavelengths in which we could pick out the Sun Ghosts from their surroundings!"

"The spools!" deSilva cried. "They should show ..."

"They do show toroids, Ghosts ... hundreds of them! Interestingly there were no anthropoid shapes, but perhaps they didn't make them because our psi patterns indicated we weren't seeing them.

"But oh the confusion in that herd when we blundered right into them without so much as a by-your-leave, toroids and 'normal' Ghosts scattering out of our path ... all because we couldn't see that we were right in the middle of them!"

"You crazy Eatee!" LaRoque shouted. He shook his fist at Bubbacub. The Pil hissed back but remained still, the fingers of each hand flexing against one another as he watched Jacob.

"The monomolecule was designed to decay just as we were leaving the chromosphere. It slumped in a thin layer of dust on the force field at the rim of the deck, where no one would notice it until Bubbacub could return with Culla and vacuum it up. That's right, isn't it, Culla?"

Culla nodded miserably.

Jacob felt distantly pleased that sympathy came as easily as amoral wrath had earlier. A part of him had begun to get worried. He smiled reassuringly.

"That's okay, Culla. I have no evidence to connect you with anything else. I watched the two of you when you did it and it was pretty clear you were under duress."

The Pring's eyes rose. They were very bright. He nodded once again and the chattering from behind the thick lips subsided slowly. Fagin moved closer to the slender E.T.

Donaldson rose from picking up the recording spools.

"I think we'd better make some provisions for custody."

Helene had already moved to the telephone. "I'm taking care of that now," she said softly.

Martine sidled up to Jacob and whispered. "Jacob, this is an External Affairs matter now. We should let them handle it from here."

Jacob shook his head. "No. Not just yet. There's a bit more that needs out."

DeSilva put down the phone. "They'll be here shortly. Meanwhile, why don't you go on, Jacob? Is there more?"

"Yes. Two items. One is this."

From the bag on the table he pulled Bubbacub's psi helmet. "I suggest this be kept in storage. I don't know if anyone else remembers, but Bubbacub was wearing it and staring at me when I warped out aboard the Sunship. Being made to do things makes me mad, Bubbacub. You shouldn't have done it."

Bubbacub made a gesture with his hand that Jacob didn't try to interpret.

"Finally, there's the matter of the death of chimpanzee Jeffrey. Actually, it's the easiest part.

"Bubbacub knew almost everything there was to know about the Galactic technology in Sundiver; the drives, the computer system, the communications . . . aspects which Terran scientists haven't even scratched.

"It's only circumstantial evidence that Bubbacub was working on the laser communications pylon, spurning Dr. Kepler's presentation, when Jeff's largely remote-controlled ship blew up. It wouldn't convict in a court of law, but that doesn't matter since Pila have extraterritoriality and all we can do is deport him.

"Another thing that'd be hard to prove would be the hypothesis that Bubbacub planted a false lead in the Space Identification System . . . a system linked directly to the Library at LaPaz . . . creating a false report that LaRoque was a Probationer. Still, it's pretty clear that he did. It was a perfect red herring. With everyone sure that LaRoque did it, nobody bothered to really do a detailed double-check of the telemetry on Jeff's dive. Right now I believe I recall that Jeff's ship went into trouble almost exactly when he turned on his closeup cameras, a perfect delayed trigger if that was the technique Bubbacub used. Anyway, we'll probably never know. The telemetry is probably missing or destroyed by now."

Fagin fluted. "Jacob, Culla asks that you stop. Please do not embarrass Pil Bubbacub any further. It would serve no purpose."

Three armed crewmen appeared at the door. They looked at Commandant deSilva expectantly. She motioned for them to wait.

"Just a moment," Jacob said. "We haven't dealt with the most important part, Bubbacub's motives. Why would an important sophont, a representative of a prestigious galactic institution, indulge in theft, forgery, psychic assault, and murder?

"Bubbacub had personal grudges against both Jeffrey and LaRoque, to start with. Jeffrey represented an abomination to him, a species that had been uplifted a mere hundred years before and yet dared to talk back. Jeff's 'uppityness' and his friendship with Culla contributed to Bubbacub's anger.

"But I think he hated what chimpanzees represent

224

most of all. Along with dolphins, they meant instant status for the crude, vulgar human race. The Pila had to fight for half a million years to get to where they are. I guess Bubbacub resents us having it 'easy.'

"As for LaRoque, well, I'd say Bubbacub just didn't like him. Too loud and pushy, I suppose . . ."

LaRoque sniffed audibly.

"And perhaps he was insulted when LaRoque suggested that the Soro might have once been our Patrons. The 'upper crust" in Galactic society frowns on species who abandon their clients."

"But those are just personal reasons," Helene objected. "Haven't you got anything better?"

"Jacob," Fagin began. "Please . . ."

"Of course Bubbacub had another reason," Jacob said. "He wanted to end Sundiver in a way that would put into disrepute the concept of independent research and boost the status of the Library. He made it seem that he, a Pil, was able to make contact where humans weren't, concocted a story that made Sundiver out to be a bungled operation. Then he faked a Library report to verify his claims about the Solarians and ensure that there would be no more dives!

"It was the failure of the Library to come up with anything that probably irked Bubbacub the most. And it's faking that message that'll get him in the deepest trouble back at home. For *that* they'll punish him worse than we ever would for killing Jeff."

Bubbacub rose slowly. He carefully brushed his fur flat and then clicked his four-fingered hands together.

"You are ver-y smart," he said to Jacob. "But seman-tics bad . . . aim too high. You build too much on small stuff. Hu-mans shall al-ways be small. I shall speak your kaka Terran tongue no more."

With that he removed the Vodor from around his neck and tossed it idly on the table.

"I'm sorry, Pil Bubbacub," deSilva said. "But it appears that we're going to have to restrict your movement until we get instructions from Earth."

Jacob half expected the Pil to nod or shrug but the alien performed another movement that somehow conveyed the same indifference. He turned away and marched stiffly out the door, a small stubby, proud figure leading the large human guards.

Helene deSilva picked up the bottom of the "Lethani relic." She weighed it carefully in her hands, thoughtfully. Then her lips tightened and she threw the object with all her might against the door.

"Murderer," she cursed.

"I've learned my lesson," Martine said slowly. "Never trust anyone over thirty million."

Jacob stood in a daze. The exalted feeling was draining away too quickly. Like a drug, it left behind it an emptiness—a return to rationality but a loss of totality as well. Soon he would begin to wonder if he had done right in releasing everything at once in an orgiastic display of deductive logic.

Martine's remark made him look up.

"Not anyone?" he asked.

Fagin was nudging Culla into a chair. Jacob went over to him.

"I'm sorry, Fagin," he said. "I should have warned you, discussed it with you first. There may be . . . complications to this thing, repercussions that I didn't think out." He brought a hand to his forehead.

Fagin whistled softly.

"You unleashed that which you have been restraining, Jacob. I do not understand why you have been so reticent to use your skills, of late, but in this instance justice demanded all of your vigor. It is fortunate that you relented.

"Do not worry too much about what has happened. The Truth was more important than the damage done through minor over-eagerness, or through the use of techniques too long dormant."

Jacob wanted to tell Fagin how wrong he was. The "skills" he had unleashed were more than that. They were a deadly force within him. He feared that they had done more harm than good.

"What do you think will happen?" he asked, tiredly.

"Why I believe that humanity will discover that it has a powerful enemy. Your government will protest. How it does so will be of great importance, but it will not change the essential facts. Officially the Pila will disown Bubbacub's unfortunate actions. But they are peevish and prideful, if you will excuse a painful but necessarily unkind description of a fellow sophont race.

"That is just one result of this event-chain. But do not worry overmuch. You did not do this thing. All that you did was make humanity *aware* of the danger. It was bound to happen. It always *has* happened to wolfling races."

"But why!"

"That, my most esteemed friend, is one of the things I am here to try to discover. Though it may be of little comfort, please note that there are many who would like to see humanity survive. Some of us . . . care very much."

20.

MODERN MEDICINE

Jacob pressed against the rubber rimmed eyepiece of the Retinal scanner, and once again saw the blue dot dance and shimmer alone in a black background. Now he tried not to focus on it, ignoring its tantalizing suggestion of communion, as he waited for the third tachistoscopic image.

It flashed on suddenly, filling his entire field of view with a 3-D image in dull sepia. The gestalt he got in that first, unfocused instant was of a pastoral scene. There was a woman in the foreground, buxom and well fed, her old-fashioned skirts flying as she ran.

Dark, threatening clouds loomed on the horizon, above farm buildings set on a hill. There were people on the left . . . dancing? No, fighting. There were soldiers. Their faces were excited and—afraid? The woman was afraid. She fled with her arms over her head as two men in seventeenth-century body armor chased her, holding high their matchlocks with bayonets sharp. Their . . .

The scene blacked out and the blue dot was back. Jacob closed his eyes and pulled back from the eyepiece.

"That's it," Dr. Martine said. She bent over a computer console nearby, next to Physician Laird. "We'll have your P-test score in a minute, Jacob."

"You're sure you don't need any more? That was only three." Actually, he was relieved.

"No, we took five from Peter to have a double-check. You're just a control. Why don't you just sit down and relax now, while we finish up here."

Jacob walked over to one of the nearby lounge chairs, wiping his left cuff along his forehead to remove a thin sheen of perspiration. The test had been a thirty-second ordeal.

The first image had been a portrait of a man's face, gnarled and lined with care, a story of a life-time that he had examined for two, maybe three seconds, before it disappeared again, as seared as any ephemera could be into his memory.

The second had been a confusing jumble of abstract shapes, jutting and bumping in static disarray . . . somewhat like the maze of patterns around the rim of a sun-torus but without the brilliance or overall consistency.

The third had been the scene in sepia, apparently rendered from an old etching of the Thirty Years War. It was explicitly violent, Jacob recalled, just the sort of thing one would expect in a P-test.

After the overly dramatic "parlor scene" downstairs, Jacob was reluctant to enter even a shallow trance to calm his nerves. And he found that he couldn't relax without it. He rose and approached the console. Across the dome, near the stasis shell itself, LaRoque wandered idly as he waited, staring out at the long shadows and blistered rocks of Mercury's North Pole.

"May I see the raw data?" Jacob asked Martine.

"Sure. Which one would you like to see?"

"The last one."

Martine tapped on her keyboard. A sheet extruded from a slot beneath the screen. She tore it off and handed it to him.

It was the "pastoral scene." Of course now he recognized its true content, but the whole purpose of the earlier viewing was to trace his reactions to the image during the first few instants he saw it, before conscious consideration could come into play.

Across the image a jagged line darted back and forth, up and down. At every vertex or resting point was a small number. The line showed the path of his attention during that first quick glimpse, as detected by the Retinal Reader, watching the movements of his eye.

The number one, and the beginning of the trace, was near the center. Up to number six the focus line just drifted. Then it stopped right over the generous cleavage presented by the running woman's bosom. The number seven was circled there.

There the numbers clustered, not only seven to sixteen, but thirty through thirty five and eighty two to eighty six, as well.

At twenty the numbers suddenly shifted from the woman's feet to the clouds over the farmhouse. Then they moved quickly among the people and objects pictured, sometimes circled or squared to denote the level of dilation of the eye, depth of focus, and changes in his blood pressure as measured by the tiny veins in his retina. Apparently the modified Stanford-Purkinje eye scanner he had devised for this test, from Martine's tachistoscope and other odds and ends, had worked.

Jacob knew better than to be embarrassed or concerned by his reflex reaction to the pictured woman's breast. If he'd been female his reaction would have been different, spending more time with the woman, overall, but concentrating more on hair, clothes, and face.

What concerned him more was his reaction to the overall scene. Over to the left, near the fighting men, was a starred number. That represented the point at which he realized that the image was violent, not pastoral. He nodded with satisfaction. The number was relatively low and the trace darted immediately away for a period of five beats before returning to the same spot. That meant a healthy dose of aversion followed by direct instead of covert curiosity.

At first glance it looked like he'd probably pass. Not that he ever really doubted it.

"I wonder if anyone will ever learn how to fool a P-test," he said, handing the copy to Martine.

"Maybe they will, someday," she said as she gathered her materials. "But the conditioning needed to change a man's response to instantaneous stimuli . . . to an image flashed so fast that only the unconscious has time to react . . . would leave too many side effects, new patterns that would have to show up in the test.

"The final analysis is very simple; does the subject's mind follow a plus or zero sum game, qualifying him for Citizenship, or is it addicted to the sick-sweet pleasures of a negative sum. That, more than any index of violence, is the essence of this test."

Martine turned to Physician Laird. "That's right, isn't it, Doctor?"

Laird shrugged. "You're the expert." He had been allowing Martine to slowly win her way back into his good graces, still not quite forgiving her for prescribing to Kepler without consulting him.

After the denunciation downstairs, it became clear that she had never prescribed the Warfarin to Kepler at all. Jacob recalled Bubbacub's habit, aboard the *Bradbury*, of falling asleep on articles of clothing, carelessly left on cushions or chairs. The Pil must have done it as a subterfuge to enable him to plant, in Kepler's portable pharmacopoeia, a drug that would cause his behavior to deteriorate.

It made sense. Kepler *was* eliminated from the last dive. With his keen insight he might have detected Bubbacub's trick with the "Lethani relic." Also his aberrant actions would have helped in the long run to discredit Sundiver.

It hung together, but to Jacob all of these deductions tasted like a dinner of protein-flakes. They were enough to persuade but they had no flavor. A bowl full of suppositions.

Some of Bubbacub's misdeeds were proven. The rest would have to remain speculation since the Library representative had diplomatic immunity.

Pierre LaRoque joined them. The Frenchman's attitude was subdued. "What is the verdict, Doctor Laird?"

"It's quite clear that Mr. LaRoque is not an asocially violent personality and that he does not qualify for Probation," Laird said slowly. "In fact, he betrays a rather high social conscience index. That may be part of his problem. He's apparently sublimating something and he would be well-advised to seek the help of a professional at his neighborhood clinic when he gets home." Laird looked down at LaRoque sternly. LaRoque merely nodded meekly.

"And the controls?" Jacob asked. He had been the last to take the test. Dr. Kepler, Helene deSilva, and three randomly selected crewmen had also taken their turns at the machine. Helene hadn't given the test a second thought and had taken the crewmen with her when she left to supervise the hurried pre-launch checkout of the Sunship. Kepler had scowled as Physician Laird read him his own results privately, and stalked off in a huff.

Laird reached up and pinched the bridge of his nose, just below the eyebrows.

"Oh, there isn't a Probationer in the bunch, just as we expected after your little show downstairs. But there are problems and things I don't quite understand, bubbling in the minds of some of the people here. You know, it's not easy for a country sawbones like me to have to fall back on his internship training and look into people's souls. I would have missed half a dozen nuances if Dr. Martine hadn't helped. As it is, I find it hard to interpret these hidden darknesses, especially of men I know and admire."

"There's nothing serious, I hope."

"If there were you wouldn't be going on this rush-job dive Helene's ordered! I'm not grounding Dwayne Kepler because he has a cold!"

Laird shook his head and apologized. "Forgive me. I'm just not used to this. There's nothing to worry about, Jacob. You had some awfully strange quirks in your test but the basic reading is as sane as any I've ever seen. Decidedly positive-sum and realistic.

"Still, there are some things that confuse me. I won't go into specifics that might cause you more worry than they're worth while you're on this dive, I'd just appreciate it if you and Helene would each come and see me when you get back."

Jacob thanked the man and walked with him, Martine, and LaRoque toward the elevator.

High overhead, the communications pylon pierced the stasis dome. All around them, beyond the men and machines of the chamber, the blistered rocks of Mercury sparkled or shone dully. Sol was an incandescent yellow ball above a low range of hills.

When the elevator car arrived, Martine and Laird entered, but LaRoque's hand on his arm kept Jacob back until the door had closed, leaving the two of them alone.

Pierre LaRoque whispered to Jacob.

"I want my camera!"

"Sure, LaRoque. Commandant deSilva disarmed the stunner and you can pick it up any time, now that you're cleared."

"And the recording?"

"I've got it. I'm holding onto it, too."

"You have no business . . ."

"Come off it, LaRoque," Jacob groaned. "Why don't you just once cut the act and give someone else credit for some intelligence! I want to know why you were taking sonic pictures of the stasis oscillator in Jeffrey's ship! And I also want to know what gave you the idea my uncle would be interested in them!"

"I owe you a great deal, Demwa," LaRoque said slowly. The thick accent was almost gone. "But I have to know if your political views are at all like your uncle's before I answer you."

"I have a lot of uncles, LaRoque. Uncle Jeremy is in the Confederacy Assembly, but I know you wouldn't be working with him! Uncle Juan is pretty big on theory and very down on illegality . . . my guess is that you mean Uncle James, the family kook. Oh I agree with him about a lot of things, even some things the rest of the family doesn't. But if he's involved in some sort of espionage plot, I'm not going to help to dig him deeper . . . especially in a plot as clumsy as yours appears to be.

"You may not be a murderer or a Probationer, LaRoque, but you are a spy! The only problem is figuring out who you're spying *for*. I'll save that mystery for when we get back to Earth.

"Then, maybe, you can visit me; you and James can both try to talk me out of turning you in. Fair enough?"

LaRoque nodded curtly.

"I can wait, Demwa. Just don't you lose the recordings, eh? I have been through the very hell to get them. I want to get that chance to persuade you to hand them over."

Jacob was looking at the Sun.

"LaRoque, spare me your moanings. You haven't been to hell . . . yet."

He turned away and headed for the elevators. There was time enough for a few hours under a sleep machine. He didn't want to see anyone until it was time to leave.

PART VII

In all evolution there is no
transformation, no "quantum leap," to
compare with this one. Never before has
the life-style of a species, its way of
adapting, changed so utterly and so swiftly.
For some fifteen million years the family
of man foraged as animals among animals.
The pace of events since then has been
explosive . . . the first farming villages . . .
cities . . . supermetropolises . . . all this
has been packed into an instant on the
evolutionary time scale, a mere 10,000 years.

John E. Pfeiffer

21.

DÉJÀ PENSÉ

"Have you ever wondered why most of our starships jump out with crews that are seventy percent female?"

Helene handed Jacob the first liquitube of hot coffee and turned back to the machine to punch out another for herself.

Jacob peeled back the outer seal on the semi-permeable membrane, allowing steam to escape while keeping the dark liquid contained. The liquitube was almost too hot to hold, in spite of its insulation.

Trust Helene to think up another provocative topic! Whenever they were alone together, as alone as one could get on the open deck of a Sunship, Helene deSilva had never missed a chance to engage him in mental gymnastics. The odd thing was that he didn't mind a bit. The contest had lifted his spirits considerably since they had left Mercury ten hours before.

"When I was an adolescent, my friends and I never really cared about the reasons. We just thought it was an added bonus for being a male on a starship. 'Of such thoughts are pubescent fantasies born . . .' Who was it who wrote that, John Two-Clouds? Have you ever read anything by him? I think he was born in High London, so you may have known his parents."

Helene sent him an accusing glare. Jacob had to fight back, for the nth time, a temptation to tell her that the expression was endearing. It *was*, but what fully-grown female professional wanted to be reminded that she still had dimples? It wasn't worth getting a broken arm, anyway.

"Okay, okay," he laughed. "I'll stay on the subject. I suppose the male-female ratio has to do with the way women respond better to high acceleration, heat and cold . . . better hand-eye coordination and superior passive strength. That must make them better spacemen, I guess."

Helene sipped from the siphon of her liquitube. "Yes, all that's part of it. Also most fems appear to be more immune to Jump-sickness. But you know those differences aren't all *that* big. Not enough to make up for the fact that more males volunteer for spaceflight than females.

"Besides, more than half of the crewmen on in-system ships are male, and seven out of ten on military craft."

"Well, I don't know about commercial or research ships, but I'd think that the military selects for an aptitude for fighting. I know it's still not proven, but I'd guess that . . ."

Helene laughed. "Oh, you don't have to be so diplomatic, Jacob. Of course mels make better fighters than fems . . . statistically that is. Amazons like me are the exception. Actually, that *is* one factor in the selection. We don't want too many warrior types aboard a starship."

"But that doesn't make sense! The crews on starships go out into an immense galaxy that hasn't even been fully explored by the Library. You have to face a wild variety of alien races, most of them temperamental as hell. And the Institutes don't forbid fighting among the races. They couldn't even if they tried, judging by what Fagin says. They only try to make it tidy."

"So a starship with humans aboard should be ready for a fracas?" Helene smiled as she rested her shoulder against the wall of the dome. In the mottled red light of the upper chromosphere in hydrogen alpha, her blonde hair looked like a close fitted ping cap. "Well you're right, of course. We do have to be ready to fight. But think for a moment about the situation we face out there.

"We have to deal with literally hundreds of species whose only thing in common is the one thing we lack, a chain of tradition and uplift stretching back two billion years. They've all been using the Library for aeons, adding to it, albeit slowly, all of the time.

"Most of them are cranky, hyper-mindful of their privileges, and dubious of that silly 'wolfling' race from Sol.

"And what can we *do*, when we are challenged by some two-bit species whose extinct patrons uplifted them as talking, obedient riding steeds, who now own two little terraformed planets that sit right astride our only route to the colony on Omnivarium? What can we do when these creatures with no ambition *or* sense of humor stop our ship and demand an incredible *forty* whale songs as a toll?."

Helene shook her head and her eyebrows knotted.

"Wouldn't it be *nice* to fight, at a time like that! A great beauty such as Calypso, filled to the brim with things badly needed by a struggling little community, and with an even more precious cargo of . . . stopped dead in space by a pair of tiny, ancient hulks that were obviously bought, not built, by the "intelligent" camels aboard!" The woman's voice thickened, as she remembered.

"Picture it. New and beautiful, yet primitive, using only the tiny portion of Galactic science we'd been able to absorb when she was refitted, mostly in the drives. . . stopped by hulks older than Caesar but made by someone who used the Library all his life."

Helene stopped for a moment and turned away.

Jacob was moved, but even more he felt honored. He knew Helene well enough, now, to know what an act of trust it was for her to open up like this.

She's been doing most of the work too, he realized. She asks most of the questions—about my past, about my family, about my feelings—for some reason I've been reluctant to ask about her, the person inside. I wonder what's been stopping me? There must be so much in there!

239

"So I suppose the idea is not to fight, because we'd probably lose," he said quietly.

She looked back and nodded. She coughed twice, behind a closed fist.

"Oh, we've a couple of tricks we think we might surprise somebody with sometime, simply *because* we haven't had the Library and it's all they've known. But those tricks have got to be saved for a rainy day.

"Instead, we flatter, fawn, bribe, sing spirituals . . . tap dance . . . and when that fails, we run."

Jacob imagined meeting a shipload of Pila.

"Running must be awful hard at times."

"Yes, but we have a secret way of keeping cool," Helene brightened slightly. For a moment those appealing recesses reappeared at the corners of her smile. "It's one of the biggest reasons why the crew is mostly women."

"Now come on. A fem is just about as likely as a mel to take a poke at someone who insulted her. I don't see that as much of a guarantee."

"Nooo, not normally." She eyed him again with that "appraising" expression. For an instant she seemed about to go on. Then she shrugged.

"Let's sit," she said. "I want to show you something."

She led him around the dome and across the deck to a part of the ship where none of the crew or passengers were, where the circular deck floated two meters away from the shell of the ship.

The sparkling glow of the chromosphere refracted eerily where the stasis screen curved away below their feet. The narrow suspension field allowed light to pass, but twisted it slightly. From where they stood, part of the Big Spot could be seen, its configuration changed considerably since the last dive. Where the field intervened, the sunspot shimmered and rippled with new pulsations, added to its own.

Slowly, Helene lowered herself to the deck and then approached the edge. For a moment she sat with her feet inches from the shimmering, holding her knees under her chin. Then she placed her hands behind her on the deck and allowed her legs to drop into the field.

Jacob swallowed.

"I didn't know you could do that," he said.

He watched as she swung her legs languidly. They moved as if in a thick syrup, the snug sheathing of her shipsuit rippling like something animate.

She lifted her legs straight out and up above the level of the deck, with apparent ease.

"Hmmm, they seem to be all right. I can't push them down very deep, though. I guess the mass of my legs shoves a dimple into the suspension field. At least they don't *feel* upside down when I do it." She let them drop again.

Jacob felt weak in the knees. "You mean you've never done that before?"

She looked up at him and grinned.

"Am I showing off? Yes I guess I was trying to impress you. I'm not crazy though. After you told us about Bubbacub and the vacuum cleaner I went over the equations carefully. It's perfectly safe, so why don't you join me?"

Jacob nodded numbly. After so many other miracles and unexplainable things since he left Earth, this was rather small, after all. The secret, he decided, was not to think at all.

It did feel like a thick syrup that increased in viscosity as he pushed downwards. It was rubbery and pushed back.

And the legs of Jacob's shipsuit felt almost, disconcertingly, alive.

Helene said nothing for a time. Jacob respected her silence. Something was obviously on her mind.

"Was that story about the Finnila Needle really true?" she asked at last, without looking up.

"Yes."

"She must have been quite a woman."

"Yes, she was."

"I mean in addition to being brave. She had to be brave to jump from one balloon to another, twenty miles up in the air, but . . ."

"She was trying to distract them while I defused the Torcher. I shouldn't have let her," Jacob heard his own voice, remote and faded. "But I thought I could protect her at the same time . . . I had a device, you see . . ."

". . . but she must have been quite a person in other ways as well. I wish I could have met her."

Jacob realized that he hadn't said a word aloud.

"Um, yes, Helene. Tania would have liked you." He shook himself. This was getting no one anywhere.

"But I thought we were talking about something else, uh, the ratio of females to males on starships, wasn't that it?"

She was looking at her feet. "We *are* on the same topic, Jacob," she said quietly.

"We are?"

"Sure. You remember I said there was a way to make a largely female crew more cautious in dealing with aliens . . . a way to guarantee that they'll run rather than fight?"

"Yes, but . . ."

"And you know that humanity has been able to plant three colonies so far, but transportation costs are too great to carry many passengers, so increasing the gene pool at an isolated colony is a real problem?" She spoke rapidly, as if embarrassed.

"When we got back the first time and found that the Constitution stood again, the Confederacy made it voluntary for the women on the next jump instead of compulsory. Still, most of us volunteered."

"I . . . I don't understand."

She looked up at him as she smiled.

"Well, maybe now isn't the time. But you should realize that I'm shipping out on Calypso in a few months and there are certain preparations I have to make beforehand.

"And I can be as selective as I want."

She looked straight into his eyes.

Jacob felt his jaw drop.

"Well!" Helene rubbed her hands on her lap and prepared to stand up. "I guess we'd better be heading back. We're pretty near the Active Region, now, and I should be at my station to supervise."

Jacob hurried to his feet and offered her his hand. Neither of them saw anything funny in the archaism.

On their way to the command station, Jacob and Helene stopped to examine the Parametric Laser. Chief

242

Donaldson looked up from the machine as they approached.

"Hi! I think she's all tuned and ready to go. Want a tour?"

"Sure." Jacob hunkered down next to the laser. Its chassis was bolted to the deck. Its long, slender, multi-barreled body swung on a gymballed swivel.

Jacob felt the soft fabric covering Helene's right leg brush lightly against his arm as she stepped over beside him. It didn't help him keep his thoughts straight.

"This here Parametric Laser," Donaldson began, "is my contribution to the attempt to contact the Sun Ghosts. I figured that psi was getting us nowhere, so why not try to communicate with them the way they communicate with us—visually?

"Well now, as you probably know already, most lasers operate on just one or two very narrow spectral bands, particular atomic and molecular transitions, mostly. But this baby will punch out any wavelength you want, just by dialing it in with this control." He pointed to the central of three controls on the face of the chassis.

"Yes," Jacob said. "I know about Parametric Lasers, though I've never seen one. I imagine it has to be pretty powerful to penetrate through our screens and still look bright to the Ghosts."

"In my other life . . ." deSilva drawled ironically (she often referred to her past, before jumping with the Calypso, with defensive sardonicism) ". . . we were able to make multicolored, tunable lasers with optical dyes. They put out a fair amount of power, they were efficient, and incredibly simple."

She smiled. "That is, until you spilled the dye. Then, what a mess! Nothing makes me appreciate Galactic science more than knowing I'll never have to clean a puddle of Rhodamine 6-G off the floor again!"

"Could you really tune through the whole optical spectrum with a single molecule?" Donaldson was incredulous. "How did you power a . . . 'dye laser,' anyway?"

"Oh, with flashlamps sometimes. Usually with an internal chemical reaction using organic energy molecules, like sugars.

243

"You had to use several dyes to cover the whole visible spectrum. Poly-methyl coumarin was used a lot for the blue and green end of the band. Rhodamine and a few others were dyes for tuning in red colors.

"Anyway, that's ancient history. I want to know what devilish plan you and Jacob have cooked up this time!" She dropped down next to Jacob on the deck. Instead of looking at Donaldson, she fixed Jacob with that disconcerting appraisal.

"Well," he swallowed. "It's really quite simple. I took along a library of whale songs and dolphin-ditties when I boarded *Bradbury*, in case the Ghosts turned out to be poets along with everything else. When Chief Donaldson mentioned his idea of aiming a beam at them to communicate, I volunteered the tapes."

"We'll be adding a modified version of an old math contact code. He rigged that one up too." Donaldson grinned. "I wouldn't know a Fibonacci series if one came up and bit me! But Jacob says it's one of the old standards."

"It was," deSilva said. "We never used any of the math routines, though, after the Vesarius. The library makes sure everyone understands each other in space, so there was no use for the old pre-Contact codes."

She pushed lightly on the slim barrel. It rotated smoothly on its swivel. "You aren't going to let this thing swing freely when the laser is on, are you?"

"No, of course we'll be bolting it firmly, so the laser beam fires along a radius from the center of the ship. That should prevent those internal reflections you're probably worryin' about.

"As it is, we'll all want to be wearing these goggles when it's on." Donaldson pulled a pair of thick, dark, wraparound glasses from a sack next to the laser. "Even if there were no danger to the retina, Dr. Martine would insist on it. She's a positive bug on the effects of glare on perception and personality. She turned the whole base upside down, finding bright lights no one even knew were there. Blamed them for the 'mass hallucination' when she arrived. Boy did she change her tune when she *saw* the beasties!"

"Well, it's time for me to get back to work," Helene announced. "I shouldn't have stayed so long. We must be getting close. I'll keep you men posted." Both men rose as she smiled and departed.

Donaldson watched her walk away.

"You know, Demwa, first I thought you were crazy, then I *knew* you had it all together. Now I'm starting to change my mind again."

Jacob sat down. "How's that?"

"Any mel I know would grow a tail and wag it if that fem so much as whistled. I just can't believe your self-control, is all. None of my business, of course."

"You're right. It isn't." Jacob was disturbed that the situation was so obvious. He was beginning to wish this mission was over so he could give the problem his undivided attention.

Jacob shrugged. It was a mannerism he'd made a lot of use of since leaving Earth. "To change the subject, I'd been wondering about this internal reflection business. Has it occurred to you that somebody might be pulling a big hoax?"

"A hoax?"

"With the Sun Ghosts. All someone would have to do is smuggle aboard some sort of holographic projector . . ."

"Forget it," Donaldson shook his head. "That was the first thing we checked. Besides, who'd be able to fake anything as intricate and beautiful as that herd of toruses? Anyway, a projection like that, filling our whole view, would be given away by the columnated rim cameras on flip-side!"

"Well, maybe not the herd, but what about the 'humanoid' Ghosts? They're rather simple and small, and the way they avoid the rim cameras, spinning faster than we can to stay overhead, is pretty uncanny."

"What can I say, Jake? Every piece of equipment carried aboard is carefully inspected, along with everyone's personal items as well, for that very reason. No projector's ever been found, and where could anyone *hide* one on an open ship like this? I'll admit I've wondered about it myself at times. But I don't see any way anyone could be pulling a hoax."

Jacob nodded slowly. Donaldson's argument made sense. Also, how could one reconcile a projection with Bubbacub's trick with the Lethani relic? It was a tempting idea, but a hoax didn't seem very likely.

Distant spicule forests pulsed like waving fountains. Individual jets fenced with one another along the rim of the slowly thobbing supergranulation cell that covered half the sky. In its center lay the Big Spot, a huge eye of black, rimmed by areas of hot brightness.

About ninety degrees around the deck from them, a group of dark silhouettes stood or knelt near the Pilot Board. Only the outlines could be made out against the bright crimson blaze of the photosphere.

Two clumps of shadow could be distinguished from those near the command station. The tall, slender figure of Culla stood slightly to the side, pointing ahead at a tall, wispy filament arch that hung, suspended, over the Spot. The arch grew slowly, perceptibly closer as Jacob watched.

The other identifiable clump of shadow detached itself from the crowd and began to creep in fits and starts toward Jacob and the chief. It was rounded on top, bigger above than below.

"Now there's where you could hide a projector!" Donaldson motioned with his chin toward the bulky, massive silhouette as it creeped toward them with a swaying, twisting motion.

"What, Fagin?"

Jacob whispered. Not that it would make any difference, with the Kanten's hearing what it was. "You can't be serious! Why he's only been on two dives!"

"Yeah," Donaldson mused. "Still, all of those branches and such. . . I'd have sooner searched Bubbacub's undies than have to pry in there after contraband."

For an instant Jacob thought he caught a bit of a burr in the chief engineer's voice. He stared at his neighbor but the man had on his poker face. That in itself was a small miracle for Donaldson. It would be too much if the man were actually being witty.

They both rose to greet Fagin. The Kanten whistled a cheery response, showing no sign that he'd overheard them.

"Commandant Helene deSilva has expressed the opinion that solar weather conditions are surprisingly calm. She said that this will be of great value in solving certain solonomical problems unrelated to the Sun Ghosts. The measurements involved will take very little time. Much less than the time we will be saved, by these excellent conditions.

"In other words, my friends, you have about twenty minutes to get ready."

Donaldson whistled. He called Jacob over and the two men set to work on the laser, bolting it into place and checking the projection tapes.

A few meters away, Dr. Martine rummaged through her space-crate for small pieces of apparatus. Her psi helmet was already on her head and Jacob thought he could overhear her softly curse, "Damn it, this time you're going to *talk* to me!"

22.

DELEGATION

" 'What is their purpose, these creatures of light?' the reporter asks. But he'd do better to ask, 'What purpose has man?' Is it our job to scramble on our metaphorical knees, ignoring the pain with chin upthrust in childish pride, saying to all the universe: 'See me! I am man! I crawl where others walk! But isn't it great that I can crawl anywhere?'

"Adaptability, the Neoliths claim, is the 'specialization' of man. He cannot run as fast as a cheetah, but he can run. He cannot swim as well as an otter, but he can swim. His eyes are not so sharp as a hawk's nor can he store food in his cheeks. So he must train his eyes and create instruments from bits and pieces of tortured earth; not only to let him see, but to outrun the cat and to outswim the otter as well. He can walk across an arctic waste, swim a tropical river, climb a tree and, at the end of his journey, build a nice hotel. There he will clean up and then boast of his accomplishments over dinner with his friends.

"And yet for all recorded time our hero has been dissatisfied. He yearned to know his place in the world. He shouted aloud. He demanded to know *why* he was here! The universe of stars only smiled down at his questions with profound, ambiguous silence.

"He longed for a purpose. Denied, he took his frustration out on his fellow creatures. The specialists around him knew their roles and he hated them for it. They became his slaves, his protein factories. They became the victims of his genocidal rage.

"'Adaptability' soon meant that we needed no one else. Species whose descendents might one day have been great became dust in the holocaust of man's egoism.

"It is only by the slimmest of luck that we became environmentalists shortly before Contact . . . thus keeping from our heads the just wrath of our elders. Or *was* it luck? Is it an accident that John Muir, and those who followed, appeared soon after the first confirmed 'sightings'?

"As the Reporter lies here, in a bubble, in a swaddling of deceptive pink vapor all around, he wonders if the purpose of man may be to be an example. Whatever original sin drove our Patrons off, long ago, is being paid off in a comedy.

"One hopes our neighbors are edified, as well as amused, as they watch us crawl about, gaping in wonder and often resentment at those who are fulfillment incarnate, without ambition."

Pierre LaRoque took his thumb off the recording button and frowned. No, that last part wouldn't do. It sounded almost bitter. More whiney than poignant. In fact, all of it would have to be reworked. There was too little spontaneity. The sentences tried too hard.

He took a sip from the liquitube in his left hand, then began absently stroking his moustache. In front of him the brilliant herd of spinning toruses rose slowly as the ship righted itself. The maneuver had taken less time than he'd expected. Now there was no more time to digress on the plight of mankind. He could, after all, do that any day.

But this, this was extraordinary.

He pressed again on the switch and brought up the microphone.

"Note for rewrite," he said. "More irony, and more

on advantages of certain types of specialization. Also mention the Tymbrimi . . . how they're more adaptable than we'll ever be. Keep it short and upbeat on outcome if *all* humanity participates."

Heretofore the rising herd had consisted of little rings, fifty or more kilometers away. Now the main body came into view, along with a small sliver of the photosphere. The nearest torus was a bright, spinning, blue-green monster. Along its rim, thin blue lines swiftly mixed and shifted, like meshing moire patterns. A white halo shimmered all around it.

LaRoque sighed. This would be his greatest challenge. When holos of these creatures were released everyone and his chimp butler would be tuning in to see if his words measured up. Yet he felt the inverse of what he must make *them* feel. The deeper the ship went into the Sun, the more detached he became. It was as if none of it was really happening. The creatures didn't seem real at all.

Also, he admitted, he was scared.

"Pearls of serendipity they are, strung on necklaces of lambent emerald. If some galactic galleon once foundered here, to leave its treasure on these feathery, fiery reefs, its diadems are now safe. Uncorrupted by time, they sparkle still. No hunter will carry them off in a sack.

"They defy logic, for they should not be here. They defy history, for they are not remembered. They defy the power of our instruments and even those of the Galactics, our elders.

"Imperturbable as Bombadil, they ignore the passing of oxygen and hydrogen in their incessant bickerings, and take nourishment from the most timeless of fonts.

"Do they recall . . . could they have been among the Progenitors, back when the galaxy was new? We hope to ask, but for now they keep their counsel to themselves."

Jacob looked up from his work when the herd came into view again. The sight had less effect on him than it had the first time around. To experience the emotions he'd felt during that first dive he'd have to see something *else* for the very first time. And to see anything anywhere near as impressive, he'd have to Jump.

It was one of the drawbacks of having monkeys for ancestors.

Still, Jacob could spend hours looking at the lovely patterns the toroids made. And for a few moments at a time, when he remembered the significance of what he was seeing, he was awe-struck once again.

The computer board on Jacob's lap bore a shifting pattern of curving, connected lines, isophotes of the Ghost they'd seen an hour before.

It hadn't been much of a contact. One isolated Solarian had been caught by surprise as the ship came out from behind a thick wisp of filament near the edge of the herd.

It darted away from them, then hovered suspiciously at a few kilometers distance. Commandant deSilva had ordered the ship turned so that Donaldson's Parametric Laser could bear on the fluttering creature.

At first the Ghost had backed away. Donaldson muttered and cursed as he adjusted the laser, to carry the various modulations of Jacob's contact tape.

Then the creature reacted. It's (tentacles? wings?) shot out from the center as if snapped taut. It began to ripple colorfully.

Then, in a flash of brilliant green, it was gone.

Jacob examined computer readouts from that reaction. The Solarian had presented the rim cameras with a good view. The earliest recordings showed that part of its rippling was in phase with the bass rhythm of the whale melody. Jacob was now trying to find out if the complicated display it emitted just before jetting away had a pattern that might be interpretable as a reply.

He finished drawing the analysis program he wanted the computer to pursue. It was to look for variations on the whale-song theme and rhythm in three regimes, color, time, and brightness across the surface of the Ghost. If it found anything definite he'd be able to set up a computer linkup in realtime during the next encounter.

That is, if there *was* a next encounter. The whale song had only been an introduction to the sequence of scales and mathematical series Jacob had planned to

251

send. But the Ghost hadn't stuck around to "listen" to the rest.

He put the computer board aside and lowered his couch so that he could look at the nearest toroids without moving his head. A pair of them swung slowly by at forty-five degrees from the angle of the deck.

Apparently the "spinning" of the torus creatures was more complicated than had been previously thought. The intricate, swiftly changing patterns that swept rapidly around the rim of each represented something in their internal makeup.

When two of the toroids touched each other, nudging for better positions in the magnetic fields, there was no change in the rotating figures. They interacted with each other as if they weren't spinning at all.

The pushing and shoving became more pronounced with time as they transited the herd. Helene deSilva suggested that it was because the active region they were above was dying out. The magnetic fields were getting more and more diffuse.

Culla dropped into the couch next to him, bringing his mashies together in a clack. Jacob was starting to recognize some of the rhythms Culla's dental work made in various situations. It had taken a long time to realize that they were part of a Pring's fundamental repertoire, like facial expressions for a human being.

"May I shit here, Jacob?" Culla asked. "This ish my firsht opportunity to thank you for your cooperation back on Mercury."

"You don't have to thank me, Culla. A two-year secrecy oath is pretty much de rigueur for an incident like this. Anyway, once Commandant deSilva got orders from Earth it was pretty clear that no one would be going home until they signed."

"Shtill, you had every right to tell the world, the galaxy. The Library Inshtitute hash been shamed by Bubbacub'sh actionsh. It ish admirable of you, the dishcoverer of hish . . . mishtake, to show reshtraint and let them make ammendsh."

"What will the Institute do . . . besides punishing Bubbacub?"

Culla took a sip from his ubiquitous liquitube. His eyes shone.

"They will probably cancel Earth's debt and donate

252

Branch shervices free for shome time. A longer time if the Confederacy agreesh to a period of silence. I cannot overshtate their eagernesh to avoid a shcandal.

"In addition, you will probably be rewarded."

"Me?" Jacob felt numb. To a "primitive" Earthman, almost any reward the Galactics chose to give would be like a magic lamp. He could hardly believe what he was hearing.

"Yesh, although there will probably be shome bitternesh that you did not keep your dishcoveriesh more private. The magnitude of their generoshity will probably be invershe to the notoriety Bubbacub'sh case getsh."

"Oh, I see." The bubble was burst. It was one thing to get a token of gratitude from powers-that-be, and quite another to be offered a bribe. Not that the value of the reward would be any less. In fact, the prize would probably be even more valuable.

Or would it? No alien thought exactly the way a human would. The directors of the Institute of the Libraries were an enigma to him. All he knew for certain was that they wouldn't like to get a bad press. He wondered if Culla was speaking now in his official capacity, or simply predicting what he thought would happen next.

Culla suddenly turned and looked up at the passing herd. His eyes glowed and a short buzzing came from behind the thick, prehensile lips. The Pring pulled the microphone from the slot next to his couch.

"Excushe me, Jacob. But I think I shee shomething. I musht report to the Commandant."

Culla spoke briefly into the microphone, not moving his gaze from a position about thirty degrees to their right and twenty-five degrees high. Jacob looked but saw nothing. He could hear a distant murmuring of Helene's voice filling the region of the head of Culla's couch. Then the ship began to turn.

Jacob checked the computer board. The results were in. The previous encounter had elicited nothing recognizable as a reply. They'd just have to keep on doing as they had before.

"Sophonts," Helene's voice rang out over the intercom, "Pring Culla has made another sighting. Please return to your stations."

Culla's mashies clacked. Jacob looked up.

At about forty-five degrees, a tiny flickering point of light began to grow just beyond the bulk of the nearest toroid. The blue dot grew as it approached until they could make out five uneven appendages, bilaterally symmetric. It loomed up swiftly, then stopped.

Sun Ghost manifestation, type two, leered down at them in its gross mockery of the shape of a man. The chromosphere glowed red through the jagged holes of its eyes and mouth.

No attempt was made to bring the apparition in line with the flip-side cameras. It would probably have been futile and besides, this time the P-laser took precedence.

He told Donaldson to continue playing the primary contact tape, from the point where the last contact broke off.

The engineer raised his microphone.

"Everyone please put on your goggles. We're going to turn on the laser now." He put on his own, then looked around to make sure everyone in sight had complied (Culla was exempted; they took his word for it that he was in no danger). Then he threw the switch.

Even through the goggles, Jacob could see a dim glow against the inner surface of the shield wall as the beam punched through toward the Ghost. He wondered if the anthropomorphic figure would be more cooperative than the earlier, "natural-shaped" manifestation had been. For all he knew, this was the same creature. Maybe it left, earlier, to "put on its make-up" for this present appearance.

The Ghost fluttered impassively while the beam from the Communication Laser shone right through it. Not far away, Jacob could hear Martine curse softly.

"Wrong, wrong, wrong!" she hissed. Her psi helmet and goggles made only her nose and chin visible. "There's something but it's not there. Dammit! What in hell's the matter with this thing!"

Suddenly, the apparition swelled like a butterfly squashed flat against the outside of the ship. The features of its "face" smeared out into long narrow strips of ochre blackness. The arms and body spread until the

254

creature was nothing but a ragged rectangular band of blue across ten degrees of the sky. Flecks of green began to form, here, and there, along its surface. They dodged about, mixed and coalesced, and then began to take on coherent form.

"Dear sweet God in heaven," Donaldson murmured.

From somewhere nearby Fagin let out a whistling, shivering, diminished seventh. Culla began to chatter.

Across its length, the Solarian was covered with bright green letters, in the Roman alphabet. They spelled:

LEAVE NOW. DO NOT RETURN.

Jacob gripped the sides of his couch. Despite the sound effects of the E.T.'s, and the hoarse breathing of the humans, the silence was unbearable.

"Millie!" he tried as hard as he could not to shout. "Are you getting anything?"

Martine moaned.

"Yes . . . NO! I'm getting *something*, but it doesn't make sense! It doesn't correlate!"

"Well try sending a question! Ask if it's receiving your psi!"

Martine nodded and pressed her hands against her face in concentration.

The letters immediately reformed overhead.

CONCENTRATE. SPEAK ALOUD FOR FOCUS.

Jacob was stunned. Deep inside he could feel his suppressed half shivering in horror. What he couldn't solve terrified Mr. Hyde.

"Ask it why it'll talk to us now and not before."

Martine repeated the question aloud, slowly.

THE POET. HE WILL SPEAK FOR US. HE IS HERE.

"No, no I can't!" LaRoque cried. Jacob turned quickly and saw the little journalist, scrunched, terrified near the food machines.

HE WILL SPEAK FOR US.

The green letters glowed.

"Doctor Martine," Helene deSilva called. "Ask the Solarian why we shouldn't come back."

After a pause, the letters shifted again.
WE WANT PRIVACY. PLEASE LEAVE.

"And if we do come back? Then what?" Donaldson asked. Grimly, Martine repeated the question.

NOTHING. YOU WON'T SEE US. MAYBE OUR YOUNG, OUR CATTLE.

NOT US.

That explained the two types of Solarians, Jacob thought. The "normal" variety must be the young, given simple tasks such as shepherding the toroids. Where, then, did the adults live? What kind of culture did they have? How could creatures made of ionized plasma communicate with watery human beings? Jacob ached at the creature's threat. If they wanted to, the adults could avoid a Sunship, or any conceivable fleet of Sunships, as easily as an eagle could a balloon. If they cut off contact now, humans could never force them to renew it.

"Pleashe," Culla asked. "Ashk it if Bubbacub offended them." The Pring's eyes glowed hotly and the chattering continued, muffled, between each word he spoke.

BUBBACUB MEANS NOTHING. INSIGNIFICANT. JUST LEAVE.

The Solarian began to fade. The ragged rectangle grew smaller as it slowly backed away.

"Wait!" Jacob stood up. He stretched out one hand grabbing at nothing.

"Don't cut us off! We're your nearest neighbors! We only want to share with you! At least tell us who you are!"

The image was blurred with distance. A wisp of darker gas swept in and covered the Solarian, but not before they read one last message. With a crowd of "young" gathered around it, the adult repeated one of its earlier sentences.

THE POET SPEAKS FOR US.

PART VIII

In ancient days two aviators procured to
themselves wings. Daedalus flew safely through
the middle air and was duly honoured on his
landing. Icarus soared upwards to the sun till the
wax melted which bound his wings and his
flight ended in fiasco. . . . The classical authorities
tell us, of course, that he was only 'doing a
stunt'; but I prefer to think of him as the man
who brought to light a serious constructional defect
in the flying-machines of his day.

From *Stars and Atoms*, by Sir Arthur Eddington
(Oxford University Press, 1927, p. 41)

23.

AN EXCITED STATE

Pierre LaRoque sat with his back to the utility dome. He hugged his knees and stared vacantly at the deck. He wondered, miserably, if Millie would give him a shot to last him until the Sunship got out of the chromosphere.

Unfortunately, that wouldn't be in keeping with his new role as a prophet. He shuddered. During his entire career he had never realized how much it meant to have only to comment, and not to have to shape events. The Solarian had given him a curse, not a blessing.

He wondered, dully, if the creature had chosen him in an ironic whim . . . as a joke: Or had it somehow planted words deep within him that would come out when he got back to Earth, shocking and embarrassing him?

Or am I just supposed to spout out my own opinions as I always have? He rocked slowly, miserably. To foist one's ideas on others by dint of personality was one thing. To speak clothed in a prophet's mantle was quite another.

The others had gathered near the command station to discuss the next step. He could hear them talking and wished they'd just go away. Without looking up, he could feel it when they turned and stared at him.

LaRoque wished he were dead.

"I say we should bump him off," Donaldson suggested. His burr was very pronounced, now. Jacob, listening nearby, wished the ethnic languages fad had never caught on. "There'll be no end of the trouble that man'll cause if 'e gets loose on Earth," the engineer finished.

Martine chewed on her lip for a moment. "No, that wouldn't be wise. Better beam Earth for instructions when we get back to Hermes. The feds may decide to use up an emergency sequester allotment on him, but I don't think anyone would get away with actually eliminating Peter."

"I'm surprised you react that way to the chief's suggestion," Jacob said. "One would think you'd be aghast at the idea."

Martine shrugged. "By now it must be clear to all of you that I represent a faction in the Confederacy Assembly. Peter is my friend, but if I felt it was my duty to Earth to put him out of the way, I'd do it myself." She looked grim.

Jacob wasn't as surprised as he might have been. If the chief engineer felt a need to put up a layer of flippancy, to get through the shock of the last hour, many of the others had dropped all pretense. Martine was willing to think about the unthinkable. Nearby, LaRoque didn't pretend to be anything but scared as he rocked slowly, apparently oblivious to them all.

Donaldson raised his index finger.

"Did you notice that the Solarian didn' say anything at all about the message beam? It passed right through im and he didn't seem to care. Yet earlier, the other Ghost . . ."

"The juvenile."

". . . the juvenile, definitely reacted."

Jacob scratched his earlobe. "There's no end to mysteries. Why has the adult creature always avoided being in line with our rim instruments? Has it got something to hide? Why all the threatening gestures on all the previous dives, when he was capable of communi-

260

cating ever since Dr. Martine brought her psi helmet aboard months ago?"

"Maybe your P-laser gave it an element it needed," a crewman suggested, an Oriental gentleman named Chen, whom Jacob had met only at the start of the dive. "An alternative hypothesis would be that it was waiting for someone of reasonable status to speak to."

Martine sniffed.

"That's the theory we were working on on the last dive, and it didn't work. Bubbacub faked contact, and for all of his talents Fagin failed . . . oh, you mean Peter . . ."

The silence could be cut with a knife.

"Jacob, I sure wish we could have found a projector," Donaldson smiled wryly. "T'would have solved all our problems."

Jacob grinned back, without humor. "Deux ex machina, Chief? You know better than to expect special favors from the universe."

"We might as well resign ourselves," Martine said. "We may never see another adult Ghost. Folks were skeptical about all of these stories about 'anthropomorphic shapes' back on Earth. It's just the word of a couple dozen sophonts that have seen them, plus a few blurred photos. In time it may be all put down to hysteria, despite my tests." She looked down gloomily.

Jacob was aware of Helene deSilva standing next to him. She had been strangely silent since calling them together a few minutes before.

"Well at least this time Sundiver itself isn't threatened," Jacob said. "The solonomical research can go on, and so can studies of the toroid herds. The Solarian said that they won't interfere."

"Yeah," Donaldson added. "But will he?" he gestured at LaRoque.

"We have to decide what to do next. We're drifting near the bottom of the herd now. Do we go up and keep poking around? Maybe Solarians vary among themselves as much as we humans do. Maybe the one we met was a grouch." Jacob suggested.

"I hadn't thought of that," Martine commented.

"Let's put the Parametric Laser on automatic and

add a portion in coded English to the communication tape. It'll beam into the herd as we spiral leisurely upward, on the off chance that a friendlier adult Solarian might be attracted."

"If one is, I sure hope it doesn't scare me out of my codpiece like that last one did," Donaldson muttered.

Helene deSilva rubbed her shoulders as if fighting a chill. "Has anyone else got anything to say 'en camera'? Then I'm going to settle the humans-only part of this discussion by ruling out any precipitate action concerning Mr. LaRoque. Just everybody keep your eyes on him.

"This meeting is in recess. Think about ideas on what to do next. Someone please ask Fagin and Culla to join us at the refreshment center in twenty minutes. That's all."

Jacob felt a hand on his arm. Helene stood next to him.

"Are you all right?" he asked.

"Fine ... fine." She smiled without much conviction. "I'd just ... Jacob, would you come to my office with me, please?"

"Sure, after you."

Helene shook her head. Her fingers dug into his arm and she pulled him along in a fast walk toward the closet-sized cubbyhole in the side of the dome that served as a captain's office. When they were inside she cleared a space on the tiny desk and motioned for him to sit. Then she closed the door and sagged back against it.

"Oh, God," she sighed.

"Helene ..." Jacob started forward, then stopped. Her eyes blazed blue up at him.

"Jacob," she was making a concentrated effort to be calm. "Can you promise me you'll do me a favor for a few minutes and not talk about it afterwards? I can't tell you what it is until you agree." Her eyes appealed silently.

Jacob didn't have to think. "Of course, Helene. You can ask anything. But tell me what's the ..."

"Then please, just hold me." Her voice trailed off in a cry. She came up against his chest with her arms

262

tucked in in front of her. In mute surprise, Jacob put his arms around her and held on tightly.

Slowly he rocked her back and forth as a series of powerful tremors ran through her body. "Sshhh . . . It's all right . . ." He spoke reassuring nonsense words. Her hair brushed his cheek and her smell seemed to fill the tiny room. It was heady.

For a time they stood together silently. She moved her head slowly on his shoulder.

The tremors subsided. Gradually her body relaxed. He stroked the taut muscles of her back with one hand and they loosened one by one.

Jacob wondered who was doing whom the favor. He hadn't felt this peaceful, this calm, for Ifni knew how long. It moved him that she trusted him so.

More, it made him *happy*. There was a bitter little voice below that was gnashing its teeth at this moment, but he wasn't listening Doing what he was doing now felt more natural than breathing.

After a few more moments, Helene lifted her head. When she spoke her voice was thick.

"I've never been so scared in all my life," she said. "I want you to understand that I didn't *have* to do this. I could have been Iron Lady for the rest of the dive . . . but you were here, available . . . I had to. I'm sorry."

Jacob noticed that Helene made no effort to back away. He kept his arms around her.

"No problem," he spoke softly. "Sometime later I'll tell you how nice it was. Don't worry about being scared. I just about went out of my skin when I saw those letters. Curiosity and numbness are my defense mechanisms. You saw how the others were reacting. You just had more responsibility is all."

Helene didn't say anything. She brought her hands up and put them on his shoulders, without creating a space between them.

"Anyway," Jacob went on, brushing free locks of her hair into place. "You must have been more startled lots of times during your Jumps."

Helene stiffened and pushed back from his chest.

"Mr. Demwa, you are intolerable! You and your constantly mentioning my Jumps! Do you think I've ever been as scared as that?! Just how old do you think I am?"

Jacob smiled. She hadn't pushed back hard enough to shake off his arms. Obviously she wasn't ready for him to let go.

"Well, relativity-wise . . ." he began.

"*Fuck* relativity! I'm twenty-five! I may have seen more sky than you have but I've experienced a hell of lot less of the *real* universe than you . . . and my competence rating says nothing about how I feel inside! It's *scary* having to be perfect and strong and responsible for people's lives . . . for *me* at least, it is, unlike you, you impervious, imperturbable, once-upon-a-time hero-oaf, standing there calm as you please, just like Captain Beloc on Calypso when we ran that crazy fake blockade at J8'lek and . . . and now I'm going to go highly illegal and order you to kiss me, since you don't seem about to do it on your own!"

She looked at him defiantly. When Jacob laughed and pulled her toward him, she resisted momentarily. Then her arms slid around his neck and her lips pressed up against his.

Jacob distantly felt her tremble again. But this time it was different. It was hard to tell *how* it was different, since he was busy at the moment. Enchantingly so.

Suddenly, agonizingly, he realized how long it had been since . . . two very long years. He pushed the thought aside. Tania was dead, and Helene was beautifully, wonderfully alive. He held her tighter and answered her passion in the only way possible.

"Excellent therapy, Doctor," she teased as he tried to comb the knots out of his hair. "I feel like a million bucks, though I'll admit you look like you've been through a wringer."

"What's . . . urk, what's a 'wringer'? Never mind, I don't want any explanations of your anachronisms. Look at you! You're *proud* of making me feel like a bar of steel that's been melted and bent out of shape!"

"Yup."

Jacob didn't suceed at suppressing a grin. "Shut up and respect your elders. How much time do we have, anyway?"

Helene glanced at her ring. "About two minutes. Damned awkward time to have a meeting. You were just starting to get interesting. Who the hell called it at such an inconvenient moment?"

"You did."

"Ah, yes. So I did. Next time I'll give you at least a half hour, and we'll investigate matters in more detail."

Jacob nodded uncertainly. It was hard to tell, sometimes, at what level this fem was kidding.

Before she unlatched the door, Helene soberly leaned up and kissed him.

"Thank you, Jacob."

He caressed the side of her face with his left hand. She pressed against it briefly. There was nothing to say when he brought the hand away.

Helene opened the door and looked out. There was no one in sight but the pilot. Everyone else had probably gathered for the second meeting at the refreshment center.

"Let's go," she said. "I could eat a horse!"

Jacob shuddered. If he was going to get to know Helene better, he'd better be prepared for a lot of exercise for his imagination. A horse indeed!

Still, he dropped a little less than a foot back as they walked, so he could watch Helene move. It was so distracting that he didn't notice when a spinning torus swung past the ship, its sides emblazoned with starbursts and surrounded by a halo as white and bright as the down on the breast of a dove.

24.

SPONTANEOUS
EMISSION

Culla was just pulling a liquitube out of Fagin's foliage when they returned. One arm was enmeshed in the Kanten's leafy branches. The Pring held another liquitube in his other hand.

"Welcome back," Fagin fluted. "Pring Culla was just assisting me with my dietary supplement. I am afraid that in doing so he has neglected his own."

"No problem, shir," Culla said. He slowly pulled the tube backward.

Jacob came up behind the Pring to watch. This was a chance to learn more about Fagin's workings. The Kanten once told him that his species had no modesty taboo, so surely he wouldn't mind if Jacob sighted along Culla's arm to see what sort of orifice the semi-vegetable alien used.

He was bent over thus when suddenly Culla jerked back, pulling the liquitube free. His elbow collided painfully with the ridge above Jacob's eye, sending him backwards on his rump.

Culla chattered loudly. The liquitubes dropped from the hands that fell limply to his sides. Helene had trouble choking back a fit of laughter. Jacob hurried to his feet. His "I'll-get-even-someday" grimace at Helene only made her cough more loudly.

"Forget it, Culla," he said. "No damage done. It was my fault. I have a spare eye anyway." He resisted the urge to rub the spot where it hurt.

Culla looked down at him with shining eyes. The chattering subsided.

"You are mosht gracioush, Friend-Jacob," he said at last. "In a proper client-elder shituation I wash at fault for careleshnesh. I thank you for forgiving me."

"Tut tut, my friend." Jacob waved it aside. Actually he could feel the beginnings of a nasty bump forming. Still, it would be worthwhile changing the subject to save Culla further embarrassment.

"Speaking of spare eyes, I read that your species, and most of those on Pring, had only one eye before the Pila arrived and started their genetic program."

"Yesh, Jacob. The Pila gave ush two eyesh for esthetic purposhesh. In the galaxy mosht bipedsh are binocular. They did not want ush . . . teashed by the other young racesh."

Jacob frowned. There was something . . . he knew Mr. Hyde already had it but was holding back, still in his peevish mood.

Damnit, it's my unconscious!

No use. Oh well.

"But Culla, I also read that your species were arboreal . . . even *brachiating*, if I remember right . . ."

"What's that mean?" Donaldson whispered to deSilva. "It means they used to swing from tree limbs," she answered. "Now hush!"

". . . But if they had only one eye how did your ancestors have good enough depth perception to keep from missing when they reached for the next branch?"

Before Jacob even finished his sentence he felt jubilation. *That* had been the question Mr. Hyde was holding back! So the little devil *didn't* have a complete lock on unconscious insight! Helene was doing him good already. He hardly cared what Culla's answer was.

"I thought you knew, Friend-Jacob. I overheard Commandant deShilva explaining during our firsht dive that

I have different receiversh than you do. My eyesh can detect *phase* ash well ash intenshity."

"Yes," Jacob was starting to have fun now. He'd have to keep his eyes on Fagin. The old Kanten would warn him if he was getting into an area Culla found touchy.

"Yes, but sunlight, particularly in a forest, would have to be totally incoherent . . . random in phase. Now a dolphin uses a system like yours in her sonar, keeping the phase and all. But she provides her own coherent phase field by letting out well-timed squeaks into her surroundings."

Jacob stepped back, enjoying a dramatic pause. His foot fell on one of the liquitubes Culla had dropped. Absently he picked it up.

"So if all your ancestors' eyes did was retain the phase, the whole thing still wouldn't work without having a source of coherent light in your environment." Jacob got excited. "Natural lasers? Do your forests have some *natural* source of laser light?"

"By George that would be interesting!" Donaldson commented.

Culla nodded. "Yesh, Jacob. We call them the . . ." his mashies came together in a complicated rhythm ". . . plants. It'sh incredible that you dedushed their exishtence from sho few cluesh. You are to be congratulated. I will show you picturesh of one when we get back."

Jacob caught a glimpse of Helene, smiling at him, possessively. (Deep inside his head he felt a distant rumbling. He ignored it.) "Yes, I'd like to see it, Culla."

The liquitube was sticky in his hand. There was a smell in the air, like new mown hay.

"Here, Culla." He held out the liquitube. "I think you dropped this." Then his arm froze. He stared at the tube for a moment then broke out laughing.

"Millie, come here!" he shouted. "Look at this!" He held out the tube to Dr. Martine and pointed to the label.

"3-(alpha-Acetonylbenzyl)—4-hydroxycoumarin alkalide mix?" She looked uncertain for a moment then her jaw dropped. "Why, that's Warfarin! So it's one of Culla's dietary supplements! Well then how the hell did a sample get into Dwayne's pharmacopoeia?"

Jacob smiled ruefully. "I'm afraid that misunderstanding was all my fault I absentmindedly picked up a sample of one of Culla's beverage mix tablets back aboard the *Bradbury*. I was so sleepy then that I forgot about it. It must have gone into the same pocket where I later stashed Dr. Kepler's samples. They all went together to Dr. Laird's lab.

"It was just a wild coincidence that one of Culla's nutrient supplements happened to be identical with an old terrestrial poison, but boy did it have me going in circles! I was thinking Bubbacub slipped it to Kepler to make him unstable, but I was never very happy with that theory." He shrugged.

"Well I, for one, am relieved the whole thing is solved!" Martine laughed. "I didn't like what people were thinking about me!"

It was a minor discovery. But somehow clearing up one small, nagging mystery had transformed the mood of those present. They talked animatedly.

The only pall came as Pierre LaRoque passed by, laughing softly. Dr. Martine went to ask him to join them, but the little man just shook his head, then resumed walking in a slow path around the rim of the ship.

Helene stood next to Jacob. She touched the hand that still held Culla's liquitube.

"Speaking of coincidences, did you take a close look at the formula for Culla's supplement?" She stopped and looked up, Culla came up to them and bowed.

"If you are finished now, Jacob. I will put thish shticky tube away."

"What? Oh sure, Culla. Here. Now what were you saying, Helene?"

Even when her face was serious it was hard not to be struck by her beauty. It's the initial "falling" of love that, for a time, makes listening to one's lover difficult.

". . . I just saying that I noticed an interesting coincidence when Dr. Martine read that chemical formula aloud. Do you remember earlier, when we were talking about organic dye laser's? Well . . ."

Helene's voice faded away. Jacob could see her mouth move, but all he could make out was one word: " . . . coumarin . . ."

269

There was trouble erupting below. His channeled neurosis had mutinied. Mr. Hyde was trying to stop him from listening to Helene. In fact, he suddenly realized, his other half had been holding back its usual tithe of insight ever since Helene had hinted, in their conversation at the edge of the deck, that she wanted *him* to give her the genes she'd be taking to the stars when the Calypso jumped.

Hyde hates Helene! he realized with a shock. The first girl I've met who could begin to replace what I've lost (a tremor, like a migraine, threatened to split his skull) and Hyde *hates* her! (The headache came and went instantly).

What was more, that part of his unconscious had been holding out on him. It had seen all of the pieces and hadn't let them surface. This was a violation of the agreement. It was intolerable, and he couldn't figure out why!

"Jacob, are you all right?" Helene's voice was back. She looked at him quizzically. Over her shoulder he could see Culla, looking down at them from near the food machines.

"Helene," he said abruptly. "Listen, I left a small box of pills by the Pilot Board. They're for these headaches I get sometimes . . . could you please look for them for me?" He brought a hand up to his forehead and grimaced.

"Why . . . sure," Helene touched his arm. "Why don't you come with me? You could lie down. We'll talk . . ."

"No," he took her by the shoulders and gently turned her the right way. "Please, you go. I'll wait here." Furiously, he fought down panic at the time it was taking to get her away.

"Okay, I'll be right back," Helene said. As she walked away Jacob sighed with relief. Most of those present had their goggles on their belts, per standing orders. The competent and efficient Commandant deSilva had left hers at her couch.

When she had gone about ten meters toward her destination, Helene began to wonder.

Jacob never left any box of pills by the Pilot Board. I would have known it if he had. He wanted to get *rid* of me! But why?

She looked back. Jacob was just turning away from a food machine with a protein roll in his hand. He smiled at Martine and nodded at Chen, then started to walk past Fagin to get out onto the open deck. Behind him Culla watched the group with bright eyes, near the gravity-loop hatch.

Jacob didn't look like he had a headache at all! Helene felt hurt and confused.

Well if he doesn't want me around, that's fine. I'll make a pretense of looking for his damned pills!

She started to turn when, suddenly, Jacob tripped on one of Fagin's root pods and went sprawling on the deck. The protein roll bounced away and fetched up against the Parametric Laser housing. Before she could react, Jacob was on his feet again, smiling sheepishly. He walked over to pick up the food ball. Bending over, his shoulder touched the barrel of the laser.

Blue light flooded the room instantly. Whooping alarms howled. Helene instinctively covered her eyes behind her arm and grabbed for the goggles at her waist.

They weren't there!

Her couch was three meters away. She could picture where she was exactly, and where she'd stupidly left the goggles. She turned and dove for them, coming up again in one movement, the protectors over her eyes.

There were bright spots everywhere. The P-laser, shoved out of plumb with the ship's radius, was sending its beam bouncing about the concave inner surface of the Sunship's shell. The modulated "contact code" flashed against the deck and dome.

Bodies writhed on the deck near the food machines. No one had approached the P-laser to shut it off. Where were Jacob and Donaldson? Were they blinded in the first instant?

Several figures struggled near the gravity-loop hatch. In the flashing, sepulchral light she saw that they were Jacob Demwa and the chief engineer ... and Culla. They ... Jacob was trying to shove a *bag* over the alien's head!

There was no time to decide what to do. Between intervening in the mysterious fight and eliminating a possible danger to her ship, Helene didn't have to choose.

She ran over to the P-laser, ducking under faint, crisscrossing trails, and tore out the plug.

The flashing points of light stopped abruptly, except for one that coincided with a shriek of pain and a crash, near the hatchway. The alarms shut off and suddenly there was only the sound of people moaning.

"Captain, what is it? What's happening?" The voice of the pilot rang out over the intercom. Helene picked up the mike from a couch nearby.

"Hughes," she said quickly. "What's ship's status?"

"Status nominal, sir. But it's a good thing I had my goggles on! What the devil happened?"

"P-laser got loose. Continue as is. Hold her steady about a klick from the herd. I'll be back to you soon." She released the mike and raised her head to shout. "Chen! Dubrowsky! Report!" She peered about in the dimness.

"Over here, skipper!" It was Chen's voice. Helene cursed and tore off the goggles. Chen was over beyond the hatchway. He knelt over a figure on the deck.

"It's Dubrowsky," the man said. "He's dead. Fried through the eyes."

Dr. Martine cowered behind Fagin's thick trunk. The Kanten whistled softly as Helene hurried over.

"Are you two okay?"

Fagin let out a long note that sounded vaguely like a slurred "yes." Martine nodded once, jerkily, but she stayed clutching Fagin's trunk. Her goggles were skewed over her face. Helene took them off.

"Come on, Doctor. You have patients." She pulled at Martine's arm. "Chen! Go to my office and get the aid-kit! On the double!"

Martine started to get up, then sagged back shaking her head.

Helene gritted her teeth and hauled up on the arm she held, suddenly, snapping the older woman upwards with a gasp. Martine staggered to her feet.

Helene slapped her once across the face. "Wake up, Doctor! You'll help me with these men or so help me I'll kick your teeth in!" She took Martine's arm and supported her across the few meters to where Chief Donaldson and Jacob Demwa lay.

Jacob moaned and began to stir. Helene felt her heart

rise when he took his arm away from his face. The burns were superficial and they hadn't touched the eyes. Jacob had his goggles on.

She steered Martine over next to Donaldson and made her sit. The chief engineer was badly seared along the left side of his face. The left lens of his goggles was smashed.

Chen arrived on the run, carrying the aid-kit.

Dr. Martine turned away from Donaldson and shuddered. Then she looked up and saw the crewman with the medical bag. She held out her hands for it.

"Will you need help, Doctor?" Helene asked.

Martine spread instruments on the deck. She shook her head without looking up.

"No. Be quiet."

Helene called Chen over. "Go look for LaRoque and Culla. Report when you've found them." The man ran off.

Jacob moaned again and tried to rise up on his elbows. Helene got a cloth from the fountain nearby and wet it. She knelt by Jacob and pulled on his shoulders to get his head onto her lap.

He winced as she dabbed gently at his wounds.

"Oh . . ." he moaned and brought a hand to the top of his head. "I should've known better. His ancestors were tree swingers. He'd have to have a chimp's strength. And he looks so weak!"

"Can you tell me what happened?" she asked softly.

Jacob grunted as he groped beneath his back with his left hand. He tugged on something a couple of times. Finally he pulled out the large bag the protection goggles had come in. He looked at it, then tossed it away.

"My head feels as if it's been sandblasted," he said. He pushed himself up into sitting position, wavered for a moment with his hands on his head, then he let them drop.

"Culla wouldn't happen to be lying unconscious around here, would he? I was hoping I turned into a fighting fool after he knocked me dizzy, but I guess I just blacked out."

"I don't know where Culla is," Helene said. "Now what . . . ?"

Chen's voice boomed over the intercom.

"Skipper? I've found LaRoque. He's at degrees two-forty. He's okay. In fact, he didn't even know anything was wrong!"

Jacob moved over next to Dr. Martine and began to talk to her urgently. Helene stood up and went to the intercom next to the food center.

"Have you seen Culla?"

"Nossir, not a sign anywhere. He must be on flipside." Chen's voice dropped. "I had the impression there was a fight going on. Do you know what happened?"

"I'll get back to you when I know something. Meanwhile you'd better relieve Hughes."

Jacob joined her by the intercom.

"Donaldson will be all right, but he'll need a new eye. Listen, Helene, I'm going to have to go after Culla. Lend me one of your men, will you? Then you'd better get us out of here as fast as you can."

She whirled. "You just *killed* one of my men! Dubrowsky's dead! Donaldson is blinded, and now you want me to send someone *else* to help you harass poor Culla some more? What madness is this?"

"I didn't kill anyone, Helene."

"I *saw* you, you clumsy oaf! You bumped the p-laser and it went crazy! So did you! Why were you attacking Culla?"

"Helene . . ." Jacob winced. He brought a hand to his head. "There's no time to explain. You've got to get us out of here. There's no telling what he'll do down there now that we know."

"Explain first!"

"I . . . I bumped the laser on purpose . . . I . . ."

Helene's shipsuit fit so snugly that Jacob would never have thought she had the snug little stun gun that appeared in her hand. "Go on, Jacob," she said evenly.

". . . He was watching me. I knew if I showed a sign I'd caught on, he could blind us all in an instant. I sent you away to get you clear and then went after the goggles bag. I kicked the laser free to confuse him . . . laser light all over the place . . ."

"And killed and maimed my men!"

Jacob drew himself together. "Listen, you little nit!"

274

He towered over her. "I turned that beam down! It might blind but it wouldn't burn!

"Now if you don't believe me, knock me out! Strap me in! Only get us out of here fast, before Culla kills us all!"

"Culla . . ."

"His *eyes*, damnit! *Coumarin!* His 'dietary supplement' is a dye used in lasers! *He* killed Dubrowsky when he tried to help me and Donaldson!

"He was lying about that laser plant back on his home planet! The Pring have their *own* source of coherent light! He's been projecting the 'adult' type Sun Ghosts all along! And . . . my god!" Jacob punched at the air.

". . . if his projector is subtle enough to display fake 'Ghosts' on the inside of a Sunship shell, it must be good enough to interact with the optical inputs of those Library designed computers! *He* programmed the computers to tag LaRoque as a Probationer. And . . . and I was next to him when he programmed Jeff's ship to self-destruct! He was feeding in commands all the time I was admiring the pretty lights!"

Helene backed away, shaking her head. Jacob took a step toward her, looming large with fists tight, but his face was a mask of self-reproach.

"Why was Culla always the first to spot the humanoid Ghosts? Why were there none seen during the time he was with Kepler on Earth? Why didn't I think, before this, about Culla's reasons for volunteering to have his 'retina' read during the identity search!"

The words were coming too fast. Helene's brow knit with tension as she tried to think.

Jacob's eyes pleaded. "Helene, you've got to believe me."

She hesitated, then cried out, "Oh shit!" and threw herself at the intercom.

"Chen! Get us out of here! Never mind strap-in warning, just put on max thrust and crank up the time-compression! I want to see black sky before I blink twice!"

"Aye sir!" came the reply.

The ship surged up against them as the compensation fields were temporarily overcome, sending both

275

Helene and Jacob staggering. The Commandant held onto the intercom.

"All hands, keep your goggles on at all times from now on. Everybody please strap in as quick as you can. Hughes, report to the loop-hatch, on the double!"

Outside, the toruses began to pass by more rapidly. As each beast fell below the rim of the deck, its rims flashed brightly as if bidding them adieu.

"I should have caught on too," Helene said dismally. "Instead I turned off the P-laser and probably let him get away."

Jacob kissed her quickly, hard enough to leave her lips tingling.

"You didn't know. I'd have done the same thing in your shoes."

She touched her lips and stared past him at Dubrowsky's body. "You sent me away because . . ."

"Captain," Chen's voice interrupted. "I'm having trouble getting the time-compression off automatic. Can I keep Hughes here to help? We've also just lost maser link with Hermes."

Jacob shrugged. "First the maser link to keep word from getting out, then time-compression, then the gravity drive, finally the stasis. I guess the last step is to blow the shields, unless the other steps are sufficient. They should be."

Helene toggled the intercom. "Negative, Chen. I want Hughes now! Do what you can alone." She cut the switch.

"I'm going with you."

"No you aren't," he said. He put his goggles back on and picked up the bag from the floor. "If Culla gets to step three we're cooked, literally. But if I can stop him part-way you're the only one who'd stand a chance of piloting us out. Now please lend me that gun, it could be useful."

Helene handed it over. At this stage argument would be ridiculous. Jacob was in charge. She had no ideas of her own.

The quiet thrumming of the ship changed its rhythm, becoming a low, uneven hum.

Helene answered Jacob's questioning glance. "It's the time-compression. He's already started slowing us down. In more ways than one, we haven't very much time."

25.

A TRAPPED STATE

Jacob crouched in the hatchway, ready to dive back behind the combing at the sight of a tall, gangling alien. So far, so good. Culla hadn't been in the gravity loop.

The turnaround route to flip-side, the only route, might have been a good place for an ambush. But Jacob wasn't particularly surprised that Culla wasn't there, for two reasons.

The first was tactical. Culla's weapon operated on line-of-sight. The loop curved very tightly, so the humans could approach within a few meters without being spotted. An object thrown around the loop would travel most of the way with undiminished velocity. Jacob was now sure of this. He and Hughes had thrown several knives from the ship's galley when they entered the loop. They found them near the flip-side exit in a puddle of ammonia from the liquitubes they'd squeezed ahead of them as they walked the topsy-turvy passage.

Culla could have been waiting just beyond the door, but there was another reason he had to leave his rear undefended. He had only a limited amount of time before the Sunship reached a high orbit. After they got into free space the humans would be safe from the tossing of the chromospheric storms, and the tough, reflecting physical shell of the ship could deflect enough of the heat of the Sun to keep them alive until help came.

So Culla had to finish them, and himself, off quickly. Jacob felt sure the Pring specialist was by the computer input, ninety degrees around the dome to the right, using his laser eyes to slowly reprogram past the machine's safeguards.

Why he was doing it was a question that would have to wait.

Hughes picked up the knives. With the bag, some liquitubes, and Helene's little stunner, they composed their armory.

Classically, since the alternative was death for all of them, the answer would be for one man to sacrifice himself so the other could finish Culla off.

He and Hughes could carefully time their approach from different directions to surprise Culla at the same moment. Or one man could come in front and the other aim the stunner from over his shoulder.

But neither plan would work. Their opponent could literally kill a man as fast as he could look at him. Unlike the faked "adult" Sun Ghost projections, which were continuous output, Culla's killer bolts were discharges. Jacob wished he could remember how many he'd fired off during the fight on topside . . . or at what repeat frequency. It probably didn't matter. Culla had two eyes and two enemies. One bolt each would probably suffice.

Worst of all, they couldn't be sure that Culla's holographic imaging ability wouldn't enable him to locate them the instant they stepped out onto the floor, from reflections off the inner shell. He probably couldn't hurt them with reflections, but that was poor compensation.

If there weren't so damned much attenuation during the internal bouncing of the beam they could have tried to disable the alien with the P-laser, by letting it sweep the entire ship while the humans and Fagin crowded into the gravity-loop.

Jacob cursed and wondered what was keeping them with the P-laser. Next to him Hughes mumbled softly into a wall intercom. He turned to Jacob. "They're ready!" he said.

Thanks to their goggles they were spared most of the pain when the dome outside burst with light. Still it took a few moments to blink away tears and adapt to the brightness.

Commandant deSilva had, presumably with Dr. Martine's help, dragged the P-laser to a new position near the rim of the upper deck. If her calculations were right the beam should hit the side of the dome on flip-side exactly where the computer input was. Unfortunately, the complexity of the figure needed to go from point A to B, through the narrow gap at the edge of the deck, meant that the beam probably wouldn't harm Culla.

It did startle him though. At the instant the beam came on, while Jacob was squeezing his eyes shut, they heard a sudden chattering and sounds of movement far to the right.

When his vision cleared, Jacob saw a thin tracery of bright lines hanging in the air. The passage of the P-laser beam left a track in the small amount of dust in the air. That was fortunate. It would help them avoid it.

"Intercom on max?" he asked quickly.

Hughes gave thumbs up.

"Okay, let's go!"

The P-laser was randomly putting out colors in the blue-green. They hoped it would confuse reflections from the inner shell.

He gathered his legs and counted, "One, two. Go!"

Jacob dashed out across the open space and dove behind one of the hulking recording machines at the rim of the deck. He heard Hughes land hard, two machines clockwise from him.

The man waved once when he glanced back. "Nothing over here!" he whispered harshly. Jacob took a look around the corner of his own machine, using a mirror from the aid-kit, which had been smeared with grease. Hughes had another mirror, from Martine's purse.

Culla wasn't in sight.

Between them, he and his partner could survey about three-fifths of the deck. The computer input was on the other side of the dome, just out of Hughes' view. Jacob would have to take the long way around, darting from one recording machine to another.

The Sunship's shell glowed in spots where the P-laser beam glanced off it. The colors shifted constantly. Otherwise, the red and pink miasma of the chromosphere surrounded them. They had left the big filament minutes before, and the herd of toroids with it, by now a hundred kilometers below.

Below was actually right over Jacob's head. The photosphere, with the Big Spot in the center made a great, flat, endless, fiery ceiling above him, spicules hung like stalactites.

He gathered his legs beneath him and took off, bent over and facing away from any possible ambush.

He leapt over the P-laser beam where its path was traced in floating dust particles, and dove behind the next machine. Quickly he eased the mirror out to look at the territory now exposed.

Culla wasn't in sight.

Neither was Hughes. He whistled two short notes in the brief code they'd agreed upon. All clear. He heard one note, the fellow's reply.

He had to duck under the beam the next time. All the way across the narrow distance his skin crawled, anticipating a searing bolt of light along his flank.

He stumbled behind the machine and caught hold of it to steady himself, breathing heavily. That wasn't right! He shouldn't be so tired already. Something was wrong.

Jacob swallowed once then began to slide the mirror out along the counter-clockwise edge of the machine.

Pain lanced into his fingertips and he dropped the mirror with a cry. He stopped just short of popping the hand in his mouth, and held it, instead, a few inches away, his mouth open in agony.

Automatically, he started to lay over a light pain relief trance. The red pokers started to fade as the fingers seemed to grow more distant. Then the flow of relief stopped. It was like a tug of war. He could only accomplish so much; a counter pressure resisted the hypnosis with equal strength no matter how hard he concentrated.

Another of Hyde's tricks. Well there was no time to

dicker with him . . . whatever the hell he wanted. He looked at the hand, now that the pain was barely bearable. The index and fourth fingers were badly fried. The others were less damaged.

He managed to whistle a short code to Hughes. It was time to put his plan into effect, the only plan with any real chance of success.

Their only chance lay in getting into space. Time-compression was frozen on automatic—the first thing Culla took care of after the maser link—their subjective time would pretty closely match the actual time it took to leave the chromosphere.

Since assaulting Culla was almost certainly futile, the best way to delay the alien's murder-suicide would be to talk to him.

Jacob took a couple of breaths as he leaned back against the holo-recorder, careful to keep his ears awake. Culla was always a noisy walker. That was his best hope against out and out attack by the Pring. If Culla made too much sound out in the open, Jacob might get a chance to use the stunner he clutched in his good hand. It had a wide beam and wouldn't take much aiming.

"Culla!" he shouted. "Don't you think this has gone far enough? Why don't you come out now and we'll talk!"

He listened. There was a faint buzzing, as if Culla's mashies were chattering softly behind the thick prehensile lips. During the fight topside, half of the problem facing him and Donaldson had been avoiding the flashing white grinders.

"Culla!" he repeated. "I know it's stupid to judge an alien by your own species' values, but I really thought you were a friend. You owe us an explanation! Talk to us! If you're acting under Bubbacub's orders, you can surrender and I swear we'll all say you put up a hell of a fight!"

The buzzing grew louder. There was a brief shuffle of footsteps. One, two, three . . . but that was all. Not enough to get a fix on.

"Jacob, I am shorry," Culla's voice carried softly across the deck.

"You musht be told, before we die, but firsht I ashk that you have that lasher turned off. It hurtsh!"

"Culla, so does my hand."

The Pring sounded woebegone. "I am sho, sho, shorry, Jacob. Pleash undershtand that you *are* my friend. It ish partly for your shpeciesh that I do thish.

"Theshe are neceshary crimesh, Jacob. I am only glad that death ish near sho that I may be free of memory."

Jacob was astonished by the alien's sophistry. He had never expected such sophomore whinings from Culla, whatever his reasons for what he'd done. He was about to frame a reply when Helene deSilva's voice boomed over the intercom.

"Jacob? Can you hear me? The gravity thrust is deteriorating fast. We're losing headway."

What she didn't say was the threat. If something wasn't done soon they'd begin the long fall toward the photosphere, a fall from which they'd never return.

Once in the grip of the convection cells, the ship would be pulled downward into the stellar core. If there was a ship left, by then.

"You shee, Jacob," Culla said. "To delay me will do no good. It ish already done. I will shtay to make shertain you cannot correct it.

"But pleashe, let ush talk until the end. I do not wish to die ash enemiesh."

Jacob stared out into the wispy, hydrogen-red atmosphere of the Sun. Tendrils of fiery gas were still floating 'downwards' (up, to him), past the ship, but that could be a function of the motion of the gas in this area at this time. Certainly they were going by much less quickly. It could be that the ship was already falling.

"Your dischovery of my talent and my hoax wash most ashtute, Jacob. You combined many obshcure cluesh to find the anshwer! Tying in the background of my race wash a brilliant shtroke!

"Tell me, although I avoided the rim detectorsh with my phantomsh, didn't it throw you off that they shometimesh appeared on topshide when *I* wash on flip-shide?"

Jacob was trying to think. He had the cool side of the

283

stun gun against his cheek. It felt good, but it wasn't helping him come up with ideas. And he had to spare some of his attention to talk to Culla.

"I never bothered to think about it, Culla. I suppose you just leaned over and beamed through the transparent deck-suspension field. That'd explain why the image looked refracted. It was actually *reflected*, at an angle, inside the shell."

Actually that *was* a valid clue. Jacob wondered why he'd missed it.

And the bright blue light, during his deep trance in Baja! It happened just before he awoke to see Culla standing there! The Eatee must have taken a hologram of him! What a way to get to know somebody and never forget his face!

"Culla," he said slowly. "Not that I'm one to hold a grudge or anything, but were you responsible for my crazy behavior at the end of the last dive?"

There was a pause. Then Culla spoke. His lisp was getting worse.

"Yesh, Jacob. I am shorry, but you were getting too inquishitive. I hoped to dishcredit you. I failed."

"But how . . ."

"I lishtened to Dr. Martine talk about the effect of glare on humansh, Jacob!"

The Pring almost shouted. For the first time in Jacob's memory, Culla had interrupted somebody. "I ekshperimented on Doctor Kepler for months! Den on La-Roque and Jeff . . . den on you. I ushed a narrow diffracted beam. No one could shee it, but it unfocushed your thoughtsh!

"I did not know what you would do. But I knew it would be embarrashing. Again, I am shorry. It wash neceshary!"

They had definitely stopped rising. The big filament that they had left only a few minutes before loomed over Jacob's head. High streamers twisted and curled up toward the ship, like grasping fingers.

Jacob had been trying to find a way, but his imagination was blocked by a powerful barrier.

All right! I give up!

He called on his neurosis to offer its terms. What the hell did the damned thing *want* of him?

He shook his head. He'd have to invoke the emergency clause. Hyde was going to have to come out and become part of him, like in the bad old days. Like when he chased down LaRoque on Mercury, and when he broke into the Photo Lab. He got ready to go into the trance.

"Why Culla. Tell me why you did all this!"

Not that it mattered. Maybe Hughes was listening. Perhaps Helene was recording. Jacob was too busy to care.

Resistance! In the non-linear, non-orthogonal coordinates of thought he sifted feelings and gestalts through a sieve. To whatever extent the old automatic systems still worked, he set them off to do their jobs.

Slowly, the window dressing and camouflage was stripped away and he came face to face with his other half.

The battlements, unscalable in every past siege, were even more formidable now. The earthen breastworks had been replaced by stone. The abatis was made of sharpened needles, slender and twenty miles long. At the top of the highest tower a flag rippled. The pennant read "Loyalty." It flew above two stakes, on each of which a head was impaled.

One head he recognized at once. It was his own. The blood that dripped from the severed neck still glistened. The expression was one of remorse.

The other head set him shivering. It was Helene's. Her face was streaked and pockmarked, and as he watched the eyes fluttered weakly. The head was still alive.

But why! Why this rage against Helene? And why the overtones of suicide . . . this unwillingness to join with him to create the near ubermensch he once had been?

If Culla decided to attack now, he'd be helpless. His ears were filled with the cry of a whistling wind. There was a roar of jets and then the sound of someone falling . . . the sound of someone calling as she fell past him.

And for the first time he could make out her words.

"Jake! Watch that first step . . . !"

Is that all? Then why all the fuss over it? Why the months trying to drag out what turned out to be Tania's last ironic dig?

Of course. His neurosis was letting him see, now that death was imminent, that the hidden words had been another red herring. Hyde was hiding something else. It was ...

Guilt.

He knew he carried a burden of it after the affair on the Vanilla Needle, but how much he'd never realized. He now saw how sick this Jekyll and Hyde arrangement he'd been living with really was. Instead of slowly healing the trauma of a painful loss, he'd sealed off an artificial entity, to grow and feed on him and on his shame for having let Tania fall ... for the supreme arrogance of the man who, on that crazy day twenty miles high, thought he could do two things at once.

It had been just another form of arrogance ... a belief that he could bypass the normal, human way of recovering from grief, the cycle of pain and transcendency by which the billions of his fellow human beings coped when each suffered a loss. That and the comfort of closeness to other people.

And now he was trapped. The meaning of the pennant on the battlements was clear now. In his sickness he'd thought to expiate part of his guilt by demonstrations of loyalty to the person he'd failed. Not overt loyalty, but loyalty deep within ... a sick loyalty based on witholding himself from everybody ... all the while convinced that he was all right since he'd *had* lovers!

No wonder Hyde hated Helene! No wonder he wanted Jacob Demwa dead as well!

Tania would never have approved of you, he told it. But it wasn't listening. It had its own logic and had no use for his.

Hell, she'd have *loved* Helene!

It didn't do any good. The barrier was firm. He opened his eyes.

The red of the chromosphere had deepened. They were in the filament now. A flash of color, seen even through his goggles, sent him glancing to the left.

It was a toroid. They were back amidst the herd. As he watched, several more drifted past, their

286

rims festooned with bright designs. They spun like mad doughnuts, oblivious to the peril of the Sunship.

"Jacob, you have shaid nothing," Culla's droning, lisping voice had become background. At the mention of his name Jacob paid attention.

"Shurely you have shome opinion on my motivesh. Cannot you shee that de greater good will come of dish . . . not only for my shpecies but for yoursh and your Clientsh ash well?"

Jacob shook his head vigorously to clear it. The Hyde-induced drowsiness was something he had to fight! The only silver lining was that his hand no longer hurt.

"Culla, I must think about this for a little while. Can we retire a ways and confer? I can pick up some food for you and maybe we can work something out."

There was a pause. Then Culla spoke slowly.

"You are very tricky, Jacob. I am tempted but now I shee dat it will be better if you and your friend stay shtill. In fact. I will make certain. If either of you movesh I will 'shee' him."

Numbly, Jacob wondered what was so "tricky" about offering the alien food. Why had that idea popped into his head?

They were falling faster now. Overhead the herd of toruses stretched toward the ominous wall of the photosphere. The nearest shone in blues and greens as they swept past. The colors faded with distance. The farthest beasts looked like tiny dim wedding rings, each poised on a tiny flicker of green light.

There was movement among the nearest magnetovores. As the ship fell, one after another moved aside and "downward" from Jacob's upside-down perspective. Once a flash of green filled the Sunship as a tail-laser swept over them. The fact that they weren't destroyed meant that the automatic screens were still working.

Outside, a fluttering shape shot past Jacob, from over his head out, past the deck at his feet. Then another rippling apparition appeared, lingering for a moment outside the shell near him, its body slick with iridescent colors. Then it sped upward, out of sight.

The Sun Ghosts were gathering. Perhaps the Sunship's headlong fall had finally piqued their curiosity.

They had passed the largest part of the herd by now. There was a cluster of large magnetovores just overhead, in their line of descent. Tiny bright herdsmen danced around the group. Jacob hoped they'd get out of the way. No sense in taking anyone else with them. The incandescent trail of the ship's Refrigerator Laser cut dangerously close.

Jacob gathered himself together. There was nothing else to do. He and Hughes would have to try a frontal assault on Culla. He whistled a code, two short and two long. There was a pause and then there was an answer. The other man was ready.

He'd wait until the first sound. They'd agreed that, when they were close enough, any attack with any chance of success would have to come the instant any noise was made, before Culla could be alerted. Since Hughes had farther to go, presumably, he'd move first.

He tensed into a crouch and forced himself to concentrate only on the attack. The stunner rested in the sweaty palm of his left hand. He ignored the distracting tremors that erupted from an isolated part of his own mind.

A sound, like someone falling, came from somewhere to the right. Jacob stepped out from behind the machine, pressing the firing stud of the stunner at the same instant.

No bolt of light greeted him. Culla wasn't there. One of the precious stunner charges was gone.

He ran forward as fast as he could. If he could catch the alien with his back turned to deal with Hughes . . .

The lighting was changing. As he ran just a few steps the red brightness of the photosphere overhead was swiftly replaced by a blue-green shine from above. Jacob spared the briefest of glances overhead as he dashed forward. The light came from toruses. The huge Solarian beasts were coming up fast from below the Sunship on a collision course.

Alarms rang, and Helene deSilva's voice came on, loudly, with a warning. As the blueness grew brighter, Jacob dove over a trace made by the P-laser beam in the dusty air, and landed just two meters away from Culla.

Just beyond the Pring, the crewman Hughes knelt on the ground, holding up bloody hands, his knives scattered on the ground. He stared up at Culla dully, expecting the coup de grace.

Jacob raised the stunner as Culla swiveled, warned by the sound of his arrival. For the briefest of instants Jacob thought he'd made it as he pressed down on the firing stud.

Then his entire left hand erupted in agony. A spasm flung it up and the gun flew away. For a moment the deck seemed to sway, then his vision cleared and Culla was standing before him, eyes dull. The Pring's mashies were now fully exposed, waving at the ends of the tentacular "lips."

"I am shorry, Jacob." The alien slurred so badly Jacob could barely make out the words. "It musht be thish way."

The Eatee planned to finish him off with his cleavers! Jacob stumbled back in fear and disgust. Culla followed, the mashies clacking together slowly, powerfully with the rhythm of his footsteps.

A great sense of resignation washed over Jacob, a feeling of defeat and imminent death. It took the distance out of his backward steps. The throbbing in his hand meant nothing next to the closeness of extinction.

"No!" he shouted hoarsely. He launched himself forward, head down, toward Culla.

At that instant Helene's voice came on again and the blueness overhead took over everything. There was a distant humming and then a powerful force lifted them off the floor, into the air above the violently heaving deck.

PART IX

There was once a lad so virtuous
that the gods gave him a wish. His
choice was to be, for a day, the charioteer
of the Sun. Apollo was overruled when
he predicted dire consequences, but
subsequent events proved him right. The
Sahara is said to be the track of desolation
laid when the inexperienced driver let
his carriage pass too close to Earth.

Since then, the gods have tried
to operate a closed shop.

—M. N. Plano

26.

TUNNELING

Jacob landed on the opposite side of the computer-console, falling hard on his back to save his blistered, bleeding hands. Fortunately, the springy material of the deck cushioned some of the impact.

He tasted blood and his head rang as he rolled over onto his elbows. The deck still bounced as the magnetovores overhead jostled against the underbelly of the Sunship, filling the interior of flip-side with brilliant blue light. They touched the ship, three of them, at about forty-five degrees "above" the deck, leaving a large gap directly overhead. That left room for the Refrigerator Laser to pour its deadly beam of stored solar heat between them, downward toward the photosphere.

Jacob had no time to wonder what they were doing . . . whether they were attacking, or just playful. (What a thought!) He had to take advantage of this respite quickly.

Hughes had landed nearby. The man was already on his feet, stumbling in shock. Jacob hurried up and took the man's arm in his . . . avoiding contact between their wounded hands.

"Come on, Hughes. If Culla's been stunned we might both be able to jump him!"

Hughes nodded. The man was confused, but he was willing. His movements were exaggerated, though. Jacob had to guide him the right way, hurrying.

They came around the curve of the central dome to find Culla just rising to his feet. The alien wavered but as he turned toward them Jacob knew it was hopeless. One of Culla's eyes flashed brightly, the first time Jacob had actually seen one in operation. That meant . . .

There was a smell of burning rubber and the left strap of his goggles parted. He was dazzled by the blue brightness of the chamber as they fell off.

Jacob shoved Hughes back around the curve of the dome and flung himself after the man. At any moment he expected a sudden pain in the back of his neck, but they stumbled together all the way to the gravity-loop hatch and fell within, safe.

Fagin moved aside to let them in. He trilled loudly and waved his branches.

"Jacob! You are alive! And your associate as well! This is better than I'd feared!"

"How . . ." Jacob gasped for breath. "How long since we started falling?"

"It has been five, perhaps six minutes. I followed you down after regaining my wits. I may not be able to fight but I can interpose my body. Culla would never have enough power to cut his way through me to get above!" The Kanten piped shrill laughter.

Jacob frowned; that was an interesting point. How much power did Culla have? What was it he once read about the human body operating on an average of one hundred and fifty watts? Culla put out considerably more than that, but it was in short, half-second bursts.

Given enough time, Jacob could figure it out. When projecting his hoaxed Solarians, Culla had made the apparitions last for about twenty minutes. Then the anthropomorphic Ghosts "lost interest" and Culla was suddenly ravenously hungry. They'd all attributed his appetite to nervous energy, but actually the Pring had to replenish his supply of coumarin . . . and probably of high-energy chemicals to power the dye-laser reaction, as well.

294

"You are hurt!" Fagin fluted. The branches fluttered in agitation. "You had best take your compatriot upside and both have your wounds tended."

"I guess so," Jacob nodded, reluctant to leave Fagin alone. "There are some important questions I have to ask Dr. Martine while she's treating us."

The Kanten gave out a long whistling sigh, "Jacob, under no circumstances disturb Dr. Martine! She is in rapport with the Solarians. It is our only chance!"

"She's what!"

"They were attracted by the flashing of the Parametric Laser. When they came, she donned her psi helmet and initiated communications! They positioned several of their magnetovores beneath us and have substantially arrested our fall!"

Jacob's heart leapt. It sounded like a reprieve. Then he frowned.

"Substantially? Then we aren't rising?"

"Regrettably, no. We are falling slowly. And there is no knowing how long the toroids can hold us."

Jacob felt distantly in awe of Martine's accomplishment. She had contacted the Solarians! It was one of the epochal accomplishments of all time, and still they were doomed.

"Fagin," he said carefully. "I'll be back as soon as I can. Meanwhile, can you fake my voice well enough to fool Culla?"

"I believe so. I can try."

"Then talk to him. Throw your voice. Use all your tricks to keep him busy and uncertain. He can't be allowed more time at that computer access!"

Fagin whistled assent. Jacob turned, with his arm in Hughes' and started around the gravity-loop.

The loop felt strange, as if the gravity fields had started to fluctuate slightly. His inner ear bothered him as it never had before, as he helped Hughes traverse the short arc, and he had to concentrate to keep his step.

Topside was still red—the red of the chromosphere. But fluttering blue-green Solarians danced just outside, closer than Jacob had ever seen them before. Their "butterfly wings" were almost as broad as the ship itself.

Blue traceries of the P-laser also shone in the dust up here. Near the edge of the deck, the laser itself hummed inside its bulky mounting.

They dodged several of the thin beams.

If only we'd had the tools to unship that thing from its holder, Jacob thought. Well, it was no use wishing. He steadied his partner until he could get him into a couch. Then he strapped the man in and went looking for the aid-kit.

He found it by the Pilot Board. Since he hadn't seen Martine, it was apparent she'd chosen another quadrant of the deck to do her communing with the Solarians, away from the others. Near the Pilot Board, LaRoque, Donaldson, and the unliving body of crewman Dubrowsky lay firmly strapped in. Donaldson's face was half covered with medicinal flesh-foam.

Helene deSilva and her remaining crewman bent over their instruments. The Commandant looked up as he approached.

"Jacob! What happened?"

He kept his hands behind his back, to keep from distracting her. It was getting hard to stay on his feet, though. He'd have to do something soon.

"It didn't work. We got him talking, though."

"Yes, we heard it all up here, then a lot of noise. I tried to warn you before we impacted the toroids. I was hoping you could use it."

"Oh the impact helped, all right, It shook us up but it saved our lives."

"And Culla?"

Jacob shrugged. "He's still down there. I think he's running low on juice. During our fight up here he burned off half of Donaldson's face with one shot. Down there he was a miser, taking tiny pot shots at strategic places."

He told her about Culla's attack with his mashies. "I don't think he's going to run out early enough. If we had lots of men we could keep throwing them at him until he went dry. But we haven't. Hughes is willing, but he can't fight anymore. I suppose you two can't leave your posts."

Helene turned to answer a beeping alarm from her control board. She stabbed a switch and it cut off. Then she looked back, apologetic.

"I'm sorry, Jacob. But we've got all we can handle here. We're trying to get through to the computer by actuating the ship's sensors in coded rhythms. It's slow work, and we have to keep turning away to handle emergencies. I'm afraid we're slipping. The controls are deteriorating." She turned to answer another signal.

Jacob backed away The last thing he wanted to do was distract her.

"Can I help?"

Pierre LaRoque looked up at him from a couch a few feet away. The little man was constrained, his couch straps secured out of reach. Jacob had all but forgotten about him.

He hesitated. LaRoque's behavior just before the fight topside hadn't inspired confidence. Helene and Martine had strapped him in to keep him out of everyone's hair.

Yet Jacob needed someone's hands to operate the aid-kit. Jacob remembered LaRoque's near escape on Mercury. The man was unreliable, but he had talent when he chose to use it.

LaRoque looked coherent and sincere at the moment. Jacob asked Helene for permission to release him. She glanced up and shrugged.

"Okay. But if he comes near the instruments I'll kill him. Tell him that."

There was no need to tell him. LaRoque nodded that he understood. Jacob bent over and fumbled with the strap hooks with the good fingers of his right hand.

Helene hissed behind him. "Jacob, your hands!"

The look of concern on her face warmed Jacob. But when she started to get up he'd have none of it. Right now her job was more important than his. She knew this. He took the fact that she was torn at all as a great display of affection. She smiled briefly in encouragement then bent to answer a half dozen alarms that started blaring at once.

LaRoque rose, rubbing his shoulders, then picked up the aid-kit and motioned to Jacob. His smile was ironic.

"Who should we fix first?" he said. "You, the other man, or Culla?"

27.

EXCITATION

Helene had to find time to think. There must be something she could do! Slowly the systems based on Galactic science were failing. So far it had been the time-compression and the gravity thrust, plus several peripheral mechanisms. If *internal* gravity control went out they'd be helpless before the tossing of the chromosphere storms, battered within their own hull.

Not that it'd matter. The toroids that were holding them up against the pull of the Sun were obviously tiring. The altimeter was slipping. Already the rest of the herd was high overhead, almost lost in the pink haze of the upper chromosphere. It wouldn't be long.

An alarm light flashed.

There was positive feedback in the internal gravity field. She did a quick mental calculation, then fed in a set of parameters to damp it out.

Poor Jacob, he'd tried. His exhaustion had been written on his face. She felt ashamed not to have shared the fight on flip-side, though, of course, it had never been likely that they could dislodge Culla from the computer on flip-side.

Now it was up to her. But *how*, with every damned component falling apart!

Not every component. Except for the maser link with Mercury, the equipment derived from Earth technology still ran perfectly. Culla hadn't bothered with any of it. The refrigeration still worked. The E.M. fields around the hard shell of the ship still ran, though they had lost the ability to selectively let in more sunlight on flipside. Naturally.

The ship shuddered. It bounced as something bumped against it once, twice. Then a brightness appeared at the edge of the deck. Suddenly the rim of a toroid appeared, rubbing against the side of the ship. Above it, several Solarians fluttered.

The bumping became a scraping sound, loud and hideous. The toroid was livid with bright purple blotches around its rim. It pulsed and throbbed under the proddings of its tormentors. Then, in a sudden burst of light, it was gone. The Sunship tipped as its forward end, unsupported, fell suddenly. DeSilva and her partner struggled to right it.

When she looked up she could see her Solarian allies drifting away, with the two remaining toroids.

There was no more they could do. The toroid that had deserted them was just a spot of light overhead, receding rapidly atop a pillar of green flame.

The altimeter began to spin faster. On her viewscreens Helene could see the pulsing granulation cells of the photosphere, and the Big Spot, now bigger than ever.

They were already closer than anyone had come before. Soon they'd be in there—the first men in the Sun.

Briefly.

She looked up at the now distant Solarians, and wondered if she should call everyone together to . . . to wave good-bye or something. She wanted Jacob here.

But he'd gone below again. They'd hit before he could make it back.

She gazed up at the tiny green lights and wondered how the toroid had been able to move so fast.

She jerked upright with a curse. Chen looked up at her. "What is it, skipper? Shields going?"

With a cry of exultation Helene started throwing switches.

She wished they could monitor their telemetry back

on Mercury, because if they died here on the Sun *now* it would certainly be in a unique way!

Jacob's arms still throbbed. Worse, they *itched*. He couldn't scratch, of course. His left hand was in a solid block of flesh-foam and so were two of the fingers of his right hand.

He crouched again just inside the hatch of the gravity-loop, looking out onto the deck on flip-side. Fagin moved aside so he could push his new mirror, this one glued to the end of a pencil with more flesh-foam, out beyond the combing.

Culla wasn't in sight. The hulking cameras stood out against the pulsing blue ceiling presented by the laboring magnetovores. The trail of the P-laser crisscrossed, marked by scattering from dust in the air.

He motioned for LaRoque to lay down his load just inside the hatch, next to Fagin.

They took turns coating each other's necks and faces with more flesh-foam. The goggles were sealed down with extra blobs of the pliant, rubbery material.

"Of course you know this is dangerous," LaRoque said. "It may protect us from damage from a quick shot but this stuff is highly flammable. It's the only flammable substance allowed in spaceships, for that matter, because of its unique medicinal properties."

Jacob nodded. If he looked anything like LaRoque, now, they'd stand a good chance of scaring the alien to death!

He hefted the brown cannister, then sprayed a shot out onto the deck. It didn't have much range but it might do as a weapon. There was still plenty of the stuff left.

The deck jerked under them, then jounced twice more. Jacob looked out and saw that they were tipping over. The magnetovore that held up this side of the ship was rolling along lower and lower, toward the edge of the deck and away from where the photosphere covered the sky.

One of the beasts on the other side must have lost its hold, then. That meant it was almost over.

The ship shuddered and then began to right itself. Jacob sighed. There still might be time to save the ship if he could disable Culla immediately. But that was clearly impossible. He wished he could go up and join Helene.

"Fagin," he said. "I'm not the man you used to know. That man would have had Culla by now. We'd have been out of here and safe. We both know what he was capable of.

"Please understand. I tried. But I'm just not the same anymore."

Fagin rustled. "I knew, Jacob. It was to achieve this change that I invited you to Sundiver in the first place."

Jacob stared at the alien.

"You are my artful dodger," the Kanten whistled softly. "I had no idea the issues here were as critical as they turned out to be. I asked you here solely to help break the chrysalis you have been in since Ecuador, and then to introduce you to Helene deSilva. The plan succeeded. I am pleased."

Jacob was at a loss.

"But Fagin, my mind . . ." he trailed off.

"Your mind is fine. You simply have an overeager imagination. That is all. Truly, Jacob, you invent such fantasies. And so elaborate! I have never met a hypochondriac such as you!"

Jacob's mind raced. Either the Kanten was being polite, or he was mistaken or . . . or he was right. Fagin had never lied to him before, especially regarding personal matters.

Could it be that Mr. Hyde wasn't a neurosis at all but a game? As a child he had created play universes so detailed that they could hardly be distinguished from reality. His worlds had existed. The neo-Reichian therapists had merely smiled and credited him with a powerful, non-pathological imagination because the tests always showed that he knew he was playing, when it mattered that he know it!

Could Mr. Hyde have been a play-entity?

It's true that until now it never did any actual harm. It was a perpetual annoyance, but there always turned out to be a valid reason for the things it "made" him do. Again, until now.

301

"You were non-sane for a time when I met you, Jacob. But the Needle cured you. The cure frightened, so you went into a game. I do not know the details of your game; you were very secretive. But I know now that you are awake. You have been awake for perhaps twenty minutes."

Jacob clamped down. Whether or not Fagin was right, he had no time to stand here and blather about it. He had only minutes to save the ship. If it was possible at all.

Outside, the chromosphere shimmered. The photosphere loomed over their heads. The dust trails of the P-laser crisscrossed the inner shell.

Jacob tried to snap his fingers, and winced in pain.

"LaRoque! Run upstairs and get your lighter. Quick!"

LaRoque stepped back. "Why, I have it right here," he said. "But of what use . . ."

Jacob was moving toward the intercom. If Helene had some reserve of power she'd been holding back, now was the time to use it. He needed a little time! Before he could switch it on, though, an alarm filled the ship.

"Sophonts," Helene's voice rang out. "Please prepare for acceleration. We will be leaving the Sun shortly."

The woman's voice sounded amused, almost whimsical.

"Due to the mode of our imminent departure, I would recommend that all passengers dress as warmly as possible! The Sun can be very cold this time of year!"

28.

STIMULATED EMISSION

A blast of cold air blew constantly from the ventilator ducts around the Refrigerator Laser housing. Jacob and LaRoque huddled around their fire, trying to keep the cold air off it.

"Come on, baby. Burn!" A pile of flesh-foam shavings smoldered on the deck. Slowly the flames grew as they piled on more chips.

"Ha ha!" Jacob laughed. "Once a caveman, always a caveman, eh, LaRoque? Men get all the way to the sun, and they build a fire to stay warm!"

LaRoque smiled weakly, and kept piling on larger and larger shavings. The loquacious journalist had said very little since Jacob released him from his couch. Now and then, though, he would mutter something angry and spit.

Jacob held a torch into the flames. It was made from a clump of flesh-foam stuck to the end of a liquitube. The end began to smolder, giving off thick black smoke. It was beautiful.

Soon they had several torches. Smoke billowed into

the air, carrying a foul stench. They had to stand back, in the path of the air duct, to be able to breathe. Fagin moved well into the gravity-loop.

"Okay," Jacob said. "Let's go!" He hopped out of the hatchway to the left and tossed one of the smoldering brands to the end of the deck, as far as he could see. Behind him LaRoque was doing the same in the opposite direction.

With a heavy rustling, Fagin followed them out. The Kanten went straight out from the hatch to the opposite end of the deck to act as a lookout, and to draw Culla's fire if possible. Fagin had refused a coating of flesh-foam.

"It is all clear," the Kanten whistled softly. "Culla is not to be seen."

That was good and bad news. It localized Culla. It also meant the alien was probably working to bolix up the Refrigerator Laser.

It was getting COLD!

Once it had begun, Helene's scheme made perfect sense to Jacob. Since she still had control over the screens surrounding the ship, (the crew were alive to prove it), she could let in heat from the Sun at whatever rate she wished. This heat could be sent directly to the Refer Laser and pumped back out into the chromosphere, plus waste heat from the ship's power plant. Only this time the flow was a torrent, and directed downward. The thrust had stopped their fall and they had begun to climb.

Naturally, such meddling with the ship's automatic heat conrol system had to be inaccurate. Helene must have decided to program the mechanism to err in the direction of coldness. In that direction mistakes would be more easily corrected.

It was a brilliant idea. Jacob hoped he'd get to tell her so. Right now it was his job to make sure it had a chance to work.

He edged around the dome until he reached the point where Fagin's view was cut off. Without looking around, he threw two more of the brands to different parts of the deck ahead of him. Smoke boiled from each of them.

The chamber was getting hazy from the smoke released so far. The trail of the P-laser beam shimmered brightly in the air. Some of the weaker trails were disappearing, attenuated by cumulative passage though the smoke.

Jacob moved back into Fagin's cone of view. He had three more smoldering brands. He backed up onto the deck and tossed them at different angles over the top of the central dome. LaRoque joined him and threw his as well.

One of the torches passed directly over the center of the dome on its way over. It entered the x-ray beam of the Refrigerator Laser and vanished in a cloud of vapor.

Jacob hoped it hadn't deflected the beam much. The coherent x-rays supposedly passed through the shell with near zero contamination of the ship, but the beam wasn't designed to handle solid objects.

"Okay!" he whispered.

He and LaRoque hurried to the wall of the dome, where spare parts for the recording instruments were stored. LaRoque opened a cabinet and climbed as high as footholds allowed, then offered his hand.

Jacob scrambled up next to him.

Now they were all vulnerable. Culla must react to the obvious threat implied by the firebrands! Already visibility was dropping well below normal. The chamber was filled with a foul stench and Jacob was finding it increasingly uncomfortable to breathe.

LaRoque braced his shoulder in the top jamb of the cabinet, then offered his cupped hands to Jacob. Jacob took the boost and climbed up onto LaRoque's shoulder.

The dome was sloping here, but the surface was smooth, and Jacob had only three fingers instead of ten. The flesh-foam coating helped. It was still somewhat sticky. After two unsuccessful attempts Jacob concentrated and leapt from LaRoque's shoulder, nearly hard enough to shake the man loose.

The surface of the dome was like quicksilver. He had to flatten himself and move with scrambling speed to gain each inch.

Near the top, he had to worry about the Refer Laser. He could see the orifice as he rested near the summit.

Two meters away it hummed softly; the smoky air shimmered and Jacob wondered what the transparency safety distance was from the deadly mouth.

He turned away so as not to have to think about it.

He couldn't whistle to let them know he'd made it. They'd have to rely on Fagin's superb hearing to track his movements, and to time the distraction.

There were at least a few seconds to wait. Jacob decided to take a chance. He rolled over onto his back and looked up at the Big Spot.

Everywhere was the Sun.

From his point of view there was no ship. There was no battle. There were no planets or stars or galaxies. The rim of his goggles even cut off the sight of his own body. The photosphere was everything.

It pulsed. The spicule forests, like undulating picket fences, hurled their noise up at him, and the breakers split just above his head. The sound divided and swept around toward the irrelevencies of space.

It roared.

The Big Spot stared back at him. For an instant the broad expanse was a face, the bristled, grizzled face of a patriarch. The throbbings were its breath. The noise was the booming of its giant voice, singing a billions-year-old song that only the other stars could hear or understand.

The Sun was alive. What was more, it noticed him. It gave him its undivided attention.

Call me lifegiver, for I am your sustenance. I burn, and by my burning you live. I stand, and in standing supply your anchor. Space curls around, my blanket, and funnels down to mystery in my bowels. Time beats his scythe on my forge.

Living thing, does Entropy, my wicked Aunt, notice our joint conspiracy? Not yet, I think, for you are yet too small. Your puny struggle against her tide is a fluttering in a great wind. And she thinks I am still her ally.

Call me lifegiver, oh living thing, and weep. I burn endlessly and, burning, consume what cannot be replaced. While you sip daintily at my torrent the font runs slowly out. When it empties other stars shall take my place, but oh not forever!

Call me lifegiver, and laugh!

You, living thing, hear the true Lifegiver's voice from time to time, it is said. He speaks to you but not to us, His first born!

Pity the stars, oh living thing! We sing away the aeons in pretended joy as we toil for His cruel sister, awaiting the day of your maturity, you tiny embryo, when He turns you loose to change the way of things again.

Jacob laughed soundlessly. Oh what an imagination! Fagin was right, after all. He closed his eyes, still listening for the signal. Seven seconds, exactly, had passed since he reached the top of the dome.

"Jake . . ." It was a woman's voice. He looked up without opening his eyes.

"Tania."

She stood by the pion-scope in her lab, exactly as he had seen her so many times when he came to pick her up. Braided brown hair, slightly uneven white teeth grinning generously, and large, crinkled eyes. She came forward with surefooted grace and confronted him with fists on hips.

"It's about time!" she said.

"Tania, I . . . I don't understand."

"It's 'bout time you brought up an image of me doing something besides falling! Think it's fun doin' that over and over again? Why haven't you brought me back having some of the good times!"

He suddenly realized that it was true! For two years he'd only remembered Tania in that last instant, not thinking about their time together at all!

"Well, I'll admit it's done you some good," she nodded. "You seem to finally be free of that damned arrogance. Just think about me from time to time, for heaven's sake. I hate being ignored!"

"Yes, Tania. I'll remember you. I promise."

"And pay attention to the star! Stop thinking you imagine everything!"

She softened. The image began to fade. "You're right, Jake, dear one, I do like her. Have a good . . ."

307

He opened his eyes. The photosphere throbbed overhead. The spot stared back at him. The granulation cells pumped slowly like leisured heartbeats.

Did you just do that? he asked, silently.

The answer permeated him, drilled through his body and came out the other side. Neutrinos to cure neuroses. A most original approach.

A short whistle came from below. Before he was aware he had moved, he was slithering toward the sound and to the right, silently and without a wasted motion.

He peered over to look down on the head of Culla ta-Pring ab-Pil-ab-Kisa-ab-Soro-ab-Hul-ab-Puber.

The alien faced Jacob's left, his hand still on the open access plate to the computer-input. Though the smoke dimmed it almost to nothing, there was still a glare as the P-laser beam hit the spot.

From the left came a rustling. Somewhere to the right was the sound of running feet, LaRoque hurrying around the dome.

A few silver-tipped twigs poked out from the curve of the dome. Culla crouched and one of Fagin's shiny light receptors curled up in smoke. The Kanten gave out a high pitched keening and retreated out of sight. Culla swiveled quickly.

Jacob pulled the flesh-foam sprayer out of his pocket. He aimed and pressed the nozzle. A thin jet of liquid shot out in an arc toward Culla's eyes. In the instant before it struck, Pierre LaRoque appeared, running, his head down as he charged through the smoke toward Culla.

Culla jumped back. The spray passed in front of his eyes. At that instant a bright spark flashed at a point along its length.

With a whoosh the entire stream burst into flame. Culla stumbled backwards, hands in front of his face. LaRoque barrelled through the falling embers and collided with the Pring's midsection.

Culla almost went down in the thick smoke. Breath wheezed as he gripped LaRoque around the neck, first for balance and then closing tightly to squeeze on the man's windpipe. LaRoque struggled wildly but his momentum was gone. It was like trying to escape from a pair of boa constrictors. His face turned flush and started to puff.

Jacob gathered himself for a leap. The smoke was so thick he could hardly keep from coughing. Desperately he suppressed the urge. If Culla saw him before he could jump, the alien wouldn't bother killing LaRoque the hard way. He'd finish them both off with a look.

His muscles pressed like hard springs and he launched himself from the dome.

The midair flight was suspenseful. His own subjective version of time-compression made the transit seem slow and leisurely. It was a trick from the bad old days, and now he used it again, automatically.

When a third of the distance was covered he saw Culla's head start to turn. It was hard to tell exactly what the E.T. was doing to LaRoque at that instant. A thick pall of smoke obscured everything but Culla's bright red eyes and two flashes of white beneath them.

The eyes came up. It was a race to see who'd arrive first at a certain point in space, just above and to the right of the alien's head. Jacob wondered at what angles Culla could shoot a narrow beam.

The suspense was killing him. It was almost satirical. Jacob decided to speed things up and see what happened.

There was a flash, then a tooth jarring, numbing smash as his shoulder hit the side of Culla's head. He clutched and got a tight grip on the front of the alien's gown as his inertia carried both of them over into a crashing tumble onto the deck.

Human and alien fought for breath amidst fits of coughing as they rolled into a tangle of slashing, grabbing arms and legs. Somehow Jacob got around behind his opponent and held on tightly to the slender neck as Culla thrashed, trying to turn his head to snap with his cleavers or burn with his laser eyes.

The powerful, tentacular hands clutched back, snatching for a purchase. Jacob dodged his head aside and struggled to get Culla around, so he could get his legs into a scissors lock. After rolling almost halfway across the deck, he succeeded, and was rewarded by a lancing pain in his right thigh.

"More," he coughed. "Shoot, Culla. Use it up!"

Twice more bolts struck his exposed legs, sending small tsunamis of agony up to his brain. The pain he shunted aside and he held on, praying that Culla would send some more.

But Culla stopped wasting his shots and began to roll about faster, buffeting Jacob every time the human struck the deck. They were both coughing, Culla sounding like half a dozen ball bearings shaken in a bottle, every time he wheezed in the thick, billowing smoke.

There was no way to choke the devil! When he wasn't holding on for dear life, Jacob tried to turn his grip around Culla's throat into a strangle hold. But there didn't seem to be any vulnerable points! It was unfair. Jacob wanted to curse the bad luck but he couldn't spare the breath. His lungs could barely hold enough to make a small cough, each time the Pring rolled over on top.

Streams of tears blurred his vision and his eyes hurt. He suddenly realized that his goggles were gone! Either Culla had burned them off again in that first instant as he launched himself from the dome, or they'd been torn off during the fight.

Where the hell is LaRoque!

His arms shuddered with the strain and there was a rubbed-out pain in his abdomen and groin from the constant pounding of the cavort across the deck. Culla's coughing was sounding more pathetic and strained, and his own took on an ominous gurgle. He could feel the first stages of heat prostration and a dreadful fear that the ordeal would never end, even as their struggle brought his back up against one of the smoldering flesh-foam brands.

It smothered in a broiling release of heat as he screamed. The pain was too sudden and from too unexpected a quarter to be shunted aside. His tight grip around Culla's throat slacked for an instant of agony and the alien tore at his hands. The grip parted and Culla rolled away even as Jacob grabbed after him.

He missed. Culla scrambled farther away, then turned quickly to face him. Jacob closed his eyes and covered his face with his encased left hand, expecting a laser bolt.

He tried to stand, but something was wrong with his

lungs. They wouldn't work properly. His breath was shallow and he could feel his balance waver as he slowly rose to his knees. His back felt like charred hamburger meat.

Not far away, two meters at most, there was a loud clack! Then another. Then another, closer.

Jacob's arm fell. He no longer had the strength to hold it up. There was no use in keeping his eyes closed, anyway. He opened them to see Culla, kneeling a meter away. Only the red eyes and gleaming white teeth showed through the thick stench.

"Cu . . . Culla . . ." he gasped. Wheezing, the words sounded like tiny, failing gears. "Give up now, this is your last chance. I'm . . . warning you . . ."

Tania would have liked that, he thought. It was almost as good a parting shot as hers had been. He hoped Helene had heard it.

Parting shot? Hell, why not give Culla one! Even if he cuts my throat or drills a hole into my brain through my eyelids, I'll still have time to give him a present!

He pulled the flesh-foam sprayer out of his belt and started to raise it. He'd give Culla such a spraying! Even if it meant he'd die at that instant by laser instead of by decapitation.

Excruciating pain burst like a steel needle through his left eye. It felt like a lightning bolt crashing all the way to the back of his head and out the other side. At that same instant he pressed the release and held it in the direction Culla's head had been.

29.

ABSORPTION

Helene lifted her eyes briefly as the ship rose past the toroid herd on the left.

The greens and blues were faded, eaten by the distance. Still the beasts shone like tiny incandescent rings, specks of life ordered in their miniscule convoy, dwarfed by the immensity of the chromosphere.

The herdsmen were already too far away to be seen.

The herd passed behind the dark bulk of the filament, out of sight.

Helene smiled. If only we still had our maser link, she thought. They could have seen how hard we tried. They would have known that the Solarians didn't kill us, as some will think. They tried to help us. We *talked* to them!

She bent to answer two alarms at once.

Dr. Martine wandered aimlessly behind her and the copilot. The parapsychologist was rational, but not very coherent. She had only just returned from the opposite end of topside. She walked unevenly and muttered softly under her breath.

Martine had enough sense to stay out of their hair, thank Ifni! But she refused to strap herself in. Helene hesitated to ask her to go around to flip-side. In her present condition the good doctor wouldn't be much help.

There was a stench in the air. Helene's flip-side monitors showed only a thick billowing cloud of smoke. There had been shouting and sounds of a terrible fracas just minutes ago. Twice the intercoms had carried the sound of someone screaming. Just moments ago came a shriek that could have waked the dead. Then silence.

The only emotion she allowed herself was a detached sense of pride. The fact that the fight had lasted so long was a tribute to them, especially to Jacob. Culla's weapons should have finished them off quickly.

Of course it wasn't likely they'd succeeded. She'd have heard something by now. She clamped a lid on her feelings and told herself she was shivering because of the cold.

It had dropped to five Celsius. The less efficient her reactions got, as she tired, the more she weighted the cold side of the Refrigerator-Laser's increasingly erratic swing. The hot side would be disaster.

She answered a shift in the E.M. field that threatened to leave a window in the XUV band. It subsided nicely under her delicate control and continued to hold.

The Refer Laser groaned as it sucked heat in from the chromosphere then back out and downward as x-rays. They climbed with agonizing slowness.

Then an alarm clanged. It wasn't a drift-warning, it was the cry of a ship dying.

The stink was terrible! Worse, it was freezing. Someone nearby was shivering and coughing at the same time. Dimly, Jacob became aware that it was himself.

He came erect in a fit of hacking that set his body trembling. For long moments after he got it under control he just sat, wondering numbly how he was alive.

The smoke had begun to clear slightly near the deck. Shreds and tendrils drifted past him toward the whining air compressors.

The fact that he could see at all was amazing. He brought his right hand up to touch his left eye.

It was open, blind. But it was whole! He closed the lid

313

and touched it over and over with his three fingers. The eye was still there, and the brain behind it . . . saved by the thick smoke and the depletion of Culla's energy supply.

Culla! Jacob swung his head about to scan for the alien. He felt a wave of nausea come on and rode it out as he peered around himself.

A slender white hand lay on the floor, two meters away, exposed by the opening cloud of smoke. The air cleared a little more and the rest of Culla's body came into view.

The E.T.'s face was burned, catastrophically. Black crusts of seared foam hung in shreds from the remnants of the huge oculars. A sizzling blue liquid seeped from large cracks in the sides.

Culla was obviously dead.

Jacob crawled forward. First he had to check on LaRoque. Then Fagin. Yes, that was the way to do it.

Then hurry and get someone down here who can work the computer panel . . . if there was still a chance to reverse the damage Culla'd done.

He found LaRoque by following the man's moans. He was several meters past Culla, sitting up and holding his head. He looked up blearily.

"Oooh . . . Demwa, is that you? Do not answer. Your voice might blow my poor delicate head away!"

"Are you . . . all right, LaRoque?"

LaRoque nodded. "We are both alive so Culla must not be, no? He left his job on us incomplete so we may merely *wish* we were dead. *Mon Dieu!* You look like spaghetti! Do I look like that!"

Whatever the effects of the fight, it had brought back the man's appetite for words.

"Come on, LaRoque. Help me up. We still have work to do."

LaRoque started to rise, then wavered. He clutched Jacob's shoulder to keep his balance. Jacob choked back tears of pain. Jerkily, they helped each other up and onto their feet.

The firebrands must have burned out, because the chamber was rapidly clearing. Wisps of smoke trailed in the air, though, hanging before their faces as they staggered along the dome in a clockwise direction.

Once they encountered the P-laser beam, a thin, straight tracery in their way. Unable to go over or under, they went through. Jacob winced as the beam stitched a bloody line along the outside of his right thigh and the inside of his left. They continued.

When they found Fagin, the Kanten was comatose. A faint sound came from the blowhole and the silver chimes tinkled, but there was no answer to their questions. When they tried to move him they found it impossible. Sharp claws had emerged from Fagin's root pods and dug into the tough springy material of the deck. There were dozens, and no way to loosen them.

Jacob had other business to tend to. Reluctantly, he led LaRoque around the Kanten. They staggered toward the hatchway in the side of the dome.

Jacob gasped for breath next to the intercom.

"Hel ... Helene ..."

He waited. But no one answered. He could hear, faintly, his own words echoing from topside. So he knew it wasn't the mechanism. What was wrong?

"Helene, can you hear me! Culla's dead! We're pretty badly torn up ... though. You ... you or Chen come down ... down and fix ..."

The cold air blasting from the Refer Laser sent him into a fit of shivering. He couldn't talk anymore. With LaRoque helping, he stumbled up past the duct and collapsed to the sloping floor of the gravity-loop.

He fell into a fit of coughing, lying on his side to favor his burned back. Slowly the hacking subsided, leaving him raw and aching in his chest.

He fought off sleep. Rest. Just rest here a moment, then over and around to topside. Find out what's wrong.

His arms and legs sent tremors of sharp pain up to his brain. There were too many and his mind was too unfocused to cut all the messages off. It felt as though one of his ribs was cracked, probably from the struggle with Culla.

All of this paled beside the throbbing burden of the left side of his head. He felt as if he was carrying a hot coal there.

The deck of the gravity-loop felt strange. The tight, wraparound g-field should have pulled evenly along his

315

body. Instead it seemed to swell like the surface of the ocean, rippling under his back with tiny wavelets of lightness and weight.

Obviously something was wrong. But it actually felt good, like a lullaby. Sleep would be so nice.

"Jacob! Thank God!" Helene's voice boomed around him, but still it sounded far away—friendly, definitely, warm—but also irrelevent.

"No time to talk! Come up here *quick*, darling! The g-fields are going! I'm sending Martine, but . . ." There was a clattering and the voice cut off.

It would have been nice to see Helene again, he thought dimly. Sleep invaded in force this time. For a while he thought of nothing.

He dreamt of Sisyphus, the man cursed forever to roll a boulder up an endless hill. Jacob thought he had a way to be tricky about it. He had a way to make the hill think it was flat while still looking like a hill. He'd done it before.

But this time the hill was angry. It was covered with ants that climbed up onto his body and bit him all over, painfully. A wasp was laying its eggs in his eye.

What's more, it was cheating. The hill was sticky in places and didn't want to let him go. Elsewhere it was slippery and his body was too light to get a grip on its surface. It heaved with sickening unevenness.

He didn't remember anything in the rules about crawling, either. But that seemed to be part of it. At least it helped the traction.

The boulder helped too. He only had to push it a little. Mostly it crawled on its own. That was nice, but he wished it wouldn't moan so. Boulders shouldn't moan. Especially not in French. It wasn't fair to make him listen to it.

He awakened, blearily, in sight of a hatchway. Which hatchway he wasn't sure, but it wasn't very smoky.

Outside, beyond the deck, he could see the beginnings of a blackness, a transparency, returning to the red haze of the chromosphere.

Was that a horizon, out there? An edge to the Sun? The flat photosphere stretched out on ahead, a feathery carpet of crimson and black flame. In its depths it crawled with tiny movements. It pulsed, and filaments sewed elongated patterns above brightly waving jets.

Waving. Back and forth, on and on, Sol waved before his eye.

Millie Martine stood in the doorway, with her fist up near her mouth and an expression of horror on her face.

He wanted to reassure her. Everything was all right. It would be from now on. Mr. Hyde was dead, wasn't he? Jacob remembered seeing him somewhere, in the rubble of his castle. His face was burned up and his eyes were gone and he gave off a terrible stink.

Then something reached up and grabbed him. *Down* was now towards the hatchway. There was a steep slope in between. He tumbled forward and never remembered crashing to a halt just outside the door.

PART X

A lovely thing to see:
through the paper window's holes
the galaxy.

Kobayashi Issa
(1763-1828)

30.

OPACITY

Commissioner Abatsoglou: "Then it would be a fair statement to say that all of the Library-designed systems failed, before the end?"

Professor Kepler: "Yes, Commissioner. Every one eventually deteriorated to uselessness. The only mechanisms still working at the last were components designed on Earth, by terrestrial personnel. Mechanisms which, I might add, were declared superfluous and unnecessary by Pil Bubbacub and many others during construction."

C.A.: "You aren't implying that Bubbacub knew in advance . . ."

P.K.: "No, of course not. In his own way he was as much a dupe as the rest of us. His opposition was based solely on esthetics. He didn't want Galactic time-compression and gravity-control systems crammed into a ceramic shell and linked to an archaic cooling system.

"The reflection fields and the Refrigerator Laser were based on physical laws known by humans back in the twentieth century. Naturally he objected to our 'superstitious' insistence on building a ship around them, not only because the Galactic systems made them redundant, but also because he considered pre-contact Earth science to be a pathetic accumulation of half-truths and mumbo-jumbo."

C.A.: "The 'mumbo jumbo' worked when the new stuff failed, though."

P.K.: "In all fairness, Commissioner, I'd have to say that that was a lucky break. The saboteur believed they'd make no difference, so he didn't try to wreck them, at first. He was denied an opportunity to correct his error."

Commissioner Montes: "There's one thing I don't understand, Dr. Kepler. I'm sure some of my associates here share my mystification. I understand the Sunship Captain's use of the Refrigerator-Laser to blast out of the chromosphere. But to do so she had to boost at an acceleration *greater than the surface gravity of the Sun!* Now they could get away with this as long as the internal gravity fields held. But what happened when they failed? Weren't they immediately subjected to a force that would squash them flat?"

P.K.: "Not immediately. Failure came in stages; first the fine-tuned fields used to maintain the gravity-loop tunnel to the instrument hemisphere, 'flip-side,' then the automatic turbulence adjustment, and finally a gradual loss of the major field which compensated internally for the pull of the Sun. By the time the latter failed, they had already reached the lower corona. Captain deSilva was ready when it happened.

"She knew that to climb straight out after internal compensation failed would be suicide, though she considered doing it anyway to get her records out to us. The alternative was to allow the ship to fall, braking only enough to impose on the occupants about three gees or so.

"Fortunately, there is a way to fall towards a gravity sink and still get away. What Helene did was to try for a hyperbolic escape orbit. Almost all of the laser thrust then went into giving the ship a tangent velocity as it fell back again.

"In effect she duplicated the program that had been

considered for manned dives decades before contact; a shallow orbit, using lasers for thrust and cooling, and E.M. fields for protection. Only this dive was unintentional, and it wasn't very shallow."

C.A.: "How close did they go?"

P.K.: "Well, you'll recall that they'd fallen twice before in all of the confusion: once when the g-thrust failed, and a second time when the Solarians lost their grip on the ship. Well during this third fall they came closer to the photosphere than on any of the previous occasions. They literally skimmed its surface."

C.A.: "But the turbulence, Doctor! Without internal gravity or time-compression, why wasn't the ship smashed?"

P.K.: "We learned a lot of solar physics from this inadvertent dive, sir. At least on this occasion the chromosphere was far less turbulent than anyone ever expected . . . that is anyone but a couple of my colleagues to whom I owe a few abject apologies . . . But I believe the most significant factor was the piloting of the ship. Helene quite simply did the impossible. The autorecorder is being studied now by the TAASF people. The only thing greater than their delight with the tapes is their chagrin at not being able to give her a medal."

General Wade: "Yes, the condition of the crew was a cause of great distress to the TAASF rescue team. The ship looked like Napoleon's retreat from Moscow! With no one alive to tell what happened, you'll understand our mystification until the tapes were played back."

Commissioner Nguyen: "I can imagine. You seldom expect to get a special shipment of snowballs from hell. Can we assume, Doctor, that the ship's Commander weighted the heat pump system on the cold side for the obvious reason?"

"In all honesty, Commissioner, I don't believe we can. I think her reasoning was to keep the interior cold so that all of the records would survive. If the Refer-

Laser system erred too much the other way they'd have been fried. I believe her sole idea was to protect those tapes. She probably expected to come out of the Sun having roughly the consistency of strawberry jam.

"I don't think the biological effects of freezing were on her mind.

"You see, in many ways Helene was a bit of an innocent. She stayed up to date in her field but I don't think she knew about the advances in cryosurgery we've made since her day. I think she's going to be very surprised, a year from now, when she wakes up.

"The others will probably take it as a routine miracle. Except for Mr. Demwa, of course. I don't think Mr. Demwa would be surprised by anything . . . or consider his revival miraculous. The man is indestructible. I think by now, wherever his consciousness drifts in its frozen sleep, he knows it."

31.

PROPAGATION

In the springtime the whales go north again.

Several of the grey humps that broached and spumed in the distance had not been born when he last stood on a shore and watched a California migration pass by. He wondered if any of the grey whales still sang "The Ballad of Jacob and the Sphinx."

Probably not. It never was a favorite of Greys anyway. The song was too irreverent, too . . . beluga for their sober temperament. The Greys were complacent snobs, but he loved them anyway.

The air boomed with the noise of the breakers, crashing into the rocks at his feet. It was wet with sea water and filled his lungs with the paradoxical satiated-hungry feeling that others got from breathing deep in a bakery shop. There was a serenity that came with the pulse of the ocean, plus an expectation that the tide would always wash up changes.

They'd given him a chair, at the hospital in Santa Barbara, but Jacob preferred the cane. It gave him less mobility, but the exercise would shorten his convalescence. Three months after waking up in that antiseptic organ factory had left him desperate to get back on his feet, and to experience something that was pleasantly, naturally dirty.

Such as Helene's way of talking. It defied all logic that a person born at the height of the old Bureaucracy would have so uninhibited a mouth as to make a Confederacy Citizen blush. But when Helene felt she was among friends her language became impressive and her vocabulary astonishing. She said that it came from being raised on a power satellite. Then she smiled and refused to explain any further until he reciprocated with acts she knew he wasn't ready yet to perform. As if she was!

One month to go before the physicians would take them off of hormone suppressants, after the bulk of cell regrowth was completed. Another month before they'd be cleared for anything as rigorous as space flight. And yet she insisted on pulling out that dog-eared copy of *NASA Sutra*, wondering teasingly if he would have the stamina!

Well, the doctors said that frustration helps recuperation. Sharpens the will to get back to normal, or some such nonsense.

If Helene keeps up her teasing much longer they're *all* going to be surprised! Jacob didn't believe much in timetables anyway.

Ifni! That water looks good! Nice and cold. There *has* to be a way to make nerves grow faster! Something that helps even better than auto-suggestion.

He turned away from the rocks and slowly walked back to the patio of his uncle's long, rambling house. He used the cane liberally, perhaps more than necessary, enjoying the dramatic touch. It made being ill slightly less unpleasant.

As usual, Uncle James was flirting with Helene. She encouraged him shamelessly.

Serves the old bastard right, he thought, after all the trouble he caused.

"My boy," Uncle James threw up his hands. "We were just about to go after you, truly we were."

Jacob smiled lazily. "No hurry, Jim. I'm sure our interstellar explorer here had plenty of interesting stories to tell. Did you tell him the one about the black hole, dear?"

Helene grinned nastily and made a surreptitious gesture. "Why, Jake, you yourself told me not to. But if you think your uncle would like to hear it . . ."

Jacob shook his head. He'd handle his uncle himself. Helene could get a little rough.

Ms. deSilva was a great pilot and in the last few weeks she'd been an imaginative co-conspirator as well. But their personal relationship left Jacob dizzy. Her personality was . . . powerful.

When she'd learned, on awakening, that the Calypso had jumped, Helene had signed onto the gang designing the new Vesarius II. The reason, she announced brazenly, was to have three years to subject Jacob Demwa to a full course of Pavlovian conditioning. At the end of said time she would ring a little bell and he would, supposedly, decide to become a Jumper.

Jacob had his reservations, but it was already clear that Helene deSilva had complete control over his salivary glands.

Uncle James was more nervous than he'd ever seen him. The usually imperturbable politician seemed decidedly ill at ease. The rakish Irish charm of the Alvarez side of the family was subdued. The grey head nodded nervously. His green eyes seemed unnaturally sad.

"Um, Jacob, my boy. Our guests have arrived. They are waiting in the study and Christien is looking after them.

"Now, I hope you are going to be reasonable about this matter. There really was no reason to invite that government fellow. We could have settled this ourselves.

"Now as I see it . . ."

Jacob held up his free hand. "Uncle, please. We've been through this.

"The matter has to be adjudicated. If you refuse the services of the Secrets Registration people, I'll just have to call a family council and present the matter to them! You know Uncle Jeremy, he'll probably opt for publicly announcing the whole thing. It'd make good press, all right, but the Department of Overt Prosecutions would have the case then, and you'd have five years with a little thing in your rump going 'beep . . . beep . . . beep.' "

327

Jacob leaned against Helene's shoulder, more for the contact than for support, and flashed both hands in front of Uncle James' eyes. With each "beep" the man's aristocratic face paled a little. Helene started to giggle, then she hiccuped.

"Excuse me," she said demurely.

"Don't be sarcastic," Jacob commented. He pinched her then reclaimed his cane.

The study wasn't as impressive as the one in Alvarez Hall, in Caracas, but this house was in California. That made up for a lot. Jacob hoped he and his uncle still spoke after today.

Stucco walls and false beams emphasized the Spanish aspect. Display cases, containing James' collection of Bureaucracy-era Samizdat publications, stood out prominently among the bookshelves.

In the mantle was carved a long motto.

"The People, United, Shall Never Be Defeated."

Fagin fluted a warm greeting. Jacob bowed and went through a long, formal salutation, just to please the Kanten. Fagin had visited him regularly in the hospital. It had been difficult at first, between them—each convinced he was deeply indebted to the other. Finally they'd agreed to disagree.

When the TAASF rescue team had broken into the Sunship, as it hurtled outward on its laser-assisted hyperbolic orbit, they were amazed by the crumpled, frozen condition of the human crew. They didn't quite know what to make of the smashed body of the Pring, on flip-side. But what shocked them most was Fagin, hanging upside down by those small sharp spikes in his root-pods while the laser still put out its potent thrust. The cold had not ruptured almost a quarter of his cells, as it had the humans, and he appeared to have come through the pounding ride through the photosphere unscathed.

In spite of himself, Fagin of the Institute of Progress —the perpetual observer and manipulator—had become, himself, a unique personage. He was probably the only sophont alive anywhere who could describe what it was like to fly, hanging upside down, through the thick, opaque fire of the photosphere. Now he had a story of his own to tell.

It must have been painful for the Kanten. Nobody believed a word of his tale until Helene's tapes were replayed.

Jacob said hello to Pierre LaRoque. The man had regained much of his color since their last meeting, not to mention his appetite. He'd been wolfing down Christien's hors d'oeuvres. Still confined to his chair, he smiled and nodded silently to Jacob and Helene. Jacob suspected LaRoque's mouth was too full to talk.

The last guest was a tall, narrow-faced man with blonde hair and light blue eyes. He rose from the couch and offered his hand.

"Han Nielsen, at your service, Mr. Demwa. On the basis of the news reports alone I am proud to meet you. Of course, Secrets Registration knows everything the government knows, so I am doubly impressed. I assume, though, that you have called us in to deal with a matter that the government is not to know?"

Jacob and Helene sat on the couch across from him, their backs to a window overlooking the ocean.

"Yes, that's correct, Mr. Nielsen. Actually, there are a couple of matters. We'd like to apply for a seal and for adjudication by the Terragens Council."

Nielsen frowned. "Surely you must realize that the council is barely an infant at this point. The delegates appointed by the colonies have not even arrived! The Confederacy b . . . civil servants" (Had he been about to say the dirty word 'bureaucrats'?) "don't even like the idea of having a supra-legal Secrets Registration to enforce honesty above secular law. The Terragens is even less popular."

"Even though it's been shown that it's the only way to deal with the crisis we've faced since Contact?" Helene asked.

"Even so. The Feds are reconciled to the fact that it will eventually take jurisdiction over interstellar and interspecies affairs, but they don't like it and they're dragging their feet every step of the way."

"But that's just the point," Jacob said. "The crisis was bad before this debacle on Mercury, bad enough to force the creation of the Council. But it was still manageable. Sundiver has probably changed that."

Nielsen looked grim. "I know."

"Do you?" Jacob rested his hands on his knees and leaned forward. "You've seen Fagin's report on the probable reaction of the Pila to Bubbacub's exposed peccadilloes on Mercury. And that report was written well before this whole business regarding Culla came to light!"

"And the Confederacy knows everything," Nielsen grimaced. "Culla's actions, his weird apologia, the whole capsule."

"Well after all," Jacob sighed. "They are the government. They make foreign policy. Besides, Helene had no way of knowing we'd live through that mess down there. She recorded everything."

"It never occurred to me," Helene said, "until Fagin explained, that it might be better if the Feds never found out the truth, or that the Terragens Council might be better suited to handle this mess."

"Better suited, perhaps, but what do you expect us ... the Council to do? It'll take years to build up acceptance and legitimacy. Why should they risk it all by intervening in this situation?"

For a moment no one spoke. Then Nielsen shrugged.

From his briefcase he pulled a small recording cube, which he activated and placed in the center of the room, on the floor.

"This conversation is under seal by the Secrets Registration. Why don't you start, Dr. deSilva."

Helene ticked off points with the fingers of her hand.

"One, we know that Bubbacub perpetrated a crime in the eyes of both the Library Institute and his own race by falsifying a Library report, and perpetrating a hoax on Sundiver; to wit: that he had communicated with the Solarians and had used his 'Lethani relic' to protect us from their wrath.

"We think we know Bubbacub's motives for doing what he did. He was embarrassed by the failure of the Library to reference the Sun Ghosts. He wanted to rub the 'wolfling' race's collective nose in its inferiority, as well.

"By Galactic Tradition this situation would resolve itself by both the Pila and the Library bribing Earth to

330

'keep its mouth shut.' The Confederacy would be able to choose its reward with few strings attached, though the human race would have to face enmity from the Pila in the future simply because their pride had been hurt.

"They could still increase their efforts to remove provisionary-sophont status from our Clients, the chimps and dolphins. There has been talk of placing humanity under some sort of 'adoptive' Client status . . . 'to guide us through this difficult transition.' Have I summed up the situation fairly well, so far?"

Jacob nodded. "Fine. Except you left out my own stupidity. On Mercury I accused Bubbacub publicly! That little two-year pledge we signed was never taken seriously, and the Feds have waited too long to put an emergency sequester on this case. Probably half of the spiral arm knows the story by now.

"That means we've lost what little leverage we would have had with the Pila by blackmail. They'll hold nothing back in their efforts to get us 'adopted,' and they'll use 'reparations' for Bubbacub's crime as an excuse to force us to accept all kinds of aid that we don't want."

He motioned for Helene to continue.

"Point number two; we now know that the one behind this fiasco was Culla. Apparently Culla never intended that humanity discover Bubbacub's pecadillo. He had his own blackmail scheme in mind.

"By encouraging Jeffrey's friendship he got the chimpanzee to try to 'liberate' him, thus enraging Bubbacub. Jeffrey's subsequent death left Sundiver in such a state of confusion that Bubbacub would be encouraged to think that anything he did would be believed. It's possible that Dwayne Kepler's apparent mental deterioration was part of this campaign, induced by Culla's 'glare psychosis' technique.

"The most important part of Culla's plan was the hoax of the anthropomorphic Ghosts. That part was magnificently executed. It fooled everybody. With talents like those, it's not hard to see why the Pring think they can take on the Pila in a bid for independence. They're one of the most deceptively potent races I've ever come across or heard of."

"But if the Pila were Patrons to the Pring," James objected. "And if they uplifted Culla's ancestors from

331

near animals, why wasn't Bubbacub aware of the possibility that the Ghosts were Culla's hoax?"

"If I may be allowed to comment on this," Fagin fluted. "The Pring were allowed to select the assistant who would accompany Bubbacub. My institute has independent information that Culla was a figure of some importance, on one of their terraformed planets, in an artistic endeavor that we have, until now, not been able to witness. We had attributed the Pring secretiveness on this matter to habit patterns inherited from the Pila. Now, however, we might conjecture that it is the Pila themselves who were not to witness the art. In their complacent superiority, the Pila must have cooperated unknowingly by denigrating their Clients' endeavors."

"And this art form is?"

"The art form must, logically, be holographic projection. It is possible that the Pring have been experimenting for most of the hundred millennia of their sentience, in secret from their Patrons. I am in awe of the dedication it would have taken to keep a secret for so long."

Nielsen whistled lowly. "They must want their release awful bad. But I still don't understand, though I've listened to all of the tapes, why Culla pulled these pranks with Sundiver! How could the hoax of the anthropomorphic Sun Ghosts, the death of Jeffrey, or trapping Bubbacub into his error ever help the Pring?"

Helene glanced at Jacob. He nodded. "This is still your part, Helene. You figured most of it out."

Helene took a deep breath.

"You see, Culla never intended that Bubbacub be exposed on Mercury. He snared his boss into lying and pulling that stunt with the Lethani relic, but he expected him to be believed, here at least.

"If his plan had carried through he would have reported two assertions to the Library Institute; one, that Bubbacub was a fool and a liar who had been saved from embarrassment by the quick thinking of his assistant, and two, that humans were just a pack of harmless idiots and should be ignored.

"I'll cover the second point first.

"On the face of it, it is obvious that no one out there would believe this crazy story of 'man-shaped ghosts' fluttering around in a star, especially when the Library has no mention of them!

"Imagine how the galaxy would react to a tale about plasma creatures which 'shake their fists' and miraculously avoid having their pictures taken so there can be no proof they exist! Having heard that, most observers would never bother to examine the evidence we did have, the recordings of toroids and of the *real* Solarians!

"The galaxy on the whole looks on Terrestrial 'research' with amused contempt. Culla apparently wanted Sundiver to be laughed out without a hearing."

Across the room, Pierre LaRoque blushed. No one said anything about the remarks he'd made on "Terrestrial research" over a year back.

"The quick explanation Culla gave, when he tried to kill us all, was that he faked the Ghosts for our own good. If we looked foolish we might make less of a splash when we announced life in the Sun . . . a splash that would give humanity more publicity in a time when we should be studying quietly to catch up with everyone else."

Nielsen frowned. "He may have had a point."

Helene shrugged. "It's too late now.

"Anyway, it seems, as I have said, that Culla intended to report to the Library, and to the Soro, that humans were harmless idiots and, more importantly, that Bubbacub had been a *party* to that idiocy . . . that he had believed in the Ghosts and lied on the basis of that belief!"

Helene turned to face Fagin. "Is that a fair summary of what we discussed, Kant Fagin?"

The Kanten whistled softly. "I would think so. Trusting in the 'seal' of the Secrets Registration organization, I will state confidentially that my Institute has received intelligence regarding activities of the Pring and Pila that now make sense in the light of what we have here learned. The Pring apparently are engaged in a campaign to discredit the Pila. Therein lies an opportunity and a danger to humanity.

"The opportunity is that your Confederacy could offer evidence of Culla's betrayal to the Pila, so that those sophonts may show how they have been manipulated. If the Soro then came down against the Pring,

333

Culla's race would be hard pressed to find a protector. They might be lowered in status, their colonies eliminated, populations 'reduced.'

"There might be immediate rewards for humanity in this act, but it would do little to change the long range enmity of the Pil. Their psychology does not work that way. They might suspend their attempts to have humanity 'adopted.' They might be willing to accept restraints on the reparations they will insist on paying for Bubbacub's crime, but in the long run it will not win their friendship. Owing humanity a debt will only increase their hatred.

"In addition, there is the fact that many of the more 'liberal' species, on whose protection humanity has so far relied, would not appreciate your providing the Pila with a Casus Belli for another of their Jihads. The Tymbrimi might withdraw their consulate from Luna.

"Finally there is the ethical consideration. It would take long for me to discuss all of the reasons. Some of them you would probably not understand. But the Institute of Progress is anxious that the Pring not be devastated. They are young and impulsive. Almost as much so as humanity. But they show great promise. For the entire species to suffer terrible depredations, because a few of its members engage in a scheme to end a hundred millennia of servitude, would be a terrible tragedy.

"For these reasons I would recommend that Culla's crimes be placed under seal. Certainly rumors would soon drift about. But the Soro will be aloof to rumors bandied about by the likes of men."

Fagin's chimes tinkled softly as a breeze came in the window. Nielsen was staring at the floor.

"No wonder Culla tried to kill himself and everyone else aboard the ship, when Jacob figured him out! If the Pila get official testimony on Culla's actions, the Pring are probably doomed."

"What do you think the Confederacy will do?" Jacob asked.

"Do?" He laughed humorlessly. "Why they'll offer the evidence to Pila with bended knee, of course. Ifni! It's a chance to keep them from 'giving' us a full sector Library Branch and ten thousand technicians to staff it! It's a chance to keep them from 'giving' us modern

ships that no human engineer could possibly understand and no human crew could operate without 'ad-
visors.' It'd put off indefinitely those damned 'adoption
procedures'!" He spread his hands. "And it's pretty
clear that the Confederacy won't stick its neck out for
the race of a sophont who killed one of our Clients,
damn near wrecked our hottest project, and attempted
to make humans look like idiots among the peoples of
the galaxy!

"And when you get right down to it, could you blame
them?"

Jacob's Uncle James cleared his throat to gain their
attention.

"We can try to put the entire episode under seal,"
he suggested. "I am not without influence in some circles. If I put in a good word . . ."

"You can't put in a good word, Jim," Jacob said.
"You're a participant in this mess, in a minor way. If
you try to involve yourself the truth will eventually
come out."

"What truth is that?" Nielsen asked.

Jacob frowned at his uncle then at LaRoque. The
Frenchman had imperturbably begun to nibble on more
hors d'oeuvres.

"These two," Jacob said. "Are part of a cabal whose
aim is to undermine the Probation laws. That's the
second reason I asked you to come. Something's going
to have to be done and Secrets Registration is a better
first step than going to the police."

At the mention of the police, LaRoque stopped nib-
bling at his tiny sandwich. He looked at it then put it
down.

"What kind of cabal?" Nielsen asked.

"A society, consisting of Probationers and certain citizen sympathizers, dedicated to the secret manufacture
of spaceships . . . spaceships with Probationer crews."

Nielson sat upright. "What?"

"LaRoque is in charge of their astronaut training program. He's also their chief spy. He tried to measure the
calibration settings of a Sunship's Gravity Generator.
I have the tapes to prove it."

"But why would they want to do such a thing?"

"Why not? It'd be the most powerful symbolic protest imaginable. If I were a Probationer, I'd certainly participate. I'm sympathetic. I don't like the Probation laws one bit.

"But I'm also realistic. As it stands the Probationers have been made into an underclass. Their psychological problems are a stigma that follows them everywhere. They react in a very human way, they gather together to hate the 'docile and domesticated' society around them.

"They say, 'You Citizens think I'm violent, well then by damn I *will* be!' Most of the Probationers would never do anything to hurt anybody, *whatever* their P-tests say. But faced with this stereotype they become what they're reputed to be!"

"That may or may not be true," Nielsen said. "But given the situation as it stands, for Probationers to get access to *space* . . ."

Jacob sighed. "You're right, of course. It can't be allowed to happen. Not yet.

"On the other hand, we can't allow the Feds to whip up public hysteria over this either. It'd just aggravate matters and put off a later, more severe form of rebellion."

Nielsen looked worried. "You aren't going to suggest that the Terragens Council get involved in the *Probation laws*, are you? Why that'd be suicide! The public would never stand for it!"

Jacob smiled sadly. "That's right, they wouldn't. Even Uncle James would have to recognize that. Today's Citizen won't even consider changing the status of Probationers, and as things stand the Terragens has no authority.

"But what is the domain of the Council? Currently it's administration of extrasolar colonies. Eventually it's to include supervision of all extrasolar affairs. And there's where they can meddle in the Probation laws, symbolically at least, without threatening anyone's peace of mind."

"I don't know what you mean."

"Well now I don't suppose you've ever read Aldous Huxley, have you? No? His works were still popular when Helene was brought up, and my cousins and I were . . . required to study some of them in our youth—damned difficult at times, because of the strange period referents, but worth it for the man's incredible insight and wit.

"Old Huxley wrote one piece titled *Brave New World* . . ."

"Yes, I've heard of it. Some sort of dystopia, wasn't it?"

"Of a sort. You should read it. There are some uncanny prophecies.

"In that novel he projects a society with some unpalatable aspects but with, all the same, a self-consistency and its own form of honor—akin to the ethics of a hive, but ethics nonetheless. When man's diversity keeps throwing up individuals who don't fit into the conditioned pattern of the society, what do you suppose Huxley's state does with them?"

Nielsen frowned, wondering where this was leading. "In a hivelike state? I'd guess that the deviants were eliminated, killed."

Jacob raised a finger. "No, not quite. The way Huxley presents it, this state has wisdom, of sorts. The leaders are aware that they've set up a rigid system that might fall before some unexpected threat. They realize that the deviants represent a control, a reserve to fall back on in times of trouble, when the race would need all of its resources.

"But at the same time, they can't keep them hanging around, threatening the stability of the culture."

"So what did they do?"

"They banished the deviates to islands. There they were allowed to pursue their own cultural experiments undisturbed."

"Islands, eh?" Nielsen scratched his head. "It is a striking idea. Actually, it's the inverse of what we're already doing with the Extraterrestrial Reserves, exiling the Probies from geographically controllable areas and then allowing E.T.'s in to mingle with the Citizens who come and go at will."

"An intolerable situation," James muttered. "Not only for the Probationers, but for the extraterrestrials, as well. Why, Kant Fagin was just telling me how much he'd like to visit the Louvre, or Agra, or Yosemite!"

"All shall come in time, Friend-James Alvarez," Fagin

trilled. "For now I am grateful for the dispensation which enables me to visit this small part of California, an undeserved and extravagant reward."

"I don't know if the 'islands' idea would work that well," Nielsen said thoughtfully. "Of course it's worth bringing up. We can go into all of the ramifications another time. What I'm having trouble figuring out is what this would have to do with the Terragens Council."

"Extrapolate," Jacob urged. "It just might ameliorate the Probationer problem, somewhat, to set up some sort of island coventry in the Pacific, where they could pursue their own path without the perpetual observation they undergo everywhere today. But it wouldn't be enough. Many Probationers feel that they are emasculated from the start. Not only are their parentage rights limited by law, they are also excluded from the most important adventure mankind has ever undertaken, the expansion into space.

"This little imbroglio LaRoque and James were engaged in is a prime example of the problems we'll face, unless a niche is found for them, so that they can feel they're participating."

"A niche. Islands. Space . . . good lord, man! You can't be serious! Buy another colony and give it over to Probationers? When we're still in hock up to our ears for the three we've got? You must be an optimist if you think that could pass!"

Jacob felt Helene's hand slide into his own. He barely glanced at her, but the expression on her face was enough. Proud, alert, and just on the edge, as ever, of laughter. He twined his fingers with hers to cover the most area, and squeezed back.

"Yes," he said to Nielsen. "I *have* become somewhat of an optimist lately. And I think it could be done."

"But where would we get the credit? And how do you salve the wounded egos of half a billion Citizens who want to colonize, when you're giving space to non-Citizens?

"Hell, colonization wouldn't work anyway. Even the Vesarius II will carry only ten thousand. There are almost a hundred million Probationers!"

"Oh not all of them will want to go, especially if they get a place on the islands as well. Besides, I'm sure all they're looking for is fair treatment. A share. Our

338

real problem is that there's not enough colony room, or transport."

Jacob smiled slowly. "But what if we could get the Library Institute to 'donate' the funds for a Class Four colony, plus a few Orion type transports specially simplified for human crews."

"How do you expect to persuade them to do that? They're obligated to compensate us for Bubbacub's hoax, but they'll want to do it in a way that serves their purposes, like making us totally dependent on Galactic technology. In that they'd be supported by almost every race. What could make them change the form of their reparations?"

Jacob spread his hands. "You forget, we now have something they'll want . . . something very precious that the Library Institute can't do without. Knowledge!"

Jacob reached into his pocket and pulled out a slip of paper.

"This is a ciphered message I received a little while ago from Millie Martine on Mercury. She's still restricted to a chair, but they wanted her back there so badly that they let her travel over a month ago.

"She says that full dives have been resumed in active regions. She's already been down once, in charge of the effort to re-establish contact with the Solarians. So far she's been able to avoid telling the Feds much about what she's found, waiting instead to confer with Fagin and myself.

"Contact has been made. The Solarians talked to her. They are lucid and have a very long memory."

"Incredible," Nielsen sighed. "But I'm getting the impression you think this will have political implications relating to the problems we've discussed here?"

"Think about it. The Library will believe they can force us to take reparations on their terms. But if it's handled right we can blackmail them into giving us what we want instead.

"The fact that the Solarians are talkative and can remember the distant past—Millie hints that they remember dives into the Sun by ancient sophonts, so long ago that they might have been the Progenitors themselves—means that we have found a prize of unprecedented proportions.

"It means that the Library must try to find out everything they can about them. It also means that this discovery will get a great deal of publicity."

Jacob grinned.

"It'll be complicated. First we've got to play to the impression they already have that Sundiver is one big fiasco. Get them to assign us a Library Investigation Patent to the Sun. They'll imagine it will only make us look more idiotic. When they realize what we have, they'll have to buy it from us at our price!

"We'll need Fagin's help to finesse it properly, plus all of the savvy of the Alvarez clan and the cooperation of you Terragens people, but it can be done. Uncle Jeremy, in particular, will be glad to know that I'm going to dust off my long dormant skills and get involved in 'dirty politics' for a while, to help."

James laughed. "Just wait til your cousins hear! I can see them shuddering already!"

"Well tell them not to worry. No, I'll tell them myself when Jeremy calls a family council on this. I'm going to make certain that this whole mess is settled within three years. After that I'm retiring from politics, permanently.

"You see, I'll be going on a long trip about then."

Helene let out a small gasp and pressed her fingernails into his thigh. Her expression was indescribable.

"One thing I'm going to insist on," he said to her, wondering if he could, or wanted to, suppress the urge to laugh or the roaring in his ears. "We'll have to find a way to take along at least one dolphin. Her limericks are awfully dirty, but they may buy us supplies in a few ports while we're out there."

ABOUT THE AUTHOR

DAVID BRIN was born in Southern California in 1950 and attended the California Institute of Technology, where he majored in Astrophysics and History. He has subsequently received his Ph.D. in Astrophysics. He has worked as an electrical engineer for Hughes Aircraft Research Labs, and is presently a college Physics professor. His second novel, STARTIDE RISING, was recently published by Bantam Books and he is currently at work on his third, THE PRACTICE EFFECT.

Mr. Brin lives in San Diego, California.